CHIAROSCURO

THE MOUSE AND THE CANDLE

A VAMPIRE NOVEL

MATTHEW S. COX

CURIOSITY
QUILLS PRESS

A Division of **Whampa, LLC**
P.O. Box 2160
Reston, VA 20195
Tel/Fax: 800-998-2509
http://curiosityquills.com

© 2016 **Matthew S. Cox**
www.matthewcoxbooks.com

Cover Art by Eugene Teplitsky
http://eugeneteplitsky.deviantart.com

ISBN 978-1-62007-745-0 (ebook)
ISBN 978-1-62007-769-6 (paperback)

Chiaroscuro

*[kee-ahr-uh-**skyoo r**-oh]*

1. *The use of deep variations in and subtle gradations of light and shade, esp. to enhance the delineation of character and for general dramatic effect.*

2. *The distribution of light and shadow in art, particularly painting.*

3. *A study of light and shade.*

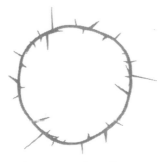

TABLE OF CONTENTS

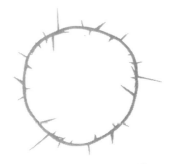

CHAPTER ONE

ORDINIS SANCTI MICHAELIS

March 4ᵗʰ 1885 Saint-Jean-de-Maurienne, France

Devoted to his preparations, **Father Antonio Molinari** weathered the bumps and sways of a moving coach while attempting to decipher the rather rushed handwriting of Pope Pius IX. The task would've been daunting even in stationary surroundings and without the horrors of Vienna still fresh in his mind. Whenever he closed his eyes to sleep, he found himself surrounded by it again: the chill upon his back, the smell of death, and the sound of fear—a pounding heartbeat in his head. His work for the Order of Saint Michael brought him face to face with sights that defied the science of mankind to explain, and the soul to withstand.

When he could no longer tolerate staring at blurry smears masquerading as words, he wiped at his eyes and sighed. Crumbled bits of red and white wax flaked onto his black pants as he rearranged the pile of missives in his lap, a modest parcel of cloth in the facing seat his only traveling companion. Warm air streaming through the window carried the scent of meadow grass and pollen.

He grasped the red-padded wall when the wheels hit a rough patch. Two lanterns hanging outside the carriage swayed and *thumped* against the sides. His surroundings pitched and rocked, and the tall grass rushed by, dotted here and there by white sheep and goats. Two teenaged boys and a dog attempted to keep them grouped; the sheep seemed compliant, but the goats went wherever they pleased.

Once the road smoothed, he settled against the plush bench and spread open the letters. The topmost, he had already read four times. A man, Henri Baudin, claimed his daughter suffered the harrowing of Satan. His words were terse, earnest, and packed with desperation. The condition of the paper, worn and refolded, supported the story it had been passed through many hands.

Beneath it laid two replies from local clergy to an inquiry Father Molinari had sent in response to the man's request. The first, penned by a Father Michaud, claimed the young woman appeared normal to him, and showed little sign of external influence. A deacon from an outlying chapel also wrote to say he believed the woman was only seeking attention. While no one claimed to have witnessed any arguments, the deacon believed she wished to delay or avoid an imminent wedding.

Somehow, the case had been elevated to a bishop who had seen fit to refer it to Molinari's immediate superior, Cardinal Benedetto.

He'd barely set his bundle down in his room before the summons came.

"No rest for the wicked... or the righteous." He rubbed fatigue from the bridge of his nose, offering a halfhearted smile at his belongings, as if the lump might answer.

He could learn nothing new from the letters, and tucked the papers into his sacred book. The pope had gotten wind of what happened in Vienna and, at least from what he had been able to discern from the overly fancy writing, wanted assurances he had dispatched the creature back to Hell. It had little bearing on the reason for his current journey, and could at least wait until he had the luxury of a solid chair and a table bereft of bouncing.

The wagon lurched forward and right, forcing him to grab the seat to avoid tumbling off.

"I am sorry, Father," yelled the driver. "Did not see that hole."

Molinari waved at the windowless wall above the empty bench. "No harm, Paolo. When do you expect we will arrive?"

"Within the hour, Father."

He reclined, braced his arm against the wall, and closed his eyes until a sharp forward lurch snapped him from his brief rest. Outside, horses nickered and shifted. The coach had stopped a few paces from the front of a sizeable but not extravagant house. He stretched, grabbed his book, and reached for the door. The driver opened it from the outside before he could touch it.

"We are here, Father." The grey-clad man removed his beret and bowed. "Welcome to Saint-Jean-de-Maurienne."

Father Molinari eyed the front door, plain and brown like most of the façade. Gnarled wood pillars blotched with dark stains and flaking white paint supported the roof overhanging the porch. Walls of stacked stone seemed at peace with the environs, as though the house had always been here. He lost a few seconds studying a thread of moss growing in the cracks, entertaining the momentary hope that Satan surely could not have influenced such a pastoral place. Perhaps, as in the claim of stigmata in Luxembourg, this would also prove false.

"*Grazie*, Paolo."

The man stood from his bow. "It is a pleasure to assist the Church. How is your French?"

"Ah, a little rusty." Father Molinari chuckled. "Enough to get me in trouble, I suspect."

An older man in a loose white shirt appeared in the doorway, skin darkened from many days in the sun. He ambled out to the edge of the porch wearing an expectant look.

"What have you learned from the locals along the way?" Father Molinari tucked the book under his arm and headed to the house.

"Rumors, Father. They circle like buzzards over a dying man. Some say Josephine is taken by madness. A few believe the Devil has touched her." The coachman gestured to his left at a distant cluster of buildings, the town proper. "Father Michaud thinks she is seeking attention."

Molinari raised an eyebrow at the modest steeple overlooking the town. "So he does not believe the case to be genuine? Curious that Cardinal Benedetto took such a keen interest."

"That is strange, Father?" asked Paolo.

"It is, my friend." Molinari smiled. "It often takes four priests, a bishop, and an act of God to get his attention. Not until a dozen witnesses were confirmed in Vienna, did he send me."

"Grace of God," said the coachman. "You returned in good health."

Father Molinari blessed himself and offered a slight bow. "He was with me."

Paolo walked with him to the front of the house, but stopped short of setting foot on the porch step. "Two priests say there is nothing here. No bishop is involved. That leaves one reason for his eminence to send you."

Molinari mumbled to his side as he took the porch. "Indeed. I was in the area."

"Father," said the older man in French. "Thank you for coming so quickly."

"C'est la volonté de Dieu." Father Molinari smiled. "Henri Baudin?"

"Yes. The will of God." Henri backed up, holding the door for him. "Please, come in."

He stepped through the foyer to a family room of white plaster walls and humble furnishings. Amateur oil paintings of the surrounding countryside lent touches of green, orange, and yellow to the otherwise earth-toned dwelling. Thick, dark-stained wood trusses across the ceiling seemed to shrink the room, invoking an urge to duck his head. The scent of dried flowers mingled with another odd, earthy fragrance he couldn't quite place right away.

Henri approached, hesitated, and ran his fingers through a short silvery-black beard. "Father...?"

"Antonio Molinari. You look troubled."

"Oui. Non. I..." A nervous smile played upon Henri's lips. "I had expected someone... older."

Ahh, but for the things I have seen, I am old. "I am older than I look, Mr. Baudin." He glanced about at the room, an archway to an interior hall and the kitchen, stairs on the left leading up, and a passage on the right to a studio full of easels. *Ahh, paint... that's the smell. It is quiet here. Not the chaos one would expect from such a report.* "Please, tell me what troubles your daughter."

Henri gestured to a padded chair and took the metal one beside it. Once Molinari sat, Henri leaned forward, elbows to his knees, and spoke in a somber half-whisper.

"Three months ago, Josephine disappeared. What they say is true enough. It was the night before her wedding. We were to have the ceremony on her seventeenth birthday. She returned two days after her wedding date, devoid of clothing and sense. It is my belief my daughter had been wandering the woods and fields for some time."

Molinari nodded. "The local priest, Father Michaud, believed she may be nervous about her wedding? What happened when you found her?"

"Josephine fainted in my arms. I brought her home and put her in bed. She awoke the following morning as though nothing happened. When I asked her where she had been, she denied ever leaving. She is... too insistent on resuming the wedding. Marcel called on her and left somewhat abruptly. He claims she is not herself. I, too, can see it. My Josephine is... not so bold."

"Oh?" Molinari eyed the dark beams overhead and the numerous small oil paintings of nature scenes.

"She has always been a quiet soul, lost to her own world. Kind." Henri shook his head. "She has never been... excited about anything."

"Hmm." Father Molinari tapped a finger to his chin, thinking. "Do you recall anything strange or traumatic happening to her in the days before she ran off?"

Henri looked up, steel-grey eyes searching the air for answers. "She was emotional the week before the wedding would have occurred. She kept asking her mother if she approved of Marcel."

"Your wife..."

"Went to God during childbirth." Henri made the sign of the cross. "She was too old, yet we were gifted with a daughter. Despite her age, Olivie thought of a baby only as a blessing."

"You have my condolences."

Henri bowed his head. "Thank you, Father. Josephine was obsessed. All her life she has lived as if under the burden of guilt. Always with her head down. My daughter became increasingly distraught in the days leading up to her disappearance. She said she had to know that her mother would approve of him. Father Michaud thinks she is seeking attention."

"It would indeed be kinder if that were the case." Molinari exhaled. "May I see Josephine?"

"Of course, Father." Henri gestured at the archway in the left wall. "She is in her studio."

Father Molinari stood. He shifted around to face behind him, but grasped the chair at an onrush of sudden vertigo. The distant wide arch wavered and pulled away. He blinked and shook his head; when he opened his eyes, everything appeared normal.

"Father, are you all right?" Henri grasped his arm as if to keep him from fainting.

"I..." He rubbed his head. "Have not been obtaining sufficient rest these past few days. I am fine." He smiled. "In there, yes?"

Henri nodded.

Five strides brought him to an archway twelve feet wide, separating the front room from a secluded area filled with sunlight and eight easels. Two held blank canvases, the rest paintings of fields, flowers, and a river in various stages of completion. Red spots on the floor by one of the easels resembled blood, though looked more like the castoff from reckless strokes.

A thin, barefoot girl with thick jet hair down to her waist laced through with green ribbons stood with her back turned. Paint smears adorned the sleeves of her plain white dress, which looked on the threadbare side. She held a wooden palette in her left hand, a brush in her right, and flitted over the canvas like an excited sprite, dabbing bright green paint onto the scene of a meadow.

Molinari stilled, watching her. She made triumphant grunts and happy squeaks, with the occasional 'a-ha' or giggle when paint seemed to strike the canvas in a way that pleased her. A number of older canvases, half covered by grey cloth, lay on the floor against the wall at the far end. They appeared to be attempts at portraits, all of the same middle-aged woman, though her impressionistic techniques that lent themselves to the landscapes did not translate well to the human figure. Based on the lack of portraits in the house, and the attempt to cover these, he assumed she considered them failures.

"My dear, there is someone to see you," said Henri behind him.

Josephine whirled. Her large grin flickered through alarm to embarrassment. "Father! I am in rags. This is my painting dress; it is not for guests."

"I am pleased to meet you, Miss Baudin." He approached and rendered a slight bow. "I am Father Antonio Molinari. Your father is… concerned about you."

"He should be concerned about manners." She gathered some yellow paint on the brush and poked some flowers into the grass. "Well. I suppose you are already here. I'm sorry my father's letter has taken you so far away from where you would rather be."

"You are quite gifted." He clasped his hands behind his back and approached. "The scene comes alive with light."

"Thank you, Antonio." She kept dabbing, not looking back. "I have been painting since I was twelve."

Henri stifled a gurgle and made an apologetic face.

Molinari ignored the informal address. "Your father seems to think you have suffered an ailment of the spirit. Disappeared into the woods for days."

"He is worried and does not wish to be alone when I marry and go to live with Marcel."

Pink paint, more flowers.

"He tells me Marcel is worried too."

"I know you think the ones in the back *look* like a twelve-year-old made them." Josephine sighed. "I wished to give Henri a picture of my mother, but none are fit to see the light of day."

Father Molinari raised an eyebrow.

"What do you think, Antonio?" Josephine stepped back with a smile. "Should I add a goat or sheep?"

The crisscross lace up the front of her dress hung open enough to expose a little skin, also daubed with paint. Her emphatic work left her breathing hard, and the way she'd angled herself gave him a clear view of her cleavage. That the area between her breasts was as tan as the rest of her caused him to shift with awkward discomfort. He snapped his gaze up to her wide brown eyes. She grinned.

"Do you like?"

Father Molinari coughed.

"The painting?" Josephine tilted her head, nothing but innocence in her eyes.

He surveyed the line of a white stone wall through rolling grassy fields, and a small church tucked against the side of a grassy mountain at the top of a long trail. On the left, the hint of a distant village spread over the deep part of a valley. "It is quite pastoral. Have you been there?"

"*Non.*" She giggled and spun about. "Usually, I paint what is outside here, but today I let my imagination go." Josephine gasped with sudden inspiration and dabbed in a small, plain building at the other end of a garden opposite the church.

The same wobbly sense of vertigo came over him as he stared at the painting.

"Father?" asked Henri.

"The fumes." He smiled. "The windows are not open."

Josephine glided to a table and set the palette and brush down before wiping her hands on a scrap of cloth. "I am so sorry my father has bothered you. There is nothing wrong. I am excited for my wedding and cannot wait for the day. Oh, Henri, you shall not be alone. Soon, I shall have two boys and you will be sick to death of the screaming." She giggled. "Marcel's house is not so far away that you can never visit."

Father Molinari furrowed his eyebrows. This girl struck him as exuberant, animated, and a little odd. Not at all like the somber creature Henri had described. Never mind her continued use of 'Henri' to address her father, or her utter disregard for his title. It again made no sense to him how the letter could've made it to Cardinal Benedetto's desk. Aside from the brash impropriety of youth, she seemed fine.

She grinned, bounced on her toes, and clasped her hands behind her back. "Father Molinari, will you be joining us for dinner?"

He forced away a yawn. "I should not seek to impose upon you any further. I believe I will spend the night in town before returning to Rome in the morning."

Josephine nodded at him and glanced at Henri. "I must clean up. Good evening, Antonio."

Hmm. Odd. She did not insist I stay for dinner. It is only polite to decline at first.

Both men turned their heads, following the dainty sprite as she all but skipped out of the studio and vanished into an inner hallway.

Henri opened his mouth, but Father Molinari raised a hand. "It is no bother at all, Henri. Think nothing of it. I do not see anything that gives me suspicion that Satan is involved."

"Please, Father." Henri teetered on the verge of tears. "This is not my Josephine. This is not how she has been for seventeen years. A girl does not change like this overnight. Is there nothing more you can do?"

Molinari paced about the easels. It did seem strange that she failed to finish so many... or started one on a whim as if taken by a random muse. As his gaze swept over the stack of paintings against the wall, the dizziness came on again—enough to cause a swoon, which Henri caught.

"Father, are you unwell?"

He raised a hand in a delaying gesture and stumbled to the back of the room. "I do not mean to insult your daughter's ability, but do you recognize who this is supposed to be?"

Henri shrugged. "Perhaps Olivie, but it could be any woman with brown hair. The features are..." The man waved his hand about as if trying to pluck a word from the air.

"Indeed." Father Molinari chuckled, hoping Henri did not take offense. He tugged at the cloth covering the stack, catching himself after the fact with no idea why he had done so. A strip of color in the back attracted his attention, for the painting there appeared done by a different hand altogether. "What is that?"

He took a knee and pulled the canvases forward before extracting the one, which seemed to have been placed in the back to hide it. Henri gasped as it came into view. The painting depicted a garden fountain surrounded by dark crimson roses. A beautiful woman well into her forties stood before the basin, arms extended in welcome. She wore a black dress one might expect to see at a funeral, and her smile held as much sadness as joy. At her feet lay the bloodstained body of a young man, stabbed in the chest and with his heart removed, dropped on the ground at his side like so much offal. Two male infants, both their throats cut, had been posed in his arms in a mockery of paternal cradling.

Josephine knelt beside him, gazing up at the woman with a worshipful expression. She held a gleaming dagger in both hands, which she appeared about to thrust into her own chest.

Henri clamped a hand over his face to stifle a horrified shout. Tears streamed down his face. When his shaking fingers slipped away from his mouth, he pointed. "T-that is Olivie... my wife. And Marcel. Who has painted this?"

No sane student of art would imagine the same hand created this piece as everything else here. What he held could stand against the great masters, so realistic the fabric sprang from the canvas. He glanced back at the red spatters on the floor, which matched the horrible gore at the bottom.

Henri dug his fingers into Molinari's sleeve. "Forgive me, Father. Do you believe me now?"

He tucked the painting out of sight as soft footfalls scuffed outside, and flipped the cloth back in place not a second before Josephine, now in a much newer-looking green dress, poked her head in and smiled.

"Still here, Antonio?" She looked at Henri. "I'm going to the river to fetch meat."

Father Molinari patted Henri on the shoulder. "Josephine, would you mind if I walked with you?"

"Are you not tired from so much traveling without a proper bed?" She shrugged one shoulder and spun to face the back hallway. "If you wish."

After a meaningful look to Henri, he followed her out onto the back porch and down a few steps to grassy meadow. Perhaps a hundred yards away, a creek cut through the green. Josephine headed toward a tiny wooden shack on the bank.

"Why did you become a priest?"

He smiled. "It is my calling."

She turned, walking backwards while smiling at him. "Oh? Did you not want a family of your own? Children?"

He held back a pang of doubt. True, if he had any regrets in his life, it was that.

"Is that why you came out here on such short notice?" She whirled forward, swishing her dress around like a girl half her age. "You wanted to protect an innocent child? Does it make you feel less guilty?"

"I have nothing to be guilty for." He tried not to hear the grumbles of his mother, lamenting being denied grandchildren.

Josephine stopped at the shack, which turned out to be only waist-high like a doghouse, and lifted the roof. Inside, several cuts of meat hung on ropes in the water. "My mother would approve of Marcel if she were alive, don't you think?"

"Henri likes the lad. I dare not say what your mother would think, but I trust your father's opinion."

She reeled up a lamb shank. "I think you waste yourself on the Church, Antonio." She closed the hatch and smiled up at him. "Do not take this the wrong way, for I am betrothed, but you are quite handsome. You should have no trouble at all finding a woman to bear you the children you so desperately want."

He took a breath and held it. "Not all men desire families. Some desire to serve God."

"Oh, stop lying to yourself." She giggled. "Lying is a sin, no? How did your mother feel when you told her you were to join the priesthood? Crushed, I bet."

Father Molinari stood in stunned silence for a few seconds as she skipped off in the direction of the house. He hurried up behind her.

She stopped. "Why did you join the Church?"

He gazed out across the meadow. "For years, it was everyone's opinion that my mother was barren. My parents had tried for a long time to have a child, and they thought it impossible. Mother prayed to God every night for months to grant her a baby... and He finally saw fit to answer."

A wry smile curled her lips. "Are you so sure it was him? If the same thing happens to two different people, one who prays and one who does not... the man who prays thinks it God's doing, while the other thinks it luck." She twirled a lock of ebon around her finger. "Henri did not pray for a child, and yet here I am."

"It was Him. I have felt the calling since I was young. I knew I would dedicate my life to His service to thank Him for what He did for my family."

"And by doing so, deprive your line of heirs, deprive your mother of her wish for grandchildren. You are being cruel to her. She is devastated. Why else do you imagine she indulges in so much wine?"

"How..." Molinari grabbed her arm. "How could you possibly know?"

Josephine's face drooped with sorrow. "It is how I would feel if one of my sons did such a thing. To throw his life away. You should give her what she wants, Antonio. She doesn't have much time left."

He stared at her, unable to think of anything to say before she resumed walking to the house.

Again, as he caught up to her, she stopped. "You are handsome, Antonio. I am too young for you, and engaged, but there are at least six women in this town alone who would adore you." She sighed. "But I suppose you find your work too important."

"What I do is necessary. It is His will. There are evils in this world—"

She rolled her eyes. "You really believe that, don't you?"

Warmth rushed over his face. "I have seen—"

"People like you see what they want to see. Anything to keep up the lie."

"What lie?" He scowled.

"God." She smirked. "Fat priests sit back and take taxes, just like any other government. It's all for money. But there's more. You're proud of what you do. You think you're better than the others because you work for *the Vatican*." Josephine puffed her chest up. "That little country priest couldn't possibly know **anything**. But you, you've *seen things*. You think Michaud a simpleton."

He drew in a breath to deny it, but... he had thought ill of the local priest. The ride back from Vienna had left him triumphant. A vampire destroyed. He'd outsmarted the fiend—as well as his poor information—and come out alive. "It's God's work. I protect the innocent. The creatures I have destroyed dwell in the shadow of Satan. They—"

Josephine traipsed along. "You *enjoy* it, Antonio. You covet the thrill of the chase as much as a rich man covets gold. You could not bear the thought of life as a normal person, without access to the *secrets* of the Vatican. It makes you feel superior to everyone... and you *love* it."

He followed, eyebrows furrowed together, mulling her words. *How does this girl know these things? My mother's fondness for wine... my*—he gazed at the clouds—*forgive me, Father, pride.* He resolved to confess to Cardinal Benedetto as soon as he could. The young woman before him was right. He had been prideful. Surely, he could allow himself a little glory? He *had* done God's will. He *had* destroyed an abomination. He *had* been called to serve. Father Molinari narrowed his eyes. She seemed to know him too well... the lack of courtesy... the painting... she didn't want him to stay for dinner. In fact, she appeared quite eager for him to depart.

Josephine stopped at the steps to the porch. "I did not think it possible, but that dark look upon your brow has made you even more handsome. You should go to town before I become unable to keep my promise to Marcel." A playful wink hinted at exaggeration. "Or do you wish to be in your own bed as soon as possible? Really, you should not worry about me. My mother cannot wait to see my sons." She beamed.

"Josephine?"

"*Oui?*" She paused with one foot on a step.

"May I see your hand a moment?" He secreted a phial of holy water from his pocket.

She offered her left, the one not holding the dripping piece of meat. "I am not wearing a ring."

He examined her palm.

"What, now you are a mystic reading life lines?" She giggled.

Father Molinari poured a bit of water into her hand. In an instant, her skin reddened and bubbled to a blister. Josephine dropped the lamb, shrieked at the top of her lungs, and shoved him away.

He flailed his arms, unprepared for the strength behind the little woman that flung him airborne. He crashed into an array of boxes and tools propped against the porch railing, dragging most to the ground with him. Not until his gaze fell upon a streak of dark crimson did the lance of pain searing through his flesh reach his consciousness. Father Molinari stared in horror at a three-inch rake tine protruding through the back of his hand. He gasped.

The soft *thuds* of her running fell silent.

"Josephine, what has—" Henri yelped as if he too was shoved aside.

Father Molinari wheezed through his teeth and shifted his weight to his knees. He grasped the rake and worked his hand up the iron spike; every muscle in his back locked at the sensation of it grating through flesh and scraping across the bones inside his palm.

Henri tromped down the three steps and grabbed his shoulders. "Father! What happened?"

"You are right, Henri." He cradled his left hand to his chest, forcing it into a fist. Again, he sucked air through his teeth. "She is... possessed."

A door slammed upstairs.

Henri helped him up and brought him to the pump where they washed his hand. After wrapping the wound in linen strips, Father Molinari made his way to the coach, past a snoozing Paolo on the front porch. He rifled through his belongings, collecting a purple stole with two crosses in gold trim, his sacred book, and a large eight-inch crucifix amulet.

He returned to the house, where Henri waited at the bottom of a stairway to the second floor. Molinari followed the man up to a narrow hallway with a curved ceiling that ran the length of the house. He halted at the top and braced his hand to the wall to fend off another, stronger, pall of vertigo. The narrow corridor seemed to twist, as if the far end drifted away, walls stretching. Blur obscured the ceiling as paintings darkened. A small vase perched on a sky blue table along the right side felt as though it watched him. Dryness parched his throat, and trickles of sweat slipped down from his armpits. He steeled his mind against the disorienting spin, remaining still until the hall shifted back to rights.

Henri, oblivious to the strange energy in the air, stopped at the third door on the right and knocked. "*Ma Fille*, we're coming in to see you."

Both men jumped at a heavy *slam* from behind the door.

Henri gestured as if to say 'you first.'

Father Molinari grasped the knob and flung the door open. Josephine sat on a cushioned bench on the far side of the room, back turned, running a brush through her long, black hair. She looked over with a curious expression, as though nothing unusual at all had occurred. Her hand still bore the red burn where the water had touched, the only thing that made Molinari not feel like he'd talked himself into giving purpose to his visit.

He opened his book, cradling it in his left hand while raising his crucifix pendant in the right. "I command you, unclean spirit, along with all your minions now attacking this servant of God, by the mysteries of the incarnation, passion, resurrection, and ascension of our Lord Jesus Christ, by the descent of the Holy Spirit, to flee this child of God in whom you have unjustly resided."

Josephine let out a soft huff and continued brushing her hair.

Blood oozed from the wound, trickling down Father Molinari's arm as he raised the book and launched into a recitation using a voice a touch short of a shout.

"I command you, unclean spirit, along with all your legions now assailing this servant of God, by the mysteries of the incarnation,

20

passion, resurrection, and ascension of our Lord Jesus Christ, by the grace of the Holy Spirit, by the coming of our Lord for judgment, that you release this humble servant of God. I command you to obey me, I who am a minister of God, despite my failures. Nor shall you be emboldened to harm in any way this creature of God, or her family, or any of God's children. Begone, unclean spirit."

She stopped brushing long enough to roll her eyes at him. "Perhaps you are the one who is possessed, Antonio. Believing in such nonsense."

He caught a glimpse of unease in her expression. Fear. He advanced, letting the crucifix dangle on its chain, and produced the holy water flask from his pocket. He eyed the door, which Henri moved in front of. Molinari took another step forward and used his thumb to turn the flask into a sprayer as he flung it back and forth, repeating his chant.

Josephine screamed as though he pelted her with boiling oil. She hurled her brush at him, which missed, and crossed her arms over her face. He continued spraying and chanting, raising his voice to shout over her wails.

She drew her knees up and spoke in a tiny child's voice. "Daddy, please make him stop!"

Father Molinari repeated the chant, adding, "May the blessing of almighty God, Father, Son, and Holy Spirit, come upon you and remain with you forever."

She hissed, flinching from the spray. "Your pitiful God is not here, Antonio."

"Begone, unclean spirit!" He returned the flask to his pocket and held up the crucifix.

The voice of a man issued forth from the slender girl. "You will die before the month is out. Leave France and scurry back to your self-righteous hole in Italy, little priest."

He held the crucifix higher and drew a breath to repeat the invocation.

A small mirror leapt off the bureau behind her and smashed across his forehead. He staggered back into Henri's arms, dazed from the hit. Josephine cackled.

"Your blood will spill, Antonio. What will your dear mother say then? Go home and take what you desire most. God is not listening."

The hairbrush floated off the ground and hurled itself at him from behind, striking him between the shoulder blades. He let out an *oof* and fell to one knee. Small statues, music boxes, and three paintings launched themselves at random while Josephine alternated between the giggles of a child, a young woman, and the deep laughter of a man.

Father Molinari let the crucifix drape against his chest and clutched his book in both hands, trying to shield his face from the onslaught.

"We drive you from our sight,

Unclean spirits,

All infernal minions,

All wicked legions,

All of Satan's servants."

"Go away!" roared Josephine.

A great invisible force smashed into Father Molinari, flinging him out into the hallway. Henri landed next to him on his back, legs in the air. A second later, the door slammed hard enough to crack the plaster around it.

"Josephine!" yelled Henri, clambering to his feet.

"*Pleaca! Nu vreau să-l văd!*" shouted a woman's voice. "*Scoate-l afară din casa mea!*"

Molinari took a few breaths and got up. "Romanian, I think."

Henri wept. "My daughter is lost."

"No." Molinari hurled himself against the unyielding wood. "I will not rest until she is saved."

He bumped the door again. Josephine shouted something else in Romanian that sounded decidedly less polite.

Henri gave him a nod, and the two men charged the door at the same time. It gave under their combined strength, and they stumbled in.

Josephine hung in the air, extending her arms up to the side. The tilt of her head mocked the crucifixion. She laughed. Two windows, one on either side of her, exploded inward in a torrent of glass needles.

Molinari ducked, letting off a wail of pain as a dagger shard stabbed through the rake wound, pinning his hand to the sacred book. He looked up after the rain of glass subsided. Henri grasped the piece of glass and pulled it loose. Molinari winced, but nodded his thanks.

Both of Josephine's eyes had gone black from corner to corner, and her gaping mouth held a cloud of ebon vapor.

"Unclean spirit, I command you," yelled Father Molinari.

Josephine gurgled and moaned, twisting and trashing in a parody of Jesus on the cross. Wailing became laughing. "What powerful God could not climb down? You worship a pathetic fool."

Molinari shouted, "In the Name and by the power of Our Lord Jesus Christ, may you be driven from the sight of God and from the souls made in the image and likeness of God and redeemed by the mercy of the Divine Lamb."

"She is mine. She gave herself to me willingly." The same man's voice, deeper still, echoed from the mouth of the girl.

Father Molinari flipped pages. "Lord, have mercy."

"Christ, have mercy," said Henri.

"O God the Father of heaven," said Molinari.

"Have mercy upon us," said Henri.

Josephine moaned and squirmed. "Go away! You cannot have this vessel! I've seen your death, Antonio. If you do not leave, you will die. Your precious God leads you to your doom."

Molinari raised his voice over her. "O God the Holy Ghost have mercy upon us."

"Have mercy upon us," whispered Henri.

Father Molinari sprayed Josephine with holy water. "Holy Mary."

"Pray for us," said Henri.

"Holy Mother of God," said Molinari.

"Pray for us," repeated Henri.

Josephine wailed, gliding around in the air in an effort to evade the relentless spray. Father Molinari recited the Litany of Saints, grateful for Henri responding where he knew, but continuing despite the gaps when the man's reply was a guess. With each saintly name, Josephine's wails intensified, alternating between anger and taunting laughter. Henri put himself in the path of several books launched at Molinari. After a second recitation, Josephine ceased floating and collapsed to her knees, slumped forward as if inebriated beyond coherence.

Father Molinari advanced and placed his hand on her forehead.

"God, by your holy name save me, your lowly servant. By your might, defend my cause."

Josephine went limp, a tendril of drool hanging from her lower lip.

"I command you, unclean spirit. Leave this place and do not return." He closed his eyes. "Christ, God's word made flesh, commands you!"

She shuddered, emitting a voice both male and female. "Mine."

"My daughter..." whispered Henri. "Fight it. Come back to me."

Molinari held the crucifix high and moved it up to down, left to right. "The sacred sign of the cross commands you!"

She hissed.

"Our Lord Jesus Christ commands you!"

She gurgled. Two crucifixes on the walls—the only items in the room that hadn't flown about—scratched as they rotated, inverting themselves. Henri trembled. Furniture downstairs rumbled, as if every chair, table, and bureau in the entire house jumped up and down in place.

"All the Saints command you!"

Josephine flopped over sideways, sprawled on the rug. She lay as if dead for a few seconds, and burst into normal-sounding tears.

Henri looked up with hope in his eyes. Molinari shook his head.

"This is the house of a child of God. Begone, unclean spirit." Father Molinari took a knee and set down the book. He placed his right hand on Josephine's head and pressed the end of his stole to her throat. "See the Cross of the Lord. Begone you hostile fiend! Lord, heed my prayer."

"Please, God," whispered Henri.

"Away," rasped Josephine. "Go away."

The upended crucifixes whirled about on their nails, racing clock hands. Dread gathered like a leaden weight in his stomach. Something unnatural had entered this house. The reek of hundreds of bad eggs washed over the room. Henri gagged; Father Molinari's eyes watered from the awfulness of it. He palmed the young woman's listless head, and repeated his invocation, commanding the spirit out in the names of God, Jesus, the Holy Spirit, and all the saints in turn.

Josephine's back arched. She coughed and sputtered as if drowning. Thick, black liquid splashed up and out of her mouth. It splattered on her dress, but then exuded as a vapor into the air. The vestige of a human face with horns and glistening glass-like teeth manifested at the top of the cloud, gazing at Molinari with sheer hatred. It receded from the crucifix in his hand, and rushed off to the corner, where it cowered against the wall.

Henri quivered, pale as a corpse. Josephine appeared to have fainted.

Molinari advanced on the black fiend.

"We drive you from our sight, unclean spirits, all infernal minions, all wicked legions, all of Satan's servants. Begone from this house and never return!"

It rose up to a height of nine feet, baring claws and hissing. Father Molinari stood his ground, confident that God would protect him. He raised the crucifix.

"May God banish you back to the abyss where you and all of your unclean servants have been condemned to dwell for eternity. I cast thee out from this place!"

The shadow entity collapsed inward, emitting a howl of anger as it melted into a cloud that seeped into the floorboards. Seconds later, the house seemed... different. More youthful. Cleaner.

Father Molinari slouched, again grimacing as the wicked pain in his hand flared.

"Mmm," muttered Josephine as if waking from an endless sleep. "Father..."

"My daughter." Henri fell to his knees and gathered Josephine in his arms.

Father Molinari approached and poured holy water over the back of her hand. It ran without effect over her skin and dribbled to the floor. He smiled and offered Henri a comforting nod.

"Father," yelled Paolo from outside in Italian. "Do you require assistance?"

"It is gone," said Molinari in French. He stood, favoring his wounded hand, and moved to the shattered window. *Dio ha prevalso.*

The coachman bowed and made the sign of the cross.

Josephine curled in a ball, clinging to Henri and sobbing. "Father, please forgive me."

"Worry no more of it," said Henri.

"No." She glanced up at Molinari, tears streaming down her cheeks. "Father... I must confess. I went into the woods wanting to talk to my mother's spirit. I opened myself to the Devil."

Father Molinari put his good hand on her shoulder. "Do not let your grief for your mother be a doorway for Satan. Trust in God that He saw fit to bring her to Him when He did. You are the blessing she had asked for. Rejoice in the life you have been given."

Henri helped Josephine to her feet.

"Thank you, Father." Henri bowed his head. "I shall be forever in your debt."

Father Molinari gathered his book. "Be forever indebted to God, for it is He whose light banishes the darkness."

He let himself out as Henri tended to his daughter.

Once Molinari reached the porch, he took a great breath of sweet, fresh air. Paolo met him at the steps and followed him to the coach.

"Have you ever seen such a thing?"

Father Molinari removed his stole and folded it into a neat bundle before glancing up at the broken windows. "Too many times, my friend. Too many times."

CHAPTER TWO

A DISQUIET BREAKFAST

March 6th 1885 Saint-Jean-de-Maurienne, France

A **plate of toast and jam sat beside the Pontiff's** letter on a table at a small inn. Father Molinari nibbled between sips of black coffee and reading. His heartbeat throbbed in his wounded hand, a clean and proper bandage tight to his skin. The innkeeper's wife, Daphne, had insisted on attending to it for him. Bad enough it seemed every adult in town had stopped in to thank him, but Pascal refused to accept payment for his lodgings or food.

Neither he nor Daphne would hear a word of protest that they deserved to earn their livelihood. As if his unwanted celebrity had not been enough to unsettle his nerves, the pope's letter to Cardinal Benedetto requested a personal debriefing of the events in Vienna. *It disturbs me more His Holiness does not question the existence of such creatures at all, but wishes to know the details.* He closed his eyes and rested his face in his unwounded hand. *What secrets we keep from the world.*

The ring of a tiny bell announced a new arrival. From his seat, his back to the wall of a plastered archway, he could not see the front. Yet out of reflex, Father Molinari braced for more enthusiastic villagers. A pair of country priests in plain black walked in, a young blond followed by a shorter, paunchier bald man who appeared a decade or two his senior. As they approached, he folded the Pontiff's letter and tucked it into his sacred book.

"Good morning, Father," said the younger priest, in Italian. A wooden cross tilted from his chest as he bowed. "May we join you?"

"Good morning, Fathers," Molinari replied in kind and gestured at the three empty chairs at his table. "Please."

"I am Father Callini, and this is Father Renault. Our church is in Briançon to the south."

The older priest bowed and took a seat. "It is an honor, Father Molinari. I pray the Baudin girl is well?"

"She will be at the chapel three times a week for months seeking absolution." Father Molinari shook his head. "Her soul is safe."

Both local priests made the requisite sign of the cross as Daphne walked over and set down a cup of water for each man. Her gaze lingered a little too much on Molinari for his comfort, and he looked down with a cough. The woman had to be in her later forties, not to mention married, not to mention he was a priest.

Daphne smiled at the new arrivals. "Would either of you care for coffee?"

Fathers Callini and Renault politely declined, but thanked her for the water.

"May I ask what happened to your hand?" asked Father Renault.

His Italian felt far worse than Molinari's French, so he answered in the man's native tongue. "There were complications during the exorcism."

The men nodded.

"We have heard you are considered an expert in investigating claims of miracles, demons, and other beasts." The young priest leaned in, eyebrows rising.

Father Renault eagerly drained his glass; the water seemed to exude from his bald scalp as soon as he swallowed it.

"I have often investigated claims of that nature, though most bear little authenticity."

"What of the Baudin girl?" asked Father Callini. "They say she spoke in tongues."

Father Molinari took a long, slow sip of his coffee. "All claims are not from those who seek notoriety."

"It was authentic?" Sweat ran in trails over Father Renault's jowls. "A demon, here?"

Molinari raised his unhurt hand. "Some manner of unclean spirit that the Holy Father saw fit to banish. I can say no more. Mademoiselle Baudin would appreciate your discretion."

Both priests nodded.

"We have found something you should see." Father Callini glanced to his right at Renault, with the expression of a boy who wished to please his parent. "We have captured a creature."

"What sort of creature?" Father Molinari eyed his remaining toast, but decided not to eat in front of those abstaining.

Father Renault leaned close and lowered his voice to a whisper. "A vampire."

Molinari blinked. "You two"—he gestured with his coffee cup at the men—"subdued and captured a vampire, intact, without so much as a scratch on you?" He suppressed a chuckle.

"It is sick and weak," said Callini. "I believe only recently turned. It came *to* us. Perhaps it seeks release from its torment."

"A perfect opportunity for study." Renault's chair creaked as he twisted to get Daphne's attention. "Please, Madame, might I ask you for a refill?"

Molinari leaned back, teasing at his chin with his index finger. Once the innkeeper's wife had poured the water and walked out of earshot, he shook his head. "I must confess I find it somewhat implausible that two men, even priests, with no prior experience could have bested such a creature. I have had encounters with them before. Recently, in fact. Vienna, less than a month ago."

Father Renault, despite looking close to fifty, gaped with the wide eyes of a child enthralled in a story. "What happened?"

"I sent its soul, if it had one, to wherever it is that the souls of such beasts go." He seized a bit of toast, waving it about. "They dwell in the shadow of Satan, out of the sight of God."

"You destroyed it?" Father Callini stared at him with awe. "You seem in good health, less the hand."

"Only a fool confronts a vampire on its own terms. They are far less dangerous at three in the afternoon." Father Molinari chuckled, and took a bite of toast.

"We would be honored if you would validate our find," said Renault. "We do not crave fame, merely greater knowledge for His work."

"I was to depart today, to return to Rome."

"We are from Briançon, which is closer to Italy," said Father Callini. "You could stop on the way. At worst, you tell us we have made a mistake, and you enjoy a bed for the night. At best, you will not have passed an opportunity to examine another such fiend up close."

Father Molinari studied the pattern of light glinting through the jam on his toast. As tired as he was, as much as he craved a night or two of peace in his room at the Vatican, he could not deny the sudden interest that sprang up within him. "All right. I will accompany you."

The priests popped up in their seats, smiling.

"Excellent!" Father Callini grinned. "God has truly sent you to us."

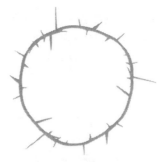

CHAPTER THREE

UNHALLOWED GROUND

March 9th 1885 Briançon, France

The coach glided to a halt in the shadow of a stone church set atop a craggy shelf overlooking a town sprawled through grassy hills. Mountains to the west blocked the setting sun from view, peaks aglow beneath a pinkish sky. Firelight flickered within the windows of homes down the grade; the only sign of life on the winding road up to the church had been an old man and a pair of mules.

Father Molinari descended from the coach and took a deep breath of cold air laced with the fragrance of pollen. Some aspect of this place haunted him, quickening his heart, though he could not set his gaze upon any obvious cause. Indeed, he was right to come here as much as he feared for his life. He clasped his crucifix, tracing his fingers over the cold metal. Something about the vista before him seemed familiar, the church, the modest farm, a small outbuilding beyond. He stared at it, gripped by an inexplicable dread. As if to let go of the coach doorjamb would commit him to a fate inexorable once set in motion. His heart pounded, and he forced himself to look away.

Yea though I walk through the shadow of the valley of death, I shall fear no evil.

The local priests dismounted their horses, handing the reins to a tow-headed boy of about fifteen in a pale tan tunic. He cast a wary glance at Molinari before leading the animals around the left of the church. Near the back of the side yard, a long rickety roof covered four stable stalls. One bearded black goat in the shadow east of the building chewed something while staring at him. Molinari studied his hand as if mystified by it, and released his grip. The uneasiness in his belly intensified. He lowered his arm at his side.

The Lord my God is my savior. I trust in Him to guide me.

"It is no grand affair like you are used to." Renault gestured at the front doors. "But it is what we have, and we are thankful for it."

Callini trotted over, all but bouncing in his boots. "Father Molinari, would you care to rest the night or see it right away? It is quite an honor for us to have a visitor of your stature."

Paolo set about unhitching the horses. "By your grace, Fathers, may I avail of your stables?"

"Of course," said Renault.

"May as well lay eyes on the beast immediately." Father Molinari started for the church, but halted at a hand on his arm.

"My apologies, Father." Callini indicated the smaller building a hundred yards west, on the far side of a garden patrolled by chickens. "We could not bring the fiend onto consecrated ground."

"Yes, yes." Renault nodded. "The beast gave off smoke and screamed when we tried to bring it inside."

"Very well." Molinari set his belongings back in the coach. "Lead the way, Fathers?"

They crossed through fields of cabbage, carrots, and beets to a masonry structure built in a similar, but less ornate style than the church. Most of the inside space contained farming tools and bags of seed, as well as a small hand-operated grist mill. Father Renault made his way to the opposite wall and opened a door, which led to a spiral stairway down.

"There are rooms below intended for monks." Renault paused at the opening. "We have confined the creature in one, where it can do no harm and is away from the sunlight."

"The Devil shall miss no opportunity to deceive." Father Callini held up a finger. "Do not trust thine eyes."

Father Molinari blessed himself. "For even Satan disguises himself as an angel of light."

Renault, lantern in hand, led the way down seven turns, and opened a door at the bottom. Beyond laid a narrow hallway with four doors on each side and one at the end, all but one open. Two metal hooks held a thick wooden beam to the door, nailed in place by an amateur's hand. Only the closed room had such a bar. He trailed the two priests into the hallway, entering a cloud of thick, moist air permeated with the stink of must.

The hair on the back of Molinari's neck rose. With each step deeper into the earth, his unease mounted. Renault stopped at the closed door. Flickering lamplight wavered on the walls, casting the man's jowls in grotesque shadow. He hesitated at touching it, as if petrified of what lay inside. Up close, it became clear they had nailed the hooks in place themselves. The nails looked more bent than driven. Father Molinari's throat tightened with worry. Any vampire he'd tangled with could rip the door open with ease.

The heavyset priest glanced at Molinari as if seeking counsel.

Father Callini sidled up at his left, terror warring with eagerness in his countenance. At Molinari's nod, Renault lifted the bar from the hooks and set it upright against the wall. He unlocked the door with an iron key and gave it a push.

Molinari, hands clenched to fists to keep them from shaking, approached the creaking portal. The sight within the eight-by-ten foot cell took the breath from his lungs.

Huddled at the center of the rear wall, shivered a tiny wisp of a girl. Pale, with dark chestnut hair and the face of an angel, she clutched a ragdoll to her chest. Her white silk nightdress bore smudges and dirt where her knees had pressed it to the floor. Bare toes peeked out from the hem. A length of chain emerged from between her feet and curved around to the wall at her side where it secured to a ring.

Molinari's heart beat in long, labored thuds as he glanced at a frayed bundle of rope on the right side of the room, and to a red velvet cord a little more than two feet in from the door. The child drew herself in tight. Faded bruises circling both wrists tugged at his heartstrings. Too-wide green eyes seemed to stare straight into his soul.

"What in the name of God is this?" Molinari caught himself yelling.

He made to rush in, but the priests grabbed his arms.

"Father, no," yelled Renault. "It is a deceiver."

"Do not step past the line." Father Callini indicated the red cord. "That is as far as its claws can reach."

Molinari threw them off, but held his ground. "What have you done? She is a child!"

"It is a beast." Father Renault made the sign of the cross over himself.

"I will not be part of this madness." Molinari again tried to approach, but the younger man held him back. "Release this child at once."

"Father, look," whispered Renault. "She smells your wound."

His struggle with Callini ceased. Molinari glanced at his bandaged hand, at the blood soaked into the fabric. The child stared with rapt attention at the cloth. He moved his hand from side to side as if waving a treat at a dog. The girl tracked it as an earnestness took over her features. She shifted her weight, a light clatter of chain on stone accompanying the slight movement.

Father Callini took note of his testing the girl's reaction and let go. Molinari entered the room, but stopped where the velvet rope crossed from wall to wall. He held out his injured hand. The child's expression fell to a sad pout.

"Please, help me," she whispered in French.

"It tries to deceive," whispered Callini. "God will give you strength."

Father Molinari's face warmed with anger. "This cannot be. You are mistaken. What crime could such a small child have committed to be treated in such a manner?"

Callini reached in and unwound the bandage. The girl appeared transfixed by the dripping wound. Such silence permeated the room that the *pat* of a droplet striking stone seemed loud. She set her doll down and braced her hands flat against the stone on either side of her. Weak red luminescence lit her eyes. Her lips twitched and tiny fangs extended.

"No..." Molinari stared in horror as the child balanced up on her toes and slid forward onto her knees.

The chain dragged behind her as she crawled; small shackles intended for a woman's wrists bound her ankles. She sniffed at the air for a second before she lunged, emitting a mixture of childish pleading mewls and angry canine growls. Her fingertips came within a half-inch of the demarcation after the tether cut her leap short. She could not get her face close to the droplets. After a few seconds of futile straining, the girl wiped at them with her hand and licked her palm.

Molinari took a step back, covering his mouth. Tears rolled from his eyes. Images of an arrogant Viennese man in a frilled collar, pale as death, cruel, and responsible for dozens of murders flashed through his mind. His laughter echoing at a party—the arrogant disdain with which he flung a dead woman from a bridge into the river, fanged mouth gaping open in the last seconds of his existence. How could God allow such a fate to befall an innocent?

The child whined and whimpered, reaching for Molinari. Glowing eyes faded and surged, as if a child and something else warred for control. *She* begged for help—*it* demanded food.

"It wants you to feel sorry for it," said Renault. "We have been providing it cow and pig blood, but only enough to forestall a second death."

"It looked startlingly close to alive when we found it." Callini puffed up his chest, proud of himself. "We have determined that their power diminishes when they are deprived of the ability to gorge themselves."

She whined, grabbing the stone and pulling herself into the tether a few times. Father Molinari glanced at the abandoned doll and crumbled a fist into his mouth, unable to stop crying. He lowered himself to a squat and reached his unhurt hand forward.

"Careful," said Renault in a stern tone. He grasped Molinari's shoulder as if ready to pull him back at a second's notice.

The girl placed her tiny hand in his, skin cold as death. She gripped two of his fingers and stared into his eyes. "Please help me."

He held her hand for a few minutes, unsure what to think. Every so often, she leaned in the direction of his wound and struggled at her chains. Molinari released her hand and stood.

"This defies all understanding. This cannot be. I wish to try an exorcism. Perhaps there is enough innocence left within her."

"She's d—" Father Renault withered away from Molinari's glower. "Of course, Father."

The girl shuffled backwards, chain jingling, and gathered her hands at her chin, cowering like a waif about to suffer a beating. It was the same pose she had been curled in when the door opened.

Father Renault closed and locked the cell after they backed out. Muted sobbing echoed through the stone hallway, clawing at Molinari's heart.

Less than an hour later, Molinari led the way back to the cell in full mass regalia, flanked by Fathers Callini and Renault, also in their vestments. Renault bore a thurible, already lit and exuding incense. Callini carried an aspersorium of holy water. Frantic clattering in the cell silenced as their steps resonated through the underground passage.

Again, Renault removed the bar and unlocked the door. The girl sat closer to the right rear corner, hands clasped about the chain between her ankles. She stared up at Molinari with such need in her eyes that he could not bear her gaze. He looked down. After a moment, he knelt upon the cold stone, as close as the other priests permitted to the red cord, and set out three candles. Callini held an aspergil over his head, and flung holy water on her. She shot him an annoyed scowl.

Molinari raised an eyebrow.

"It resists the touch of God," whispered Renault.

Callini stood at his left, dunked the aspergil, and flung more holy water upon the girl. "Should it not burn and writhe?"

"The one in Vienna did so," said Molinari. A spark of hope filled his heart. "As did one in Genoa. Perhaps this one is not lost to us." He kissed the OSM embossed in the leather-bound prayer book and set it on a cloth in front of him. "Our Father, who art in Heaven…"

She hid most of her face behind her knees, staring at him as he recited the Lord's Prayer. Throughout the recitation of the rites of Exorcism, she occasionally cringed or shivered, but maintained a fearful, if not unimpressed, look.

Father Renault shook the thurible, creating a rhythmic clattering of tiny chains on the brass vessel. The cell soon filled with incense smoke, which seemed only to make the living cough. Molinari led into a repetition of the rite that had freed Josephine Baudin. All the while, Father Callini flung holy water at the child. She gave him sour glances and wiped her face whenever it hit her there, but her skin did not blister or smoke.

Impending futility fueled Molinari's resolve. He powered through a third recitation, his voice rising, despite resignation clear in the hearts of Callini and Renault.

The girl stood and crept forward with tiny, shuffling steps. She waved her arms to keep balance when the tether went taut, staring at Molinari with a forlorn expression. Even if she were to lunge, her hands would only find the sacred book, which he assumed she could not bear to touch. Once more, the weight of guilt crushed his soul, and he averted his gaze to the tendons rising from her too-pale feet. The sight of such a small child in shackles infuriated him, even if she was… tainted.

God grant me the strength to ensure whatever fiend stole this waif from her bed in the middle of the night will suffer an eternity of Hell.

"It ignores your prayers, Father," said Callini with a trace of a sigh. "The rite is not working."

Molinari clenched his jaw, barely resisting the urge to sigh. The man had a talent for stating the obvious.

The girl managed to kneel without falling, and folded her hands as if in prayer.

Father Callini growled and worked the aspergil as if a lash, throwing holy water on her while tracing an X pattern in the air. Her eyes shut harder as if she fought to hide pain.

"It mocks us," yelled Callini.

"We are wasting our time." Father Renault stopped waving the censer.

Molinari raised a hand to quiet the priests, watching her lips move. The girl recited the Lord's Prayer in French at a level beneath a whisper. All three men waited in silence until she finished and looked up, defeat plain on her face.

The child lowered her hands into her lap. "*Il ne écoute pas.*"

"God does not listen to creatures from the depths of Hell." Renault rattled the censer at her. "You who are a fiend in the guise of innocence. You who have stolen the flesh of—"

"Enough." Molinari blew out the candles. "I have been sent here for a reason. I will find it."

She covered her face with her hands and sniffled.

Callini and Renault backed out of the cell and waited for him to gather his things. Molinari avoided looking at the distraught child; his mind raced for something—*anything*—he could do as he walked out into the hall.

CHAPTER FOUR

BY ORDER OF ROME

March 9th 1885 Briançon, France

Father Callini slammed the cell door. The *bang* echoed into silence, followed by a drag of chain on stone and soft crying. Father Molinari traced his thumb over the spine of the sacred book. Perhaps something in the Vatican library could address this, but would they regard it a waste of Holy See resources? A lost cause? All his training and vows called out to him to put her down while she was weak and harmless, but his heart and soul said he could not.

"Tell me all you know of this child." Molinari tucked the book under his arm.

"We were in the southeast, ministering to a shepherd's wife. She had fallen ill with fever, and the family asked for prayers." Callini paused with a somber frown. "The woman's condition appeared to worsen. We stayed late into the night, praying for her health."

Renault set the bar on the door after locking it. "Mrs. Galliard's fever broke, and she was able to rest. The creature found us not long after we left the house to return here."

Father Callini chuckled. "It walked right up to us, asking for help."

"It seems the mother taught it to trust the clergy." Renault did not share his associate's amusement. "Perhaps the help we can give it is release."

"We have too much to learn." Callini waved him off. "The creature's instinct is good. We *will* help it, but not until we have nothing more to learn. Beasts of this kind are not as rare as we have been led to believe. Think of the benefit of knowing their every weakness."

A blade of guilt slid through Molinari's heart as the child wept on the other side of the door. He stiffened with as much authority as he could project in his posture and voice.

"The Vatican will want complete documentation of this. You are correct in your estimation of the value of this knowledge. By order of Cardinal Benedetto, you will do nothing to this creature unless I am present to document the results. Is that understood?"

Both men bowed to him. "Yes, Father."

Callini vibrated in his boots with excitement. "Perhaps I can accompany you to Rome when we are done?"

"Perhaps." Molinari glanced again at the door. At least now he understood why this place unsettled him.

Something tugged at his soul as they navigated the cottage full of farm tools. He glanced back at the locked door. *She is a vampire. She only appears as a child. She will use her appearance as a weapon. I must not lower my guard.*

"Please help me." The muffled whisper of a child's voice teased at the back of his mind.

He hesitated, unsure if he heard it, imagined it, or if the creature *did* something. Vienna made the sixth vampire he'd seen, and the third he had destroyed himself. Not once before had he possessed a shred of pity or remorse for what God commanded him to do. Not even with the young woman in Switzerland, who couldn't have been much older than Josephine Baudin. Despite her visible age, her soul had blackened. She had done unspeakable things, and would have killed again without hesitation. Father Molinari clenched his jaw at Josephine's—no, the demon's—words. He *had* been prideful. He squeezed the wound on his hand. *Thank you Father for revealing my sins.*

The ceiling held no answers, though his being here felt *right*. He tasted jam, remembering the unusual spate of curiosity that caused him to agree to come here.

He closed his eyes. *"Deus operatur in viis arcanus."*

"Amen," said both priests.

Father Molinari hung his head as they stepped outside and took in the cool breeze of the predawn morning. *God, grant me the wisdom to do your will. Heavenly Father, please stay the hands of these men until I find the answer you wish me to see.*

They walked to the church in silence, and made their way to a small door behind the altar that led to a stairway to the second story. Renault headed to his chambers while the younger Callini had the energy to show Molinari to a modest guest room before retiring. Molinari removed the borrowed vestments and handed them to Callini before undoing his shoes and collapsing on a plain bed. A bland, beige ceiling had no more information than the dark stone of the underground chamber.

He lay for some time, no closer to sleep. Patches of sunlight crawled down the wall and settled on the floor. Renault's snoring reverberated through the corridor, as loud as if a bear had secreted itself under his bed.

"Father, I am your instrument. I beg of you to guide me."

CHAPTER FIVE

A HEART TOO BURDENED

March 10ᵗʰ 1885 Briançon, France

Father Antonio Molinari's eyes snapped open. The windows of the small room remained as dark as when he'd lain down however long ago. His mind filled with the thoughts of a frightened, lonely child chained in a dank underground cell. No matter how much he tried to think of her as a creature that dwelled without knowledge of God, the guilt remained, cold and unrelenting.

He'd been back from Vienna for only hours when Cardinal Benedetto sent him to Josephine's house. Before that, the frivolous claim of Stigmata in Luxembourg. It had been at least six months since he'd spent more than two consecutive nights in his own bed and at least two since he'd slept soundly.

"Perhaps I have gained the ability to sleep in a moving coach more than I realize."

He rolled on his side, cheek brushing over coarse linen. At the back of his mind, a little girl struggled with her bindings and cried out for her mother. He tried to picture her with glowing red eyes, fangs, and claws. A monster that needed to be locked away. Each time, the beastly visage faded to that of a weeping little girl who couldn't understand why the priests treated her this way.

What was she doing right now? Was she pacing? Sucking her thumb? Singing to her doll and telling it everything will be all right? *Probably crying. Perhaps she is asking God why this is happening to her.* After tossing in bed for another few minutes, he sat up. Sleep would not have him.

Father Molinari donned his shoes and strode to the door. Careful to remain quiet, he crept down the hall to the stairs. A narrow door at the bottom opened to the room where the priests kept their cloaks and had hung the keys for the monk cells on a peg. The delicate jingle of iron raised the hackles on his neck as though the cathedral bells of Rome had erupted in the middle of the night. Renault's snoring continued unabated, echoing through the vaulted ceiling. With the keys bundled under his arm, trapped in an embrace of silencing cloth, he took a lantern and flew down the central aisle in the church. Once outside, he hurried across the garden to the outbuilding. A handful of goats froze like statues watching him pass.

The silence within surprised him. He had expected screaming, or at least crying and the thrashing of chain. He closed the outside door and fumbled his way among the tools to the inner door. It creaked as he pulled it open, and the clink of metal on stone sounded from below. Molinari stepped through and drew it closed behind him, so a casual observer wouldn't notice.

He kept his hands out to the walls as he made his way down the spiral staircase. *This is foolish. Why am I sneaking around like a thief? How on Earth does this seem like a good idea? Unexplained urges may as well be the hands of Satan.* He stopped at the base of the stairs, and fumbled around until he managed to light the lantern. Odd feelings had served him well in Vienna; the man his superiors suspected of vampirism turned out to be a mere thrall. He'd sensed something amiss before giving himself away, a delay that afforded him the opportunity to find the real undead.

After making the sign of the cross, he approached the cell and listened to silence.

The wooden bar was heavier than Renault made it look, though Molinari had little difficulty moving it. After setting it on end and resting the ponderous board against the wall, he turned the key in the lock. Still, no sound came from within. He lingered with his hand against the door, waiting for his intuition to guide him one way or another. Eventually, uncertain of anything, he pushed the door in. The girl sat as she did when he'd first seen her, against the far wall, knees bent up. He glanced at the ring in the wall, tracing the chain until it disappeared under her nightdress. The sight of it filled him with anger in defiance of his knowing what she was.

"*Bonjour, Père,*" she whispered.

He approached, but stopped at the cord.

"I do not wish to be bad." She lowered her head. "I will not harm you."

Father Molinari squinted. "Many times have I heard creatures of darkness make such promises."

"Do you think me a creature of darkness?"

He looked down.

"You do not know what to think." Chain rattled as she shifted her legs to the side. "You are not the same as the others. You want to help me, like *Maman* said."

"I have never seen one of your kind so young." He studied her, searching for any trace of deceit. "What is your name, child?"

The girl wobbled to her feet and curtsied. "I am Sabine Caillouet, and I am eight years old. My father is Auguste Caillouet, and my *maman* was Véronique Caillouet née Favreau."

He tucked his injured hand behind his back. "The sight of my wound seemed to draw forth your true nature."

"*Non.*" She whined. "The priests want me to starve. The bad voice comes and tells me to do bad things, but I do not listen to it."

"They are giving you blood."

"It is from cows or swine." She scrunched up her face. "It is like nothing. They laugh at me when I ask for more. They are cruel."

Father Molinari found himself halfway through the cell before he realized she could reach him.

"You are nice to me. I will not listen to the bad feeling." Sabine sat on the floor.

Father Molinari lowered himself and sat next to her, rigid as a hunter about to have tea with a lion. She tugged at her nightdress to hide the shackles on her legs, as if embarrassed by them.

"I am lonely since *Maman* died. May I sit closer?"

"It is a sin to lie, Sabine. I fear you are trying to trick me."

She stared at her toes. "It is not as the bad priests say. I am not a monster. Papa did this. I am frightened and alone."

"Your father is a vampire?"

"*Oui.*" She gazed at him; a droplet of blood gathered at the corner of her right eye and ran down a porcelain cheek.

Without thinking, he reached his arm out and she crawled into his lap, curling up with her head against his chest. The cold, bony little figure trembled. Father Molinari ran his hand through her tangled chestnut-brown hair, horrified at how she felt.

"Would you tell me what happened to your mother?"

She shivered and shook her head. "I cannot. I must concentrate. The feeling wants me to do bad things." Little fingers clutched into his shirt, clinging tight, and she cried.

"I will find a way to help you." He glanced up. "You are not affecting my thoughts, are you?"

"*Non.*" She sniffled. "May I please have a little blood?"

Father Molinari raised his head, a subtle cringe away from the creature in his lap. There it was. The game. Not all hunters use stealth or strength—some use guilt. Now he thought himself the idiot stuck in a lion's cage between the beast and the way out, and it was hungry. What would she do if he tried to leave? Her face, so drawn and grey, hovered mere inches from his throat. He had seen how fast vampires could move. He wouldn't have a chance.

"I will not be angry if you refuse." She put a hand to her stomach. "I would not ask, but it hurts."

"The bite will cloud my mind and turn me to the dark."

"*Non.*" She looked up, eyes widening. "Papa brought us people for feeding. We take only a little, and he makes them forget. The bite does not curse them."

Every fiber of his being cried out to run, yet he found himself mesmerized by the innocence in her eyes. The desperate need for... love? Food? Mercy? He set a hand on her foot, cold as ice, and slid his fingers up to the metal locked about her leg. Not even a vampire child deserved to be treated like this.

"I swear in the eyes of God, I will not harm you." Her expression seemed earnest, desperate, and frightened.

He squinted. *She does not dwell in the eyes of God... but she is a child. How can she not?* His indignation receded. Her features, drawn and wan, wounded him. He turned his gaze away. "You may take a small amount."

"*Merci.*"

Father Molinari leaned his head to the side, but she grasped his arm with both hands and drew his hand to her mouth. He sat rigid as she nipped the bandage away and sank her tiny needles of fangs into the skin around where Josephine had stabbed him. Pain lasted for a fraction of a second before the area went numb. She cradled his hand to her face, holding on, peering up at him with gratitude in her eyes as she sucked on the wound.

After a moment, she pulled down his sleeve, repositioned her mouth over his wrist, and bit again. Within seconds, the skin sealed over the stab wound, though lingering pain hinted damage beneath the surface remained. She emitted soft moans and suckled. He had watched vampires feed before; twice, he nearly got himself killed when he could not bear to witness the act and gave himself away with a noise of disgust. Never in his life had he seen one of the creatures take such precious care with the process.

Sabine stopped herself two minutes later, pulling back and looking up at him, bloody fangs exposed in a gaping mouth. She breathed in heavy gasps; for an instant, the look of a predator gleamed through her emerald eyes, but innocence returned. Her fangs retracted, and she licked the trail of blood from his forearm.

Color spread over her skin, a subtle shift from deathly grey to pale flesh. Trails of once-deflated veins lifted along the tops of her feet and down her arms. Her cheeks warmed with a faint pink hue. To look at her now, she would seem alive at a cursory glance. Her arm beneath his touch remained chilly, but no longer did he hold a diminutive moving corpse. Sabine studied her hands, marveling at the change.

It would be a kindness to destroy her before she becomes like the ravening fiend in Vienna. How long can a little mind resist?

She rewarded him with a heart-melting, grateful smile. Father Molinari almost soiled his pants when she leapt up and wrapped her arms around him, but all she did was hug.

"*Maman* was right. A real priest will help me." She made a sour face at the door. "Those men are not priests. They're supposed to help children, not shut them in locked rooms."

He cradled her, unsettled by how *normal* she acted. The dichotomy of her calm demeanor in contrast to her dismal situation left a large knot in his stomach. He kept stroking her hair, a gesture that appeared to calm her.

"How is it you came to be wandering alone?"

Sabine curled her toes into his leg, and sniffled. "*Maman* prayed to God to take back what Papa had done to me. When God did not, Papa said she went mad and ran into the sun."

"I'm sorry." He brushed his hand over her hair.

"Is *Maman* with God now?" She lifted her head to look him in the eye. "Lying is a sin."

He took a long, deep breath. "Taking one's own life is a mortal sin. However, it is debatable if a vampire has a life to take. Perhaps the two cancel each other and she wanders in limbo, neither damned nor welcomed to paradise."

"I think you are right." Sabine laid her head against his heart again, hands clutched at her chest. "I heard her voice. She told me to go outside and find a priest, but they are bad."

For some time, he held her in silence. Eventually, Sabine became groggy and settled in as if to sleep.

He glanced at the door. "I must return to my room before I am noticed here."

"Please do not leave me like this." She pulled on the chain. "I am scared."

"If I am seen here, they may do something rash." He stood and set her on her feet. "I give you my word I will do everything in my power to help you."

Sabine clamped onto his leg, whining like the child she appeared to be. "Please don't go."

He peeled her away and held her hands. "I must. Sometimes we must do things we find unpleasant because they are necessary."

She pouted and shuffled to the rear wall, where she plopped down. "I will trust you."

Father Molinari retrieved the lantern from the floor and hovered in the corridor, watching her try to get comfortable on the stone. The task appeared more difficult now that she had a touch of life within her. His head swam and balance became elusive. *How much blood had she taken?* With a heavy heart, he pulled the door closed, locked it, and set the bar in place. All of it seemed overkill for such a little girl, though the Milano vampire had hurled a coach at his mentor, Cardinal Alfieri.

He hurried back to his room, chasing away the gnawing fear of what sinister plan might be rattling around her tiny head.

CHAPTER SIX

KNOW THINE ENEMY

March 12ᵗʰ 1885 Briançon, France

Fathers Callini and Renault allowed him to rest well into the afternoon, and busied themselves with local affairs for most of the eleventh. He spent much of the day in quiet prayer, beseeching God for a sign of what to do with such an untenable situation. They visited Sabine once after the sun went down, to offer a cup of cow's blood. She read Molinari's hinting glance, and did not converse with them during the short encounter.

The previous night had come with insomnia again. At sleeping most of the day and finding himself awake at night, he at first feared allowing the child to bite him released the curse of vampirism into his blood. How could he have been so foolish to trust her? Had her undead nature had given her guile beyond her years? From the instant he'd laid eyes on her, her pathetic appearance had tugged at his heart. She must have sensed it. All it took is one bite. Soon, he'd be her servant or worse—an undead as well.

Losing half the day made sense after he pondered. He'd been awake most of the night and on the road more than not these past weeks. He rubbed his arm where she'd bitten him, sensing no pain or tenderness anywhere except the knife wound. It seemed whatever dark magic she possessed had only mended the skin. The center of the hand was a poor site from which to draw blood. He traced a finger over the tender part. *The only reason for her to bite there would have been to close the wound.* Father Molinari rewound the old bandage to hide the miraculous healing.

"A favor for a favor?"

Last night, once the priests had retired, too worn out from their duties in Briançon to bother with 'testing' the vampire child, he'd repeated his nocturnal visitation. Sabine had been thrilled to see him, though she had begged for another drink, which she took with a dainty nip and perfect manners. He spent a few hours with her afterward. If not for the plain stone walls and chain, it would have felt as if he'd looked after an ordinary girl.

The morning of the twelfth came with a heavy head. He loathed the idea of leaving her alone down there, but feared the reaction of the local priests if they caught him with her or if he suggested anything contrary to the doctrine of burn and purge. What he wanted to do was bring her to Rome, and hope that Cardinal Benedetto had access to some ancient secrets that might free her from the curse of darkness.

Increasing protectiveness towards her—a feeling she existed as a child rather than a *creature*—sent him soul-searching. He fasted through breakfast, kneeling by the lone window of his small bedchamber, and prayed. Between recitations, spontaneous invocations beseeching wisdom and guidance, he meditated in quiet.

In these times, he saw her smiling face upon the backs of his eyelids. An innocent child in desperate need of protection. Logic warned him she had charmed him. He knew firsthand the effect a vampire's will could exert on the living. Some could plant seeds of ideas, some gave orders, and others could radiate beauty and charm that made everyone regard them with worshipful eyes.

His guilt questioned his training. In all the records he had seen in Rome, no member of the *Ordinis Sancti Michaelis* had once documented a vampiric child. It seemed unlikely such an event had never happened before. Perhaps they were either too well hidden or destroyed by their own kind? Surely, a creature with the power of a vampire and a lack of maturity would have been noticed. A misbehaving boy throwing a tantrum over a denied treat was one thing, but if said boy could tear people in half when he didn't get his way...

Molinari shivered.

"Our father in Heaven, grant me the wisdom to do your will."

He repeated the Lord's Prayer again before lapsing into silent meditation. Moments later, a light knock at the door opened his eyes.

"Enter."

The door emitted a *squeak*. Father Callini approached. "*Buon pomeriggio*, padre."

"And a good afternoon to you, father." Molinari smiled. "I am guessing you long for an excuse to use Italian."

"I fear it may rust." Father Callini smiled. "We missed you at morning bread."

Molinari stood. "I have fasted in hopes of receiving guidance."

"Come; please join us for an afternoon meal."

He followed to the end of the upstairs hall where a small dining area contained a table, six chairs, and the bountiful smell of fresh-baked bread. Father Renault sat at the far end, and waved as they walked in. The teen who had taken the horses laid out plates of still-warm bread and cheese once they took their seats, still giving Molinari a wary look.

"My apologies, my son. Have I done something to cause you alarm?"

"Tristan is concerned the demons may stalk their greatest adversary," said Father Renault over a mouthful. "He fears a force of darkness looms over your shoulder."

Father Molinari chuckled. "There are days when I fear the same, though I have faith in God to protect me."

Callini mumbled his agreement, not bothering to attempt to form words while chewing.

"I am sorry, Father," said Tristan. "They say you have battled many demons. It seems that the forces of Satan would seek to strike you down." He fidgeted with a bit of bread on his plate. "The creature we have captured... It is not right."

"Yes." Father Molinari took a bite of cheese. "There is much going on here I cannot begin to understand."

"Agreed." Father Renault wagged a slice of bread. "We are free of responsibility in the village today and plan to conduct some tests, with your observation, of course."

Molinari lost the urge to eat his last piece of cheese. "What manner of tests?"

Father Callini dabbed at his mouth with a napkin; crumbs fell down his shirt. "Merely to evaluate some of the standard folklore... except for crossing running water. It would not be worth the risk to let the creature out of its cell. It's already broken the rope we secured around its wrists."

"We couldn't find a manacle small enough," said Father Renault.

"She chewed through." Molinari still stared at the off-white square on his plate. "If she had the strength to burst rope of that thickness, she'd have snapped the manacles by now, torn the door from its hinges, and likely done unspeakable things to the both of you."

Renault and Callini exchanged glances.

"I ask that you consider your actions in this matter." Molinari picked at the cheese. "While she does appear to have been afflicted with the curse of vampirism, I am hopeful there may still be a trace of the person she once was."

"You are sentimental," said Renault with a smile. "As much as you have encountered, I understand your want to see hope where there is none. The girl that creature once was, is gone. The shell of a person has been filled with evil."

"The humane thing to do will be to end its torment and send it to God." Father Callini made the sign of the cross.

"You cannot send it to God." Renault held up a hand while he finished chewing. "Those fiends do not have souls. The girl is already lost."

"It feels *wrong*." Molinari pushed his plate away. Phantom fangs pierced his wrist. *Am I losing my appetite? I seem loathe to rise with the sun. What is next, will the daylight burn me?* He pulled the plate back and took the cheese. "There are..." He grumbled, and pointed at the men. "Do not speak of what I am about to tell you."

The priests nodded.

"There are over three hundred and eight cases of vampirism as recorded by my brethren in the Order. Not once in four centuries has there been a single instance of this, a child. I am at a loss to explain how such an atrocity has never been documented before. My hope is that her condition is curable. She has not had time to lose her innocence. The darkness has nothing to grab hold of. No deceit, no greed, no hate." He tossed the last bit of cheese in his mouth. "No desire for power or to control others."

"I wish I could retain your optimism, Father." Renault blessed himself. "Have you considered they have some manner of organization and are not mere simple beasts?"

At watching him devour his food, Tristan fetched more bread.

Molinari accepted a slice. "Yes. I have considered that. It is possible that there is some manner of code they follow which forbids it. Perhaps villagers simply destroy them when they occur and do not wish to speak of such things. Yet, you have seen with your own eyes blessed water does not burn her."

"Holy ground did." Callini raised an eyebrow as if to say 'check.'

Molinari lowered the flap of rye from his mouth. "I will not abide torturing an innocent child."

"It's not a child, Father." Callini stood. "It is a wolf in sheep's clothing."

Renault helped himself to two more pieces of bread and some cheese. *The way that man eats, he should be enormous.* Molinari half-smiled and considered his recent blood loss. He, too, claimed another hunk of cheese. They ate in silence for a time. Once everyone had their fill, Tristan collected the empty plates and carried them out. Renault seized a bread heel from the serving tray in the middle of the table and gnawed on it as they made their way down the hall, down the stairs, and outside.

I must not shut my mind to the possibility I have been deceived.

Back and forth, his thoughts wandered over his two clandestine visitations. Both had presented her with ample opportunity to kill him, yet she did not. She had struggled at the chain, seeming to have no more strength than a delicate child her age should have. Why had she not torn herself loose? It could not be starvation; he had given her blood. He gazed up at puffy white clouds while a warm breeze rolled over the garden, lofting the scent of growing vegetables and damp goat. One of the animals trundled by, pursuing Renault in hopes of a bread crust.

Heaviness settled within Father Molinari's chest. *God sent me here for a reason, but what* is *it? We are men of God, yet what we do feels like the work of Satan.*

Bread and cheese swirled at the back of his throat, pushed up by guilt and dread. Callini opened the inner door and led the way down the spiral stairway. Father Renault approached the cell and hefted the bar out of its cradle. While Father Callini muttered prayers of protection, Renault unlocked the latch and pushed the door in.

Sabine lay curled on her side, feet against the wall, hands clutching the chain a few inches shy of the ring. It appeared as though she'd fallen asleep while struggling to free herself. She remained inert, unresponsive to the activity at the door. Molinari stepped in, drawing gasps from the others as he crossed the red cord without hesitation.

"Be careful," whispered Callini after a quick attempt to grab Molinari missed.

"When was the last time you confronted a vampire?" asked Molinari.

"Only this one." said Renault, sounding defeated.

"It is not the mere absence of light." He stooped and grasped her forearms. Her skin seemed neither warm nor cold, her body limp like a rubber doll's. "They are inherently tied to day and night. Even if the sun cannot reach them, they sleep."

Callini gasped again as Molinari rolled her to lay flat on her back in a position that appeared more comfortable. "If it wakes up, it will kill you. Come back out of its reach at once."

"She cannot wake now. There are many hours of daylight remaining." He retrieved her doll, and put it in her arms before grabbing the rope that had bound her arms. Once back at the entrance to the chamber, he held it up to their examination. "Frayed. Chewed through. Nothing more than an ordinary child could have done."

"An 'ordinary' child with sharp fangs." Callini glanced away and down.

"So a hunter who finds a vampire in the day can destroy them with no risk?" Renault raised an eyebrow.

"That axiom is not without its failures." Molinari spoke in a low tone, a hair more than a whisper. "There are documented instances of premature waking. One case comes to mind where three of the fiends shared a nest. Six of our order went in, one left alive. They were confident the vampires would remain helpless, but as soon as the first began its death throes, the other two sprang from their beds and set upon them."

"I would like to understand how that is possible," said Callini.

Renault looked downcast. "We'd have to capture another one."

"There is another component, I think." Molinari glanced at Sabine. "One I do not yet fully understand."

Father Renault tiptoed over to Sabine, shaking as if the slightest unexpected noise would stop his heart. He dangled a clove of garlic over her face, but the child did not react in the slightest. He seemed unable to tolerate the proximity any longer and backed away.

"We should return once she is awake. Your tests will be meaningless now." Molinari pulled the door closed. "You should also consider permitting her small amounts of human blood."

The priests gasped.

"Unholy!" whisper-yelled Renault.

Molinari raised his hands. "What good will your information do if it is tainted by unnatural circumstances?"

"Everything about this is unnatural." Callini folded his arms. "What you are suggesting is against God."

"So is chaining a little girl in a basement." Molinari glared at him. "Use your head. If vampires could exist happily on animal blood, do you not think they would do so? If none of them made meals of humans, would we even know of their existence?"

After a moment of meek silence, Renault muttered at the floor. "It's not a little girl, it's a vampire."

"It would be in their best interest to remain as discreet as possible, would it not?" Molinari waved about. "There is something lacking in the blood of beasts. It does not sate them. What if her weakened state alters her reaction to your tests? Our brethren fighting the more dangerous ones will not have the luxury of their prey being a step from death's door."

"I-I can't believe I'm about to agree to this, but how do you suggest we go about doing that?" Father Callini ran a hand over his head, smoothing his hair. "We do not know if the bite carries the curse. I will not permit it to touch me."

To lie is to sin. "I have heard tell of some who are able to feed without killing. Their victims did not turn."

"You have proof of this?" asked Renault.

"I do not. It is but rumor." Molinari smiled. "However, there is a simple solution to that problem. An intermediary vessel. A chalice or bowl."

Renault fidgeted.

Callini nodded. "It is something to consider, but I must pray on whether or not to give such a creature blood is an affront to God."

It cannot be. Father Molinari bowed his head in quiet reflection.

"Let us return once the sun has set." Renault gestured at the stairs.

Hours later, after a supper of sausages and stewed cabbage, they made their way back. Father Molinari paused at the entrance to the cottage beyond the garden and stared up at dark clouds racing through an indigo sky. Distant wind howled at the mountain peaks, though no breeze moved around the garden. Far off in Briançon, a hand bell rang in a slow, repetitive *pang-pang*. The moon, stark and pale, peeked through the gaps whenever the gloom allowed. An unusual chill in the air chased him inside, and they shuffled underground in silence.

Again, with lantern raised, Renault led the way into the depths. With each step down, Molinari's gut churned with guilt. Walking into a cloud of Renault's sausage-laden belch almost brought his meal back into the world.

Sabine's forlorn weeping reached halfway up the stairs, burdening Molinari's already tattered conscience. Jingling chain and rhythmic clicking hinted at pacing. Father Callini set a small leather knapsack down near the cell and stepped back.

Renault gasped at the realization he'd forgotten to replace the bar and nudged the door open with a trembling hand. He relaxed once Sabine came into view, still safely tethered. She stood near the back wall, clutching the ragdoll to her chest. Her cheeks bore thin trails of dried blood from the corners of her eyes.

"Thank the Lord the chain has withstood its wrath," said Renault.

Father Callini removed a bulb of garlic from his knapsack. Sabine made a petulant face at him. He approached the line and held it out. The girl stared.

"It wants to kill you," whispered Renault.

"*Non.* I think he is a bad priest. He is mean to me." She teetered closer.

"Your manipulation will not work on me, fiend." Father Callini tossed the garlic to the ground at her feet.

Sabine ignored it.

"Maybe one bulb is not enough?" Renault raised an eyebrow.

Callini poked him in the side. "Well, if you'd not have protested having none left for cooking, I'd have brought the entire string."

Renault rubbed the spot, scowling. "It is a sin to waste food."

Sabine crouched and picked up the garlic, sniffing at it. "*Ca ne me dérange pas.*"

Callini winced at her rapid French.

"She says it does not bother her." Molinari dipped a quill and took notes on a sheet of vellum in Italian. *Garlic... no noticeable reaction.*

She leaned to the side to send a pleading look around Callini.

Father Renault stepped up to the red cord and threw holy water on her.

Sabine frowned.

"Holy water does not do anything either," said Renault.

"It is water." Sabine wiped her arms off. "I do not like it because it is wet, and I am cold."

Both priests glanced back at Molinari, kneeling by his papers and book, writing: *Child vampire has no reaction to holy water. No sign of burning. No smoke.*

"Is this normal for vampires?" asked Callini.

"In prior meetings..." Father Molinari paused to finish writing a word. "Except in Vienna, the effect of holy water bore striking similarities to the effect of strong acid upon a mortal body."

"What happened in Vienna?" asked Renault.

Molinari did not look up from his jotting. "The creature never made it out of its bed. I did not need to use holy water."

"Why do you think this one does not burn?" Callini looked back and forth between him and the girl.

"Why do you talk as if I am not here?" Sabine shuffled forward until the chain stopped her. "I can hear you, but you do not care what I think."

Father Callini glared, eyebrows furrowed as his brain chewed on her French.

Renault blinked, then laughed. "Well then, darkling, what is your thought?" He folded his arms.

"I think the water is blessed of God. I pray for Him to help me. I have not turned my back on Him, so the water does not hurt."

"Some part of her is tainted by Satan still," muttered Molinari. "How long can she hold it at bay?"

"Some part? I think all... but that would be something to test. Though, it may take years." Father Callini rubbed his chin.

Sabine's expression collapsed with sadness. "*Non. Merci.* Do not keep me shut in here forever. I am lonely."

Renault's eye twitched. Callini frowned, unimpressed. Molinari sent an imploring look at the dark stone overhead as Callini took a large crucifix from the bag and held it aloft. Sabine regarded it with casual disinterest.

"Begone unclean spirit," said Callini.

"I would love to." Sabine pulled her nightdress up off her feet. "Please unlock me, and I will do so."

"The Crucified Christ has no effect." Callini lowered his head in defeat.

"Perhaps you lack faith." Molinari stood.

Callini stepped back as if slapped. "How can you say such a thing?"

"You invoke from where you know she cannot reach you. You do not put your trust in God as a shield and sword." He took the crucifix from Callini's hand. "By hiding out here, you prove this."

Molinari entered the cell, Callini and Renault too stunned to attempt to stop him. He held the crucifix up and advanced to within inches of the child. She smiled up at him.

"It is not screaming or cowering in the light of God," said Renault.

"She is also not harming me," said Molinari. "Child, does the sight of our Suffering Lord cause you any distress?"

Sabine nodded. "Yes, Father. It is bad what they did to Jesus, but he had to give himself to save us."

Renault made a squealing noise. Callini grumbled.

"You are correct, girl." Molinari winked. "However, I mean physical pain."

She shook her head, her long, thick hair dancing about. "*Non.*"

Callini removed a wooden stake from the bag. "I have read that to destroy a vampire, one must sever the head after driving a wooden stake through the heart. If one simply pierces the beast, it serves only to immobilize them until the implement is withdrawn."

Sabine tripped over her shackles in her haste to back up. She scurried into the wall, shaking.

"I'm not going to do that." Molinari frowned. "If you wish to test that, you will need to do it yourself. The fiend in Vienna exploded into flames as soon as I impaled it."

"*Non!*" Sabine covered her face in her hands and bawled. After a moment, she kicked at her legs, trying to get away.

Father Callini stared at her, knuckles creaking on the wood. He breathed in and out in sharp, harsh gasps. When he entered the cell and crossed the cord, Sabine screamed. Molinari leapt in front of him.

"Wait."

"Wait?" Father Callini's face reddened. "You tell me to do it myself and then say wait?"

"I didn't think you had the nerve." He glanced back at the sniveling child. "If there is any hope to redeeming her, I do not want to do something that drastic until I have exhausted all options. True, a darkness attacks her soul. Do you think a child this age could have *wanted* this? Most of these fiends crave power. They are humans who gave themselves willingly to the dark, who have walked away from God. I must try to purge this evil and reach out to the soul trapped within."

Father Callini backed up. "I do not know whether to pray for you, or pity you. A fool searches for light and hope where there are none."

Renault pursed his lips and shifted his weight.

Molinari left the cell to retrieve his sacred book from the hallway. "There are some secret rites I have yet to try. Incantations we have closely guarded for centuries. If I am not successful with them, I would ask the two of you to accompany me back to Rome, with this child. Cardinal Benedetto may be able to offer some counsel."

"Dangerous." Father Renault's jowls wobbled as he shook his head. "How would we travel with such a creature in any sense of safety?"

"I would not harm you." Sabine sniffled and wiped her face. "Even after you have been so cruel to me."

"It says what you wish to hear." Father Callini tossed the stake at the bag. "We can wait for it to sleep, and seal it in a casket for transport."

She pouted.

Molinari shooed them to the stairway. "I am not permitted to allow those outside the Order to witness these rites."

"Praise God, we cannot let you risk yourself." Father Renault broke out in a heavy sweat.

"I have spent eleven of my thirty-two years battling the darkness. If I do not feel threatened by this child, you should not fear. I trust in God as my protector. He is the light leading me through the dark. Seal the door if you must, but allow me the solace I need for my attempt to save her soul."

The priests exchanged a nervous glance. Renault ended the stalemate first by reaching in and setting a lantern on the floor before pulling the door shut. Sabine twitched as the lock *clicked*. Molinari stared at the door, at the two-by-eight foot patch of cell Sabine could not reach, and the short distance beyond where only her hands could go.

He tensed when the girl shuffled over and put her arms around his waist. "Thank you for staying with me. I do not like it in here."

God guide me and keep me in our hour of need.

He glanced down at the beautiful, innocent smile aimed up at him. If deceit indeed lurked behind those shimmering green eyes, he had nowhere to go. Her smile proved infectious, and he patted her on the head.

Father Molinari had no doubt God would protect him.

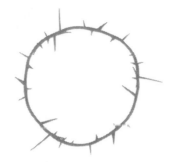

CHAPTER SEVEN

MERCY KILLING

March 12th 1885 Briançon, France

On his knees in the middle of the room, Father Molinari steeled himself and pulled the lantern closer. Eye to eye with the unliving child, he clung to his faith and set the sacred book on the ground. Sabine stood, calm and quiet, watching as he flipped to the last three-quarters, navigating the tome by tugging at red silk ribbon bookmarks. She spun back and forth, letting her limp arms fly. After a few minutes, she shifted her weight onto one leg and traced her foot from side to side while he skimmed over page after page of Latin rites. He searched for one of the old incantations, which might afford some manner of relief to her situation.

"What are you doing?" She tilted her head.

"I am trying to help." He flipped three pages to the start of the next section. "Some of these haven't been spoken aloud since the 1300s."

"Are they magic?" Sabine crouched and crawled up alongside him, peering at the book.

The jingling of chain dragging clenched the jaws of guilt around his heart. He glanced down at her twig-thin legs, as if the enmity radiating from his eyes could shatter the metal. Vampire or not, Sabine was a child.

Is she affecting my thoughts?

"It looks like magic." She tried to pronounce some of the words, but sounded like a three-year-old learning to speak.

"Some people think the Vatican libraries hold such things." He smiled and winked.

"Do they?" Her eyes went wide.

"Well." He turned another page. It was easy to pretend she was a normal child, not locked in a cell, not undead. "I think if there are, they would be things to fight demons with. Since there are no demons running around in broad daylight anymore, they don't need them. Perhaps they are dangerous, so they guard them close."

Sabine covered her mouth and gasped.

"Or maybe people have wild imaginations."

"*Maman* told me vampires are only in storybooks." She picked at her doll's dress. "Are other monsters 'only in storybooks?'"

"I have not seen a dragon." He smiled. "Okay, give me a moment of quiet."

She nodded.

He shifted around to face her, held his hands out, and chanted from the book. The Latin passage beseeched Saint Luke and Archangel Michael himself to lift the darkness from the subject of the prayer. Sabine listened patiently, at one point closing her eyes and concentrating as if her fervent wish might tilt the scales of fate in her favor.

Father Molinari finished the passage with little hope it had done any good. Stagnant air grew thicker with the stink of burning lantern oil. Perhaps he had not been given all the information. If there was any so-called 'magic' in this rite, it may require certain preparations he had not the time nor the training to make. Reagents, oils, candles, perhaps sacred symbols. He pinched the bridge of his nose. *I am falling into a pit. Am I giving serious thought to the arcane?*

"I do not feel different."

He ran a hand over her hair. "How do you feel?"

She frowned at her knees, whispering. "Hungry."

God in Heaven, please grant me the wisdom to help this lost soul.

"How has such a cruel thing been done to you?" He pulled her into his lap, cringing as the chain slid over his leg.

"Papa put the bad feeling in my head after he and *Maman* yelled at each other for a whole night. I had never heard Papa so angry. When they quieted, Papa found me hiding under my bed. He picked me up and held me. He said bad things about *Maman*, and left me on my bed, but I did not sleep until the sun came." She stared at his arm as he rolled his sleeve back. "When *Maman* saw me the next night, she fell and cried."

Sabine grasped his arm, drawing his wrist to her lips. Her fangs elongated as she opened her mouth. Molinari looked away, wincing as the little needles tore his skin. She suckled at his wrist, and the vein in his arm swelled.

A moment passed before she lifted away and licked blood from her lips. "*Maman* was so sad. She prayed and prayed, asking God to help me." Sabine leaned down and drank again.

He offered a silent prayer for her mother's soul. "Her guilt drove her to the sun."

She nodded without breaking contact.

The door swung open.

Molinari and Sabine jumped like a pair of lovers caught in the act.

"God in Heaven," said Callini.

Father Renault went bug eyed. "Poor Father Molinari! She's charmed him. God forgive us. W-we never should have played with such a monster."

Sabine pulled away, and cowered behind him.

"Calm yourselves." Molinari stood, raising his hand. "She is no threat."

"You've been seduced." Father Callini dove on his bag and grabbed the stake. "Fools we were! We must destroy it before it kills us all."

Renault made the sign of the cross. "Forgive us, Father, for leaving you alone with this monster."

Molinari held up both hands. "You are overreact—"

Father Callini rushed in, stake raised. Sabine screamed and scurried backwards. Father Molinari jumped into him, knocking him against the wall. He grabbed the young priest by the forearms, wrestling.

"Renault..." Callini gurgled.

The heavier man thundered in, though he hesitated at the red cord. Callini had perhaps a ten-year advantage in youth, though seemed an even match in strength. Molinari twisted and pushed, trying to force him to the door.

"Calm yourself, Callini!" he shouted, straining to pin the man's arms to the wall.

"Go away!" wailed Sabine. "Don't hurt me."

Renault, covered in sweat, surged over the red cord. He roared, grabbing Molinari from behind. For an instant, his collision crushed the two smaller men into the stones, drawing a wheezing gurgle from Callini.

"Forgive me, Father." Renault heaved back, dragging Molinari away. "Kill it now!"

Callini twisted out of Molinari's grasp, taking one step closer to the screaming child before Molinari kicked him in the groin and knocked him to his knees with a beet red face. Renault got his arms around Molinari's middle, squeezing the air out of him. Sabine crawled away from Callini, dragging herself in an arc to the door until the chain stopped her. She kicked and screamed at the shackles as her hands slipped over the smooth floor.

"Don't push her!" yelled Molinari. "If she fears destruction, she may give herself to Satan to survive. It is not too late for her."

"*Non! Merci!*" yelled Sabine, breaking into sobs. "*Maman! Maman!*"

Molinari growled and drove his fist into Renault's gut. The big man wheezed sausage-laden air over Molinari's hair and careened ass-first into the wall. Molinari jumped on Callini's back before he could stand, grabbing the wrist of the arm that held the stake.

"Satan has him!" Callini bashed at the side of Molinari's head with an elbow, trying to knock him away. "He is too strong!"

Renault gasped for air. At the sight of Sabine prostrate within inches of his foot, he screamed at a woman's pitch and hustled to the door. Molinari rolled to the side, threading an arm around the younger priest's neck. Shoes scuffed at the stone; the scent of mildew flooded his lungs. Sabine stared at Molinari, pleading. Her skin had enough color that she appeared how she must have been in life; her limbs, though still dainty, looked fuller. *With each feeding, she seems more alive. Am I hallucinating?*

Callini flung him off in his moment of doubt and scrambled upright. He lunged at the girl, driving the stake into the floor a split second after she sprang back. Callini grabbed the chain and dragged her closer. Molinari staggered upright, stepping in to a kick to the young priest's stomach that lifted him off his feet. Sabine scurried to the corner and cowered. Renault lumbered to his feet. Molinari slugged him in the jaw, knocking him back to the floor. Callini pushed himself up to his knees, holding his belly. Molinari spun around, fist cocked.

"Stop! You are *priests*!" yelled Sabine. She cowered against the wall, eyes wide with horrified disbelief. "You're not supposed to hit."

Callini gasped and wheezed, bracing his hand on the wall. The stake slid from his fingers and *clattered* to the floor. Molinari kicked it at the door, but it hit the wall instead and remained in the cell. Callini surged to his feet with a right hook, catching Molinari in the ear and knocking stars into his vision. Rather than follow up, the younger man brushed past him and went for the stake.

Molinari shook off the daze, and tackled Callini into the stone. "You will not harm her. She is an innocent!"

Callini got his fingers on the stake a split second before Molinari grabbed his arm. The young priest's free left hand seized Molinari's wrist.

Sabine covered her ears, shaking her head and whispering, "*Non.* Be quiet. I will not listen. Do not say such things of *Maman.* I do not trust you, leave me alone."

Renault stumbled upright and seized Molinari by the shoulders. Sabine, screaming, thrashed at the chain. Her continuous pleas for the men to stop fighting went unheeded. Rather than be hauled away, Molinari lunged and drove his fist into Renault's breadbasket. The big man gawped and hit the ground like a sack of potatoes. When Molinari whirled to face Callini, a flash of pain lanced through his chest. The world seemed to drag to a standstill. The blond priest's face warped with rage, terror, and regret, frozen as an instant stretched to a minute.

Molinari glanced down at himself, at the handle of a misericord impaled to the hilt near his breastbone. Strength melted out of his legs, and he rolled backward to the ground. Sound took on a watery quality as if he'd plunged into a lake. Sabine bawled. A hollow wooden *clonk* came from the right.

Callini loomed over him, his expression horrified. "My God, my God, what have I done?"

Father Renault wheezed. Molinari's leg twisted as something heavy crawled past him.

A chain jingled behind his head.

He lifted a hand to his chest, easing his fingers around the plain wooden handle of the blade jutting out of him. An ache deep within throbbed in time with his heartbeat. *The wound is mortal.*

Antonio Molinari closed his eyes. "Father, into your hands I commend my spirit."

CHAPTER EIGHT

UNTO DARKNESS

March 12ᵗʰ 1885 Briançon, France

The ringing of a chain on stone changed to the slap of a taut leash striking the floor. A childish grunt strained nearby and let off with a sigh. Molinari drifted out of time. His hand slipped from the blade and flopped on the ground.

"Do it now," said Renault, his voice echoing to infinity.

Molinari thought of Heaven.

Sabine struggled to pull herself forward. The nice priest lay inches from her fingertips. When the blond man glanced at the stake, she pushed herself upright and glared at him. His eyes went wide as their gazes locked. Father Molinari's blood had filled her with warmth and hope. Days without either had not broken her trust *Maman's* prayer would be heard. Papa had done something bad, but God could not blame her for it.

These men wanted to kill her. What sort of priest carries a knife?

"Go away!" Her shackles rattled as she stomped. She wanted him to go away. She wanted them both to go away. Something tugged at her thoughts, not the *bad feeling,* but a sense of exertion that manifested in time with a glazed look on the priests' faces.

Father Callini stumbled to the side and rushed out of the cell. The pudgy man screamed again and slammed the door closed. Sabine flung herself on her chest, ignoring the *snick* of the iron lock and heavy *thud* of the wooden bar.

"Father, please!" She pulled herself forward until metal bit into her heels. "Father Molinari! Wake up!"

A child's voice hammered at the side of Molinari's consciousness. Pain in his chest, worse than any he could recall, took the feeling from his legs and left him dizzy. The child cried out again. He peeled one eye open and twisted his head toward the sound. A little hand flailed on the far side of a blurry red cord.

"Wake up!" she wailed. "Come closer."

With a grunt, he flung his weight to the side. He grabbed at the stone floor, his hand sliding more than pulling him. Nothing existed but the need to move forward. He tried to push with his feet, but couldn't tell if he moved them or imagined it. Something picked at the tips of his fingers. Small hands.

Closer. Closer...

He heaved with the last of his strength, collapsing flat. At the sense of a child grasping his arm, he stopped trying to move.

Sabine got both her hands around his wrist and held on; the leash let her use her entire body to pull him closer. The bad feeling offered to make it easier. It showed her visions of being strong enough to snap her chains, pull him with ease, or break down the door. Sabine thought of her mother, and begged God to let her be nice to the man who had shown her kindness. Blood trickled down her feet as the manacles bit into her skin. She reached up and grabbed his shirt, pulling and screaming.

Father Molinari snapped out of his delirium as small fingers clenched a fistful of fabric at his collarbone. He moaned and dragged himself another few inches back. Sabine collapsed on top of him for a few seconds before moving to kneel beside his head. He looked up at her, filled with remorse for being unable to spare her.

"I'm sorry... I have failed."

A tiny hand covered his mouth. "It is my fault you are dying."

No. Don't...

Blackness.

Sabine thought back to what Papa had done to *Maman*. She raised her right wrist to her mouth and slit it deep with her fangs. Holding the wound over Father Molinari's mouth, she grasped her forearm and squeezed the thick blood onto his lips and tongue. She did not want him to die. She wanted him to come back to her. Drops hit his teeth, filtering through the gaps. By the fifth one, he began to lap at it. At the tenth, he opened his mouth wide.

"Thank God. It is working." She grinned.

Father Molinari reached up; his hand engulfed hers. She held her wrist over his mouth, afraid to stop before she'd given him enough to save his life.

He pulled her arm down and sucked the blood from the cut. The sense of energy flowing out of her felt good at first, it meant she was helping. He fed with increasing fervor, clutching her arm like a starving dog on a bone. Her eyes widened with fear as her skin grew paler before her eyes.

"Enough. You should stop now." She pulled away, but his hunger would not release her. "Father, please... stop!"

He grasped her arm with his other hand, holding her in a painful grip as he drew the life out of her. Snaps and crunches jarred the bones of his face. Sabine screamed. She tried to kick him in the head, but the chain held her feet too far away. She wailed and pulled, at the verge of panic. The bad feeling in her head made itself known: accept what it offered or perish. She could be strong enough to save herself.

Sabine slapped at his face and pounded at his chest. "Father, stop! You are killing me!"

A sense of energy moving inside her seemed to peel up from her legs, flow through her chest, and siphon down her arm.

The feeling in her mind, the dark tempter, grew stronger. She withdrew from it.

"*Maman* would not like that." Her eyes fluttered.

Molinari snarled, biting, sucking.

She pulled with all the natural strength of an eight-year-old waif—no match for a grown man. Her mother's voice spoke in her thoughts; the comforting sound held back her panic. Her body grew heavy and leaden, but she continued to ignore the bad feeling as the cell blurred and spun.

I hear you, Maman.

A tiny heartbeat rattled in Father Molinari's mind, racing with terror and overpowering the childish mewls nearby. Reason came on with a flash; the slender white arm in his hands belonged to the little girl he had so wanted to protect. He lifted his mouth from her wrist, staring in horror at the pallid skin. Sabine collapsed across his chest, as limp as a doll. Seconds later, she rolled off to the side and onto her back.

Father Molinari sat up, shocked into numbness by what he had done. Her once-lifelike body now looked worse than it did when he had first laid eyes on her, sunken and grey. A hint of her skull showed through her cheeks; her collarbones, so thin and brittle, protruded clear upon her neck. His attempt to breathe brought notice to a frigid needle through his chest, the handle of a narrow dagger. His fingers curled around it, but his brain refused to believe. With a wincing grunt, he yanked the misericord loose and the wound closed. He wasted only a second staring at the weapon before it slipped out of his grasp and fell to the floor.

"Sabine!" he yelled.

She remained still; the cut at her wrist released a slow ooze of dark red. He picked and pawed at her, unsure of what to do. He cradled her lifeless form to his chest. His body wished to cry, but nothing ran from his eyes. He clasped the back of her head and drew her face to his shoulder, patting her on the back and rocking her.

"Please, God, no..." He tried to put his wrist in her mouth. "Take some back..."

Her head lolled to the rear, fangs half extended. Every muscle in his body locked and burned. The child slid down and rolled away. Molinari tried to stand, but the plain grey walls spun in circles. He grabbed his head and screamed as agony crackled through every nerve. The world of color became one of black and white. After a bright flash, the intricacies of the stonework magnified a hundred times; every pit and pore became clear in excruciating detail, as did the scraping of a dozen scuttling insects in the corner. Another flare of blinding light came with a roasting inferno over his skin. He collapsed flat, back arched, and howled until the noise scratched his throat raw and blood pooled in the back of his mouth.

His body had turned traitor, convulsing and thrashing out of control. Scratching rats, creaking bones, and tearing flesh tormented his thoughts; things he should not have been able to hear bombarded him at an impossible volume. He raked his nails down his chest, writhing and wailing until he succumbed to the mercy of unconsciousness.

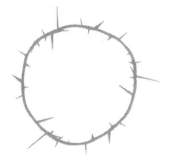

CHAPTER NINE

LA PETITE MÈRE

March 13th 1885 Briançon, France

Father Antonio Molinari glided at the speed of a full run through the rocky meadows surrounding Briançon. The grass, an arm's length below, rushed by fast enough to blur, yet no wind touched his face. Yellow flowers passed like comets. Snow-capped mountains to the west shimmered in the setting sun.

Tristan emerged from the green up ahead, a distrustful glower etched on his face. He glowed as if illuminated by light that existed only to him. The boy rotated in place, facing him as Father Molinari flew past. Somewhere far away, a melodic little girl's voice sang:

Frère Jacques, frère Jacques...

He hovered to a standstill and put his legs down; his body rotated upright. Father Molinari looked to the sky, and witnessed the last few seconds of a red-orange sun slip behind the mountain. He reached at it, not wanting the daystar to flee from him. Wind fluttered his billowy white shirt, the loose ties at the ends of his sleeves whipping about.

Dormez-vous? Dormez-vous?

Molinari glanced in the direction of the singing child. At first, she seemed to be behind him, then to his left, then above. He squinted at the peak as the sky darkened from burnt umber to indigo and black.

Sonnez les matines! Sonnez les matines!

He raised his arms, staring down at his hands covered in blood. Fingers clenched into fists. The wind rose to a gale, beating the meadow like waves of an emerald ocean. When he looked up again, no trace of the sun remained beyond the Alps.

Ding, dang, dong. Ding, dang, dong.

"What has become of me?" He sank to his knees and sat back on his heels. "God, I am your servant. I beg of thee a sign."

His bones became a ponderous weight dragging him over backwards. Sight failed him, and the meadow vanished to an impenetrable night. Rather than hard earth, his head landed upon a cushion.

"*Frère Jacques, frère Jacques*

Dormez-vous? Dormez-vous?"

Father Molinari opened his eyes. Sabine's face hovered over his. She sang in a soft, childish tone while cradling his head in her lap. Her blue lips barely moved. Dark, sunken eyes held great sorrow.

"*Sonnez les matines! Sonnez les matines!*

Ding, dang, dong. Ding, dang, dong."

The child grinned. She had the look of a moving corpse, her skin cold and grey, though her smile brightened his heart. Tiny, claw-like fingers combed through his hair. His body didn't react with even the slightest movement when he tried to sit up.

"Good morning, Father." She reached down and patted the bloody spot on his chest. "Do not be afraid. You will not be moving for a while. It was the same when I woke from the sunset dream."

She sang the rhyme again, using a bit of cloth torn from his shirt to dab blood from his chin.

"What...?" he wheezed.

"The bad priest has gone mad. He tried to hurt you. I made them go away."

He cringed from a ripple of pain twinging up his back. "M-made?"

"*Oui.* I wanted them to go away, and they went." She leaned down and studied him, poking and picking at his shirt. "Do you feel better?"

"I feel... nothing at all right now."

She smiled. "That is good. I prayed for you. We are not safe here."

Father Molinari managed to lift one arm. At the sight of his own grey skin, a great weight crushed his heart inward. Gasping and wheezing, he grabbed at nothing in an effort to sit. Sabine held him down, shushing him as if he were a tantrum-throwing toddler.

"Shh... It is all right." She cradled his head again. "I did not want you to die."

He grabbed his chest. Probing found no mark where the blade had pierced his flesh. His fingertips came away clean.

"If the pain is gone, it will not be long." She rubbed his shoulder. "You will feel like every spider in the whole world walks on your skin. And *voila*! You will be okay."

He moaned.

"You will have a bad feeling." She poked the back of his head with one finger. "It lives in here, and it will tempt you like the Devil. *Maman* says do not listen to it."

Warmth, as if a cooked sausage had been placed upon his chest, brought his eyes to the crucifix hanging around his neck. The metal radiated heat. Though it did not burn, it pierced his soul. He bit his lip to weather the tidal wave of guilt. Eyes closed, he held back a wail of anguish. He recalled Callini's expression when he had mentioned faith. Now was not the time to be a hypocrite.

Father Molinari clasped his fingers around the hot gold, clutching the crucified Lord in a tight fist. *God has led me here for a reason. All that happens is His will.*

The warmth seemed to lessen.

Tingles, pins and needles, swam over him. Sabine did her best to hold him through a second wave of convulsions. Though her meager weight did little to arrest the spasmodic flailing of his legs and arms, she did keep his head from banging into stone. When the fit ceased, a feeling as if a great mound of earth had been lifted from his body came over him. He sat up and drew his feet close, resting his right elbow on the peak of his knee. Sabine clapped. Her deep green eyes sparkled with happiness, despite her ghastly countenance. With wild hair and a filthy nightgown, she resembled a doll forgotten in an attic for a century. The door, the only way out of the cell, remained closed. Despite the feebleness of the flame inside it, the lone remaining lantern illuminated their cell like midafternoon. He stood, surprised at his lack of dizziness, and walked to the exit.

A knot of hunger twisted inside him, a feeling as though he'd gone a week without food. He grunted as his hands slapped the door. The hollow wooden *clonk* echoed in the hall outside. Remembering it opened inward, he tried the knob, which rattled immobile—locked.

Sabine wobbled to her feet, creeping to the end of the chain. "The bad priests will come back. They did not send the boy to feed me."

"Perhaps they will leave us here for eternity." Father Molinari pounded a fist on the door. A glimmer of an idea formed. He *could* break it. It wouldn't take much effort. Something dark and evil slithered around in his thoughts as if a tempting serpent coiled on his shoulders, peering around one side of his head, then the other. His mind filled with visions of the door breaking to splinters.

"No."

He stumbled away and slipped in semi-dry blood. A short distance past the red cord, the crimson coated the floor save for tiny tongue marks. He looked down at Sabine, who continued smiling up at him with adoration. The sight of the shackles on such small legs ignited a fire of rage within him. He pictured the metal snapping in his fingers.

Father Molinari fell to one knee. "No. I will trust in the Lord, my God."

Chains clattered as Sabine ground her big toe into the floor. "They will come for us."

"In the middle of the day when..." He shuddered. "*We* cannot move."

She shook her head. "They will not wait. The young one is mad with guilt."

He dragged himself closer to her and grasped the chain. Mortal strength failed to snap it. He took hold of the tether leading back to the wall, and pulled himself hand over hand down its length until he could brace his feet on the stone. For several minutes, he strained and wrenched, but the ring refused to yield. He studied the metal links in his hands, certain the priests had expected their prisoner to be stronger than a living man. Futility, guilt, and fear sent a wet trickle down his cheek. He dared not wipe it and look.

He knew he would see blood.

Sabine shuffled up behind him and put a hand on his shoulder. "Do not cry, Father."

"I have failed."

She knelt beside him. "Please, Father. Do not give up. Help me."

"You have so much hope in your eyes." He embraced her, patting her back and staring at his sacred book, still on the floor. "Perhaps there is enough for both of us."

CHAPTER TEN

FORBIDDEN GROUND

March 14th 1885 Briançon, France

O ne hour dragged into the next. He sat in the spot they'd found her each time they'd come to visit. Sabine crawled into his lap, content to cling in silence while staring at the door. After holding her awhile, he grew tired of the sight of metal around her ankles. Despite how thin she had become, he could not work the manacle past her heel. Sabine kept still, tolerating his likely painful effort with the patience of a saint. Molinari relented, and sighed. He didn't bother trying to break them open, knowing it futile. His angry gaze slid across the floor, stalling on the shadow of a bloody misericord, stretched long from the lantern. He attempted to jimmy the lock with the knife, but the tip snapped off.

She frowned. "You broke it."

"I have not had much practice at the arts of *legerdemain.*"

Sabine yawned and nodded, settling into his chest. Fatigue came out of nowhere, spreading over him like a dense blanket dragging him beneath the surface of a dark ocean. In what seemed an instant later, he awoke to Sabine gripping two fistfuls of shirt at his shoulders and bumping his head against the wall.

The fear in her eyes stole the words from his mouth. Footsteps echoed outside, accompanied by the clatter of lanterns. Father Molinari eased her out of his lap and set her between his back and the wall. Little fingers clutched into his side as the scent of paraffin seeped into the room.

Sabine gasped and shivered. "They want to burn us."

He patted her hand and stood, stalking up to the door with careful, quiet steps. Renault and Callini whispered outside. For once, Renault was not so eager to be the one to lift the bar. Pottery clinked on the floor; Molinari pictured two large jars of lamp oil. *They mean to open the door just enough to throw them in.* He held his hand an inch from the knob, and waited. Wood scraped on metal. Renault grunted, and the hollow *clonk* of the large beam hitting stone echoed in the hall.

Sabine rattled her chain, whimpering.

Click.

Molinari grabbed the knob and hauled the door in with a rush of smoky air. The pudgy priest stood dumbfounded at the sight of him, sweaty jowls hanging open. Father Callini waited a pace behind, working to take the glass shroud off a lantern.

The scent of the heavyset man plunged into Father Molinari's lungs and teased the raging hunger lurking in his gut. He lunged forward and pounced on Renault, knocking him into a stumble across the narrow hall and slamming him into the opposite wall. Callini yelped and jumped back, raising the lantern as well as a crucifix.

A wave of heat swept over Father Molinari's body, distracting him enough for Renault to shove him away. The big man stooped to grab one of the pottery jugs. Molinari caught him with a wild haymaker. Knuckles smashed into the side of the older man's head, sending him staggering into the cell, unconscious on his feet. Renault fell over like a board with a meaty *slap.*

"Back!" yelled Callini.

The younger man's blood called out to him. Each pulse throbbing through his veins echoed in Molinari's heart. Amid a blur of flailing limbs, a streak of gold, and screaming, the wonderful taste of lifeblood filled his senses, somewhere between a perfect steak and raw power. Fingers raked at his head and arm, a fist hit him in the chest. Nothing mattered but the explosion of energy flooding through him.

When sense returned, he found himself kneeling astride the corpse of the younger priest, the man's throat torn to shreds, lifeless eyes staring at the ceiling. He covered his face with two crimson hands, and emitted a wail of contrition before collapsing across the body, sobbing tears of blood.

"God in Heaven, what have I done?"

Grief waned as soft whimpers and moans of pleasure emanating from the cell reached his consciousness. Molinari pulled himself to his feet and approached the doorway, dreading what he would see inside. No portion of his mind could attribute a sight to *those* noises coming from such a small child that he would not want to scrub from his mind.

Sabine crouched over Renault, who lay flat on his back, and suckled from his neck. The essence of her eager noises changed in Molinari's mind; no longer seeming lustful, they were the joyful sounds a child would make while savoring an expensive confection. His shoes scuffed as he trudged in. Sabine looked up with a bloody grin, her little fangs as long as could be.

Color had returned to her skin, a light tan she must have had at the time her father murdered her. The sight of her so lifelike warmed his heart and lessened the guilt at what he had done to Callini. Despite not remembering more than fleeting glimpses and shouts, he had—without a doubt—killed a man. Not merely a man, a priest.

"I have not taken his life." Sabine opened her mouth, stretching her jaw from side to side as her fangs retracted. "It is a sense you have when drinking. You can feel when you must stop."

"I…" He sank to his knees. "You look…"

"He is very big. I am very small." Sabine crawled over and clung to him. "I did not have to hurt him to become strong again."

"Are you strong enough to break free?"

"*Non.* I am a little girl. I cannot break this"—she waved her foot around to shake the manacles—"without disobeying God."

"I have disobeyed Him." Father Molinari hung his head, sniffling into the crook of her neck.

"Papa said the first time is not to blame." She squirmed up to peer over his shoulder. "*Maman* killed a woman when she awoke, but it was not *Maman*. She was a wild animal."

"Did you..."

Sabine shook her head. "No. Papa was strong enough to hold me still. Élodie fed me from a cup until I became myself again."

Molinari held her out to arms' length and looked her in the eye. "Who is Élodie?"

"She is one of Papa's housekeepers."

He winced. "She knows of the vampires? She will create panic."

"*Non.* She does not speak." Sabine clutched her hands to her chest, shivering. "She is timid like a mouse."

"Poor child." He brushed a hand over her ankle and across her foot. "Do you know where they keep the keys?"

"Did you search their pockets?" She blinked.

He rushed to the remains of Father Callini and rummaged through his clothes, collecting a rosary, a few coins, and the key to the cell door. After finding nothing of use, he stooped and performed the Last Rites.

"The fat one does not have the key," yelled Sabine. "Perhaps it is in the church? I want very much to leave this room."

He made the sign of the cross over the fallen Father Callini. "I lack the wisdom to know if you were right. I pray that if you were, justice finds me swift and sure." Molinari got up and leaned his head into the cell. "I will return as fast as I am able. Wait here."

"Where would I go?" She stomped, acting upset at his obvious joke for only two seconds before smiling.

The spiral stairs passed in a blur. At thirty-two, he hadn't considered himself slow or aged, but his body seemed to possess the energy of an eighteen-year-old—and beyond. Sprinting through the moonlit garden had the paradoxical effect of making him feel more alive than he'd been in years. Ahead, the church loomed like an onyx cutout of sky, where no stars shone through. A sight that had once lifted his soul unsettled his nerves.

Father Molinari slowed to a trot and then a cautious walk as he neared the wall surrounding the humble house of God. He circled to the right, rounded the corner, and came up to the wrought iron gate. Reaching for it burned as though he'd stuck his hand near the mouth of an oven. As his fingertips passed among the bars, the back of his hand seared with blisters and erupted with smoke.

He let off a primal yelp of pain, jerked back, and cradled his arm to his chest. No scent had ever disgusted him more than the fragrance of his own charred flesh. If the key to Sabine's chains lay within the church, there it would stay.

"God, guide me." He backed away.

Perhaps Tristan would come to investigate and he could convince the boy to fetch the key? *No... what if he runs and alarms the entire town?* Father Molinari spread his fingers; charred flesh hissed and popped as it regenerated. The temptation reared itself again. He could tear the chains apart. Metal could crumble like matchsticks in his hands. He shut his eyes and forced it away.

"Enter ye in at the strait, for wide is the gate, and broad is the way, that leadeth to destruction, and many there be which go in thereat."

Focused on his task, he ran back to the outbuilding and rummaged through gardening tools until he found a large sledgehammer. He gripped it near the head and jogged down the spiral stairs. After pausing to apologize yet again to Father Callini, he entered the cell.

Sabine sat in the middle of the room, head forward, feet poking out from under her nightdress. She perked up as he strode in, but her face twisted in confusion as he went past her.

"Did you find the key?"

"No. If it is in the church building, we cannot reach it." He hefted the sledge. "Stay back."

He swung in the manner of a croquet mallet, with as much strength as he could put behind it. Metal struck metal with a resounding *clang*. Father Renault didn't react, though his chest continued to rise and fall with slow breaths. Molinari brought the hammer around a second time, driving it into the peg to which the ring attached.

Again and again he hammered at it, mixing angles from head on to sideways glancing blows. Sabine covered her ears. The crunch of weakening stone, a sound he should not have heard, gave him pause.

My ears are sharper. My eyes more focused. I am not the least bit tired after all this labor. What manner of justice exists that the absence of God grants such boon? He clenched his eyes shut, and repeated the Lord's Prayer in his mind.

The chain rattled.

"It is not broken," said Sabine. "Please hit it more."

In his untiring hands, the hammer proved the victor within the hour, and the peg snapped. He dropped the tool and gathered the child in his arms. Three feet of loose chain and a four-inch ring dangled at his side, but he had freed her from the cell at least.

After collecting his sacred book, he carried her up the narrow stairs. She squirmed with anticipation as they crossed the outbuilding. As soon as the cool night breeze lofted her hair, she raised her hands and giggled in delight. He walked along the road that passed in front of the church and led to the valley below where the citizens of Briançon proper slept.

Father Molinari could not bear the idea of Paolo seeing him like this. Of course, the point was moot, as both the coach and the man were on holy ground. Sabine ceased giggling, and clamped her arms around his neck. He could not stay here, and the town would be the first place checked when Renault recovered or when Tristan found Callini dead.

Of the few people he knew in France, he could think of only one who might be inclined to help despite his... condition. He jogged down the road, skipping the turn down to Briançon, and took a northerly route. Sabine rested her head against his shoulder, and whispered a child's rhyme to herself.

He ran for hours in silence broken only by the jingle of the chain hanging from Sabine's legs or a weak voice when she sang to herself in a soft half-whisper. Debating which unsettled him most between not growing tired after sprinting so long, killing a priest in a blackout, or that he carried a tiny undead child, left him unsure of himself. Had he done God's will, or had Satan seduced him?

"It will be morning soon," said Sabine.

Father Molinari slowed to a walk and considered the countryside. "We have at least an hour, perhaps two."

"Yes." She tilted her head to the side, eyes widening. "But we do not have a place to hide. When the sun comes up, it will be too late to find our bed."

He grumbled.

"That is how *Maman* gave herself to God." Sabine looked down and sadness emerged in her voice. "I do not wish to die."

He squeezed her, more to comfort himself, unable to speak the thought she already had.

"There." Sabine pointed past his face to the left. "Do you hear the chickens?"

A few seconds of silence passed before the soft clucks of hens reached his ears. He moved in the direction she had indicated. The trees thinned within a few minutes of travel, revealing the shapes of village huts. Sabine reeled in the chain like an anchor, bundling it in her lap to keep it quiet. Molinari circled the village until an old root cellar cover caught his eye. It seemed promising only due to the sight of the burned and empty hut beside it.

He crept to the door and set the child down on her feet. She crawled under as he lifted the door, and descended stairway rickety plank staircase step by step while sitting. He waited for her to reach the bottom before climbing after, lowering the door without a sound.

Barrels and sacks lined the sides of an underground space twelve feet deep and five wide. Two wooden trusses reinforced the ceiling, bedecked with cured meats and cheeses hanging by ropes. The combined scent and fragrance of the food overwhelmed him to gagging. It took a moment of concentration to force his senses to mute the flavor in the air. Given the quantity and condition of the provisions, someone had appropriated the root cellar for their own needs. Molinari spent a moment constructing a 'nest' of grain sacks behind a row of barrels, sufficient to offer them cover in the event someone walked in during the day.

He crawled in first, and Sabine pulled herself up on his chest.

"Thank you for saving me," she whispered, and settled down.

At what cost? One man is dead by my hand. My soul may be damned. Father Molinari shut his eyes. "May His will be done."

"Amen," whispered Sabine, already sounding groggy.

He reached up and adjusted the canopy of empty burlap over their heads.

With any luck, the sun would come and go, and they would not be seen.

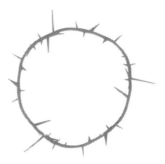

CHAPTER ELEVEN

THE DEVIL WHISPERS

March 15ᵗʰ 1885 French Countryside

Vampiric sleep had one quite noticeable advantage over the repose of mortals. No amount of guilt, excitement, or an uncooperative brain could stave it off. The instant the hour struck, his body became wooden and a sense of vertigo overtook him as if his soul plummeted down into the earth.

Father Molinari jolted awake; though hours had passed, it felt as though he'd only begun to fall. Sabine sat on his chest, facing him. She twisted and pulled at the shackle on her right leg, trying to squeeze it over her heel. When he opened his eyes, she gave up and smiled.

"Morning," she chirped.

"Or evening." He scratched behind his ear.

"Morning sounds more cheerful." Sabine stuck out her tongue.

He traced a finger over the chain. "When I first saw you, I didn't think that would be able to hold a vampire. I expected you'd be strong enough to snap them."

"*Non.* I am small. The bad feeling wants me to, but *Maman* said I shouldn't trust it."

"Good girl." He managed a smile. "Your mother was wise."

"I miss her." Sabine lowered her head.

He lifted her hair out of her face. "She knew enough to trust in God to protect her. I am sure she watches over you."

Sabine looked up with sad eyes, though a trace of a smile formed on her lips. She twisted around and crawled over his legs to the end of the barrel wall. He propped himself up on his elbows, staring at the serpent of chain trailing after her over the dirt as she moved out of sight. He went through the motions of stretching, though it did nothing for him. Part of his mind remembered the scent of spiced meat and cheese as appealing, but his gut balked with nausea at the thought of eating.

Metal clattered over wood. He glanced to his right, finding Sabine near the top of the stairs.

She emitted a soft grunt, and the trapdoor creaked. "It is dark."

"Then we shall be on our way with all due haste." He rolled forward and stood.

Sabine gasped. She tried to back up in a hurry, but the chain tangled her legs and she fell clear off the rickety stairway, landing on her back with a *whump* that terrified him, until he assumed a broken neck could do her no worse. She didn't hesitate, and crawled backwards with frightened gasps.

Molinari ducked behind the barrel as the cellar door opened upward, revealing the outline of a stocky woman in a plain green dress and white apron. The woman's quiet singing came to an abrupt halt at the sight of Sabine struggling to retreat.

"*Mon dieu!*" cried the woman. "Child, what has happened to you?"

The woman rushed down into the root cellar and hurried over to the girl. Sabine flattened her back against a barrel, wide eyed.

"Oh, you poor, poor dear." She covered her mouth, stooped, and picked up the trailing chain. "Who has done such a thing?"

A breath, perhaps a fleeting shadow, made her look to her side–right at Molinari.

Before the woman could scream, Sabine lunged forward and grasped her chin, pulling the woman's face around to make eye contact.

"Sleep." Sabine lowered her arm, continuing to gaze into the woman's eyes with focused intensity. "Sleep."

"What? Michel, where are…" The village woman collapsed on her side, unconscious.

Molinari pulled himself out of their hidden alcove and walked over, an accusing glower upon his face.

She shifted her legs to one side. "I did not listen to the bad feeling. Small tricks do not need it. She would have made panic in the village."

He grasped her under the arms and lifted her onto her feet. "We should go."

"We can take a little blood before?" She tilted her head like a child asking permission.

Hunger did dwell within him. That it strengthened when he looked at the sleeping, defenseless woman made him turn away. "It is wrong."

"Why?" Sabine blinked. "We must have nourishment, and we do not have to hurt her. We can make her forget us."

Father Molinari put a hand to his face and pulled it down, leaving his mouth covered. *What horror have I become?* "What darkness is this?"

Sabine twisted side to side, smiling. "Papa taught me how to make people forget. You look very close into their eyes." She stood on tiptoe, peering up at him. "You want them to forget, and a squishy thing moves inside your head."

He scowled.

"*Non.* It is not bad." She lowered herself to stand flat and giggled. "If they do not remember us, they will not have scary dreams and we do not have to harm them."

"This is against God. It is against everything I have ever known." Still, he could not deny the way this woman's life force called out to him.

"*Maman* said it is okay. God made wolves to eat deer, and the deer must die for this. We are better because we do not have to kill anyone." Sabine moved to kneel beside the woman.

The sight of her, around his age, and helpless, filled him with distaste. He couldn't quite bring himself to look at her neck, much less her cleavage, and threw an awkward glance at the wall.

Sabine lifted the woman's left arm. "At the wrist. We need only a little. It does not taste as bad as you think. In it, you will feel the life."

He knelt next to Sabine. Lower to the ground, the scent of the blood within the woman nudged past his sense of impropriety. While his thinking mind recoiled, his need guided his hands. He grasped her arm and held the tender skin of her wrist to his nostrils. The thrum of her pulse awakened a feeling he likened to lust. With each pulse, a creaking pressure in his cheeks grew. A sharp point jabbed him in the tongue. His jaw snapped open in shock. After a second of gawking, he raised his fingers to his mouth and touched the sharp points of fangs.

It was not a dream.

As gently as he could, he bit down. The instant blood touched his tongue with the flavor of honey and berries, a sense of her living soul spread through him. Her heartbeat echoed in his mind. Beyond the simple sense of fluid entering his mouth existed a tingling of rushing energy. He swallowed the first mouthful; warmth slid down his throat, gathering at his heart and forming a core of heat. Father Molinari let himself drift into the ecstasy of the most intense pleasure he had ever known.

A sudden weakening in the flow made him open his eyes.

Sabine had attached herself to the woman's other wrist. He marveled at his ability to feel the woman's life force ebbing out from two places. The nature of the flow changed as he drank and her pulse sped up. He felt as though he floated with her down a great torrent, gaining speed as he approached a waterfall he could not see as much as *feel*.

"Can you sense it coming up ahead?" whispered Sabine.

Molinari forced himself to pull away from the woman's arm. "Yes."

"*Maman* said it is the point of no return. We must always stop before we cross it."

Sabine's whispery voice drifted into the chaotic swirl raging in his mind.

The river current slowed as Sabine ceased feeding.

Her tiny hand placed warm upon his cheek. "Stop now."

He leaned up and licked a stray trickle of blood from her arm before staring at the wound. Did he truly possess the fangs that had made those two holes?

Sabine glanced at the seeping blood. "You must want the bite to close."

What am I doing? No sooner did horror and regret at what he had done—and enjoyed—collided in his heart, the puncture marks shrank away to faint pink dots. "Is this… magic?"

"I do not know." Chain links clinked over each other as she lowered herself nose to nose with the woman. She thumbed the villager's eyes open and stared into them. "Thank you for letting us have some blood. You did not see anyone in your cellar."

"Is it that simple?" Father Molinari put a hand on the child's back.

"*Oui.* It is quite simple when they are sleeping. A bit more difficult when awake." She sat back on her heels. "It does not work on vampires. I tried to make Papa remember being nice, but my head hurt."

"We need to go." He grabbed a bit of burlap from the shelf and wiped up all traces of blood on the woman's arms.

Sabine stood and reached for him, a child's unmistakable request to be picked up.

Father Molinari obeyed. "Hold on while I climb."

She clamped her arms around his neck and clung. He crept up the swaying stairs and lifted the door a few inches, enough to peer out. A handful of people moved among small homes, peals of inebriated laughter came from the far side of buildings. Chickens, geese, and a handful of goats roamed free. One small dog took notice of him and barked. He made a shushing noise. The animal tilted its head and zipped away.

Once he trusted no one would see them, he climbed out and lowered the door closed. Every jingle of the chain hanging at his side made him wince. He slid an arm under Sabine's legs to support her weight, and sprinted into the night.

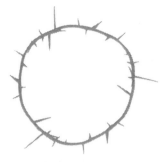

CHAPTER TWELVE

PENITENCE

March 18ᵗʰ 1885 Saint-Jean-de-Maurienne, France

Dim lamplight flickered from the windows of the modest home of Henri Baudin. Father Molinari approached the porch, praying in his mind that he had followed God's will by coming here. With only a few minutes more than an hour until sunrise, he had put all his faith and trust in what had felt like their only option. Slow-moving clouds lit azure in the moonlight reflected from the upstairs windows. A smile caught him off guard. Henri had already replaced the glass.

He shifted Sabine from laying sideways in both arms to sitting on his left, crossed the porch, and knocked.

Henri appeared at the door within a moment. "Father? By God, what has happened? Were you waylaid? Come in, come in."

"Thank you, Henri."

Father Molinari stepped into the main room. Moonlight turned the paintings black and grey, sapping the warmth of their forest scenes. Josephine glided in from a hallway at the back of the room. She seemed to want to run to the stairs leading up, but hovered in a patch of shadow.

"*Allo,*" said Sabine.

"Why hello, little miss." Henri smiled at her. "And who is this adorable one?"

"I am Sabine Caillouet."

Josephine padded closer, drawn by the sound of the child's voice. She kept her gaze low, her posture carrying a mournful air. She curtseyed. "Father Molinari."

Henri's mirth faded to shock at the sight of the chain. "What is the meaning of this?"

"I apologize for disturbing your home with my trial of faith, but I must ask a favor of you." He set Sabine down. "How is Josephine?"

"Why is this child in manacles?" Henri gawked.

"She was..." Father Molinari held his breath for a few seconds. "In the company of those who wished her harm. I..."

"He saved me." Sabine threw her arms around him.

"Me as well." Josephine stooped, hands on her knees. A hint of a smile played upon her lips. When the shackles rattled, she looked ready to weep.

Sabine grinned up at her. "He is a *real* priest, like *Maman* said."

"How are you feeling, child?" asked Father Molinari.

"I am tired and ashamed." Josephine looked downcast. "It is fortunate that Marcel has forgiven me. He is..."

Henri blessed himself. "He was as concerned for her wellbeing as was I." He blinked with inspiration. "Father, would you be so kind—"

"I am not sure if..." Father Molinari shook his head. "No, I cannot. I am sorry. I would give anything to be able to, but I am caught up in a matter that cannot wait."

"Oh." Henri looked downcast.

"This child's life is in danger." Father Molinari took her hand and walked to the kitchen slow enough for her to keep up.

Josephine hid her mouth in her hands at the rhythmic *click click* of the child's shortened gait. She hurried to grab the chain so it did not drag.

Sabine smiled at her and held her free arm out for balance. "I am sorry for making you walk so slow."

"It is all right, child." Father Molinari squeezed her hand.

In the kitchen, he let go, and Sabine shuffled over to the nearest chair.

Molinari glanced at Josephine, who sent the most peculiar stare at him. "What troubles you, my child?"

"Father, may I speak to you... in confession?" Josephine clasped her hands in front, still staring at the floor.

"Of course." Molinari glanced around.

"The porch?" Henri gestured at a door in the back of the kitchen.

"*Oui.*" Josephine hurried out.

"Forgive me, Henri. I—"

The elder Baudin made a shooing motion. "Go... It is no bother."

Sabine grinned, appearing content to wait in the chair.

Father Molinari bowed and crossed to the door Josephine had used.

The young woman stood at the top of the porch steps, toes curled over the edge. She had her arms folded, gaze downcast, and trembled as if close to tears.

Father Molinari approached and faced to the side, offering a bit of privacy.

Josephine blessed herself. "Bless me Father, for I have sinned. My last confession was three months and nine days ago."

"May the Lord be in your heart and help you confess your sins with truth and desire to become closer to Him." Father Molinari made the sign of the cross.

She sniffled and wiped at tears. "Father, I have committed the sin of envy, and of blasphemy. I... have expressed anger at God for taking my mother's life. I shouted at Him in anger. I sought to speak to the dead."

Molinari rubbed the spot where the rake had pierced. *Please Father, forgive my trespass if to hear this child's confession in my state is an affront.* "How have you committed the sin of vanity?"

"I wished to gift a portrait of my mother to my father. For many years, I have tried to paint her... and—" She sobbed. "You have seen them. They are sad blotches that look more like flowers than a person. When I allowed Satan into my heart, he showed me visions. He gave me the skill to paint that... ghastly thing. He said I would be famous.

All the world would know my work." Josephine looked up. "I only wanted to see my mother since I had never before, yet... I was tempted. I have—"

Sabine's high-pitched scream broke the calm from a second-floor window.

Father Molinari sprinted into the house, racing past Henri, who ambled toward the stairs from the sitting room. He followed the sound of crying to Josephine's bedroom and pulled the thin door the rest of the way open.

Sabine knelt on the floor near the bed with a scattering of dolls around her. The masterful painting depicting the murder of Marcel and his two sons lay in front of her, half under the bed. A swath of dirty cheesecloth wrapped it, pulled away enough to show the gory details.

The child wept into her hands, shaking from the sight. "Father! It is awful. Who would make such a bad picture?"

Molinari swooped in, almost tripping on the chain, and bundled her in his arms. He made a quick pass with his black sleeve to wipe the blood tears from her fingers and face before Henri arrived, out of breath, at the door.

"My God," wheezed Henri. "I had thought I burned it."

Josephine ran in, wide-eyed. She collapsed on her knees at her father's side, and grasped his waist. "I am sorry! It is my fault. I lied. You could not remember, and I said you had already burned it. I... wanted to keep it"—she looked down—"out of pride... vanity."

"But..." Henri grasped her shoulders.

Sabine sniffled, visibly regaining her confidence. She reached forward and pulled the cheesecloth over the canvas. "It is evil. The woman is smiling at what has happened."

"It is horrific," said Josephine. "Ghastly. Unthinkable. I could never do such things as it depicts... but the technique—"

"Is not your work," said Father Molinari. "This is a product of temptation. Your hand did not create this abomination."

"It promised me I could make such wonderful paintings..." Josephine shivered.

Sabine rolled back from her knees to sit, chain clinking, and looked up at them. "To do evil while you cannot help it is one thing, but to keep such a horrible, horrible thing because you *want* to..."

"Yes." Josephine wept into her father's side. "It is a sin. Vanity."

"Josephine?" Sabine scooted over to the young woman. "*Maman* says if you ask God to forgive a bad thing, and you are sorry in here"—she patted her hand on her heart—"He will listen."

Henri mumbled, "To keep such a thing is to invite it."

"No!" Josephine leapt to her feet. She rushed over to grab the painting, cloth and all. "I will burn it myself! I will not harm my children... or Marcel. Or take my own life."

"Josephine. Charge yourself with the protection of your family. Renounce temptation wherever it may lurk. I would like you to spend the afternoon tomorrow in prayer, and reflection."

She bowed. "Yes, Father."

Molinari put his hand on her shoulder. "God, the Father of Mercy, through the death and the resurrection of His only begotten son, has sent the Holy Spirit among us for the forgiveness of sins. May God give you pardon and peace. I absolve you from your sins in the name of the Father, and of the Son, and of the Holy Spirit."

"Amen," said Josephine and Henri at the same time.

Sabine stood and grabbed Josephine's sleeve as she went past carrying the painting. "Do not uncover it. You should not look at it again. Please take it straight outside and set it to fire."

Henri put his hand on his daughter's back and guided her through the door. "I shall return in a few minutes."

Father Molinari waited for the Baudins to leave, then dabbed a few more traces of blood from Sabine's hands.

She clung to him. "I fear I will see her babies in my dreams."

"Shh." He picked her up and rocked, patting her back. "Josephine did not paint that. She will not harm her children."

Sabine nodded, smiled, and snuggled against him. He carried her downstairs, returning to the kitchen. By then, the flicker of a small fire danced in the backyard. Molinari took a seat with Sabine in his lap. She curled up, content and smiling.

Josephine entered first, followed by Henri.

Father Molinari glanced at him, hoping his unease remained hidden. "Do you have a basement?"

"A wine cellar. Yes." Henri filled the narrow hallway between front room and kitchen. "Why do you ask? Are you hungry?"

Father Molinari grasped the crucifix hanging from his neck. "Henri, I cannot in good conscience ask this favor of you and allow you to remain ignorant of recent events. On the other hand, such truths defy the common man and may drive sanity from the mind."

"You expelled a demon from my daughter. I saw the crucified Lord spin upon the walls, and windows break. I saw my only flesh and blood become another person, and you have returned her to me." Henri sat at the table. "I am listening."

Sabine turned the other way in Molinari's lap to face Henri. He recounted the tale of meeting the two priests and their claim of a captured monster. Josephine brought water for everyone as he spoke, and joined them at the table.

"When they opened the cell, I could scarcely believe my eyes for what they had captured seemed like no monster."

Henri leaned forward, eyes widening. "What was it?"

Father Molinari gathered Sabine's hair from her face and pulled it back over her shoulders.

"No..." Henri covered his mouth. "What was wrong with them?"

Josephine muttered a quiet prayer, staring at Sabine as if she wanted to hug her forever.

"That was my first thought as well." He closed his eyes. "God has led me to a place where I fear the slightest misstep may cost both of us our immortal souls. This child needs help, and I was there to offer it."

Henri's hair gathered in white tufts between his fingers as he rubbed his head. "I do not understand."

"You have seen the work of demons." Father Molinari squeezed Sabine's shoulder, making her smile. "This child has been cursed."

"She is possessed?"

"No. I ask you to trust in God and that I am still the man you knew."

"You are possessed?" Henri sat stiff.

Sabine perked up and opened her mouth; her fangs lengthened.

Josephine's eyes bulged.

"My God." Henri stared at her. "Vampires?" His gaze darted up to Molinari.

"Yes, Henri. Father Callini mistook my compassion as the work of Satan. He saw her only as a creature whom God no longer acknowledged." He picked at the hole in his shirt. "Misericord. A fatal wound."

Henri blessed himself. "You are *both* vampires? How is it you are sane and talking?!"

"Vampires?" Josephine gasped. "But you are a priest. You speak His name in sacrament. How can such a thing exist?"

"I have come to learn there are degrees. This child's innocence has somehow remained. God has seen fit to protect her. There is an inner pull, a draw toward darkness. My faith is my shield. I trust in the Lord that he will guide us out of the shadow of death, though I know not the path to walk. It may take me some time to come to terms with what has happened and find my way. May we shelter in your wine cellar?"

"You do not plan to feast upon the people of Saint-Jean-de-Maurienne?" Henri tapped his fingers. "To tear out the throats of the unsuspecting?"

"No, Henri. We are nothing like the creature I destroyed in Vienna. This child is innocent, and I *will* save her. I swore an oath to the Order to protect humanity from the very thing I have become, yet I am in command of my mind. I am no beast, as were the few I had encountered before."

"We do not want to hurt anyone." Sabine bowed her head in a demure pose.

Josephine's hand slipped from covering her mouth to grasping her throat. "She... looks so innocent. I do not feel malice."

"The whispers are afraid of God." Sabine fidgeted with her nightdress, gaze downcast. "It is not so different. You did not give yourself to become a painter. You were still there. As am I."

Josephine sniffled, but gave Henri a wary nod.

"The sun shall rise soon." Henri rubbed at his beard, the coarse scratching as loud as a brush upon stone. "You pulled my daughter from the clutches of damnation only to wind up in your own peril. I cannot turn my back on you. Can you give me your word in the eyes of God you shall do no harm here?"

Father Molinari clutched his crucifix. The hot metal cooled a little with his resolve to trust in Him. "As the Lord is my witness, we shall do no harm."

The table creaked as Henri pushed himself to his feet. "This way."

Josephine remained seated, eyeing the two untouched glasses of water. He led them to a small brown door in the corner of the kitchen. Behind it, a stairway too narrow for a man to navigate without turning sideways led down to a fifteen-foot square room. Three shelves laden with dusty wine bottles stood against the walls, and a worktable littered with corks sat to the right at the bottom of the steps. The air smelled of damp wood and moss. Stones of many sizes and colors left the curved ceiling a patchwork of hue and texture. Sabine shuffled forward, holding her hand up to touch the corks protruding from bottles.

Henri returned in a few minutes with four cloth sacks packed with straw, which he dropped and patted into the shape of a bed.

"I'll get you some blankets." Henri paused midway up the stairs. "Do you need blankets?"

"*Merci*," said Sabine. She sat on the straw. "This is much nicer than stone or dirt."

"Please, that would be most kind of you." Father Molinari lowered himself next to her and removed his shoes. He let them dangle from his fingertip, arm draped over his knee.

"What is wrong?" She scooted close, putting an arm across his shoulder.

"I have forgiven Father Callini for taking my life, though I cannot forgive myself for taking his."

Sabine furrowed her eyebrows. "Do not listen to the bad thoughts. They will make you sad. I am sorry I forgot to warn you it would happen. I was so frightened I did not think. You did not want to kill him. It is not your fault. No more than a starved dog is guilty of stealing food."

His mind taunted him with an image of Sabine tearing a man's throat out. He pulled her into a tight hug. *Thank God she was spared this guilt.* When he let go, she smiled at him. He set the sacred book on the worktable above and behind him, and knelt on the bare stone floor.

"My God, I am sorry for my sins with all my soul. In choosing to do wrong
and failing to do good,
I have sinned against you whom I should love above life itself.
I firmly intend, with your grace,
to do penance,
to sin no more,
and to avoid temptation.
Our Savior Jesus Christ,
suffered and died for our sins.
In his name, my God, have mercy."

Henri returned with blankets, keeping silent as Father Molinari prayed. He set them on the floor and retreated. When he finished reciting the full Penitent's Prayer, he kissed the crucifix and let it drape on his chest.

Sabine crawled around, arranging the heavy wool blankets over the straw-filled sacks. The rattle of her chain awakened the darkness lurking in the back of his mind. Visions of how easy it would be to seize her and tear the offending metal apart taunted him. Anger bubbled in his heart. How *dare* anyone do such a thing to a child!

He distanced himself from rage and repeated the Penitent's Prayer, adding a recitation of a prayer for protection.

"Father?" Sabine flopped on the bed. "Does God hear our prayers?"

"Yes, he does." Father Molinari stood, dusted his knees off, and reclined on the cushion. Despite being dead, the comfortable softness struck him as a vast improvement over bare ground or stone. "Why do you ask?"

She curled up against his chest. "Every day after Papa hurt me, *Maman* would pray, asking him to take away the curse." She sniffled. "He didn't listen."

He patted and rubbed her back as she broke into quiet sobs.

"Sabine?"

She composed herself and raised her head. "Yes, Father?"

"You have heard the story of the creation of the world?"

"Mmm." She nodded.

"Do you believe God made the Earth in seven days?"

"Of course." Sabine drew her eyebrows together. "What sort of question is that?"

He couldn't help himself, and tapped a finger on the tip of her nose. "What is a day to God?"

She tilted her head. A look of confusion spread over her face.

"For almighty God who always was, and always will be, do you think a 'day' might be longer than twenty-four hours?"

Sabine pursed her lips, looked down, bit her lip, and shrugged. "I do not understand."

The fast approach of their unnatural sleep sent heavy tendrils crawling through his limbs. He tucked the blanket around her, and lay down. "I believe He is listening, but we should not expect Him to answer on our time."

She didn't react, already asleep.

"God save us both," he whispered, and closed his eyes.

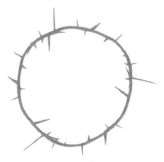

CHAPTER THIRTEEN

COUSIN BERTRAND

March 19th 1885 Saint-Jean-de-Maurienne, France

Another dreamless day passed as an instant of void. The beat of clicking metal and ringing chain seemed to greet Father Molinari within seconds of his laying down. Sabine shuffled across the basement to the stairway, looking happy despite being hobbled. He leaned upright and wiped a hand down his face. Disobedient limbs moved under protest, as though his body fought consciousness. In the quiet of Henri Baudin's wine cellar, his heartbeat overpowered the distant scratching of an unseen rodent.

Clonk, clonk, clonk.

He looked up as the ring at the end of the chain bounced up the stairs. "Where are you going?"

"The sun is setting," said Sabine, in a reverent whisper. "I wanted to watch the light in the clouds."

She should not be awake yet, much less… chipper. He reached out, intending to call her back, but fell face down on the stone floor. When next he opened his eyes, he found himself alone—and alert. Father Molinari sprang to his feet and rushed up the stairs. Sabine sat at the table in the kitchen, hands folded in her lap, watching Henri pace about. She swung her legs idly, feet nowhere near the floor. Both glanced at him as he walked in.

"Good evening, Father," said Henri. "I was about to come check on you."

"How much time has passed since Sabine woke?" Father Molinari eased himself into an open seat.

"The better part of an hour. She played for a time with Josephine, but my daughter now sleeps." Henri cast a helpless look at the pantry. "I would offer you food…"

Molinari held up a hand. "I understand. It is more than I have a right to ask of you that you allow us the use of your home. I do not wish to further burden your daughter. If we—"

"Josephine is leaving tomorrow morning. She will be staying with Marcel and his parents." Henri hovered by the counter, a guilty look aimed at Sabine.

Did she fear for her safety, or is it Henri's doing? No matter. For all I know, he is right to protect her. Father Molinari smiled. "I pray she has the strength to forgive herself."

"Thank you." Henri's somber expression brightened. "I told Marcel you have brought a sick child to stay here, and suggested she, being weakened from her ordeal, would be better removed for a few days."

Father Molinari nodded. "Our condition is not contagious." The mesmerizing *click-click* of the child's swinging legs lulled him into a fog. *Is it? Perhaps her influence touched my blood from the moment I let her drink.*

Henri approached Sabine, a trace of worry in his step. She lifted her gaze to maintain eye contact, smiling at him.

"Thank you, Monsieur Baudin. You are kind to let us sleep here."

He stooped beside her chair and placed a hand on her chest. "Are you certain of which you speak? She does not appear to be anything but alive." Henri lowered his arm. "There is a heartbeat."

Molinari cringed at the first memory he would have as a vampire, the sight of the small—and visually dead—Sabine curled on her side. As grey, withered, and lifeless as a thousand year old mummy. No heartbeat. "I do not understand this myself." He covered his chest with one hand, detecting a slow, but evident, thumping. "There seems to be a mechanism by which the body uses blood as fuel, the heart must continue to beat even in death… to distribute it."

Sabine got to playing with fruit from a basket in the middle of the table.

Henri scratched his chin. "My cousin Bertrand should be able to help remove those fetters."

"Oh, *oui, merci!*" Sabine looked up. "I do not like them. It feels like I have been stuck forever."

Father Molinari stood and collected her in his arms. "Of course. The sooner, the better."

"Come." Henri hurried to the front of the house, grabbed a coat and cap, and went outside for only seconds before ducking back in. "I will need a lantern."

Molinari carried her to the porch, finding the crisp night air relaxing. Between the stars and moon, the path was clear. Perhaps the world was not so dark to vampires? Sabine bounced in his arms, grinning.

"He is a nice man." She laid her head on his shoulder. "Like you."

"I…" He smiled.

Adoration sparkled in the green of her eyes. How could this be a monster of the night? *She is a sick child.* Nothing more. God had sent him to help her. He looked at the heavens above. How else could Henri's letter have arrived on the desk of Cardinal Benedetto? *May He guide me.*

Henri returned with a lit lantern, holding it chest-high as he made his way past. The light source made the immediate area seem like broad daylight, though beyond twenty feet or so, everything turned black. Feeling safe enough here not to worry about what may lurk in the darkness, Father Molinari kept close to Henri as they navigated the uneven dirt path to a wagon-worn trail leading into the heart of Saint-Jean-de-Maurienne. Glowing bugs drifted inches above the dark meadow grass, which wavered in a light breeze. Sabine whispered to herself, counting them.

After zigzagging for a short while, the path gave way to cobblestones. Small houses and businesses clustered together around a handful of streets. Few people were out and about at night, though the presence of a moving lantern attracted faces to windows.

Sabine frowned into her lap. "*Maman* said I should trust priests. Why were they mean to me? I have not hurt anyone."

"They could not know how different you are from what people imagine a..." He squeezed her. "God protects you."

She flicked a bit of chain side to side. "Is it because *Maman* prayed, or because I do not listen to the bad feeling?"

"Both." Father Molinari lifted her chin with one finger.

Sabine lowered her head. "If I am a bad thing, I should be put to rest. I do not want to hurt anyone."

"Your trust in God will keep you from darkness." He followed Henri around a leftward turn.

She held her feet up. "If I am not bad, why did they put me in prison?"

"Fear, child." He sighed. "Fear. They are weak of mind and weak of faith." *I am strong of faith, yet that strength has led me to what?*

She remained quiet while Henri led them through the town. Molinari's mind wandered around in circles, searching for an answer to his greatest question: was this God's plan, or had he succumbed to Satan? Demons often disguise their voices as those of children to lure the unwary—one of the first things he had learned in the Order.

A middle-aged man with a soot-colored wraparound beard and dark clothes gasped, startling Father Molinari away from his doubts. "*Mon dieu!*" He ran up and grabbed the shackles around Sabine's bony legs. "What are you doing to this child?"

"He has rescued me!" Sabine clung to Molinari. "He protected me from bad men."

The stranger blessed himself. "*Pardonnez-moi.*" He bowed to Father Molinari. "I shall fetch the *Gendarmerie* right away."

"*Non,*" said Sabine, in a creepy-calm tone. "No police."

"No... police..." The man stared into space, motionless as they walked past.

Henri shot a worried look to Molinari, and hastened his steps.

Three cross streets passed in silence before Henri turned right onto a winding road with a severe uphill grade. A cluster of barrels stacked against a house at the bottom bore the scars of frequent mishaps with burdened wagons coming down the hill. Unseen chickens flustered and clucked. In the distance, a lone dog bayed at the moon, startling a blackbird from a nearby eave. Molinari carried Sabine, slowing to accommodate the effect of the incline and age on Henri's pace.

After passing about twenty buildings, Henri stopped at a large house, white with dark beams showing through the wall. A cantilever roof over the front protected a porch bearing clock-shaped signs as well as a few huge wooden keys painted silver or gold. He rapped twice on the door, and waited.

Sabine blinked at a key as tall as she was. "What lock opens to that?"

Father Molinari chuckled. "It is not real. It is for decoration."

"Oh." She looked to her left as the door opened.

A thin man in a white shirt and brown vest, older than Henri, squinted in the lantern light. Clumps of white hair stranded from his scalp like spider silk in the wind; his left eye opened twice as wide as the other. Black finger-shaped smears marred his shirt, in the same place he scratched at his chest at the sight of them. He coughed; the sickly-sweet scent of pipe tobacco flooded Molinari's nostrils and throat as strong as if he'd toked himself.

"Henri?" croaked the older man, scratching more fervently.

"Bertrand, forgive me for visiting unannounced at such an hour." Henri gestured to his rear. "This is Father Antonio Molinari of the Vatican, and..."

"Sabine Caillouet, sir." The child attempted to mimic a curtsey while being held. She lifted one foot to display the handcuffs. "Monsieur Baudin said you would help me."

Bertrand's left eye shrank as narrow as the right, but he waved them in. The front room had a shopkeeper's counter in front of shelves of various bins full of clock parts and seemingly random wooden shapes. Henri hung the lantern on a peg protruding from a support post, causing shadows to sway back and forth for a few seconds.

"Why are you bringing a bound child to my shop?" Bertrand coughed and pounded his chest three times. "It is suspicious you do not summon the police. What nefarious business are you involved with, cousin?"

"I am afraid the police cannot be involved," said Molinari. "This is a matter of the Church, and one that we must maintain in confidence. This girl was taken by men who were to use her for dark purposes."

Bertrand squinted at Henri.

"Cousin…" Henri spread his arms wide. "If we meant this girl harm, why would we be here to get her loose?"

"Something is not as you are telling me, but I cannot leave the little lady in such a state." Bertrand gestured at the counter. "Set her there."

Father Molinari lowered Sabine and the chain fell upon the wood with a heavy *clatter*. She spread her feet apart as far as she could, about four inches. Bertrand affixed a jeweler's glass to his eye socket and gathered her leg in his hand. He studied the keyhole for a few seconds while making appraising grunts.

"You sound insulted." Father Molinari raised an eyebrow.

"Bah," said the old man. "I've known some boys her size who could pick locks like these with a butter knife." He cackled, and winked. "I used to be one of them."

Henri laughed. "But a clockmaker is honest work."

Bertrand ducked and opened cabinet after cabinet. In a moment, he paused in his rummaging to glance up. "I got too old for taking chances."

Sabine braced her hands on the counter behind her back and tilted her head from side to side. Chain clicked and clattered on the wood as she tapped her foot. Henri helped himself to a small baguette from a basket, and cringed from its audible staleness. Bertrand selected a long, fine tool and held it up to the light. Satisfied, he stood and hovered over her. Within ten seconds of inserting the implement in the keyhole, the hasp around her left ankle popped open. The other surrendered in five.

"Hah!" said Bertrand. "I've still got the touch."

"Thank you!" yelled Sabine. She leaned up and wrapped her arms around Bertrand, clinging to him like a limpet.

Bertrand emitted a startled yelp, which faded to a dazed, dopey grin an instant later. His eyes rolled up into the back of his head, and his smile got wider.

"Sabine?" asked Molinari. "What are you...? Oh, you're not." He pinched the bridge of his nose. "That is rude."

She released him. Bertrand's head fell to the countertop with a loud *thud*. The skinny old man bounced up and collapsed out of sight. A trickle of blood ran down the girl's chin. She held her hands up, her face a mask of surprise and contrition.

"*Oups!*"

Henri gawked at her, and swallowed hard.

Father Molinari suppressed the urge to yell, and rushed around the counter. Bertrand appeared alive, though unconscious, still with a vapid grin. He gathered the man and carried him across the room to a cushioned chair.

Sabine pulled her knees to her chin and hid her face in her nightdress. Already, the redness from around her ankles had faded.

Henri crept up alongside Molinari. "Is he...?"

"No. He is..." Molinari tilted his head. "I believe he fainted... from pleasure."

"What?" Henri blinked.

"There is a peculiar property of the bite. It seems to numb the recipient. When she fed from me, it was upon the wrist." He held up his arm. "It hurt only for an instant, replaced by a mild euphoria. Either your cousin is weak of body or a bite to the neck provides a much stronger feeling."

Henri paled. "Can we agree not to test this?"

"I am sorry," whispered Sabine. "I have not had anything to drink in days. I could not help myself." She sniffled. "I only wanted to hug him, for he was being nice to me."

"Look at him." Henri gestured at Bertrand. "He's probably having the best dream he's had in ten years."

"Let us hope." Father Molinari moved to the counter and picked Sabine up. "Thank you, Henri, for bringing us here. I shall arrange for some money to—"

"No need, Father." Henri waved him off. "No moral man could have left her in such a state, and I am still in your debt. Will Bertrand remember what has happened?"

Molinari pursed his lips. "I cannot say, but would he believe it?"

"Perhaps not." Henri nodded, and walked to where he'd hung his lantern. "We should probably leave."

"Wait." Father Molinari put the child down on her feet.

She darted around the room, giggling, skipping, and doing pirouettes.

He gathered the chain from the counter. "It would not be wise for anyone to find this here. If people come looking for us, it may cast a pall of suspicion on your cousin. He has done enough and does not deserve further hardship."

"Down the well?" said Henri with a shrug.

"I do not think that would be safe." Molinari studied the metal. The sight of it sparked a waft of rage at the two priests. Sabine had fed from Renault but not killed him. He'd taken almost all of Callini's blood before his sense returned. How much longer would it be before the need overtook him? "May I bury this on your land?"

Henri took the lantern. "Certainly, Father."

"Margaret?" Bertrand sat up. "Where are you?"

"You were dreaming, cousin." Henri went to the old man's side. "Margaret passed a long time ago."

"Oh." The old locksmith seemed to gain ten years in his face as his happy expression faded to the look of a man who yearned to crawl beneath the earth. "It was a nice dream." He gazed into nothingness a few seconds before perking. "Is the girl all right?"

"I am." Sabine skidded to a halt in front of Bertrand, and curtseyed proper. "Thank you, sir."

"I will visit again tomorrow, cousin, and bring some provisions. Now I know why your baguettes taste like your mother made them... because she did."

"Bah." Bertrand waved dismissively at Henri and stood. He patted Sabine on the head and trudged over to Molinari. "Whatever business goes on here, I pray the foul souls who treated that girl so poorly are brought to justice."

Father Molinari gazed down. "And as they continued to ask him, he stood and said to them, 'Let he who is without sin among you be the first to throw a stone.'"

"Amen," said Sabine.

"Hmph." Bertrand scratched at his chest. "No stones for me, I'm afraid. I suppose you know best."

"Misguided, but with good intentions," muttered Father Molinari, in Italian. He reached for the child, but she took a step back.

"*S'il vous plait, je peux marcher?*" She offered a pleading, innocent look while bouncing on her toes.

"I suppose you've been rather looking forward to walking." Molinari smiled.

"*Oui.*" She skipped to the door. "And running."

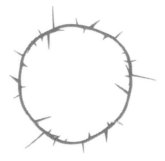

CHAPTER FOURTEEN

CAIAPHAS

March 19th 1885 Saint-Jean-de-Maurienne, France

Henri's cottage came into view beyond a small patch of woods after twenty-some odd minutes of walking. Sabine raced off through grass as high as her shoulders, squealing with delight. Thick, brown hair trailed after her, no doubt collecting all manner of burrs and seeds. Father Molinari slowed, taking in the scene of the property. He wondered if Henri or Josephine had painted the images hung inside. Perhaps both?

How different the blue-cast walls look in the moonlight. He closed his eyes and imagined his first arrival: bright skies, hilly meadows covered in oceans of emerald grass as far as the eye could see, and the painfully white house. *I pray Paolo a safe return to Rome.* Had his coachman been the one to find Father Callini's body? Would he have remained in the church's guesthouse with Tristan, waiting for Molinari's return, only to have Renault stagger in whenever he recovered from Sabine's feeding?

Distant giggling opened his eyes. Sabine vanished into the field behind the cottage. If not for it approaching midnight, the scene could've been a normal girl frolicking in a garden. He wandered after her in no great hurry, and paused at the rear corner of the house's stacked-stone wall. Henri diverted to a small shed and returned a moment later with a shovel.

"You can bury the chain over that way somewhere." He handed him the tool while waving to the east with his other hand.

Father Molinari trudged off, attention focused on the little sprite zipping among wildflowers, seeming hesitant to pick one, preferring to caress and sniff at them. She paused, facing sideways. Between her delicate frame and puffy hair, she resembled an enormous dandelion wrapped in white.

He marched about thirty paces from the house and sectioned off a square patch of sod, which he levered up and out of the way before digging a hole deep enough to conceal the chains.

With the grass patted back in place, he grasped the shovel at the neck and wandered to the house. Sabine emerged from the tall grass at a slow walk, her hands together in front of her, cradling a large yellow and black butterfly with a hint of blue along the rear of the wings.

"Father, *la papillon* let me touch her!" She spoke in an excited whisper, grinning.

He stooped to examine the creature, which shifted and climbed over her fingers. "It is beautiful."

"*Oui.*" She followed him to the back porch.

Henri sat in a wooden chair, legs up on a stool. Heavy eyelids threatened to close at any second. Sabine padded over to him, holding up her find.

"Monsieur Baudin, look what I have found."

Henri muttered and smiled.

"I should let her go home where she belongs," whispered Sabine, and tiptoed back to the meadow.

Father Molinari settled in a chair separated from Henri's by a small, round table bearing two bowls, one empty, one with a few assorted nuts. For a while, he reclined and watched Sabine racing back and forth. She adored the freedom of nature.

"*Dio, come hai potuto permettere una cosa del genere?*" Father Molinari mumbled into his hand.

"What?" asked Henri, in French.

Sabine ran in great skipping leaps, tripped, and rolled into the weeds, laughing.

"I am asking Holy God how he could allow such a thing to happen. She is so innocent... even cursed."

Henri cleared his throat and let his feet down. Wakefulness seemed to surge within him—to a point. "The priests always say 'God has a plan.' When Olivie died giving birth to Josephine, they said it was 'God's plan.'"

A tip of fang brushed Father Molinari's tongue. *Is this part of God's plan?* "Olivie was called to sit beside Him in the Kingdom of Heaven." He sighed. "Sabine is neither of Earth nor Heaven. She is an innocent trapped in somewhere that is not dark, nor is it light."

"At least she has you there with her," said Henri. His head drooped back.

Soft, childish singing floated from the tall grass, emanating from where a trace of chestnut hair glided among white flowers. Molinari closed his eyes. *What would you have me do, Lord? I am yours to command.*

"You have changed, Father. Cynical." Henri snapped out of a catnap. "That girl does not seem to be a creature of darkness to me. God must have given her strength."

"Suffer little children and forbid them not to come unto me; for of such is the kingdom of heaven."

"Jesus will have to welcome her," whispered Henri. "He said so himself."

"I feel like Caiaphas now, the adversary of Christ." Father Molinari examined his hands, a touch paler than they should be.

"You are being melodramatic, Father." Henri's eyes wrinkled with a smile. "God has a plan. It took me many years to accept it. Perhaps you can yet save the child's soul."

"I am not sure if I have defied or followed Him." Molinari rubbed a metronome finger over his lips, back and forth.

Henri settled down in the chair and closed his eyes. "You think perhaps she affected your mind like Étienne's?"

"Étienne's?"

"The man who wanted to summon the police." Henri opened one eye. "She made him go away."

"I admit I have thought such." He stared at the girl, twirling around and around, dancing with herself. "Yet I cannot sense an ounce of malice in her."

"Then you are following His plan." Henri offered a sleepy smile.

"Henri?"

"*Oui?*" He mumbled, half awake.

"Would you be so kind as to purchase some clothing for Sabine in the morning? I have some money to give you. We are taking enough of your charity."

"Mmm." Henri lapsed into snores.

Sabine ran through the meadow and rushed to Molinari's side, extending a cluster of periwinkle blue flowers. "For you."

Her happiness echoed within his heart as sadness. Deprived of life—and death—she seemed blissful. For all her running around, she did not breathe hard or appear flushed. Dirt smeared her bare feet and much of her nightdress. Bits of plant matter and flowers clung to her hair.

"Thank you, Sabine. They are quite pretty." He accepted the offering, fighting his urge to look away from her out of guilt.

An old rumor surfaced in the back of his thoughts. A member of the Order, a century and a half ago, catalogued success in curing a recent 'infezione vampirica' by destroying the creature responsible for biting a young woman.

"Will you read me a storybook?" Sabine tilted her head.

The sight of her wide, angelic eyes kept the idea of killing her father mute. He couldn't bring himself to spoil the moment of innocence by reminding her of what they were.

"Of course." He took her hand and led her inside. "If I can find one."

"In the front room, there is a bookshelf." She pulled him forward. "I will show you."

She wove through the kitchen and an archway beyond, heading for the room with the landscape oil paintings. He took a seat while she headed to the shelf. After pacing and deliberating for several minutes, she chose a book and crawled with it into his lap.

Grimm's Fairy Tales, in the original German.

Henri stumbled in the door, mumbled something incoherent, and dragged himself upstairs to his bedroom. Father Molinari caught himself exhaling, certainly now only a gesture of dread.

"Can you read this?" She traced a finger over the title.

"Yes, but do you understand German?"

Sabine shook her head, tossing her hair about.

"Well..." He smiled. "You will have to forgive me then if I read slow."

"Of course." She settled her head onto his shoulder. "We have time."

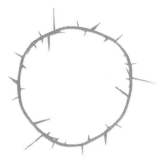

CHAPTER FIFTEEN

DESCENT

March 20ᵗʰ 1885 Saint-Jean-de-Maurienne, France

Vampire dreams had a vividness Father Molinari had never thought possible. Since the moment of his change, periods of undead sleep had passed in flashes of instantaneous blackness. This dawn, he walked among olive trees for hours, lurking in the shadows of a place neither day nor night. Every sight or smell from the texture of the sand beneath his bare feet to the wind on his face or the fragrance of the plants inundated him, more real than real. The trees had a surreal glow, as if a mad artist had painted them with daytime lighting against a midnight sky. A vision of a man in a white robe, his back turned, knelt and prayed in the center of the grove, lit by an impossible light as though the moon concentrated all its effort on a spot ten paces across. Stars pierced the indigo sky, blurry, oscillating nimbuses of light that sickened him whenever he looked up.

Father Molinari walked along pathways of sand between the trees. He reached out, feeling the urge to prostrate himself before the supplicant, but could not suffer the touch of the light. Father Molinari drew back a smoking hand and clutched it to his chest. His shout of pain got no reaction from the kneeling man.

The shock of rejection snapped him awake. He stared up at the ceiling, barely aware of its distance from his face. Sabine's weight pressed into his side; her cheek rested at his left breast. When he peered down at her, he found her eyes wide and her mouth grinning.

"You were talking in your sleep." She moved to kneel beside him.

"What did I say?" Instinct brought his hand to his face, though no sleep crumbs had formed.

"You kept asking me to take a cup away from you." She looked puzzled. "Are you thirsty?"

A trace of hunger swirled through his innards like a malcontented serpent. "It seems so."

She jumped to her feet as he sat up. "Look, look!" Sabine scampered over to the worktable and pointed.

"I can't..." The instant he desired to see what she pointed at, the dark basement changed. Only Sabine seemed to be in color, but the walls, floor, wine shelves, and table appeared in perfect detail. It occurred to him at that instant Sabine's eyes glowed red. He raised a hand to his face, catching crimson light in his palm. "What have I done?"

"It is okay. God lets us see in the dark. I did not have to listen to the bad feeling." She bounced on the balls of her feet. "Look what Henri has brought."

He stood and approached. A pair of small shoes, plain hose, and a gauzy white child's dress lay folded on the table next to a dark long-sleeved girl's overcoat with black buttons.

"It's about time you stopped running about in a nightdress. You can save it for sleeping as it should be."

She glanced down, appraising her garment. "It is a bit dirty."

"Go on then, get dressed."

He started away, but stopped when she said *"Non."*

"What?" He whirled around, raising an eyebrow. "You cannot stay barefooted and half dressed for the rest of your l... life."

Sabine extended her arm, pointing at the clothes with her whole hand. "I cannot wear such beautiful things when I am like this."

"Oh, Sabine..." He took a knee at her side and ran a hand over her hair. *I do not know that I shall ever find a way to undo what has been done. Such a thing is likely impossible.* "If I am ever able to rid you of this curse, I will buy you finer clothes than these."

She set her little fists against her hips and let off an exasperated sigh. "*Non.* I cannot wear new clothes when I am so filthy." She gestured down her front, splaying her toes for effect. "Look at me. I am like an urchin. I must have a bath before I can put on new clothes."

"A bath."

"*Un bain.*" She folded her arms. "With rosewater and perfumed oils."

Father Molinari raised both eyebrows. "You have such things at home?"

"*Oui.*" Sabine made a contemplative face, and clasped her hands in front of her. "But, I am not home, so I will manage without a servant to wash me."

"Will you now?" He covered his mouth to conceal a barely-contained chuckle.

Molinari traced his fingers over the smooth pages of the sacred book, reassured by the lack of heat or pain. He had not opened it since his death. Despite his crucifix still only irritating and warm to the touch, the idea of opening *that* book had felt disrespectful. For how many years had he hunted abominations, and now he was one—or was he? Enough moonlight filtered through the four-pane window to let him read. The tiny room adjacent to the back porch had thin walls with so much moss gathered in the mortar grooves that the green fuzz appeared to knit the stones together. Henri admitted the bathing vessel was Josephine's idea, but he didn't trust the upstairs floor to hold it and she demanded privacy. The idea of bathing in this room during winter was ridiculous. As far as Henri was concerned, the river was all he needed, but he had been gracious enough to help cart buckets of heated water in, and left them to the use of the bath chamber.

Water sloshed in the bronze vessel behind him. Only Sabine's head rose above the edge, though he still shifted with discomfort. Despite her tender years, it seemed wrong to be in the same room with someone else's child while they sat in the bath. Perhaps she, too, was wary in these surroundings, for she had refused to be alone. He considered the possibility it wasn't so much she was frightened as she did not wish to be separated from him. An odd fear for a girl her age. He glanced at her, wondering what horrors she'd witnessed in that house before fleeing. Might now be a good time to mention his idea?

She sang in a hushed whisper. Her morose voice echoed within the bathtub and took on watery vibrato. From the splashing, he wondered if she cleaned herself or simply played. Alas, Henri possessed neither scented oils nor rosewater to offer her, a shock that had left her on the verge of an outburst. But after only a brief twisting of her features, she sighed and thanked their host for the use of the tub.

The thought of what might happen if she ever had a tantrum sent him straight to his book. Much to his dismay, little within it had specific relevance to vampires. One passage read like a blessing intended to bar demonic forces from entering a house. Another was a re-sanctification rite to restore holy ground. The irony of it struck him with a smile. Assuming God granted him the ability to render the blessing, he could make a house such that it would destroy him to enter.

Listening to her play in the bathwater, like an ordinary eight-year-old, made it impossible to read with any degree of comprehension. The priests had kept her prisoner for three weeks according to their dinner conversation. But for the grace of God at them hearing a rumor of his arrival, she may have already been put to the stake. He could not bring himself to hurry her along. This moment of childish purity soothed his soul as much as it seemed quite needed for her as well.

He considered Tristan, and stared at a patch of pale plaster in front of him while offering a silent prayer for the boy's sanity. *Do not let him be the one to find Callini.*

"*Maman* had bath oils from Paris," said Sabine.

He flipped pages, though continued to stare at the wall. "I am sorry for what happened to your mother."

"I know." Water sloshed; the tub rang with the hollow *thud* of a leg or elbow banging it. "Are we to stay with Henri? Will Josephine bring Marcel to meet me?"

"I do not think he will come. To protect us, Henri has told them you are sick."

The lapping of water faded. "Am I sick?"

"Perhaps I am a fool chasing a wish, but I would like to think you can be cured."

After a moment of silence, soft sobs echoed in the tub.

Father Molinari looked over. "What is wrong?"

She had moved onto her knees and turned herself to face him, though her head hung so only her hair showed over the rim, bobbing with the rhythm of crying. He could not see, but assumed she covered her face.

"Do you think I am a creature?"

"No. No..." He glanced at the floor. "You are still... much to my relief, still very much a little girl despite being—"

"A vampire." She straightened. Two tiny hands gripped the rim of bronze, one on either side of her chin as she peered at him. Thin trails of red ran down her cheeks. "Papa made us all like this. Is it like a sniffle?"

"I'm afraid it's not quite so simple." *Perhaps impossible.* "I have read rumors of a way to end the curse, but..."

"What?" She perked up.

"It may not work, and I am not sure it is appropriate to mention to you." He clasped the crucifix around his neck. "I would have to do something bad."

"You would have to hurt someone?" She sat back, pushed away from the wall, and slid into the middle of the tub where she smeared soap on her arms and chest after rinsing her face.

"That depends on if you regard a vampire as a some*one*."

Sabine made a series of contemplative faces as she washed. "If a person listens to the bad feeling and gives away their soul, does God consider them a person? *People* have souls."

"A person who surrenders their soul turns their back on God." He kissed the crucifix and murmured a blessing.

"Where does their soul go if they listen to the bad thing?" She flung water on herself to chase away suds. "Does it go to Hell?"

"I do not know. If not Hell, then oblivion." He couldn't bear to look at her. "There is a chance, however small, that if I destroy the vampire who took your life, you would be released from the curse."

Sabine huddled down, hiding behind the bathtub wall save for her eyes. Her voice sounded tiny and meek when at last she spoke. "You would kill Papa?"

Father Molinari winced. "I... If the rumor is true, it might... but—"

"He is not Papa now." She shivered. "He is not a nice person anymore."

He looked at her. "It does not horrify you that I speak of such things? Of destroying the last of your family?"

"*Non.*" She fidgeted with the water in front of her knees. "Papa became strange and mean one day. He yelled at *Maman* for opening the curtains. Soon, we only saw him at night. He put heavy drapes over all the windows. *Maman* became sick soon after. I did not know they were vampires... not until Papa hugged me. My neck hurt, and then I had to stay inside all the time."

"Sabine..." A trickle of warm blood ran down Father Molinari's cheek. How a man could kill his own daughter—even if she was technically not 'gone'—was beyond any trace of his understanding. Surely, the man she knew of as 'Papa' could no longer be in possession of any semblance of a soul.

"If you kill it... kill Papa, will I stop having to hurt people?" She curled up and hid her face behind her knees. "Papa is already dead, isn't he?"

"The man he was, yes." He ran a hand through his hair. The gesture made him feel normal, if nothing else. "I do not know. Even if the curse is not lifted, he must answer to God for what he has done to you."

"I am afraid of the creature that took his skin." Sabine lifted one leg from the water and ran the soap up and down her calf and foot. "He does not act like Papa anymore. That is why I tried to get help from the priests." She looked down and swished her hand through the water for a little while before swiveling around to put her back to him. "*Maman* told me to run away."

"After she had immolated herself?" He straightened, mouth not quite closed.

"What is *immolé?*" asked Sabine.

Father Molinari hung his head. "After she went to God."

"*Oui.*" After soaping and rinsing her other leg, she squirmed around to look at him. "Please, will you wash my hair?"

"I am not sure it is appropriate, Sabine. I am no relation to you."

Her lips curled into an innocent grin, fangs bared. "You are my family now, Father." The mirth faded, leaving her mouth a flat line. "You are all I have in the world."

CHAPTER SIXTEEN

GLIMMER OF HOPE

March 26th 1885 Briançon, France

Fate proved somewhat fortunate in that the Caillouet Manor House sat at the far northeast of Briançon, well removed from the church in which he had spent his last night as a breathing mortal. Sabine, in her new clothes, led him along a road, which consisted of little more than two lines of dirt in the grass. The closer they got to the imposing wrought iron gate, the tighter she squeezed his hand.

Ivy devoured the brickwork of a decorative wall that cut across the path some hundred and fifty yards from the door. The wagon path split, passing around both sides of a fountain at the center of the front yard. He imagined dozens of coaches and their drivers standing about while the area's well-to-do hobnobbed inside. Fair bet, it had been some time since a soiree happened in this place.

"You should hide here."

Sabine grabbed his arm. "I am more afraid of being alone than I am of Papa. God will protect us."

He pulled open the breast of his long coat, checking on a pair of stakes. Two bottles of holy water at his belt were bath-warm to the touch, even through glass. Molinari removed the stopper from one and touched the lip. The water on his fingertip could have been hot tea.

After tucking his crucifix amulet under his black vest and cinching the top button, he took Sabine's hand. Rather than risk noise at the gate, he climbed the waist-high wall to the side and lifted the child up and over. Nothing stirred in the dark as they crossed the long, open lawn. The once-white marble fountain in the center of the courtyard had darkened with moss.

He took in the ruin of it, wondering how long it had been.

Sabine glanced off in the distance.

"*Maman's* rose garden is over there." She pointed past the house's right corner. "She used to sing to me in the grove. It was so pretty there. I can still see the sun in the trees and hear the birds when I dream."

Father Molinari swallowed. The taste of ale repeated in the back of his throat. He said a prayer for the drunken man now several sips low of blood. A burglar two alleys over had been free of drink, and perhaps still sleeping off the effects of their meal. The image of Sabine dabbing blood from her lips with a pink silk napkin would haunt him for some time.

This is not the advantage I like to have when facing these creatures. He ran over the scenario in Vienna again. An old brick house with boarded up windows, and a monster who never imagined he'd be found. *Arrogance was his demise. He laired alone. I pray this one makes the same mistake.*

Sabine followed close, a hint of trembling in her arm by the time they stepped up on the porch among large white columns strangled by ivy. Her family had money, something he'd assumed at her talk of scented bath oil and servants.

"I suppose you *can* take it with you..." he whispered.

"*Quoi?*" She looked up.

"Nothing important."

Knocking seemed foolish. Going through a window looked implausible. He tested the front door and found it unlocked. *Of course. A thief is merely a self-delivering meal.*

They stepped in to a large foyer done in black and white marble. Two nude male statues flanked them, modesty preserved by strategic fig leaves. One held a large wine jug, the other a spear. If not for his vampiric eyes, the room would have been pitch black. Beyond a grand hall and a dining room with service for forty, a trace of light seeped through the gap of a heavy, burgundy curtain blocking an archway. He released her hand and waved her behind him as he advanced, as quiet as hard shoes allowed. On crossing the ballroom, he listened at the curtain for a moment before risking a peek. The light seeped in from a half-closed door on the opposite wall of the next room between two wingback chairs.

Sabine tugged at his pant leg. He stooped. She leaned up and whispered in his ear, a wisp of air leaving her throat so faint the ears of a vampire almost failed to register her words.

"Papa is in his study."

He brushed the curtain aside and slipped in. Massive paintings decorated the sitting room, otherwise adorned with dark red velvet wallpaper. Small tables held candles and decanters of dark red liquid. His nose said blood, but his brain struggled to grasp the how of it. While he had never trained in the medical arts, he knew blood would not keep long out of a body. Some part of him cringed inside at the thought of tasting it days old and room temperature.

"*Merci*, Élodie." A man said, genteel and bored. "Has there been any further word?"

"No, sir. The fat one did not know anything," replied a whispery, high-pitched woman.

A second later, the female voice sucked in a breath and squeaked. The sound made Father Molinari picture a servant cringing from the threat of a physical blow. He pulled one of the stakes from his coat and rushed forward, figuring his only chance would be surprise.

The door swung wide and struck the wall with a *slap*. A slender, foppish man in a teal brocade suit sat with his white-gloved hand coiled like a striking serpent. Near him cowered a young woman who appeared as delicate and fragile as a china doll brought to life. Her underdeveloped chest and straight blonde hair made her look young, perhaps sixteen. Plain grey servants' clothes covered everything but her face and hands, which she held up in a defensive stance.

Father Molinari sprinted forward, snarling as he raised the wooden implement of doom. The man sprang from the seat with alarming speed, leaving Molinari skidding to a halt against the back of a now-empty chair.

"And who is this that I have the pleasure of entertaining?" The man, now between him and the exit, raised his chin and eyebrow.

"Caiaphas," said Molinari.

"An interesting name. Biblical, correct?" The man smiled. "You've an Italian look to you. I am quite surprised the *Abandonato* would send an 'emissary' so soon. Quite a shame. Your features are quite becoming. Dark eyes, that sharp nose... Ah, such a waste. I am Auguste Caillouet. May I enquire as to the reason you are in my home?"

The servant girl backed into a corner where she slipped behind floor-to-ceiling red curtains.

"I am an agent of the Lord. He to whom you must answer for your transgressions."

Auguste blinked. His mouth opened a few seconds of silent shock, after which he burst out laughing. "Oh, you Italians... So pious. Has no one bothered to inform you that your God is no longer watching?"

Father Molinari stalked toward him. Stakes worked on vampires, Vienna had proven that. He wasn't sure about the head-cutting bit, as the body had gone up in flames soon after being impaled. What other things might pose a fatal hindrance to a vampire's continued existence, he did not know. Regardless, he ought to have the upper hand with both God and a stake on his side.

Auguste circled sideways, a matador taunting a bull. "You are a strange one, Caiaphas. You smell new. Have you walked among us for two full days yet? Surely, you must have been presented to the conclave?" He startled at a tiny gasp. When he noticed Sabine half-hidden behind the doorjamb, he opened his arms wide—to Father Molinari. "Ah... you have brought my daughter back to me."

Darkness dwelled within the grey eyes glimmering at Father Molinari, the same darkness he beheld in Vienna. This being in front of him was no longer a man; he had given away any trace of that which had made him human.

"*Non.*" Sabine whimpered and shrank behind the wall.

"Foul corruptor!" Molinari clenched the stake. "What depravity have you committed upon your own daughter, an innocent child?"

He charged, but the taller, thinner man blurred out of the way, leaving him stabbing a tapestry. Auguste's light chuckle incensed him and brought temptation to the back of his mind. A little desire would grant him speed or strength, enough to destroy the mocking face before him. Enough to protect the innocent child.

Satan harrows my mind. I shall not turn away from God.

"Let us be reasonable here, Caiaphas. It is unseemly to have such a quarrel amongst our own kind. Certainly, I can make room among my coterie for you." Auguste winked. "Of course, you will need to much better attend to a sense of fashion. I do think those dark and serious looks of yours would turn many heads."

"I have no interest in your foul temptations." He gripped and released the wood, eyeing Auguste. "For what you have done to your own child, you must answer to Him."

"You do realize you are a vampire, do you not?" Auguste grasped his frilled lapels, looking amused.

Father Molinari leapt again, swiping the stake through an insubstantial blur of fabric, gone before the point touched. This time, Auguste spun around and grabbed him by the neck, lifting him off his feet in a casual one-handed grip. He gurgled from reflex more than need of air, and brought the stake down into a vice grip around his wrist.

"My, you do have such unrefined manners." Auguste squeezed Molinari's arm until his hand opened and the stake fell. "I am trying my best to be civil." He tilted his head and smiled. "Since you have returned Sabine home, I would find it most unpleasant to have to destroy you."

Father Molinari struggled at the hand around his throat, though the man may as well have been a statue. *God grant me the strength...*

Auguste lost interest in controlling his arm, since the stake was well out of reach. Molinari palmed a phial of holy water, warm in his hand, as the other vampire carried him across the room and pressed him against the wall.

"Papa, do not hurt him!" yelled Sabine. "You have killed *Maman* already!"

Auguste closed his eyes and seethed. "Véronique's choices were her own."

"Because you *made* her," Sabine shouted from behind the wall. "You killed her heart."

For an instant, Father Molinari thanked God he had no further need of air. Auguste's grip weakened, letting him slide down until his feet touched floor. Though the pressure no longer crushed his neck, the man did not release him.

"Why, Auguste? What darkness had grasped your soul that you poisoned your own child?"

Sabine's father snapped his eyes open. "Poisoned? I did nothing of the sort. I would not have her betray me as my wretch of a wife had."

"Stop lying!" yelled Sabine, in tears.

Father Molinari tugged at the arm holding him. "I did not mean literal poison. You cursed your child with darkness. Why?"

"Véronique... She took the gift I had given her and betrayed me with another. I surprised them... in my own bed." Auguste shuddered, twisting his head to stare at the door. "I could not bear the thought of my daughter becoming a treacherous woman... I had to protect her. Now, I shall keep her innocent. Forever."

"Fool," said Molinari. "You have not protected her innocence, you have devoured it."

Auguste snarled, baring fangs. "Now then, Caiaphas. You have entered my home, and brought violence. I will suffer not your lectures of an invisible man who lords over—"

Father Molinari flung his right arm up, dashing holy water into Auguste's eyes.

Smoke poured from the alabaster face. The older vampire wailed; his voice twisted deep into a range well below what a human throat should produce. Hands clasped to his blistering skin, he staggered back. Father Molinari advanced, spraying water in the sign of the cross.

"In the name of God the father, the Son, and the Holy Spirit, I command you to the shadowy abyss from whence you came. Ye who have denied God. Ye who have chosen to dwell amongst sin and shadow."

Auguste backpedaled, flailing his arms. Thick, grey smoke peeled from his sleeves. Holes appeared in his cheeks, exposing bone. His eyes flared with crimson light. All traces of humanity fled; he lunged forward, hissing, baring fangs.

Father Molinari leapt to the side, far too slow to avoid a tackle that knocked him once more against the wall. He lost the holy water while scrambling to grab claw-tipped arms. The stink of fetid flesh flooded his nostrils as he fought to keep Auguste away. Fangs inched closer to his throat. Side to side, they thrashed.

"Christ, God's word made flesh commands you to Hell."

Auguste laughed; a deep, demonic sound reverberated through the den. Plaster crumbled behind Molinari and the tapestry tore from its bar above their heads, draping over them. The stench of burned skin grew nauseating. Auguste smiled with gleeful delight as they grappled. Faint steel-blue light lit the fiend's eyes. Muscles beneath the other vampire's skin had the hardness of stone, yet moved.

"You are weak, Italian. Too new." Auguste opened his mouth; strands of flesh stretched like melted cheese over gaping holes in his cheeks.

Father Molinari focused on his faith, tuning out the urge in the back of his mind telling him he would die if he did not call upon the darkness for power. This vampire had given in to Satan. He had a great advantage in speed and strength. *What chance do I have of surviving?*

"The Lord is my strength and my shield." He strained, twisting left and right.

The tapestry slipped off and draped to the ground as the two men whirled through the room and slammed against the desk. Starbursts of fizzling pain ran up and down his spine from the hard wooden edge. Small objects behind him fell and rolled.

"Pathetic." Auguste surged, and shoved him. "You are as weak as a mortal."

Molinari fell back, sliding across the desk. Auguste pounced on top of him and raked elongated claws through his shoulder. Blood sprayed from the rip across his chest. Auguste's snarl became a pitiful yelp as if he had touched a red-hot plate. Father Molinari's destroyed vest fell open, exposing the crucifix. He grasped the warm metal and held it up on its chain.

"Yea, though I walk through the valley of the shadow of death, I fear no evil. Thou art with me. Thy rod and thy staff comfort me."

Auguste scurried back, crossing his arms before him. More smoke wisped from his skin, as if standing in the path of an intense ray of heat.

Molinari sat up, keeping the crucifix directed at Sabine's father. "Lord God in Heaven, strike this fiend from your sight. Protect your children who supplicate themselves at your feet." He slid to the end of the desk and stood.

"What? How is this possible? You are one of us!" Auguste wailed. "There is no God."

"He who created all sees your sin. In your own house, you have brought evil upon those whom you were supposed to protect." Molinari thought back to his comments on faith. Callini had doubted. The fiend before him proved him correct. Bolstered with the love of God, he pressed forward. "I command you, unclean spirit, back to the fires of Hell where you belong. You who cannot stand in the glory of our Lord have no place on this Earth."

Auguste screamed, shrinking into the floor as if crushed by a tangible weight.

Father Molinari drew his second stake and leapt at the fiend. In the instant the crucifix sagged against his chest, Auguste recovered enough to catch Molinari's arm. The two men slid to the floor, rolling over each other three times. With the crucifix dangling inches from his face, Auguste tried to crawl away more than fight. Molinari's shoes slipped over the carpet as he struggled to keep up. He raised the crucifix to make Auguste cringe away, growling as he fought to overpower the man and get the stake into position. Inch by painful inch, he forced it up and over the vampire's heart.

The wooden tip pushed into Auguste's breast; blood, thick and dark, welled up around it. He hissed like a panicking cat, wide eyes devoid of reason. Another more primal sound seemed to reverberate through Molinari's soul. Sabine screamed.

"I commend you to Hell!" Father Molinari shouted as he fell on the stake, driving it through to the floor.

Auguste's wail cut off to a breathless wheeze. His body tensed and convulsed. His back arched. His claws grew another half-inch. Color melted out of his face, leaving him grey. Skin dried, tightened, and creaked like ancient leather.

Father Molinari pushed himself up, grasping a shoulder full of claw wounds. Warm, sticky blood seeped through his fingers. Auguste lay still for several seconds before cracks raced through his features and large ashy flakes drifted into the air. Yellow light flared from deep within, and his body erupted with flame.

Molinari fell to his knees and dribbled holy water on the disintegrating forehead of Auguste Caillouet.

"Through this holy unction, may the Lord pardon thee whatever sins or faults thou hast committed."

The corpse hissed and squealed. All traces of flesh burned away to ash, leaving an almost-recognizable skeleton scattered in a patch of char. Father Molinari slouched in place, unsettled by the sensation of the wounds beneath his fingers sealing fast enough to perceive skin moving. A blur of white caught his eye and he looked up.

A woman with long brown hair stood five paces from him, near the covered window. Thin like Sabine, the silhouette of her willowy body showed in moonlit shadow upon a gauzy nightdress. Sadness permeated her being, though she smiled at him and bowed as if in thanks.

"*Maman?*" Sabine crept in the door. "*Maman?*"

The woman turned a sad stare at her, and faded away.

Father Molinari sat back on his heels, hands on his thighs. He glanced to his left at Sabine, who appeared ready to burst into tears. Hope swelled in his heart at the redness forming around her eyes.

"Sabine?" He leaned toward her. "Do you feel any different?"

She clasped her hands to her chest, gaze darting about the room. The desiccated bones of her father seemed to escape her notice—or care. Her breathing picked up speed, and she smiled.

"I think..." She took a step closer, grinning. "I think I feel..."

Tiny fangs grew long in the child's mouth. She froze, a look of shock on her face, and reached one little hand up to touch them. Sabine stared at a droplet of blood on her fingertip.

No... No... Father Molinari closed his eyes and bowed forward until his head touched the carpet. *God, please guide me. What must I do?* The apparition of Véronique Caillouet had smiled at him. He had taken it as a sign of success, but she had to know he had failed.

"*Non! Ce n'est pas juste!*" screamed Sabine. "*Ce n'est pas juste...*"

With a shriek of rage, she pushed a chair over and set to flinging items from the desk, hurling whatever she could get her hands on across the room. Glass shattered, small metal statues landed with heavy *thuds*, while the little girl howled with rage. When the desk lay bare, she ran to the wall and clutched at the curtains on tiptoe, seeming intent on tearing them down.

Father Molinari rushed up behind her, grabbed her arms, and held her.

"Sabine... calm yourself."

Blood trails streaked down her cheeks from her sobs. "I do not want to be calm. I do not want to be damned! I am going to be like this forever!"

"You are not damned." He pressed her hands to her chest, fighting to contain the struggling child. "Put your trust in God. Do not listen to the feeling."

She snarled, kicking her legs and twisting her body.

"Sabine!" he yelled. "Do not give in to anger and despair; they are the hands of Satan. I will not rest until I understand God's plan. Your mother smiled. That must be a good sign."

She stopped fighting. After a moment of stillness, she tried to wriggle around to face him. He released her enough to let her turn, and cradled her close. She threaded her arms around his neck and held on. "I am sorry for losing my temper."

He hugged her, surreptitiously dripping a little holy water down the back of her neck.

"I feel that." She leaned back and stuck her tongue out at him. "It is not painful, merely wet."

His heart sped up with relief, and he kissed her atop the head.

Father Molinari stood, took her hand, and walked to the curtain where the meek servant girl had concealed herself. He drew back the dense red fabric, finding only empty wall.

Sabine looked around. "Élodie has gone."

He scowled at the bones. "I must find her. I do not want her stirring up a panic in Briançon."

"She will not speak of it." Sabine pulled on his arm. "Élodie has seen everything that happened. She would be happy you have sent Papa away."

Molinari approached the door. Sabine raced after him and held her arms up.

"You do not want to walk?" He attempted a smile.

"*Non.*" Her lip quivered. "I am sad."

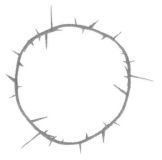

CHAPTER SEVENTEEN

GETHSEMANE

May 21ˢᵗ 1885 Saint-Jean-de-Maurienne, France

I n the void of a dream, Father Molinari walked upon scorching sand that seared his feet, though no sight reached his eyes. Light in the distance beckoned him toward a grove of olive trees arranged in neat rows. Somewhere, a noise reminiscent of an irritated camel echoed. He advanced, returning to the familiar scene of a man in white kneeling in a spot of light. Thunder creaked overhead, distant and subtle. Pop-flashes of lightning flickered here and there beyond dense clouds.

"My soul is overwhelmed with sorrow to the point of death."

The voice sounded like his, but seemed to come at him from everywhere.

"My father, take this cup from me; yet not as I will, but as you will."

Father Molinari knelt at the edge of the light, knowing himself unworthy to enter. The figure in white looked back at him. His mouth opened, releasing a blinding glow that erupted from his eyes a second later.

"Are you sleeping? Could you not keep watch for even one hour?"

Molinari sat bolt upright in Henri's wine cellar. Sabine was gone, though her nice clothes remained folded where she'd left them the morning before. He shifted to his knees and spent a half-hour in prayer, beseeching God for guidance, fortitude, and understanding. That she was capable of waking up so long before him gave him hope. Her soul remained farther from the night than his.

When he finished his prayers, he collected his sacred book and wandered upstairs to the back porch. He sat in the wooden chair by the round table, but did not put his feet up. For a few minutes, he observed the meadow behind the house, watching flitting insects and listening to the restlessness of birds. A spring breeze rushed through the trees and sent waves cascading through the wildflowers and grass. Sabine, barefoot and in her nightdress, moped about, tracing a hand through the flora without enthusiasm.

He opened the book in his lap, seeking pages by where the cloth ribbons separated them.

The book contained little he deemed helpful. Had these old rites been common knowledge among the priesthood in a time when creatures of darkness walked among men? Had some ancient tide of battle turned, forcing the minions of Satan into hiding and clouding the minds of humans? Many thought such tales were allegorical. They thought 'demons' didn't exist as real entities, and were purely tools used to convey a moral truth.

Father Molinari knew different.

A fruitless hour later, he lifted his tired stare from the page and watched Sabine traipse in the garden. His sharp, dead eyes picked out her sullen frown from a hundred yards away. Surely, she had to be thinking of her mother. Perhaps she had come to understand the depth of what her father had done to her? Such a weight could crush the heart of a grown man, much less that of a little girl.

"God," he whispered. "Why have you let the darkness enter my soul? How could you allow a child to dwell in the shadows where you do not look?"

An itch in the back of his mind agreed. *Hate God. He lies. He does not love you.*

For an instant, the crucifix around his neck heated, near to the point of pain.

"I have given my life to the service of the Lord. It has ever been my only wish to do His work." The crucifix cooled. "I have followed your will into the life..." He sighed. "Life of this child, yet I feel as if I have failed."

You deny yourself strength. Think of all the good you could do if you were as strong as Auguste, stronger even. Think of how you could protect Sabine if you had such power.

"No." He forced his hand to clench around the crucifix, despite the burn. "The Lord God made light where there is darkness. I do not understand why he tests a little child, but I am an unworthy instrument of His will."

Somewhere... there had to be secrets. Perhaps in the Vatican. He cringed. If he could not set foot in a rural church in the French countryside, the mere sight of the Holy See would likely cause him to burst into flames from afar. He would need help.

"I trust in God." He repeated the phrase until it became a chant.

You are a fool. The feeling slid side to side like a mass of jelly at the back of his brain.

"God is my light and my salvation."

The feeling receded.

When he opened his eyes, he startled at Sabine almost nose to nose with him. The look of forlorn resignation in her eyes created a cold weight within his chest. She stood with her feet together, arms at her sides, and head ever so slightly tilted to the right.

"Father, is God mad at us?" She looked down. "Should we be destroyed?"

He put a gentle hand on her cheek, tracing his thumb over her soft skin. "My child, if God wishes you destroyed, God can do so Himself... I cannot."

She looked up with a somber smile. "I am trying to be patient."

"Children and patience are not often good friends." He slid his hand onto her shoulder.

She crawled up into his lap and hugged him. "Thank you for saving me."

He cradled her little body, wracked with silent sobs, and knew that God had sent him to her. *Seven days...* He gazed up at the stars. *I, too, am being impatient.*

In time, Sabine lifted her head and wiped her tears. "Father, can we pray for Him to send us a sign?"

"Of course."

He held her hand.

"God," said Sabine. "Please watch over *Maman*, and bring her to Heaven. Please protect Father Molinari and give him strength. Please forgive the bad priests for trying to hurt me, and please don't be angry with Papa for what he did."

She opened her eyes and looked up. Her expression seemed to ask him if she'd said it right. A leaden weight settled upon his heart and tightness gripped his throat. *She did not ask anything for herself.* He bowed his head, spending a silent moment caught between rage at what Auguste had done, sorrow at the thought of a cursed child, and awe at her prayer.

He held her hands and whispered, "May God bless this child and keep her from harm."

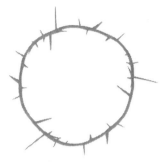

CHAPTER EIGHTEEN

LIBERTY

May 24ᵗʰ 1885 Saint-Jean-de-Maurienne, France

altering light from Henri's lantern cast fluttering shadows through the kitchen. Father Molinari sat at the table's end, half-aware of Sabine dancing in whorls through the family room while singing a nonsense song, an ill-remembered thing she must have heard from her mother. He stared into the little flame before his eyes, frustrated that his sacred book had so far proven useless. Boredom had crept in. Being confined to the night left him little opportunity for research, at least when his best sources were hundreds of miles away and on holy ground.

"What do vampires do with all this time?" He scratched at his head, and shuddered. "Things I have taken vows not to."

Sabine ceased her singing and padded in. "Father? Where is Henri?"

"He has traveled to Avignon. Josephine is due to marry tomorrow morning."

She crawled into an empty chair and smiled. "Ooh. I wish we could go. I like weddings. Especially if they are fancy and have cake and music and dancing. Will there be many people?"

"I do not know. Henri's family does not possess the same kind of wealth you are used to." He squinted at the window. "Is there no one left in your father's line to claim his fortune?"

"*Non*. They are all gone." Sabine leaned her head from side to side. "I do not want his wealth. I want *Maman* to come back. Even if we are paupers to beg for our bread."

"Wealth of the soul is the only—"

He startled at a light knock. At the creak of a door, he stood and moved to put himself between the girl and the front room.

"*Allo?*" asked a dainty feminine voice. "*Prêtre, êtes-vous là?*"

"I am. In here," said Molinari.

The young woman from Auguste's manor house crept into view. Her dark blue dress appeared a few shades shy of wealthy. Wispy blonde hair hung loose down to her waist, though she had gathered it behind her. She held a cloth bag in the crook of her left elbow, burdened by a small, heavy object inside. The mood of the room changed, as though an overwhelming sense of melancholy radiated from her.

"Élodie!" Sabine cheered and scrambled out of the chair to hug the slight woman.

The servant girl scooped her up and spun her around a few times, a hint of a smile breaking through her gloom. Élodie pulled Sabine into a tight embrace. Father Molinari put a hand over his heart at the sight of a blood tear collecting in the young woman's eye.

"Merciful God... How old are you, girl?"

Élodie set Sabine back in her chair. "I was nineteen at the time of my death. I have always appeared younger than my years. Auguste did not treat me well, even before..." She fixed him with a decidedly unmousy stare. "Thank you for destroying that horrible man."

"Our family grows..." Father Molinari swayed into a chair.

"No." Élodie shook her head. "I have not come here to stay with you. I have come to warn you. You must leave France."

Sabine sniffled. "Élo... Why?"

"Oh, *chéri*..." Élodie stooped to kiss Sabine on the head. "You would not understand. People... even—no, especially—vampires can be capricious and mean."

"We should return Henri's house to him." Father Molinari tapped his fingers on the table.

"I think it would be best for you to leave Europe as well." Élodie paced. "There are others, older and more dangerous than Auguste, calling for your head. Some wish to see you destroyed for slaying Auguste. It is against the *L'accord de l'Ombre* for a vampire to destroy another without the approval of the Conclave."

"A conclave of demons has no domain over God." Father Molinari scowled.

"I do not mean to debate the legitimacy of it. A thousand years ago, our kind warred openly with each other." Élodie paced around, apprising the décor. "They almost became extinct. To survive, they had no choice but to form the Conclave."

Father Molinari chuckled. "How sad to think that even in death one cannot escape politics."

"It is true they will hunt you... There are too many and they are too strong. Not all cared for Auguste, though many know of your work for the Church. Their desire for revenge was enough to sway the decision." Élodie cast a sad glance down. "They will likely kill Sabine if no one claims her as *la progéniture*. I cannot."

His throat tightened. "Because Auguste turned you as well?"

Élodie lifted her gaze to meet his, speaking in Italian. "Because I am a woman, and more so because of my childish appearance. I am not permitted even to speak among them. No one will claim Sabine. They would consider it an act of mercy to destroy her. I do not agree. We do not have much time. If my help is noticed, my existence is forfeit."

"I will send the lot of them to Hell." Father Molinari grasped his crucifix.

Élodie took a step back. "Do not be foolish, Father. You are perhaps a match for them one at a time, but can you fend off ten and protect Sabine at the same time?"

"I..." He slouched in the chair. "Her life is not worth the chance."

"Where would we go?" Sabine's lip quivered in anticipation of tears.

"Soon, an enormous statue will be shipped to America aboard the *Isère*." Élodie put a hand on Sabine's shoulder.

"America?" Sabine blinked. "I do not want to go to America. They all run about with guns"—she held her hands up, mimicking two pistols—"and shoot each other from the backs of horses."

Élodie patted the child on the back. "It is not all so bad. That is in the west. In the east, there is civility."

Father Molinari tapped his foot. "The monstrous head they put on display in Paris a few years ago?"

"Yes, I believe it is the same." Élodie stroked Sabine's hair. "She would be much safer across the Atlantic. There are few of our kind there, and none of them know or care about you. Better, they do not honor *L'accord de l'Ombre*."

"I have never heard of this." Father Molinari leaned forward. "You spoke to Auguste about 'the fat one.' What did you mean?"

Élodie wandered to the window, leaning forward to peer outside. "The priest you did not kill. Auguste desired for Sabine to come home. He sent me to find her. The man did not know where she had gone."

"What became of him?" asked Molinari. "Or the boy?"

"He was punished for his cruelty to Sabine." Élodie turned to face him, her expression devoid of emotion. "There was no boy. Please." She rushed to within inches of him. "You must come with me. I can help you flee Europe. I have... friends in the shipping yards and in Paris. The Conclave has long memories and short tempers."

"You killed the priest?" Sabine blinked.

"Oh, sweet Sabine." Élodie took the girl's hand. "I saw in his thoughts what they did to you... keeping you locked in that dreadful place."

Sabine gazed into her lap, whispering. "It is a sin to kill priests, even bad ones."

Élodie looked at Molinari and slid the bag from her shoulder. "Here, this is for you."

She removed a fat pouch of coins as well as a wine bottle with no label, and set them on the table. Dark fluid, too thick to be the fruit of the vine, coated the sides as it moved.

"Blood?" Father Molinari examined the bottle. "I have not been afflicted for long, but even I sense the futility of consuming dead blood."

Élodie put a hand to her mouth to suppress a noise. "Oh, forgive me. I forget you have not been taught. A drop or two of a vampire's blood added to an amount of fresh blood will preserve it for many years."

"And who used their blood to preserve this?" He raised an eyebrow.

"Auguste." Élodie attempted an innocent smile. "He has many such bottles."

Sabine stuck her tongue out and shook her head.

"I do not think it wise for us to partake of the blood of one so dark." Father Molinari set the bottle down. "There are too many things I do not know about what I am that I fear his corruption may seep from it."

"He thought a simple bite would make him a vampire." Sabine kicked her feet back and forth.

"Many mortals do." Élodie glanced up at him, a spark of attraction in her eye. Her smile bared one retracted fang for a few seconds before she bit her lower lip. "Perhaps you are wise to be cautious."

"I thank you for the gesture." He wrenched his stare away from her sapphire eyes.

"There is little time." Élodie collected the bottle. "Gather your things and come with me."

Sabine's swinging legs went still. Seconds later, she looked up with red liquid gathered in crescents beneath her eyes. The fear and sadness upon her face hit him like a punch to the stomach. She seemed to trust this woman, and though Élodie unsettled him to a degree, he did not relish the thought of a war with dozens of vampires, many likely centuries old.

"Go and get dressed, Sabine."

The child slipped out of the chair, trudged across the kitchen, and disappeared down the basement stairs.

Élodie flashed a wistful smile. "You do not trust me, but I am not offended. Perhaps in time you will see we are not all mindless savages."

"How do you propose we travel to Paris?" Molinari walked for the stairs.

"I have brought a coach." She did not turn, or appear to pay attention to him. "My drivers are discrete... and alive."

"Mortals help you?" He froze at the thought.

"Yes." Élodie winked at him. "They are quite loyal, and paid well for their service. To have the living as one's eyes and ears in the day is indispensable. Do not loathe what you have become so much that you do not exploit your advantages and guard your weaknesses. Sabine's life is now yours to protect."

Father Molinari stood in silence, staring at the blonde waif as he tried to wrap his thoughts around the concept of living people *willingly* assisting vampires.

Sabine tromped up the stairs, shoes clomping. She carried her nightdress bundled in a wad atop the sacred book. He searched for paper, ink, and a fountain pen, returning from the family room to the kitchen to write at the table.

My friend Henri,

Circumstances have arisen which require our immediate relocation. I cannot in good conscience remain here as to do so will imperil you and your family. You have my thanks for your hospitality and generosity. May God watch over you and Josephine. It seems unlikely I will return.

-Father Antonio

After setting the pen down, he blew on the letter to dry the ink, rolled it up, and tucked it between two wooden bowls. Sabine held his hand as they walked outside to a white coach trimmed in ornate gold filigree. Its appearance suggested it once belonged to Auguste. A team of two dark horses fidgeted at their approach, causing a man at the front to make soothing noises at them.

Another man, dressed like a commoner with a brown beret, removed his hat and bowed to Élodie and Sabine before opening the door. "Good evening, ladies." He offered a nod of greeting to Molinari. "Father."

Sabine squealed. "Oh, Élodie!"

The outburst ripped Molinari's attention from the coachman to the interior, where Sabine dove among a collection of dolls arranged on a dark blue plush bench. She pounced on one, apparently named 'Papi,' perhaps for the butterfly embroidered on its dress.

"You brought my dolls!" Sabine hugged Papi, and three others after flopping down in the rear-facing seat.

"I could not bear the thought of you being separated from them." She pointed to a beige lump on the far side of the seat. "There is a bag for you to pack them in."

Molinari settled in next to Élodie. She eyed the crucifix around his neck and edged as close as she could to the far wall while smiling at Sabine.

The coach lurched forward, lanterns rattling. In minutes, it bounced and swayed over the rough country roads behind the steady rumble of hooves pounding dirt. Every so often, the springs gave him the sense they would fly clear off the path. Father Molinari gritted his teeth and clung to the wall.

They drive like men who look forward to death.

Aside from Sabine whispering to her dolls, no one spoke for several hours.

"Is everything all right, Father?" Élodie turned her blank expression toward him.

"Yes. Yes. I am not fond of coach rides, especially at such speed in the dark."

Élodie giggled, a tiny, innocent noise that sent shivers down his spine.

"So," said Molinari. "What do you know of the *L'accord de l'Ombre?*"

She waved her hand about. "No different than mortals. A group of old men who think they own the world. A council of ancients who represent several countries. In the time before *L'accord*, the vampires disregarded law and morals. Strength was all that mattered. War raged in the dark. Italians, Germans, French, English... all of the Old World. I am glad I did not exist to see it."

"There are so many?" He swallowed hard. "Never could I have imagined..."

"Not so many..." Élodie looked at the roof, muttering. "At one time there were too many to count. Then only a hundred. Now? Perhaps two thousand. The agreement set up territories in rough approximation to those of the mortal world. It is all politics. Boring politics, and they do not entrust it to women." She scoffed. "They think they are keeping power from us, but I am grateful to be spared the tedium and drama."

Cardinal Benedetto would collapse over his desk.

"You are frightened." Élodie flashed a mischievous grin. "Your church does not understand us. Our kind do not seek wanton slaughter. For ages, we have lived in the shadows and you have not seen."

He glared. "I have put down—"

"Humans have killers, do they not?" She raised her nose a tick. "Being a criminal or a murderer is not limited to those whose heartbeat is more than a convenience. You have seen... oh what is the phrase? The tip of the iceberg."

Father Molinari sank in the cushioned seat, still gripping the silk from the pace of their midnight trek. Shadowy figures, trees both dead and verdant, whipped past the windows, chopping the moonlight in a fluttering glow.

"And as do groups of men who think they own the world, they have laws and decrees. Like mortals, they frown upon murder..." Élodie glanced out her window. "And we have no prisons."

"Why haven't they come for me before?" He squinted.

"You have seen only the ones who cause problems, the ones the Conclave deems... risky. This is why you were allowed to continue. They do not wish to attract attention. Mortals have always hunted us whenever we grew careless. To take revenge would only invite more scrutiny."

"I fear you are mistaken, Élodie." Father Molinari fingered his crucifix. "The vampires I have witnessed have all been creatures of darkness, standing out of the Light of God. Beasts, the lot of them. No trace of a soul."

"I would disagree with you, but in the case of Auguste, I cannot." Élodie's eyes gleamed red for a few seconds. "While he retained his *charm*, he was a monster. Those you have slain had been disowned."

Molinari thought for a moment, trying to draw forth any sense of regret from his memory of their battle. He could not. "Auguste referred to me as *Abandonato...*"

"An old Italian vampire once proclaimed his great suffering at being abandoned by God. Those who shared his feelings formed a small group separate from the Conclave." Élodie smiled. "I imagine Auguste thought your aggression political at first. It is the term they use now to refer to the Italians of our kind."

He let his head roll along the cushioned wall, peeling his gaze from the window to watch Sabine play, making two dolls waltz on the seat beside her.

They all eventually give in to the temptation. God, give me the strength to spare this one... or do what must be done when she has no soul left to save.

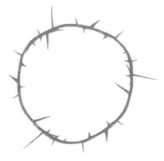

CHAPTER NINETEEN

SURRENDER TO THE DARK

May 26th 1885 Lyon, France

tiny voice drifted through the black void.
Frère Jacques, Frère Jacques.
Dormez-vous? Dormez-vous?

Father Molinari opened his eyes. Sabine, still in her 'out-and-about' clothes, lay on her side, her nose inches from his. She grinned.

"Good morning, Father. It is time to wake."

It is not morning. He pushed himself upright and scratched his head while surveying the tavern basement around them. Élodie lay on a small bed tucked against the wall, pale and lifeless. Sabine sprang up and rushed across the room. She pounced on the bed and bounced up and down atop her former serving girl.

"Élo! Élo! Élo!" Sabine grasped the woman's shoulders and shook her. "Élo! Élo! Élo!" When Élodie did not stir, she looked over at Molinari. "Something is wrong."

A sinking feeling settled in his gut. He walked over and gathered Sabine in his arms. "She is more tired than us."

Sabine beamed at him. "Father, I dreamed of the garden and birds. I was with *Maman*, and the sun was out. The grass was wet with warm dew, and we ran among lilies and roses. *Maman* had such a big smile."

He smiled. "That sounds beautiful."

"*Oui!*" Sabine leaned in and whispered at his ear. "*Maman* told me to trust in God. He is watching over me."

He set her down by the bag of dolls, and took a seat at a rickety table covered in dark stains and knife gouges. Ignoring the three burned-down candles in an iron holder, he flipped through the sacred book to a prayer of protection, and recited it in his head.

At Sabine play-acting her dolls having a conversation about finding some blood to drink, he hastened his prayer. A moment later, he turned to chide her for such dark thoughts, but a knock stalled him.

One of the coachmen, Francis, entered without waiting for anyone to open the door. In his left hand, he carried one large goblet and one small wine glass. In his right, an identical large goblet.

He set the pair on the table by Father Molinari and moved to Élodie with the remaining cup.

Blood, still warm.

"Sabine, come." Father Molinari offered her the smaller glass, and took hold of his. *Father, forgive me for what I am about to do. May you bless and keep the unfortunate soul who has given of themselves so that I may continue to... exist.*

One did not work with the Order without encountering the occasional danger. The taste of blood had not been new to Father Molinari prior to his *change*, though beforehand it had always been his own. Several unfortunate meetings between his face and hard objects replayed in his mind.

Now, it had lost its off-putting metallic twang. Within the fluid, the flavor of its former owner blossomed forth upon his senses. A woman's blood settled easy on the tongue, lingering like raspberries or something sweet. Blood from a man tasted like... power and aggression. He remembered feeding from Callini, or at least the last few seconds of it. There, he had tasted terror and guilt. The memory of it caused his unliving heart to race, flooding his limbs with the need to fight or destroy something.

Fortunately, the goblet in his hand filled his mouth with a bouquet of fruit... peaches and ginger. He prayed this woman still lived.

"Be at ease, Father. It was provided willingly." Francis returned his attention to Élodie, who had only seconds ago stirred with a soft moan.

"I... can taste the surrender." Molinari sipped again. "She gave of her own will, but not without fear."

He thought little of enjoyment, and gulped it down along with his guilt. Sabine nursed hers in small, dainty sips. Whenever she smiled, her blood-outlined teeth made him angry. He wished for Auguste to return so he could drive the stake through his heart again, and again, and again.

Warmth spread up the back of his neck and into his head. Something siphoned at his rage, beckoning him, feeding the anger, justifying it, honing it.

"Father, what troubles you?" Élodie glided over to the table, a look mixed of worry and amusement on her heart-shaped porcelain doll face.

"You see my thoughts?" He raised an eyebrow.

Sabine set her empty cup down and returned to sit with her dolls on the floor.

Élodie winked with a coy smile. "When anger glows from your eyes, I do. Two of our kind cannot see the other's thoughts, unless there is a great gap in age or power."

"The two are not the same?" He twisted the cup in his hands.

"Often they are." Élodie covered her mouth and giggled. "But I think you will find out what I mean eventually. What has so darkened the mood of a man of God?"

"Auguste." He indicated Sabine with a flick of the eyes. "Each time I look upon her..."

Élodie clucked her tongue. "Despite the opinion of the Conclave, you have done the world a kindness. Those who have reason know it is forbidden to turn one so young." She looked off to nowhere. "Those who lack reason... would not bother to try." She scowled. "The man wished to keep her innocent for eternity. Véronique's betrayal was not her fault. Another vampire influenced her thoughts, yet Auguste had such a low opinion of women he assumed she wanted..." She edged closer to him, watching Sabine play. "She was such a good child, innocent and pure."

"To look at you, I would infer the same."

"I am no longer the innocent I was." Two dark crimson trails glided down her perfect cheeks. "Auguste killed me. The things he made me do…"

"God forgives. Would you like me to hear your confession?"

"Not now. There is a limit even to His mercy." Élodie forced a weak smile. "Until I bore witness to such horrors, I didn't even believe He existed. Irony, yes? Now, if you wish to make your boat on time, we mustn't tarry."

They sat and watched Sabine play for a few minutes. A perfectly normal little girl with perfectly normal dolls—except for the trail of blood leaking from the corner of her mouth.

Father Molinari led the way to the coach, which had stopped fifteen or so paces from the front of a little tavern in a poor district of Lyon. They hurried across a section of rain-soaked cobblestones. When Father Molinari was three steps from the door, Sabine screamed. He clamped tight to her hand, spinning in the direction she faced.

Two silhouettes of men with glowing red eyes leapt from the second story roof of the tavern, sailing at them as if gliding. A third figure rushed around from behind the coach, brandishing a saber.

Élodie whirled about and leapt straight up, intercepting the two flyers before they could land on Molinari. He pushed Sabine to the ground as the swordsman stepped in with a diagonal slash, and suffered a minor slice to the arm. Sabine scampered on all fours, heading for the coach. The bladesman laughed. Moonlight glowed from a frilled white ascot at his throat; the thin-faced blond winked and lunged again.

Somewhere behind him, bodies smacked into the cobbles.

Molinari ducked to the right, evading another downward stroke, and grabbed the man's lavender coat sleeve. The figure drove his left elbow into Molinari's cheek, hard enough to knock him airborne, then pivoted and slashed at Sabine. His blade hit the wheel spokes with a *clank* as she squeaked and jumped back. Molinari growled and clambered to stand.

"Poor wretch. Be still and it will not hurt." The swordsman beckoned Sabine forward, but she refused to move.

Another man, with black hair and no sword, flew sideways in an ungainly butt-first fold. He cleared the span of the street, bounced off the front wall of the tavern, and fell among a stack of crates and barrels. Élodie let off an echoing snarl, called someone a brute, and made the kind of diminutive roar one might expect from a small lynx or cougar—no sound that should issue forth from a young woman.

Molinari didn't bother to look behind him. He rushed the assassin angling for a thrusting attack through the spokes at the child, wrapped his arms around the man's chest, and dragged him down.

"Droll," said the sword-wielder, forcing himself over onto his back.

At such close range, Molinari kept the saber out of the fight with a hand on the fiend's forearm. His attacker, a pretty man in his middle twenties, bared fangs and laughed.

"Am I to spare *two* small girls from damnation this night? You are weak." He flung Molinari off with enough force to knock him upright for two stumbling steps... and too much to allow him to retain his footing; he fell over backwards. The vampire floated to his feet as if lifted by an unseen giant, and raised the saber. "This is disappointing."

Father Molinari stuck his hand in his vest.

A fleshy slap behind him rang out in time with Élodie's cry of pain. A male laugh, tinged with mania, followed.

"Little whore. You'll die along with them."

Molinari glanced to his rear. A dark-haired man with a ponytail held his arms to the sides and sprouted four-inch claws. From lying flat on her back, Élodie sprang into the air, flipped upright, and descended in a rapid arc. The man jumped away to avoid her dive, but she moved in a blur. Her boots clicked twice on the cobbles, and she got a hold of him by the vest.

The swordsman strolled up to him, wagging the blade. "Come on, come on. At least stand up."

Wood splintered and crunched to the left as Molinari stood.

"You are a brute!" yelled Élodie. "I do not wish to destroy you, but I will not let you harm my master's child."

A man groaned. "Auguste is destroyed."

Élodie spat.

The swordsman feinted twice, moving with such speed his limbs and blade left ghost trails in the air. Temptation gnawed at the back of Molinari's brain, a starving rat desperate to be set loose from its cage. The man toyed with him, faking again.

Molinari yanked the crucifix into the moonlight. "Back, fiend!"

"*Merde!*" yelled the swordsman as his skin smoked and bubbled. His blue eyes glinted as the pupils contracted to pinpoints.

"In the name of God, I cast you back to the inferno!" Father Molinari advanced.

The fuming swordsman wailed, shielding his face with both arms. "My face! What is the meaning of this?"

Francis leapt from the top of the coach. He stole up behind the swordsman, seizing him in a bear hug while ramming a stake through his heart..

Sabine let off a high-pitched scream, sucked in another breath, and yelled, "Help!"

Father Molinari whirled toward the coach. The man who'd sailed across the street had crawled under and grabbed the girl from behind. She clung to the wheel spokes, struggling not to lose her grip.

"Back!" Father Molinari raised the crucifix at the pair. "In the name of Jesus Christ, I command you!"

Sabine shivered and shied away, though her body did not emit smoke. The vampire behind her ignited and rolled into the street, flailing at himself. Molinari stooped to retrieve the saber from the pile of ashes at Francis's feet and sprinted at the fuming vampire. The burning figure flipped over and pounced, sinking claws into the flesh of Molinari's thigh.

Growling, he plunged the saber into the man's shoulder, deadening the arm before twisting his leg out of the clawed grip. "In the name of the Holy Spirit, I send you back to Hell!" He yanked the blade free, and whirled through a beheading stroke.

The vampire's head bounced into the road with a hollow coconut-like sound. Small yellow fires still burning all over him flared up, consuming his remains in a matter of seconds.

Father Molinari flipped the blade up, glancing at a smear of dark ichor across the moon-blue glow of steel. "I suppose either stake or beheading is a viable option."

Sabine ran out from under the coach and clamped on to his side, trembling. "Father…"

"Bastards," said Élodie.

A pathetic male wheeze brought his attention around to the left. The ponytailed man fell backwards, rigid as if made of stone. In her right hand, the innocent-looking young woman clutched a pulsating heart threaded with black veins. Her fingernails shrank from razor claws to a lady's fine manicure. She walked over to Francis and flung the organ to the ground with a wet *splat*. Her satin sleeve had blackened with blood up to the elbow.

"My dress is ruined!" Élodie huffed and pointed at the still-beating lump. "Francis, please be a dear and burn that wretched thing."

Father Molinari took a knee and rubbed his thigh, waiting for the claw marks to fade. It took longer than he expected to heal, and burned while it closed. He hissed at the pain.

Élodie walked to the back of the coach, opened a trunk, and changed her gown right there in the street, all the while muttering about the lack of manners in Lyon. Father Molinari averted his eyes from her lacy underthings. By the time she'd donned a simpler gown that left her arms bare, the oozing gouges in his leg had closed, though the area remained tender.

He rubbed the wound, wincing. "You move as fast as they, and seem far too strong for such a frail body."

The servant girl offered a resigned sigh. "Observant, Father. I doubt you will ever know such things, for you must give yourself to the dark."

He reached for her, but she shied away from the pity radiating from his eyes.

"Auguste was cruel beyond measure. He did not leave me a choice. I was like you, refusing to let him take my soul. He desired a capable servant and had no use for an innocent girl. When whipping and beating failed, he left me outside, bound by a chain around my neck to a tree." She stared at the ground, her voice a whisper. "He did not come for me when the sun nipped at the horizon. I had to make myself strong enough to break free..." Her dainty hands curled into fists. "I do not think of myself as *dark* like you and your Vatican associates do. Is the want to survive a sin?"

Father Molinari didn't have a quick answer, and looked down.

"When you destroyed Auguste, my thoughts were once again my own. I am again the person I was before he enslaved my mind. Well, one now forced to hide from the sun." She rested her fingertips upon her cheek, turning to strike a pose. "Does wonders for one's complexion." Élodie shook her head, as if finding her levity uncalled for. "If a person kills when not doing so would mean their demise, is that evil?"

Father Molinari opened his mouth to answer, but she continued before he could breathe one word, a sentiment clearly borne of days of thinking.

"One who does good only out of fear they will be punished in the afterlife is not so good, no? I will remain who I am, and it is up to Him to decide if I am too *dark*. I do not blame Him for what has happened to me. I blame Auguste."

Élodie climbed into the coach.

After a moment of stunned silence, Father Molinari lifted Sabine. The child's trembling stalled at his embrace, and she snuggled tight to his side. Molinari started up into the coach, but froze with one foot inside at the sight of two women on the rear-facing bench, one with frizzy, curly red locks, the other with straight black hair. Their chosen line of work showed obvious in their poor, immodest dress. Both wore billowy tops with baggy sleeves that bared their shoulders. Their skirts, garish red for the older woman, teal for the other, bore frilled trim underlined with black lace and were short enough to expose most of their legs. The younger girl's right breast hovered precariously close to peeking over the ruffles. Perhaps sixteen, she lacked shoes.

"I am paying them to accompany us," said Élodie. "They are not to be harmed."

Father Molinari glared at her with indignation. "What manner of man do you think I am?" He flung the saber to the floor inside hard enough to make it stick and wobble, and took a seat to the right of the older prostitute.

Sabine cuddled in his lap. She sniffled and whined, but did not cry. Francis closed the door, and the coach rocked with his weight as he took his position on the roof. The redhead leaned into him, flashing an alluring smile.

He shifted, glaring at her before nodding at Sabine. "Do you mind, woman? There is a child present... and I am an ordained priest."

Both prostitutes gasped.

"Madame," asked the younger girl. "What do you intend for us to do if this man is a priest?"

"Are we to entertain *you*, mademoiselle?" asked the older woman.

Father Molinari found the upholstery to his right fascinating.

Élodie smiled. "I am being charitable. All you need do is make pleasant conversation."

The women exchanged a glance, shrugged, and began chatting about some inane rumor regarding a local actor and a nobleman's wife.

"Oh, I find that hard to believe," said Élodie. "Everyone knows actors favor men."

"Oh, Madame..." The sixteen year old emitted a demure giggle. "They favor anyone with a heartbeat and a beautiful face."

"I suppose I'm going to be disappointed then." Élodie feigned a sigh.

"But, you are beautiful!" said the older woman.

Élodie appeared to blush, and fanned herself. "You are too kind."

Father Molinari plucked Papi from the bag, and held the doll up to Sabine. Her fear lessened, and she let go of him with one arm to accept her favorite toy.

The coach trundled down a relatively flat road for an hour or more, filled with random gossip of fashion, theater rumors, people rising and falling among the social hierarchy, and all manner of dirt overheard in the boudoir of a working girl.

None of it interested him in the least. He shut his mind to his surroundings and imagined Gregorian chant.

"We will feed from them at the end of tomorrow night, and drop them off in Fontainebleau, with enough money to return home to Lyon and live well for some weeks." Élodie examined her fingernails.

"What?" The younger girl blinked. "Feed?"

"Do not worry." Élodie smiled. "It will not hurt at all, and you will not remember."

The women became quiet.

"You can make them forget?" Father Molinari glanced from them to Élodie.

"Yes. You can too. Without malice, subtle tricks of the mind do not require you surrender."

"W-what are you to do with us?" asked the older woman.

Élodie twirled a lock of her long hair around a finger and crossed her legs. "In two days, you will wake in a hotel with a substantial sum of money and return home to your lives. There is no reason for you to alarm yourselves."

"Can we all play games with the mind?" asked Father Molinari.

"To a degree." Élodie kept fidgeting with her hair. "How dark it is depends on what you do with it. If we force a mortal to sin, the stain is ours."

"M-mortal?" asked the younger prostitute.

"Oh, we are vampires." Élodie spoke without emotion or inflection. "You will give us blood... but do not worry. We shan't take it all."

The women's giggles melted to an unenthused chuckle, then silence.

"You are not laughing," said the older woman. "You are joking, yes?"

"Flying, inhuman strength, moving too fast to see... all of that you must give your soul for." Élodie tapped her foot in the air. "I do not know why some become like the one you destroyed in Vienna and others remain like people. Perhaps it can be acclimated to?" She stared at the window; her eyes caught the moonlight and glowed bright blue. "Perhaps we are all sliding to Hell, some slower than others."

"Please, let us go," said the younger prostitute. "You can keep your coins."

The older woman leveled her gaze at Molinari. "What are you going to do with that child?"

"Protect her." He ran a hand over Sabine's hair.

Sabine looked up and smiled, fangs out. "*Allo.*"

Both women screamed, clinging to each other. Once their lungs emptied, they prayed in rapid French.

Sabine gasped. "I am sorry. I did not mean to frighten you."

Élodie stared at the prostitutes until they slumped in the seat, unconscious.

"Father, forgive me." Sabine buried her face in his chest. "I'm sorry."

He rubbed her back. "You must conceal yourself. There are very few people we will be able to trust."

Sabine nodded. "Yes, Father."

May 28ᵗʰ 1885 French Countryside

Raquel, the older prostitute, sat rigid at Father Molinari's side. She folded her hands in her lap, her trembles unnoticeable amid the jostles of the coach in motion.

"Are you absolutely sure you are willing to do this?" asked Father Molinari.

"You are the priest," she said. "Is this a sin?"

Élodie laughed, a keening high-pitched giggle she muffled with her hand.

"What is funny?" Sabine perched on the far left, between the younger prostitute, Emmeline, and the wall.

Emmeline laid her arm in Sabine's lap, watching the child with pitying curiosity. Her fear had faded far faster than that of her 'street mother.'

"What these women do to earn money, and they are worried of sin?" Élodie giggled again.

Raquel's face reddened to match her hair. "You are vampires." She shivered. "If such beings exist... then God must be real." She closed her eyes. "God, please... if you let me live through this, I will never sell myself again."

Father Molinari smiled. "The first time I laid eyes on a vampire, I felt the same way. As horrified as I was that such a being could exist... the sight of it warmed my heart."

Raquel gawked at him. "That sounds backwards."

"May I?" asked Sabine.

"Will it hurt?" Emmeline tensed.

"*Oui,* but only for a moment." Sabine brushed her hand over the girl's forearm.

"Most people do not believe in vampires," said Father Molinari. "Some believe God is but a made up story... like vampires. When I encountered one, a real thing that so many people dismiss as an old wives' tale, I knew that mankind has no answers."

Raquel blessed herself. "How is it you are a priest yet a vampire?"

"All right," said Emmeline. "I want to watch."

Élodie raised an eyebrow.

Raquel turned, staring at Emmeline's arm.

"God's plan," said Father Molinari. "It is God's plan."

Sabine lifted Emmeline's wrist to her mouth, her fangs extended, and bit down. Emmeline emitted a soft yelp as blood welled at the child's lips. Seconds later, she cooed and sat limp and relaxed, a dazed smile on her face.

"You will not take my life?" Raquel looked up at Father Molinari.

"I will not, but God *will* hold you to your promise when you survive this night." He smiled.

Raquel leaned her head back, exposing her neck. Suppressing the awkward, sensual proximity to a woman, Father Molinari leaned in. A faint creak resonated through his skull as his fangs elongated. When he pressed his lips to the side of her neck, she gasped and wrapped her arms around him.

Exquisite sweetness laced with cherry and vanilla flooded his mouth and coursed down his throat. Raquel's heartbeat echoed in his head, pulsing through his entire body. He drank of her essence. He tasted her worry, which evaporated as the intoxicating effect of the bite took hold. Conscious of the approaching waterfall, he stopped well short of any point of danger. The ecstasy of the bite applied to the neck rendered her as loopy as Cousin Bertrand. Her limp, sinewy body draped into Molinari's lap. His first hasty attempt to catch her before she fell to the floor planted his hand upon her breast, which set Élodie off on another fit of giggles. He battled with gravity, attempting several futile pushes in an effort to get her to sit upright, before begrudgingly tolerating holding her.

Emmeline stared at the little face sucking blood from her arm. "She is adorable... but so, so creepy."

Sabine withdrew her fangs from the girl's arm, and licked all traces of blood from her wrist, palm, and fingers. "Thank you for letting me drink."

"I feel woozy," said Emmeline. "Am I going to become a vampire too?"

"No," said Élodie. "There is magic within the bite, which makes you feel pleasure."

Father Molinari positioned Raquel to lean on Emmeline, and sat against the wall. Vows, and years of chastity while alive were one thing, but a pretty woman close enough to feel her body heat while he pressed his face to her neck was quite another. He closed his eyes and mentally recited several prayers of contrition.

He could have taken more blood from Raquel, though he preferred erring on the side of caution for her benefit. Over the past night's ride, Élodie had explained more of how a vampire's body reacts to feeding. The more sated they are, the more lifelike they look. When 'full,' the heart would beat, imparting color and even the warmth of life to the skin. Even in death, the heart continued to pump blood throughout their bodies.

Those vampires who had welcomed the darkness burned their energy with superhuman exertion far faster than one such as he, who needed only enough blood to sustain existence. After the ambush at the tavern, Élodie had fed from three men. At least her horror at Auguste had not destroyed her distaste for killing. For himself, Father Molinari knew he could last for weeks on a good feeding, so felt no need to imperil the woman. He would never consume so much energy at once.

That would mean he had given himself fully to the dark. And if there was one thing he knew deep in his bones, in that thing now beating laggardly in his chest against all reason, is that there would be no provocation in this world that could pull him away from God.

He would never give in to the dark.

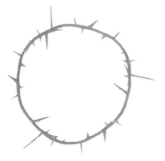

CHAPTER TWENTY

TO PASS THE TIME

May 29th 1885 Paris, France

Élodie's coach pulled to a halt in a quiet side street in the heart of Paris. Father Molinari pushed the door open, not waiting for Francis or the other man to open it for him. A chilly breeze carried the scent of the ocean through the air, tinged with the aroma of cooking fish. The food neither tempted nor nauseated him, but called forth a lingering feeling of loss as he stared down a row of streetlamps. He had been rather fond of fresh fish.

Sabine leapt from the side of the coach and landed on his back. He took a step forward from the impact and grabbed her arms before she slipped off and fell. She giggled, not protesting as he guided her to her feet.

"This is Paris?" She took a few steps, spinning around with a look of awe.

"I will pray for you," said Élodie. "Even though He no longer pays any attention to me." She handed him the bag of dolls, his book, and the large sack of coins.

"Thank you." He slung the dolls over his shoulder on a strap, tucked the coins into his vest, and clasped the book under his left arm. "Well, we are here. Now what?"

"The *Isère* will not depart for a few days. It is unlikely you will be able to leave the crate once our friends close it." Élodie waved Sabine over when she drew too close to the adjoining street. "You should spend a few hours tonight hunting. Feed until you feel you cannot drink another drop, and then fill a wine bottle. Add two drops of your blood and seal it."

Father Molinari took Sabine's hand when she ran up to him. "Do you know if consuming the blood of another vampire has any strange effects as opposed to that of a mortal?"

Élodie shrugged. "I do not know. Auguste hinted at things, though I am not so much older than you... a year or four." She winked. "As a vampire. Auguste was cruel; however, he did teach." She fidgeted at her dress. "Perhaps there is something... I could not bring myself to disobey him, no matter how repulsive his desires. When you destroyed him, a weight lifted from my heart. I am no more a mouse."

"Father, we are to sit in a box for days." Sabine craned her head back to grin at him. "What will we do?"

"Well..." Molinari ruffled her hair. "You have your dolls and I have much to reflect upon."

"For how long are we to be shut in?" She tapped the toe of her shoe on the street.

"Five or six days, depending on weather," said Élodie. "While you look for food, you should buy a storybook or two."

Sabine's face lit up. "Can we, Father? Please?"

"I expect there will not be any light." He glanced in the direction of several couples making their way down the street at the end of the alley. In particular, a man stalking the slowest pair. Molinari squinted, not liking the way the man carried himself.

"Light?" Élodie suppressed a giggle. "Darkness is our home, Father."

"Yes, yes. Sabine, wait here a moment." He started after the mugger. "I realize things are not as dark as they should be, but I cannot read in this light."

"You have but to want to." Élodie took Sabine's hand. "Your eyes will glow, but it shan't push you further to the darkness."

Father Molinari moved down the alley, keeping to the shadows as best he could while walking as fast as allowed him to remain quiet. Sabine's voice, chatting about the trip with Élodie, faded into the background as he focused on a man he somehow knew meant to harm the young couple. He turned left at the street, waited for a horse to trot by, and crossed. His quarry seemed worried about the husband, and fidgeted with a weighted sap. The thin, mousy-haired man with a protruding Adam's apple feared for his safety if his initial debilitating strike to the back of the head missed.

How do I know this? Father Molinari's heartbeat quickened in his hearing. *I am sensing this man's thoughts and feelings. God forgive me, but he means to attack them.*

The couple meandered past several twisty side streets, holding hands and sightseeing as if they were not native to Paris. Their shadow kept within ten paces, sometimes hiding, sometimes acting casual, but remaining in plain sight as he waited for a more secluded place. Molinari hurried up alongside the mugger, bumping arms on purpose.

"*Excusez-moi,*" muttered the man, acting at fault despite having been stationary.

Molinari locked eyes with him. "With me."

His desire to have the man follow washed away free will as well as any semblance of a facial expression. The robber followed him to an alley, removed from view of the street.

"W-what? Where? Who are—"

Father Molinari whirled, fangs bared, and seized him in a tight embrace. Blood tinged with the flavor of tobacco and cheap spirits filled his senses. The taste of avarice swept down his throat. Minutes passed as he held the man upright, gulping down mouthful after mouthful. The sense of energy changed in time with a hastening of his pulse. In his imagination, he flew above a crimson torrent; a waterfall raced toward him. Father Molinari slowed, taking small sips and edging as close as he had ever come to the threshold. A roar of energy flooded his ears and an urge beckoned him. *Take a little more* whispered something primal deep within him. One step over the line would bring such bliss.

Father Molinari imagined the halls of the Vatican passing. Red tapestries gliding in the wind, Cardinal Benedetto's wood-paneled office, and the beneficent smile of the aging prelate.

The darkness would not tempt him.

He lowered the unconscious figure against the wall and propped him up like a vagrant who'd passed out. After Raquel's kindness, this meal had brought him to a degree of satiety he had not yet known since death. He studied his hands, rich and tan. For an instant, he found it easy to wonder if this had all been some strange dream. A product of a sleep-deprived brain passed out in a coach on the way to a little town in the French countryside. His sharp ears caught Sabine's distant laugh. Worry pressed upon his stomach. He walked out of the alley, ignoring a handful of passersby.

Élodie's suggestion of drinking even more made him feel a touch ill.

"God in Heaven, please forgive me this trespass against all you have created. I ask you guide my wayward soul away from a life of sin and toward your radiant light."

He made the sign of the cross and hurried back to the coach.

Bells jingled as the door to a little corner shop opened. A tall woman behind the counter looked up from what she read as Father Molinari entered, guiding Sabine by the hand. The clerk had him by at least an inch in height; thick, raven locks hung to her waist, decorated by a sprig of wildflowers tucked behind her right ear. Lily white, he wondered for an instant if she were a vampire as well, but a living heart thrummed within her chest. Her strong jaw and solid figure hinted at Nordic ancestry, though nothing about her face—or bosom—could anyone dare call masculine.

"*Allo!*" yelled Sabine, waving at the woman. "I would like a book of stories."

"Oh, aren't you just adorable!" The woman set her novel down, forgetting to mark her place, and hurried around the counter. She crouched to eye level with the girl after smiling at Father Molinari. "What manner of stories would you like?"

Sabine looked around at shelves packed with books of all shapes and size, some straight, some tilted, and others set flat on top where no room remained. "One that shan't put me to sleep."

The woman covered her mouth to stifle a laugh.

"And in French." Sabine tapped her foot. "Or Italian."

Father Molinari sighed through a smile, speaking French. "Or English."

"This way, child." The woman stood and led her among the rows.

Sabine touched books here and there while navigating shelf after shelf. She paused to study an illustrated faerie on a thick blue spine. The clerk, Antoinette, suggested titles every so often, all of which received a nod from the child. *The Prince and the Pauper, Bimbi: Stories for Children, Milly and Olly,* and a fat collection of French children's poems and short stories.

Father Molinari eyed the Mark Twain book. "This one will be helpful for you to learn English." He smiled at Antoinette, who stood nearby with an armful. "These will be fine. Do you have any primers or French/English dictionaries?"

"Yes." Antoinette set the books on the counter and ran off into the back.

Sabine looked up at him. "May I?"

God forgive us. "Be polite."

She curtsied. "Yes, Father."

When Antoinette returned, Sabine emitted a gasp of wonder. "Your bracelet is so pretty! May I see it?"

The woman grinned and held out her arm. Sabine traced her fingers over the wood and brass ornament for a few seconds, her gaze focused more on the vein along the underside of the arm.

"It is very pretty."

"Thank you, little one."

Sabine opened her mouth while Antoinette glanced to her side, tallying their purchases. When the child bit down, Antoinette let out a faint squeak, and fainted.

Father Molinari caught her before she could fall. He shook his head at the expression on the child's face. She seemed halfway between ecstasy and starving dog, eyes half closed and emitting muffled coos of delight. The sight of it twisted his stomach in a knot and forced him to look away.

"Sabine...?"

"Hmm?" She did not cease feeding.

"Indulge me a small request."

Her gaze flicked up to him. "Mmm?"

"In the future, I think I shall run the blood into a cup for you."

"Mrm?" She tilted her head, scrunching her eyebrows together.

"Because it will make me feel better."

Sabine shrugged. "Mmm."

Élodie's voice drifted through his thoughts, reminding him to indulge beyond his need. Hunger was quite distant, but he nonetheless sank his fangs into the tender skin along the side of Antoinette's neck. Her blood settled on his tongue with the flavor of blueberries and vanilla. He tasted her love for knowledge and her fondness for the adorable child who'd come seeking books. Father Molinari recoiled at the sense of taking advantage of her.

Sabine suckled at the wrist while he forced himself to drink. Within a minute, they released her at the same time. He braced his hand on his stomach, overcome with a moment of queasiness not unlike having overdone it at a banquet. Sabine licked at Antoinette's arm, careful to chase down every droplet of blood.

"I am still hungry, Father, but she is weak." Sabine stretched her jaw open wide, and retracted her fangs. Her lips pursed as she sucked blood from between her teeth.

He guided Antoinette to a bench seat behind the counter and fanned her until she awoke.

"What happened?" The woman's eyes fluttered.

"I fear the air in here is stagnant, miss. You grew faint and nearly fell." He took a step back to a polite distance. His opinion of what happened took root in her mind.

"Oh. I feel so tired." She put a hand to her forehead.

Father Molinari set some coins on the counter. "This should cover the books and a little more for your generous help."

"Thank you, sir." Antoinette started to stand, but thought better of it. "Perhaps I shall sit a while. It was a pleasure meeting you and your beautiful daughter."

Sabine grinned at him.

Father Molinari pondered, and bowed. "May God watch over you."

He collected the books, and ducked the arrangement of bells at the door on the way out.

With their purchases tucked under his left arm, Father Molinari held Sabine's hand as they walked in no great hurry back to where Élodie waited. Knowing they'd spend the next week and change stuffed in a box made the open night sky something he wished to enjoy as long as possible. Sabine twisted left and right, taking in the sights of Paris.

"It is so beautiful here." She ooh'ed and ah'ed at streetlamps, fancy buildings, and a few dresses on passing women.

"It is that." Father Molinari took a deep breath, savoring the crisp air.

He'd been in Paris twice before. In one case, a small boy woke up speaking Russian with no explanation. He still spoke Russian when Molinari left. The child had no reaction to exorcism, and no amount of praying worked. He'd concluded the cause non-supernatural, and left him to the care of doctors. The second visit had been for a long, mundane, and refreshingly boring meeting with a small group of bishops who asked for guidance on what situations were worthy of the Order's attention.

That had been a pleasant vacation.

"Father!" Sabine lurched to the right, tugging at his arm. "Look..."

He snapped out of his fond remembrance, and let her pull him to the window of a jeweler's shop, where a small silver crucifix necklace hung on a wooden model of a neck. Sabine leaned her hands on the glass, and stared through her reflection at it. The bright silver caught the moonlight, almost glowing.

"I used to have one like this, but Papa took it from me." She frowned and bowed her head. A thin line of red crept down her right cheek. "*Maman* gave it to me when I was five."

The mass of gold coins in his pocket swelled against his side. Had she fancied a bauble or trinket, he might have pulled her along without a second's hesitation. He did not want to waste Élodie's generosity on frivolity, but the child was drawn to an image of the Crucified Lord. He ran a finger over where his vest concealed his amulet. Having such an item close to her could only help stave off Satan.

This must be a sign.

"Let us ask after the price." He grasped the doorknob.

Sabine's sorrowful face brightened in an instant. "Are you sure?"

"I am." He glanced up. "God has a plan."

She dabbed at her face to hide the tear, and followed him inside.

Father Molinari settled against the wall of an enormous wooden shipping crate. A bit of the iron framework of the great statue offered a hollow in which they huddled, with a little room to move around. Sabine had been terrified at the sudden idea they'd be shut in separate crates. The mortals Élodie had somehow convinced to help pried open a box big enough for them to share.

For a few days, their clandestine vehicle remained on land until they awoke one evening to find their surroundings moving and swaying. Loading of the *Isère* had occurred during daylight. Sabine crawled up on top of him soon after he started to move, trembling.

"I am afraid, Father," she whispered.

"Shh." He rocked her. "Put your trust in God, and everything will happen as it should."

"Are we still in France?" Her eyes lit up red, and she looked around. Shadows crept on the boards as her head moved. "We are at sea, yes?"

"I believe so. Do you not hear the water lapping at the sides of the ship?"

"I have never been on a boat before, not even a little one." She clung to him. "What will we do if something bad happens?"

He smiled. Though they did not need to breathe, the thought of being trapped in a huge crate inside a sunken boat was equally as unappealing. Perhaps in that case, susceptibility to drowning would be a kindness. He daydreamed of walking along the ocean floor, feeding from fish. The absurdity of it made him laugh, but he clamped a hand over his mouth.

"You are teasing me." She scowled.

"No... no." He patted her shoulder. "Fetch one of your books. Have faith. And do not make too much noise. We must remain unnoticed."

"Okay." Sabine crawled to the other end of their small 'room,' where their belongings lay bundled.

Three quarters of the way through their sixth pass at *Prince and the Pauper*, their surroundings shifted with a hard lurch that catapulted Sabine off him. She caught herself on the ironwork before flying face first into the copper skin of whatever statue's body part they inhabited.

"Father, wha—"

The world rocked the other way, accompanied by a resounding crash of water on steel. Sabine's willowy form rose sideways like a pennant. She screamed as her fingertips slipped. Father Molinari reached up, but the motion of the sea rolled him into the opposite wall.

Sabine lost her grip and fell on top of him, screaming. He shifted to put an arm around her, and they slid across the crate the other way. His head cracked against a metal strut, which left him seeing stars. Seconds later, they slid back.

"Stop screaming," he whispered, though he could not hear himself over the thundering war between ocean and boat.

She scrabbled at his shirt, trying to gain purchase before the opposite swing tore her loose. Sabine started to slip away, but stopped when her fingers hooked his belt. He braced a foot against the statue's iron skeleton, grabbed her by the wrists, and pulled her up into his arms. A splitting *crack* of thunder pounded the ship as though cannons had fired ten feet above them.

"I don't want to die," she yelled, trembling. "We are going to sink!"

Father Molinari cradled the back of her head in one hand and pulled her chin to his shoulder so he could speak into her ear. "Have faith. Pray. Let us ask God to guide us through this storm."

"I'm frightened." She bit down on his shoulder.

"Ouch!" He tugged at her. "What are you doing?"

She didn't let go, though she did not drink. *She wants to hold on.* He shifted himself around and wedged his body between two struts, a position that let him use only his legs to keep from flying around the crate. Books, dolls, and their spare clothes slid back and forth in the wrath of an angry ocean. Every time thunder crashed overhead, she twitched.

He clamped his arms around her, too tight for a breathing child to tolerate. Eventually, she released her teeth from his shoulder.

"Our Father, who art in Heaven..."

Molinari hesitated before repeating the line, waiting for her quivering voice to join in.

For hours, they prayed and prayed, until at last, the seas calmed.

Sabine held up her silver crucifix in both hands, smiling. "He is listening."

He patted her on the back. "He is indeed."

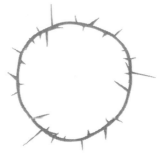

CHAPTER TWENTY-ONE

STRAYS

May 3rd 1918 Richmond, Virginia

By the flickering light of an oil lamp, Father Molinari pored over a collection of handwritten books arranged atop a mammoth oak desk. Three were written in German, one in Hungarian, two in Romanian, and only one in Italian. Works collected by the prior resident of the house, who existed now as a few traces of ash adhered to the walls of the fireplace chimney.

They had not spent long in New York. Within weeks of their arrival, he'd stumbled into Father Giuseppe, another of the Order, who recognized him. At first, the two shared laughter and fond reminiscence... Giuseppe had come to the city to disprove a claim of a weeping statue, and lingered due to a report of an exsanguinated body. It did not take long for him to question Molinari declining food, and as soon as he asked his old friend for help, the man acted as though he'd never known him.

On the off chance of a change of heart, he had not blanked himself from the priest's mind, though he did leave him unconscious. Following up on what appeared to be the work of a remorseless undead, he spent days tracking the killer while staying two steps ahead of Father Giuseppe. The fiend turned out to be a half-feral colored man who'd been made vampiric as an amusement. His change had left him crazed with fear and the unrestrained sense of darkness. The man, Jeremiah, had told him of a landowner in Virginia who had done this to him… a man with a foreign accent and fancy clothes. He had done this for no reason other than to see if the curse would affect a Negro.

Father Molinari tried to help Jeremiah overcome the dark, but he could not feed without killing—he said his mind could not resist the allure of such power, and begged Molinari to pray for him. With a heavy heart, and Jeremiah's eager welcome, Molinari had put him down, as he had the fiends before.

He stared at the books, tracing finger lines through the dust on the leather cover. He'd come south in search of the one responsible for killing Jeremiah, dreading the kind of monster who could devour another man's soul for simple entertainment. Rumors and whispers led them city by city to Richmond over the course of several years.

Élodie had been right about one thing: vampires *did* seem quite rare in the new world. So far, aside from Jeremiah, he had met two. A chatty fellow by the name of Alastair Cooke had stumbled upon them quite by chance while they searched the streets of Baltimore for food. His insistence on the use of cups for Sabine had become routine, and she no longer minded. It reassured him that she did not make the same sort of faces while sipping from a glass as she did when her lips made contact with a person.

For all observation, she may as well have been a child with a glass of grape juice.

The third vampire they had found in The States had owned their new house, likely after murdering its original occupants. He wanted to think the creature's name had been Gustav, though opportunity for conversation had been short. Rumor brought him here, and the sight of eleven Negro women, sprawled about the parlor nude and dying, made up his mind.

Gustav had been the sort of creature that enjoyed suffering. By the grace of God, Sabine had obeyed Molinari's order and remained in the woods, well removed from the scene. The horrors of the manor house were a thing better left out of her memories.

Six of Gustav's victims perished. Molinari had buried them in a small, attached cemetery among the ancestors of whatever family built this place. Each night he and Sabine prayed to God to keep them from the brink of such madness. He made sure she remembered to thank Him for everything they had, and everything he fought so hard for her not to lose.

Gustav's library contained a few books not written by mortal hands, though Molinari's grasp of Romanian was limited to hearing it and recognizing it as Romanian—understanding what it meant, not so much. Hungarian may as well have been Greek written backwards and upside down. The Italian journal inferred in vague terms that a cabal of vampires existed somewhere in the region around Naples capable of using some manner of 'blood magic.'

He raked his fingers through his hair out of frustration. The book referenced '*magia del sangue*' repeatedly, but never in any detail aside from veiled statements that they 'guarded their secrets closely,' and 'held sway over the curse.' His heart fluttered with excitement as one passage began to describe how they could inflict the curse of vampirism upon a person from a great distance, supposedly with a lock of hair, tears, and a few drops of the victim's blood—but it sounded like a charlatan's ramblings.

With a groan of exasperation, he pushed the Italian book aside and pulled the thickest of the German ones close. He reached for the lamp and twisted a small knob to extend the wick and brighten the flame. The scent of burning oil grew strong enough to leave the taste in his mouth.

Fourteen pages into what appeared to be little more than 'a day in the life' of an aristocratic vampire named Brigit—who was predisposed to complaining about everything she could—the creak of a door gave him an excuse to look up.

I have seen financial ledgers with a more compelling story. The woman hates everything.

Sabine entered from the front porch, wearing her new knee-length cotton sundress, barefoot, her hair wild, and a massive black tomcat in her arms. The animal hung straight in front of her, forelegs thrust forward and a 'help me' look on its face. Despite the ungainly posture, the cat seemed rather content, offering no sounds or squirms of protest. She pivoted and hooked a toe on the door, pushing it closed and muting the deafening chorus of crickets outside.

"Father! Come see the cat I have found." Sabine padded up to the side of the desk. Her English carried a thick French accent, but sounded passable. "He likes me."

The cat wriggled when he reached to pet it, though the animal's attempt to flee was feeble. It stared with wary emerald eyes as he scratched it atop the head.

"I have named him Gaston." Sabine shifted the cat in an effort to hold him sideways, though his weight and size threatened to pull her over.

"Curious."

"What is?" She set Gaston on the floor and knelt behind him, running both hands down his back.

The cat considered the door before falling over sideways with a heavy *thump*, and purring.

"Animals are not often tolerant of vampires." He held his fingers close to Gaston's nose. The cat regarded him with indifference.

Sabine stroked him with a continuous hand over hand petting motion. "Gaston knows we are nice." She stooped to touch her nose to the cat's head. "Don't you, Gaston? You know we are nice?"

The cat stretched with a deep "*mrrrowp.*" Secure enough to expose his belly, he purred.

"Well, I suppose you are correct." Father Molinari smiled.

Sabine kneaded her fingers through Gaston's fur. "Will you read me a story?"

Father Molinari watched her for a moment. Her delicate body, pronounced collarbones, and fragile, dainty wrists made her seem far more vulnerable and defenseless than she was. Years had passed, yet she remained the same innocent soul. *How much time has God given me to find an answer? If something threatens her, she may react like a cornered animal. The Darkness will not suffer a quiet defeat.*

At his silence, she turned her gaze upward, a trace of 'did I do something wrong' in her eyes.

"Of course. Fetch your book."

Sabine scooped Gaston up and carried him to a large burgundy sofa covered in pillows. Deposited there, the cat rolled onto his feet, watching her cross to a bookshelf. Indignation in his eyes at the cessation of her attention shone clear as day.

A set of white double doors on the left side of the room parted to reveal a tall, dark-skinned man in a black suit. Sabine, kneeling by the bookshelf, glanced at him only in passing while continuing to peruse spines and titles. The man, in his later forties with a neatly trimmed afro, approached the desk and put down a bundle of papers tied with cord.

"It is done, sir. You will need to sign these papers."

"You have my thanks, Thibodeaux." Father Molinari took the bundle and opened it. "I hope they did not give you much trouble."

"No more than usual, sir." The man shook his head. "What wit' the war on, dey got more problems than who y'all send runnin' errands."

Father Molinari examined paperwork that would transfer legal ownership of the manor house to his pseudonym, Albert DeSantis. "Madness."

"That it is." Thibodeaux nodded.

Sabine pulled a book from the shelf and hopped up on the couch. Gaston curled up at her side, his purring audible across the room.

Father Molinari signed his false name on four documents. "If this is any trouble for you, I will visit them in person."

"No trouble, sir." Thibodeaux bowed. "Dey know I do not 'ave de readin' nor de writin'."

"I pray that your family is well." He folded the papers and re-bound them with the cord.

"It would 'ave been better if God sent you a day earlier." Thibodeaux bowed his head. "But I am tankful 'e sent you at all. Times, dey be difficult, but we manage."

"I'm sorry I didn't sa—"

"My family be disquiet wi' beings such as yourselves under tha same roof, but for time being, it is tolerated. We are grateful for tha' ones you did save."

"Your family suffered under Gustav's whim. You are not obligated to stay and serve me, Thibodeaux."

Sabine peered over the back of the couch at them.

The tall man smiled. "You say my family deserve dis house, and I do not know if I should believe. Den again, never could I have dreamed de townsmen would 'ave believed you were a lost heir o' Mistah Burroughs."

Father Molinari smiled. "I can be persuasive."

Thibodeaux collected the papers, bowed, and walked out. His baritone laugh bounced off the walls well after the double doors closed.

"Come and read to me, Father." Sabine ducked out of sight.

He went over and took a seat in the middle of the couch. Sabine handed him the fat storybook from Paris and lay sideways, head in his lap, ankles crossed, and Gaston atop her chest.

"Father, is it not bad to kill a man and take his house?" She stroked under the cat's chin.

"The creature I destroyed was no man, Sabine. He took pleasure in cruelty. He murdered Thibodeaux's eldest daughter, his sister, and his sister-in-law. He drew blood from the innocent for no reason other than to cause pain and death."

She frowned. "Why would someone do that?"

"Because his soul was consumed by darkness." He plucked at her hair, pulling strands out of her face and attempting to set order to the unruly mess.

"Is God helping us?"

"Yes, Sabine."

She smiled. "I will thank him in the morning before we sleep."

"Good girl." He opened the book. "Which story would you like to hear?"

Sabine twisted her foot from side to side with a pensive face. *"La Souris et la Bougie, merci."*

"Are you not tired of it yet?"

She leaned her head back to look up at him. *"Non. Je ne me souviens pas."*

"Practice your English." He winked.

"I do not... member it."

Father Molinari smiled. *"Souvenir.* To remember."

"I do not *remember* it." She grinned. "I would like to hear that one."

"I read this to you every night while we sailed. Are you sure you forget?"

She blinked. "There is a mouse... and a candle. I do not remember the story." Her lip quivered as if an explosion of tears approached.

He patted her head. "It is okay, Sabine. No need to get upset. Mouse and Candle it shall be."

Sabine settled in and smiled.

Father Molinari flipped to a page bearing an illustration of a bipedal mouse in the clothes of a French farmer, gazing in awe at a massive (by comparison) candle. He smiled at the child resting against him, certain in only that he remained uncertain.

God guide us.

He took in a breath, and began to read aloud. "Philippe le petit was a mouse..."

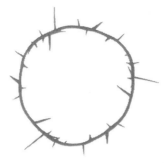

CHAPTER TWENTY-TWO

DOLLS

October 5th 1918 Richmond, Virginia

Summer had proven brutally hot, especially August. With the season now behind them, he'd taken to leaving many of the ground floor windows open to let air flow through the house. Gaston had made himself at home, often following Sabine wherever she went and even curling up with them at sunrise. The arrangement alarmed him to a degree... cats were not that loyal, or dog-like. Had she exerted some manner of influence over the beast?

Having given up on Gustav's tomes, Father Molinari debated penning a letter to Rome. The incident with Giuseppe worried him. Perhaps Cardinal Benedetto's successor—surely the man was dead or retired by now—might offer some assistance. There had always been rumors circulating of secrets the Vatican kept, even from the Order. Secrets only the Pope, now Benedict XV, and perhaps a select circle of Cardinals were aware of.

Then again, sometimes rumors were just that...

News of the events in Europe over the past several years distressed him greatly. He thought of Josephine Baudin, who had to be at least fifty by now, if she still lived amid the war. Had she born children with Marcel? If God had been generous, perhaps she was a grandmother.

Molinari's reclusiveness had kept much of the outside world from penetrating his sphere of awareness, but with the assassination of Archduke Ferdinand of Austria four years prior... it was as if all the civility of Europe existed as a rickety stack of straws, and someone had pulled the wrong one from the pile.

How little it can take for humanity to turn in and devour itself.

America had kept its distance until last year; the local gossips seemed convinced things were winding down. Allied forces supposedly rallied against the Germans, but who knew how many civilians had been trampled underfoot.

He moved to the window, watching Sabine play in the forest around their home. All through the darkness amid the trees, spots of fireflies danced. The steady chirrup of thousands of unseen insects made it difficult to hear her occasional laugh or conversation with Papi. A wave of guilt came over him. So much death going on halfway across the world, yet there he was, praising God for sparing the unlife of one little girl.

"God has a plan," he whispered, trying to believe it.

Sabine wandered in the front door, leaving it open. Gaston trailed at her heels. She looked thinner than usual, and the tint of life had almost completely left her skin. The girl resembled one of the effigies perched the windows of shops as of late, white as snow. He frowned at the back of his hand, also absent his usual tan. The quarantine had made feeding difficult. A simple trip into Richmond proper could stir up more trouble than it would be worth, assuming they found someone other than the police out and about.

She moved up to his side in silence. Her toes crept into the edge of his vision, pale against the dark blue rug. Too pale. He glanced down, smiling at the tiny silver crucifix visible through the loose neck of her dress. It settled against her skin without a hint of discomfort.

"Father, what is wrong?" She reached up and took his hand; her skin neither warm nor cool. "You seem sad."

He couldn't bear the concern in her eyes and glanced away. "The world has lost its mind."

"The world does not have a mind, it is a ball of stone and water and dirt." She tilted her head.

"The people upon it." He chuckled. "War. Why can man never be content with what he has? Why must he always crave more power? Our former homes are ravaged."

She shrugged. "Do you think Henri and Josephine are safe? I will ask God to watch over her babies." Sabine looked up. "How many babies do you think she will have?"

He put a hand on top of her head, brushing it down over the back. "Sabine, Josephine is..." *A grandmother perhaps. Henri is probably with God.* "... going to have beautiful children."

She grinned. "I would like to visit them some day."

Two quick knocks preceded Thibodeaux entering from the double doors. He paused a step in, staring at Sabine. A chill rattled through him and he looked somewhere else as he walked over.

"What news?" Father Molinari glanced at him.

"It is becoming dire, sir. Most of Richmond is sick. Dey tink it came from Camp Lee. Da' soldiers was wheezin' and coughin' afore anyone in town. A number have already died. Last I hear, dey say over two t'ousand bedridden. It's bad, sir. Dey even askin' fer colored nurses ta help. From the sound of it, da whole city be shut up tighter'n a virg"—he glanced at Sabine—"Um..."

"How tight is a verge?" Sabine looked back and forth between the men, Papi dangling from her left hand by one arm.

"Very," said Thibodeaux, unable to look at her. "Never you mind about that now, girl."

"Thank you, Thibodeaux." Father Molinari bowed his head.

His 'day man' walked out and pulled the twin doors shut behind him. Whenever he looked at Thibodeaux, looked with intent, he sensed the man's loyalty—and wariness. Though Molinari had taken a vow of poverty, he had amassed a substantial sum over the past thirty years. Initially by investing the remainder of the gold Élodie had provided, later by influencing a few bankers. Never enough to cause hardship, and never enough at once to be noticed.

Of course, he did not regard the money as his; he kept it in trust for Sabine. For now, he used it to keep her as safe as possible. In the future, perhaps she might need it. He let his head dip. Hope that God had sent him to *save* the child had faded over the past three decades. Perhaps he was a fool for taking his own wishes too literally. He had indeed saved her from the murderous priests. *Is my lot to dwell forever with an eternal child?*

"Meow," said Gaston. "Mrrr." He rubbed against Sabine's legs, ducked between them, and curled around the other way.

"Go and feed Gaston." He put a hand on her shoulder. "Then fetch your shoes. We must find something for ourselves."

"It is nice outside. Must I?" She set Papi on the sofa before collecting the cat and lugging him across the room toward the doors Thibodeaux emerged from. "I like to feel the grass."

"We are not walking to enjoy ourselves." He gazed out the window, at the dark woods.

"Yes, Father." Sabine seemed to inherit his somber mood, and slipped through. "Claudette, will you help me feed Gaston?"

Father Molinari stared at Sabine's shadow spread out from the doorway along the floor. Thibodeaux's remaining daughter hadn't said a word since they'd arrived. Not since her mother and older sister died.

"Claudette?" asked Sabine.

No... Sabine, no... back away. He rushed to the door. Sabine peered up at a slender girl with rich brown skin. So much lighter than Thibodeaux, he wondered sometimes if her mother had been her mother. The teen stared transfixed, trembling at Sabine as if one wrong move would mean her death.

"Claudette," whispered Father Molinari. "Do not be afraid."

"What's wrong?" Sabine looked back at him. "Why is she frightened of me?"

He took the child's hand and walked with her to the kitchen. Claudette shifted in place to keep them in sight, backing into the wall and clutching her hands to her chin as if in prayer. When they pushed through the kitchen door, two older women on either side of a long table looked up with far less fear, but fear all the same.

"Mister DeSantis," said the nearer woman, at least three times his weight and a head shorter. Of Thibodeaux's family, she seemed the least intimidated by them. "Child..."

"Georgia." Father Molinari bowed. "Please set out something for Gaston."

"Of course—" Georgia froze, staring past him.

Claudette appeared in the doorway, wide eyed and mute. Father Molinari offered as reassuring a smile as he could.

"Come here, girl." Georgia gestured to her niece.

Claudette slipped in, skirting the wall to keep as much distance as possible between herself and vampires, and hid behind her aunt.

"You do not look right." Georgia blessed herself.

Father Molinari studied the back of his hand. "I am aware. It has been challenging to sustain ourselves as of late due to the epidemic. I gave my word to Thibodeaux, and I have every intention of keeping it. Please trust that we do not take life."

Georgia kept her eye on him while dicing a bit of kidney and setting it on a plate for the cat.

Gaston approached the offering, and chomped it up with rapid bites.

"I am hungry," whispered Sabine.

The three women leaned back. Claudette, still staring at Molinari, crept forward. She pulled at her dress collar, exposing her flesh a little more. She leaned her head, moving her straight hair off her neck.

Father Molinari's heart drummed in a rapid three-beat, he could not pull his eyes from her, entranced by both the seventeen year old's beauty and the scent of the blood coursing through her. Sweet, like cinnamon and maple. He edged backward. Claudette approached him as if charmed into obedience. When she came within grasping distance, Molinari whirled, took Sabine's hand, and rushed through the back door that led from the kitchen straight to the outside.

"Father, my shoes..." Sabine hurried to keep up.

"It is nice out tonight." He headed for the woods. "And you like the feel of grass."

Sabine kept quiet, though the weight of her worried eyes bored into the side of his head.

Within an hour, he had slowed to a cautious walk along a wagon trail. Sabine hovered at his right side, occasionally peering into the forest with glowing eyes. He knew of several small homesteads in the area. As much as it pained him to consider, he would have to take blood from someone outside of Richmond and the influenza epidemic, and that meant either barging into a home or a long walk. A random inkling of thought whispered he could find his fill by flying, but he mentally recited the Lord's Prayer to distract himself.

"Father?" Sabine skipped ahead. "Why do we not ask Georgia and Marie and Claudette for blood?"

"It is part of our arrangement." He strode on. "I promised Thibodeaux we would never feed on his family."

"Is it because of the bad vampire who hurt them?" She ceased skipping, and trudged.

"Yes." He grumbled. "The military camp is better, but they locked it down. The city was more pleasant, but that is closed up as well now."

Sabine took his hand. "I understand."

"When we leave, the house will be theirs."

She looked up. "Are we going to Saint-Jean-de-Maurienne? I would like to see Henri."

"Not yet." A tiny square of light in the woods caught his eye. "There."

He crept through the forest in the direction of the glow. In a few minutes, the shape of a medium-sized house emerged in the gloom. A pile of wood on the right stacked as tall as the roof. Chickens and geese milled around free in the front yard.

Sabine smiled at the house, smiled up at Father Molinari, and knelt in the dirt. "Bless us, O Lord and these thy gifts which we are about to receive, through Christ our Lord. Amen."

God, please forgive us what we are about to do. Please protect these people from harm. If this is against your will, I beg of thee a sign.

Sabine stood, waiting in silence. The sight of her, skin all but glowing in the moonlight, told him he must bring her blood, and soon. He could not bear the sight of her as she progressed closer to appearing dead. He had to keep her well fed so she continued looking... alive.

He approached the front door. A moment's listening cued him in on at least two voices, likely a married couple.

A muscular man with unkempt black hair, a round belly, and a dense beard answered the knock. His loose shirt hung to one side, exposing a tuft of chest hair and his right shoulder. He seemed prepared for an antagonistic greeting at being disturbed so late at night, but at the sight of Sabine, he hesitated, confused.

"I am sorry to bother you at such an ungodly hour, but I must ask a favor of you." Father Molinari smiled. "Invite us in."

"C'mon in." He backed up as if in a trance, leaving the door open.

Father Molinari gestured at a plain wooden table in the front room. "Please, sit."

The man pivoted on his heel and walked without a word, took a seat in the nearest chair, and stared into space. Sabine wandered to the right, looking around at a peg rack full of coats, some boots on the floor, and a slow-burning fireplace.

"Father," said Sabine in French. "I thought we couldn't go inside unless they invite us in. I do not think *making* them invite us in is the same."

Molinari went left where the front room became a kitchen without a separating wall. He collected a cup from one of the cabinets. "That is an old wives' tale... probably something the vampires started to make people feel safe."

"Oh." Sabine traced a finger across the rough stone mantle.

"Come, you shall take your fill first." Father Molinari grasped the man's arm and extended his fangs.

"Daw?" asked a little voice. "Who's in our house?"

A pair of black-haired girls, one a bit older than Sabine, one about the same age and height—though more robust—appeared at a doorway leading deeper into the home. Father Molinari covered his mouth and faked a cough.

"Hi! I'm Sabine. Want to play?" She trotted over. "Can I see your dollies?"

"Daw?" asked the maybe ten-year old.

"That's fine," said Molinari, staring at the man.

"Go ahead, Sarah. Play with the nice girl." The man spoke in a distant monotone.

The sisters stared at him, the look on their faces giving away their worry something wasn't right. Sabine grabbed them each by the hand and pulled them into the hall. "Father needs to talk to your papa. They talk about grown-up things. It is not fun."

Father Molinari stood in silence, dread circling his heart at the silence coming from the back room. In minutes, multiple small voices giggling settled his nerves. He put a hand atop the man's head and tilted it back before lowering himself to feed. Salty blood, laced with the flavor of ham caused him to choke on the first mouthful. Not willing to waste any of the precious fluid, he pressed his face to the sweaty neck and drank.

Warmth spread into his chest and through his body. His muscles creaked and softened. The man's grogginess and desire for bed affected him in passing. Corpse stiffness faded to limber motion. *God save my soul.* He drank until the rushing waterfall drew near, and pulled away. The puncture wound in the man's neck faded to a mild bruise. At motion in his periphery, Molinari stood up straight and looked past the man at a well-endowed woman with generous hips in a plain blue dress.

She stared right at his bloody fangs and screamed, dropping a bundle of cloth.

Molinari widened his eyes and pushed his thoughts into her mind. "Calm yourself."

The woman closed her mouth and glanced from him to her husband. "Clem?"

"Your husband is fine, Madame. Please, sit."

Driven by compulsion, the woman advanced and lowered herself into a chair. Children's laughter no longer came from deep within the house. He cast a nervous look in that direction as he collected the woman's right arm in his hand and opened her wrist with one fang. He held it over the cup until the flow filled the vessel, then brought her arm to his mouth and suckled for a few seconds, enough for the nature of his bite to take effect and seal the wound.

"Sleep."

The woman sagged in the chair.

"Sleep," said Molinari, glancing at the man.

Clem fell forward over the table with a loud *clonk*.

Father Molinari picked up the cup of blood and hurried deeper into the house. Sabine's whispery voice filtered down the hall. She spoke as if making a doll talk to its playmate. He edged through the entrance of a tiny room with two child-sized beds squeezed on either side of a white-painted nightstand. Sabine sat cross-legged with her back to the door, holding a doll in each hand. Both girls lay slumped against their beds, unresponsive.

The ten year old lost her battle with friction, and fell flat on the floor.

Father Molinari's hands shook. Dread welled up within him. *God, please, no.* "Sabine... what have you done?"

She twisted around to smile at him. Her face remained pallid. "They became frightened when their mother screamed. I made them sleep." Sabine leaned left and placed a doll in the younger girl's lap, then did the same for her sister after pulling her upright. "You asked me not to bite anyone, and they are children like me. *Maman* would be disappointed with me if I hurt them."

He slouched with relief. Sabine stood and drew closer, mesmerized by his hand.

"I think God would be angry too." She leaned up on tiptoe, sniffing at the cup.

"Yes... yes He would." He extended his arm.

Sabine clamped her mouth over the rim, slurping up the blood before she even had the cup in her hands. She drained it as fast as she could swallow, then licked the rim, and grinned bloody teeth at him.

Color spread through her body, leaving her pale but much closer to alive.

"Please, Father, can I have some more?" She handed him the cup.

He put a hand at the back of her head and guided her to the door. "The woman should be able to spare another cupful." He lifted the girls into their beds and covered them with their blankets.

The older one stirred and opened her eyes.

He put a hand on her forehead. "Sleep, little one. You are secure in your bed."

She nodded off.

"Would it not be safer for me to bite the woman?" Sabine looked up as they walked back to the front room. "I do not want her to become sick. I can feel if there is danger."

He pinched the bridge of his nose. *Her motivation is pure. Is this my guilt which haunts me at the sight of such a thing? The horror of what she has become? My failure to break this wretched curse? God, have I failed you or are we biding time while your plan plays out?*

"I would rather you are careful than my unease risks the life of an innocent person." He looked away. "Safeguard her life."

Sabine released his hand. "Yes, Father."

He walked outside to a small water pump and rinsed the blood from the cup. Even ten steps from the front door, he had not found enough distance to avoid notice of soft sucking sounds inside the house. Father Molinari could not help but look back. To his surprise, what he had seen at the bookstore upon Sabine's face... an expression he could only describe as lust, was absent. He returned to the house long enough to replace the cup in the cabinet and went back outside. She kept a dutiful stare on the woman's face as she drank from her wrist. Soon, Sabine's skin took on the pleasant color of a fair girl from the French countryside with a mild tan.

She removed her fangs from the woman's arm and cleaned the wound before standing on tiptoe to whisper into her ear. "Thank you, Madame, for helping me stay alive. I am sorry if we have frightened you."

Sabine rushed to his side and took his hand. Father Molinari closed the door and paused to say a prayer over the house.

"Father?" asked Sabine, ten minutes into their walk home. "Why would God make vampires? To stay alive, they have to hurt people."

He gazed up at moonlit branches. Gentle wind sifted through the trees, a muted, but steady whisper above them. His ears picked out all manner of creatures going about their nocturnal routines; they were one in a long line of hunters.

"I am not sure God made vampires so much as His absence does... but he did make tigers and lions. Wolves, bears, and birds that eat fish. Many animals live upon the deaths of other animals. At least we have the choice not to kill."

The song of cicadas grew loud, emanating from everywhere. Far off among the trees, the hoot of an owl echoed. Twigs snapped, crushed by unseen things with enough weight to disturb the underbrush.

Sabine did not react to the frightening sounds, and seemed to mull his words over for a few minutes. "Why does God let bad things happen to good people? Why does he allow war?"

He stooped to pick her up, and perched her on his hip. She smiled. "When God made mankind, he gave us free will. Humans can choose to follow Him, or allow evil to flourish in their hearts. He does not force people to love Him. It is up to us. Our time on this Earth is a test of our faith."

Sabine put her hand over her little cross pendant, urgency in her eyes. "I hope we are good enough."

"Trust in Him, and follow your heart."

"I will." She rested her head on his shoulder. "And I won't listen to the bad feeling."

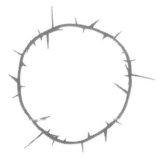

CHAPTER TWENTY-THREE

ABSOLUTION

November 13th 1918 Richmond, Virginia

The hiss of gas lamps gave way to the click and rattle of a streetcar making its way along the Fourteenth Street bridge behind him. Wind stirred up as the behemoth rumbled by, pressing into his back and fluttering the cloth of his pants. Father Molinari leaned on the banister and gazed into the blackness of the James River, focused on a point far enough removed that the shimmery reflection of yellow light did not exist. Creaking metal made the streetcar seem as if it labored to move, straining and protesting against its very existence. Clicks and taps of footsteps burdened the air with a cacophony unknown to mortal ears, a snippet or two of conversation, a demure laugh, an arrogant guffaw. He tried to tune it out. This close to the water, the stone beneath his sleeves seeped a chill into his arms.

Sabine kept close at his side, her chestnut brown hair drawn back in an arrangement of ribbons tied in a bow the color of black currant. The hissing lights turned her new dress yellow, like an artifact from a bygone age, despite being purchased only days before. She folded her hands in front of her and admired her dark stockings and shoes for a few seconds before leaning forward to peer through two spars holding up the railing.

"Be careful, Father, lest you fall in."

He closed his eyes, attention drifting among the people meandering along the sidewalk. Topics of conversation divided themselves into two primary categories that night: the end of The War, and influenza. Every so often, an amorous couple discussed other things. Each time a woman's breathless whisper suggested something he vowed never to do, a twinge of pity for Sabine pulled at him. She would never know romantic love, the joy of having a child of her own, or the satisfaction of being a grandparent.

God, how could you let this happen? Why do you leave us in this state?

"What about him?" whispered Sabine. "There is a big man walking toward us."

He glanced sideways at a potbellied man with a red nose and an unsteady gait. "No. His blood is tainted. Can you not smell it, surrounding him?"

The reek of whiskey followed the tottering figure. He bumped Father Molinari into the banister as he passed, muttering an apology to the next lamppost. Disregarding the oaf, he observed the people wandering by, waiting for a gap in the crowd. Soon, a healthy young man in an olive drab Army uniform approached, whistling. He, too, seemed fascinated by the shifting glare upon the water.

"A moment of your time, sir?" said Molinari. With a deft turn, he positioned himself to block the man from moving forward, and concealed Sabine behind him.

The soldier blinked, dazed, not managing to come up with anything before the little girl sank her teeth into his wrist. Father Molinari kept up a one-sided conversation about the German Armistice while Sabine took her meal. After, she licked at his wrist like a dog after a strange smell upon someone's clothing. Satisfied no trace of blood remained exposed, she grinned up at him as her fangs shrank away.

"Have a pleasant evening." Father Molinari bowed his head at the bewildered man.

"Yeah... you too." He rubbed the side of his head, flashed a weak smile at Sabine, and resumed walking. "Ugh... I thought I got over feeling sick. Maybe I should go back to the camp..."

Molinari caught the eye of a passing woman, a task he found far easier in a typical man's suit rather than the trappings of a priest. Whether or not he still deserved to wear such vestments, he did not know.

His mark, a plump brunette in her middle twenties, had a little wine in her but not so much that he shied away. Solitary ladies out for a walk were rare enough he did not want to waste the chance. The sooner they were home and out of sight, the better. He got her attention by complimenting the way her eyes caught the gaslight. Once she looked at him, the game was done. He slipped his arms around her while she remained dazed, and guided her to the side, back against the railing, face against the crook of her neck.

"No, please..." She pressed her hands to his chest in a feeble effort to fight him off, but once his fangs pierced, she moaned with pleasure.

Sabine giggled, a sign that people nearby stared and acted shocked at what they thought were a pair of lovers without the decorum to find a secluded place. Whenever anyone got too close, too insistently prudish, or too curious, the child made them walk away and forget.

A bounty of strawberries and chocolate swirled on his tongue, perhaps the last thing she ate. She clutched at his shoulders as he supported most of her weight. He tasted her longing, and loneliness. The ecstasy of the bite left her shaking, her eyes rolled up in her skull.

She squeaked and sighed as Father Molinari cleaned the blood from the side of her neck. The lingering effect of his feeding on top of the wine left her in no state to be upright. Warmth flooded his cheeks in time with a sense of tipsiness. He glanced at Sabine and motioned with his head before escorting the delirious woman off the bridge to the west.

She muttered something unintelligible and swayed to the side. He lurched with her, but kept her from collapsing.

"What has happened to her?" asked Sabine.

"She is intoxicated. Too much wine." He spoke loud enough for those giving him curious glances to overhear. The lamps across the bridge turned into smeared streaks of light as the liquor's effect permeated his brain.

After a short walk, he brought her to rest upon a bench beneath a grove of trees and sat with her until her faculties returned.

"Who are you?" She fanned herself. "Where... what happened?"

Father Molinari offered a pleasant smile. "We were out enjoying this beautiful evening when we saw you on the bridge. The wine seemed to have gotten the better of you, and I feared the imbalance might send you tumbling over the edge."

"Oh..." She looked at the distant span, her confusion obvious. "Thank you for... I must have blacked out."

"Shall I walk you home?" He smiled.

"That would be lovely of you, good sir." She reached out. "It is not far."

He took her hand and helped her up. Still, she teetered. "I find it unusual for such a comely woman to be walking unescorted."

"Oh, sir..." She blushed. "I do declare... you are quite the flatterer."

Father Molinari offered his elbow, and she threaded one arm through. "I speak only the truth as I see it. Emerson is a lucky man."

The woman walked for a few minutes without speaking, until the combination of blush and sadness lifted. "I do not remember who you are, nor how you know him... but he scarcely gives me the time of day."

"So I have heard." Father Molinari smiled. "Perhaps you would have more success if you spoke to him rather than fleeing whenever he approached." He caught her gaze. "You shouldn't doubt yourself, Rowena."

"Oh..." She stumbled over her feet for two steps. "Perhaps you are correct."

He smiled, following her lead through a left turn, and four houses down the next street where she stopped. Determination hardened her eyes. Sabine trailed them a few paces back, keeping to the shadows.

"I shall see him tomorrow." Rowena stood tall. "Thank you, kind sir, for escorting me home."

He bowed. She gathered her dress and hurried up the path to the front door.

"Did you make her love someone?" Sabine peered up at him.

"No." He clasped her hand and started in the direction of home. "I merely pushed aside her doubts."

A dark figure in an upstairs window backed away from the curtains as Father Molinari led Sabine up to the front door of their manor house. Despite a clean hunt, a shroud of self-loathing weighed heavy upon his shoulders. The girl raced into the house as soon as he pulled the door open, shoes *clomping* into the dark. He made his way to the study where his sacred book sat open, surrounded by the useless handwritten tomes Gustav had collected.

Gaston stood on a divan positioned by the window, arched his back, and raced off to wherever Sabine had gone, claws skittering.

The headline 'World War is ended' dominated the front of a newspaper Thibodeaux had left for him. He flopped into the chair, reading a bit about Germany's surrender, and skimming an article about the state board's plans for protecting schoolchildren from influenza. He traced his finger back and forth over the word 'schoolchildren,' losing himself to a waking dream of Sabine having a normal life. The soft *taps* of little shoes echoed from the cellar door.

What existence is this for a child? Hiding beneath a house, out of the sight of God.

He flung the paper to the side, scattering it into loose leaves, which fluttered to the ground. His fist stalled before he pounded the desk. Father Molinari pressed his knuckles to his mouth, shaking with anger, sadness, and desperation. A single blood tear crept from his right eye.

"What do you want of me?" he shouted, holding his arms out to the sides. "Is it your will I have become this? Is it your will to take a child's life?"

Energy shifted in the back of his brain. Anger gathered. Tempting. Luring.

"I have served you with all of my being!" he yelled, sweeping the books from the desk with his arm. "What must I do? Give me a sign."

Father Molinari collapsed to his knees and grabbed his hair with both hands as he let off a wail of anguish. He pictured himself hurling the entire desk through the window, and how good it would feel to let go... how good it would feel to stop denying himself the power his new existence could offer.

Faint pattering approached in a rapid cadence, and petered out to silence as a white blur neared.

"Are you so capricious you would watch her suffer for eternity for the actions of another?"

"Father..." Sabine rubbed her hand across his shoulders. "Father, are you all right?"

He clamped his arms to the sides of his head, staring down at her bare feet. Her toes gripped the carpet as she shivered. How easy would it be to revel in this undeath? Become the Lord of Richmond. Every politician under his thumb. Every woman at his whim. Every citizen his meal.

"My God, my God, why have you forsaken me to darkness?"

"Father?" Sabine slid her arm around behind his neck. "You are saying bad things."

He lowered his hands to his lap. The itch in his mind called out for anger and rage. Sabine sniffled and fell on him, sobbing. Darkness slithered around his heart, searching for something to blame for this child's sorrow. Something at which to lash out. He held his fingers in the shape of claws, but calmed. Father Molinari pictured the terrified little girl he'd first seen in a cruel cell, soft green eyes begging for mercy. He leaned forward, pressing his face into her hair.

I must save this child.

"I'm sorry for making you a vampire. You were trying to help, and they hurt you. I didn't want you to die because of me." Blood smeared over her cheeks. "I'm sorry."

Father Molinari wrapped his arms around the fragile, trembling girl. "Do not cry, Sabine. Do not waste your blood."

Her fingernails dug into his back. She squeezed herself tight to him. "I am sorry for making God angry with you. Don't blame Him. It is my fault."

"Sabine..." He ran a hand up and down her back, over smooth cotton. "I have never been angry with you."

She raised a leg, trying to crawl into his lap. He leaned back, gathered her in his arms, and stood. Cradling her, he paced back and forth, tripping over a worried Gaston the third time he passed the desk.

"Did I kill you?" Sabine leaned back to look at him, her face a mask of sorrow and bloody tears.

Father Molinari pulled a handkerchief from his pocket and dabbed at her cheek. "No. Father Callini killed me." He sighed. "Perhaps I killed myself."

Sabine's frown tore at his soul. She sat still, tolerating the attention of the cloth on her face. Her sobbing faded to sniffles. Gaston meowed and stood on two legs, pawing at his knee. Molinari carried her to the sofa and sat, the cat bounding up beside them.

"You forgive me?" She grabbed two fistfuls of her dress.

He put a finger under her chin, lifting so he could wipe blood from the front of her neck. "In order to forgive you, I would have to be angry with you. I have never once blamed *you* for what happened." A sigh escaped his throat. "What you did, you did out of love. The love of a child. Your intentions were pure."

All these years, and she still acts like a child. He shifted his weight, cradling her sideways across his lap. Sabine gathered her hands at her chest and cuddled, seeming content. *Even her mind is that of a child. She is not growing up.* He watched her 'breathe' for a few silent minutes. Though fangs lurked beneath the countenance of an angel, and the ever-present threat of darkness waited within her heart, she acted as if alive, and looked it when well fed. How long could daily prayer and a child's naiveté protect her?

She sniffled again, and bowed her head. Voluminous hair slipped forward and shrouded her face. "Is God angry with me?"

"No, child. He is not. The crux of sin lies in the spark of intention." He leaned his head back, studying the decorative painted-tin ceiling squares of caramel brown. "Keep your thoughts to God and away from the darkness. Your *maman* is watching."

Sabine smiled. "*Oui*. She is."

He did not question why her little body mimicked the act of breathing. It reassured him to feel her motion, rhythmic and regular. In the silent pause, he became aware of the air moving in and out of his lungs as well. *Perhaps the mind remembers?* Vows taken in 1874 seemed fleeting, as if they'd only happened in a dream he barely remembered. Never had he imagined he would care for a child, though he had known of a number of orphans tended by friars in the countryside. His calling had been too dangerous... too dark. In a way he could not define, this girl provided a sense of balance to what had been his life.

"God has a plan..." He chuckled, wincing at the mockery in his voice. "Henri certainly thought so. I am starting to wonder. None of this makes sense."

Sabine looked up at him and squirmed. Father Molinari relaxed his grip and let her scamper away. She walked in a deliberate line to the tall bookshelf. Like a little capuchin monkey, she climbed up three shelves, grabbed the spine of a book twice the width of her hand, and tugged it free. It fell with a loud *slam,* and she lowered herself back to the floor.

Amused, he wiped fingers over his mouth to hide his smile as she let off a diminutive grunt from the weight of the tome and carried it to him. She dropped the book on the cushions, causing Gaston to bounce and emit a warble of protest at being moved.

"Father..." Sabine stood as rigid as a soldier, feet together, and pointed at the book. "I do not understand this."

It appeared to be a textbook on chemistry, likely intended as part of a university curriculum.

He swiped dust from the cover. "Of course not, Sabine... You are eight years old, not to mention a girl, and this is science. It is far too complex a thing for you."

Sabine folded her arms. "It is the same as you not understanding the plan of God."

Gaston rolled onto his back, stretched, and meowed.

Father Molinari raised both eyebrows, tapping his fingers on the book. "Perhaps."

She ran to fetch her storybook and clambered up alongside him, an earnest look in her eye. "He has been busy stopping the war, and now has many prayers to hear in Europe. He will make time for me soon."

Tightness gripped his throat. Without asking which story she wanted, he opened to The Mouse and the Candle, and began reading.

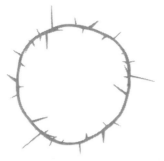

CHAPTER TWENTY-FOUR

SHADOW PLAY

December 5th 1918 Richmond, Virginia

People shivered in a fifty-degree gale blowing across the James River. Father Molinari led Sabine across the bridge into the city proper. She admired her new outfit, a port wine colored satin gown Thibodeaux had purchased earlier the same day. Her basic black shoes clicked on the sidewalk with each step.

At first, he had hesitated working on her skills with English and Math. Her memory seemed an unpredictable thing that snatched and grabbed at places and events. Of Paris and the ocean crossing, she spoke as though it happened weeks ago. Of Henri and Josephine, the same. Yet, she retained the language of the New World, though her French accent had a stubborn hold of her words. Whenever she got excited, her speech became indecipherable, stuck in a halfway point between both.

Tonight, he had decided to break from routine. The doldrums of having a manor house all to themselves, even one as modest as theirs, closed in on him. He needed air, to take her out of that place and cease dwelling on their untenable situation. Tonight, they headed to a theater.

"Is it true that the performers are not really there?" She looked up.

"They call it film, Sabine."

"Film?" She gazed down and took large steps. "What is the name of the story?"

Father Molinari pulled a folded newspaper from his pocket and held it up. "*The Blue Bird.*"

"It sounds pretty." Sabine giggled.

They stole a quick meal in a shadow beneath some trees. For expediency's sake, he allowed Sabine to bite the woman on the neck while he fed from her husband. Perhaps due to Sabine's age, the effect of her fangs left the woman insisting they hasten their plans for a baby. Taken by how adorable 'that sweet little girl' was, the woman burst into tears at the man's insistence six years of torture preceded that state.

Father Molinari smiled to himself as the man caved in and agreed to discuss the matter.

Sabine peered up at him. "Why are you smiling?"

"I think my dear, we should refrain from you biting women on the neck... or there shan't be a space of ground in this state without a crib upon it."

She squinted, adorably confused. "I do not understand."

"Nor do I." He debated how to explain the concept of lustful ecstasy to a perpetual eight year old, and how the effect likely changed when the vampire was so innocent. The man's desire for his wife had surged the instant Father Molinari's fangs broke his skin. Perhaps Sabine's essence filled the woman with a strong desire to mother someone. She'd sent Bertrand into a loving dream of his dead wife. "It is nothing. I was simply ruminating on how the effect of our bites differ."

"My teeth are much smaller." She sucked at them. "Papa called them my 'tiny needles' and thought them cute, but they made *Maman* cry."

"They were both right." He squeezed her hand, making her grin.

They left the bewildered couple staring at each other as the emotional surges of lust and motherhood faded. A short walk brought them into the heart of the city. As in Paris, Sabine gazed around at the buildings, the lights, shops, and holiday decorations.

"It is so large here. I wish *Maman* could see this."

"It is beautiful, but it is no Rome, or Paris."

She made a sputtering noise. "Of course it is not. It is America. I think it is grand. And not one cowboy has shot at us."

He chuckled.

A right turn brought them along a large street, shimmering in white and yellow light from the façade of the theater several blocks distant. Sabine followed, though she wandered around to look at everything.

The terrified scream of a woman split the calm. Sabine clamped herself to his side, staring in the direction of a shadowed alley. No one nearby reacted to the noise, too far away for normal hearing to detect. Father Molinari rushed ahead as his intent to see peeled away the darkness.

Snarling and gasping came from within the narrow gap between buildings. He rounded the corner as a hunched-over figure in pale blue satin dropped a body to the ground. Clad in the fine raiment of a gentleman, the man who had torn open the side of her neck stood and dabbed at his lips with a lavender silk kerchief. A matching ascot fluffed at his throat all but glowed in the moonlight. Frilled cuffs gave away his apparent disregard for changing fashion trends.

"Ah," said the man with a trace of French in his English. "How fortuitous."

Father Molinari rushed to the woman, who seemed to be breathing. He stooped and put a hand at her chest as her faltering heart beat its last.

"It is too late for this meal, I'm afraid." The man folded his hands behind him. "A bit famished after my trip. Shame. Of course"—he gestured—"if your guilt is too much of a burden, you *can* keep her around to replace your current companion."

"Fiend..." Molinari snapped upright. "There is no reason for what you have done. What crime did this woman commit?"

Sabine covered her mouth, and turned her head in a slow pan as if watching someone walk away through empty air.

"Consider it," said the man. "Being alone forever is no pleasure. Come, Mademoiselle Caillouet, we have quite a journey ahead of us."

"No." Sabine took a step back. "You are a bad person."

"I will not permit this." Father Molinari lunged to his feet. "You will answer to God for your crime."

"It is not your choice to make." The man flicked a dismissive wave at him and took a step toward the girl. "I represent the one who passed on the Gift to Auguste. He has claimed *la progéniture* over the girl, as she is of his line."

"No!" screamed Sabine. "You are bad. My father was a horrible, horrible man. I will not go anywhere with you." She pointed at the body. "You killed a woman. You are a murdering monster."

The man sighed, eyes closed. "Very well. I will take you with me then *after* I destroy the child's child."

In a blur, the man grabbed Father Molinari by two fistfuls of his vest and flung him across the alley into the bricks. A *crack* of bone resonated through his body on impact, however, the wall held firm. The vampire's nails grew out; ten pale yellow claws glinted as he spread his fingers wide. He did not wait, nor did he taunt. With Sabine yelling at them to stop in the background, he flung himself onto Molinari, moving with speed that rendered him difficult to see, and impossible to stop.

Sharp threads of pain pierced Molinari's side and shoulder. The man floated straight up, carrying him airborne as if suspended on nonexistent stage wires. Molinari bared his fangs and growled as the Frenchman bit into his neck and bladed fingers deepened their grasp in his flesh. He punched once, into a chest as hard as earth, before a fear of heights left him clinging. They glided up to the level of the fourth story, rolled over in midair, and crashed down, Molinari flat on his back. The French vampire leaned up, face smeared with thick, dark blood.

"Stop this at once!" shouted Sabine, stomping her foot.

"I am confused. You are so weak it is as if I am preying upon an ordinary man. Yet, you do not have a neophyte's essence in your blood." The man wiped at his chin and licked his fingertips. His blue eyes paled until the iris became indistinct from the white around it. "This is a rare treat. Tell me, *priest*, have you tasted a vampire's blood before? It truly is unlike anything else."

Father Molinari ripped his vest open to expose the gold crucifix. The French vampire hissed and leapt up. Smoke gathered at the man's chest, seeping through every seam and gap in his vest. He grabbed Molinari by his coat and hurled him. Alley stone, sky, wall, and alley stone whirled through his vision in a repeating cycle until he crashed into brickwork and slid to the ground. High-pitched squealing invaded his skull as bone knitted back in place. He shuddered from the pain and tried to force himself up. The beast within the back of his thoughts cried out in ecstasy. It reveled in his anger, his need to destroy this monstrosity.

Father Molinari turned his mind to God, and sagged limp. *Holy Father, guide me. Give me the strength to protect her.*

Sabine screamed; her voice trailed off as rapid, tiny footfalls echoed away in the narrow passage.

The darkness beckoned again. For an instant, his need to protect her tempted him. He fought to disregard the grinding agony of broken bones, and hauled himself upright by a hand on a barrel. Icy water sloshed over his fingers. A sharp child's scream cut out, followed by a smash of wood and a male voice swearing oaths in French. Rapid footsteps preceded another squeak, and something metal went bouncing over stones. Two points of crimson light sailed through the air farther down the alley, thirty feet from the ground. The dots moved away, following the *clap-clap-clap* of hard shoes on paving stones.

"Sabine!" he shouted. "Here!"

Another pair of red lights appeared close to the ground as a small shadow swiveled to look back at him. She skidded to a stop and nearly fell over in her haste to turn before sprinting in a straight line toward him.

Father Molinari placed his second hand on the barrel rim.

Sabine darted into a patch of light where a cross street let the moon leak into the alley. The French vampire swooped out of the air like an eagle on a mouse, snatching her off her feet. A brief, sharp scream pierced the night. She pedaled her legs in the air as she careened skyward.

Again, the darkness tempted him. He could fly up to grab her. All it would take is the *wanting*. Molinari released his grip on the barrel, shaking from the fear of his imminent descent beyond redemption. *Forgive me, Heavenly Father; I cannot let this horror continue.*

Sabine's terrified screams gave way to a determined shout of, "No!"

She writhed around and clapped her hand against the fiend's cheek. The man shouted with pain and agony in a deep, demonic voice no human could emit. Smoke billowed out through her little fingers before he released her and tumbled into an out-of-control head-over-boots plummet. Sabine hit the street six paces away from Molinari, landing in a short tumble before rolling out onto her back. Her abductor sailed headfirst into a wall.

Father Molinari retreated from his close call, and denied the want to fly. He grabbed the barrel with both hands behind his back, dipping his fingers in the collected rainwater.

"Blessed are you, almighty God, who gave us the living water of salvation. Grant that this water fortifies and keeps us. Renew the youth of our spirit by the power of the Holy Spirit. May we walk forever in the newness of life."

Icy water became as hot as fresh soup to his touch. Energy leeched from his chest; the bite mark across his throat burned and tingled with a powerful itch as it sealed.

Sabine dragged herself upright and hobbled over, favoring her right leg. Her fragile left wrist looked broken. A tug of darkness clawed at Father Molinari's heart, rage fueled by the sight of her hurt. He seized her by the unbroken arm and pushed her behind the barrel. She let out a whimper of pain and huddled low.

The other vampire picked himself up from a heap of rain-soaked burlap sacks. He brushed at his fancy clothes with little effect on the dirt and dampness before plucking splinters from his arms and face while sauntering over. A small char mark in the shape of a cross upon his cheek still smoldered.

"A crucifix... *Mon bon prêtre,* you are full of surprises." He halted six paces away, smiling as scuffs and scratches faded from his perfect forehead. "They will be most curious of this development. I am sure

Yves would adore meeting you, if only for the curiosity of it." His smile fell flat. "The girl, now. I will not ask again."

"That is wise of you," said Molinari. "Our answer will not change. As God is my witness, I will protect her." He swung his arm up to grab the crucifix, fully expecting not to get the chance to raise it.

The Frenchman half leapt, half flew at him, claws extended and hissing. Father Molinari made no effort to defend himself, instead grabbing the man under the arms and throwing his weight to the rear, pivoting over the barrel ridge at the small of his back.

Molinari screamed bubbles as they plunged inverted up to the waist in blessed water. Pain enveloped him as though he'd plunged into a vat of boiling tea. His eyes flared red, as did those of the Frenchman. The other vampire went from biting and clawing to struggling to get away. Sandy-brown hair unfurled from the knot he'd kept it in, wavering like seaweed around a corpse-like face that shrank in against the underlying skull. Molinari held on with all his strength, eye to eye with a disintegrating body. Small holes appeared in the man's chiseled features, widening to great wounds that oozed red blur into the water. Muscle peeled back to expose bone. The instant the head burst into a gory mess and the chest spilled open, a flare lit up the sky overhead, and the Frenchman's weight all but vanished.

He kicked to the side, using his whole body to overturn the barrel. After two tries, it tipped and he spilled out onto the street in a rush of painful, hot liquid. The blessed water sizzled and hissed as it put out the flames on the disembodied legs. In under ten seconds, the growing puddle consumed the last traces of the vampire's body. Gagging, Molinari wheezed and coughed, wide-eyed and gasping from lungs filled with liquid torture. He curled up, forehead to the street, and kissed the crucifix around his neck.

"Thank you God, for all you have given." He spat up more water. "Thank you God for all you have withheld. Thank you God for protecting me though I am unworthy."

Shaking from the pain soaked into his clothes and lingering in tiny flame trails within his throat, he bowed in supplication to God until agony lessened to discomfort. Whorls of black ash blew past; the wind claimed the last remnants of his enemy.

Sabine crept out from her hiding place. The little silver crucifix hung outside of her dress, still with small bits of burned skin adhered to it. A distinct *snap* came from her shin, and she ceased favoring the leg. Her pendant flashed in the moonlight as she stooped to offer him a hand up. He clasped it, but put no weight on her arm. Seeing her wrist no longer broken made him smile.

The holy water soaked into his clothes simmered down to a tolerable, but far from comfortable, warmth. He continued to offer thanks to God in silent prayer as he approached the dead woman.

After reciting the quick form of the Last Rites, he grasped Sabine's hand again and rushed deeper into the alley, taking the first right possible. At the end, he lifted her to the top of a wooden fence, vaulted it, and helped her down on the other side not three seconds before a few men jogged past, calling out about hearing a child's scream come from that direction.

In the moment of quiet, Sabine's calm cracked. She sniveled and whined in French. "I wanna go home. I don't wanna see a film now."

"Of course. That is an excellent idea."

He guided her through an alley cluttered with boxes and loose boards to a less populated thoroughfare a distance away. Leaving a dead woman in the middle of an alley nagged at his conscience, but there was little he could do for her now. Being seen would only cause problems for them. Sabine walked with her head down as they headed west out of the city, picking at stains and wet marks on her dress.

"Who is Yves?" asked Molinari. "Have you ever heard of him?"

Sabine nodded. "Yes. It is he *Maman* was unfaithful with." She looked up with a pleading expression. "It was not *Maman's* desire. He made her want to be with him."

He patted the back of her hand. "Yes, Sabine. I do not doubt that."

She calmed. Soon, street gave way to dirt, and buildings to trees. Away from the light and noise of Richmond proper, the girl peered up at him, mouth open, but let her gaze fall.

"What do you wish to ask?" He slowed their pace to a casual stroll.

"Why did he kill the woman?"

Father Molinari squeezed her hand. "He dwelled in darkness. I suspect he had only arrived in the States recently and was hungry. One such as him thinks nothing of taking all he needs from a single person. It was not your fault. A creature that dark would kill without regret if it suited him."

"Yes, Father, but he was here to take me." She sniffled.

"The actions of an evil man are no more caused by those who suffer at his cruelty than the wind on Earth can claim to push the stars through the heavens."

Sabine dragged her feet for a while. "I would like to say a prayer for that lady tonight."

Father Molinari smiled at the top of her head. "We shall."

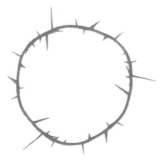

CHAPTER TWENTY-FIVE

THE GIFT

December 24ᵗʰ 1918 Richmond, Virginia

The small 'chapel' Father Molinari had set up in their house reminded him of his early days as a country priest in a tiny village north of Salerno. Its humbleness, far removed from the Vatican or the cathedral he'd lodged at in Vienna, made him feel a closeness to God he had not sensed since Sabine's attempt to save his life. He had not—for obvious reasons—tried to sanctify and bless the room as holy ground, but for his purposes, it would do.

She sat behind him, quiet and respectful as he went through the recitations for Christmas Eve mass. He smiled to himself, remembering her objection to dressing up 'just to go to another room of the house.'

Gaston curled up on the chair next to her, his loud, trilling purr a constant presence. Thibodeaux and his remaining family had gone into the city to celebrate. He did not harbor any resentment toward them. While he went through the rites of the service, he contemplated the arrangement. How difficult it must be for them to tolerate vampires in the same dwelling after what had been done to them?

He prayed for them, for the woman slain in the alley, and for Sabine.

CHIAROSCURO

Once he had finished his best attempt to remember a Christmas Mass, he led Sabine by the hand to the sitting room. After a yawning yowl of protest, Gaston dropped from his perch and trotted along after them. The house lay too far from Richmond for electricity, though he had arranged a number of shrouded candles. While even two would have lit the room enough for vampiric eyes, he'd lit twelve, filling the room with a shimmering golden aura. The dreamlike quality of the light had taken Sabine's attention from her grumbles about formal attire. Watching her gaze about with awe brought him a measure of peace and comfort. He placed a hand over his heart at a tingle of warmth within. *This is such a feeling as I should not have known. The joy of a father bringing a smile to his child's lips.* He thought back to Josephine taunting him for wanting a family. Had he sinned, or could this be God's way of granting his wish?

At the back corner near the bay window stood a small tree decorated with glass orbs and garland. Beneath it waited a box wrapped in shiny paper and topped with a bow.

Sabine gasped, looked up at him, at the present, and back up at him. She threw her arms around him and bounced.

"Oh, Father, thank you!" She squeezed herself to him. "I adore it!"

He patted her on the head. "You've not even opened it, how can you say that?"

"Because." She took a step back. "It is something you have given me."

Sabine smiled for a second more and rushed to kneel by the gift. She pulled it into her lap and spent the better part of the next ten minutes taking great care to open it without tearing the wrapping. Molinari settled into the sofa behind her, smiling as she turned the box around to work at the folded paper.

Eventually she exposed the box within, white and specked with silver spots. A squeal of joy rang out after she removed the lid. Sabine grinned back at him and gingerly extracted a porcelain doll with soft red hair, large blue eyes, button nose, and a small mouth. Its frilly dress had bands of sky blue and cream embroidered with roses.

"Father, she is beautiful!" Sabine clutched the doll in long hug before carrying it to the sofa and taking a seat beside him.

Gaston hopped up and jammed his head into Sabine's chin. She giggled and nuzzled with him. After a few minutes, the cat flopped at her side. She held the doll in one arm, and petted Gaston with her free hand. "Thank you, Father. It is a wonderful gift." She hugged him. "Do you think I can name her Véronique?"

He brushed a hand over Sabine's hair. "I don't see why not. She is your doll."

Sabine regarded the doll in silence for a moment, fussing with its dress as if mulling something. "*Maman* is named Véronique too. Is it wrong?"

"I think it means you love"—he caught himself before saying loved—"her very much."

She looked up with an adoring grin. He sat with her for a time as she introduced herself to Véronique, and promised to take good care of her. Once Sabine set to entertaining herself with her gift, and began formal introductions between Véronique, Papi, and the rest of the tribe, he moved to his desk. Thibodeaux had left a stack of a few rare books, which had arrived on order from up north. With any luck, one of them might contain some tiny snippet of helpful information. He hoped the doll to be the lesser gift he could provide her this Christmas.

Sabine's conversation with her dolls faded to background noise that comforted him as much as it alarmed him. Hearing her happy on Christmas Eve gave him hope, though the dread of what he had thus far so eminently failed at saving her from tamped it down to resigned determination.

A creak at the white double doors raised his attention from the pages of what had proven to be little more than fanciful vampire fiction. Not yet a quarter of the way through the supposed writings of one Ernesto Montaigne, 'vampire hunter,' he had already discovered four outright lies, and at least ten exaggerations.

Slender brown fingers curled around the white-painted wood. Thibodeaux's youngest daughter peeked in. Father Molinari raised an eyebrow at the look on Claudette's face. The young woman stood half in the door, still in the swan-grey dress she'd worn to church hours before. She stared at him with frightening intensity; her fear evident, but at the same time, she had the fire of a tigress burning in her eyes.

"Can I help you, Claudette?" He set a loose paper in the book and closed it.

She crept into the room and let the door glide closed behind her with a soft *click*. Her mother had to have been white, or at least, not the same woman who had given birth to the older daughter. The shape of her face, and graceful build hinted at an origin within the Islands.

She stopped at the far side of his desk, her gaze aimed down and to the side. Of all the family who stayed here, Claudette had been the most terrified of them. Even the sight of Sabine had always sent her scurrying in the other direction. Watching her approach set him on edge.

A flash of how he'd first seen her, sprawled naked on the floor and bleeding into a bowl from a cut on her neck, seared his thoughts. Claudette had the same defeated look on her face now as she had then.

"Claudette? Is there something wrong? Did something happen in the city?"

Eight small fingers curled over the back of the sofa. Sabine peered up and over at them.

"Mister DeSantis... I wish for you to help me."

He leaned back. "Tell me what troubles you, child."

Large brown eyes flicked up, fixing him with a stare. "Make me like you."

Sabine gasped.

"You know not what you ask..." He placed a hand over his heart. "Claudette... why would you want such a thing? To walk out of the sight of God for the rest of eternity?"

"I cannot live in this world, Mister DeSantis." Her resolve seemed to grow the longer she stared at him. "To my own family, I am of mixed blood... barely tolerated. To the people of Richmond, I am Negro... and to some, not even that. I am called 'mulatto.' I hate the way the white men look at me. I fear what they would do in the absence of polite company. If they merely desired to murder me, it would be kinder than what I fear lurks in their hearts."

"I can think of nothing so wrong to do to such a beautiful woman as what you ask me now." Father Molinari bowed his head. Sabine whimpered. "You are not at death's door. I cannot in good conscience take your life and cast you into godless existence."

Sabine stared with mournful eyes at him.

"Yet you do this thing to a little girl?" Claudette flung her arm to the side, in the general direction of the sofa.

"No, Claudette. It was she who... saved me from death."

The young woman looked stunned, and shifted to appraise the little face watching her.

Father Molinari leaned back in the chair and offered a brief explanation of how he'd found Sabine, leaving out the details of the fight. "I tried to protect her and wound up suffering a mortal wound. She saved my life."

Claudette slapped her hands on the desk and bent forward, staring at him. "Then save mine! It is only a matter of time, Mister DeSantis, before I am raped, or killed, or beaten in this place. I will not allow them to take away my dignity when there is such opportunity here, right in front of me. I do not want to bow to anyone, and you can give me this strength."

"That is precisely why I cannot do what you ask." He stood. "You are full of fear and you desire power. The darkness will seize your heart. You will become the sort of creature who visited such atrocities upon you and your family."

"No!" yelled Claudette. She moved around the corner of the desk and grabbed his vest. "You must do this for me, Mister DeSantis. From the day you destroyed that creature, I have felt as if something were missing from here." She slapped a hand over her heart. "I must have it back."

He took her hands, holding them together. "Claudette, you were traumatized. You still are. Please believe that neither Sabine nor I will ever be a threat to you. There is no need for you to live in fear. Nor must you surrender yourself to the fate which you seem to expect will strike when you least expect it."

Claudette lowered her gaze. "Yes, Mister DeSantis. I was, for a time, unable to sleep. I wondered if you would take my life while I dreamed. Or if I would wake to find your little one attached to my neck."

"We promised Thibodeaux we would not," whispered Sabine. "God would be angry with us if we broke our promise."

"You have no need of fear." Father Molinari smiled, patted her hand, and let go. "In time, this house and all that is in it shall belong to your family." A vision of the Frenchman disintegrating in a barrel of blessed water danced through his thoughts. "It may be time for us to move on soon."

"Please, sir!" Claudette fell to her knees and clutched herself to his legs, the side of her head pressed to his hip, weeping. "Please, give me the gift."

"Put such thoughts out of your head. You are a strong woman, Claudette. Focus your energy on finding a way for yourself in this world. Find a man if you so desire, have children, protect them as fiercely as you are able."

"And what if I do not desire children?" Claudette's voice sounded hollow, distant.

"Then do not bear any." He pulled her to her feet. "God has a plan for all of us."

"You will not make me one of you?" She glanced at the desk.

Father Molinari stepped back and half-turned away. "No, child. I cannot. You are too young. Too rash. Too beautiful. And your soul is disquiet. Satan will claim you."

"You will not give me the gift, no matter how I ask?" Claudette squeezed and released her fists.

He looked down. "No. I could not bear the cruelty of it. What you ask of me is more a sin than to murder you."

She swiped a letter opener from the desk and thrust it into her neck. Her eyes bulged as she staggered backward, forcing the point in deeper.

"Then..." Blood swam down over her collarbone, soaking into the dress. "...watch me die."

Sabine screamed.

"No!" Father Molinari shouted. He leapt upon her, seizing her arms. "Claudette, what have you done?"

He guided her to the side, laying her on the desk while knocking books to the floor. A shrouded candle fell and rolled; Sabine darted from the couch to chase it.

Father Molinari leaned his weight into her and extracted the sliver of metal from her throat. The scent of her blood, like cinnamon and maple, intoxicated him at a breath. She smiled up at him.

"Do it, Mister DeSa—"

"Forget." He stared into her eyes. Darkness swirled at the back of his mind, teasing him with thoughts of bringing her into the dark, of laying with her. He snarled at the presence. *Begone from my thoughts, Satan.* "You will forget vampires. You will forget Gustav. You will be strong. You will live in the grace of God until He calls you home."

Flashes of the manor house's fire-lit walls played backwards through her memory. All the women he'd found sprawled about or danced naked around Gustav who sat in a wingback chair, a goblet of blood in his upraised hand. Figures moved in ungainly spirals, drunken, mindless marionettes in no command of their own bodies. He sensed Claudette's terror and desire clash. Her family regarded her as lesser for her entire life. Watching them suffer had been a frightening spectacle at first, but somehow became thrilling. Revenge. She had wanted Gustav to choose her... but to him she had been just another worthless Negro. In that moment of realization, that not one of them were to survive the night, Claudette had crushed inward with guilt at betraying her family, even if it had only been a momentary flicker of her mind's desire. For a time, she had hated Molinari for saving her life, believing death her deserved punishment.

The scene rewound in fits and starts. The fire faded; music ceased; clothing returned. Daylight. Outside, a city street full of people. Claudette's memory before she'd ever laid eyes on the fiend.

He leaned down, placing his lips around the bubbling wound. He bit into her flesh, as deep as the thin blade had gone. The touch of his fangs set in motion the effect he had no word other than 'magic' to explain. Her wound closed. Such a beautiful taste lingered on his tongue, he shuddered from the torment of resisting.

The darkness within him cried out to consume her lifeblood. Her warmth permeated his body, awakening within him urges he struggled to deny. He panted through his elongated fangs, fingers digging into her perfect, smooth shoulders. Molinari closed his eyes and warred with the desire to devour her in every way imaginable.

I have sworn before God the family will not be touched.

He turned his head and let her blood fall from his lips.

"Father!" shouted Thibodeaux, amid the clattering slam of thin doors. "You gave me your word!"

"No!" yelled Sabine, holding the candle at arms' length. "Claudette is mad."

"What goes on here?" bellowed Thibodeaux. He stormed across the room.

Father Molinari put a hand on the desk, pushing himself away from the unconscious Claudette and the temptation of her warm body. She lay draped limp over the desk in the posture of a taken conquest.

"Father..." Rage simmered below the surface of Thibodeaux's voice.

"Your daughter came to me seeking the gift of eternal damnation." Father Molinari bowed his head. "I would not give it to her."

Thibodeaux narrowed his eyes.

"I have explained to you how I came to be as I am."

Pity showed itself through the dark man's anger as he regarded Sabine. "You did."

"When I refused her, she tried to take her own life." Father Molinari gestured at the bloody letter opener on the carpet. "She attempted to force me to give her that for which she asked, lest I do nothing and she perish."

"You were feeding." Thibodeaux scowled.

"It is not as it appears." Father Molinari wiped blood from his lip. "A peculiarity of our bite is that it causes the wound to mend, once we no longer desire it to remain open. I bit only to staunch her bleeding."

"Is that not exactly what you claim to have denied her?" Thibodeaux seemed ready to set upon him with physical blows.

"I did not take her blood." He looked her father in the eye. "My bite closed the wound she had inflicted upon herself. Had I not done so, she would have succeeded in killing herself."

Thibodeaux relaxed his aggressive stance, moved to his daughter's side, and took her hand. "Will she live?"

"Yes. It looks far worse than it is. She did not lose much blood. Claudette sleeps because I have taken from her the memory of what she did." He grasped Thibodeaux's shoulder. "She is in no danger. A simple bite will not harm her. The... process to create a vampire is more involved, and truth be told, I do not fully understand it myself."

Thibodeaux nodded, and collected Claudette in his arms. "What shall I do when she wakes?"

"If God is willing, she will not remember what happened to her, or that such things as vampires exist. Please see to it that she does not discover us." He glanced down at the rug while the man carried his daughter away. "Thibodeaux?"

"Yes?" He paused in the doorway.

"You have been far more of a friend and helper than I could have ever hoped for. Considering what you have been through at the hands of one such as me, I cannot find the words to express my gratitude."

Thibodeaux's unreadable expression lingered for a few seconds more before he focused his attention on Claudette.

"You do not deserve such conflict in your life. You are a good man, Thibodeaux. I shall soon cease to plague your conscience."

"You are not like him, sir." Thibodeaux faced away and took a step before pausing. "Not like him at all."

Sabine moved to Father Molinari's side. He put a hand on her back and she leaned on him.

"Go and see that Véronique is not frightened by what has happened. I must clean up this mess."

"*Oui.*" Sabine smiled and hurried to the couch.

He stared at the blood spilled on the desk, clenching his hands in fists. Temptation rose, but he forced it down and wiped the stain with a cloth.

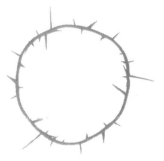

CHAPTER TWENTY-SIX

FOLLOWING BREADCRUMBS

February 8ᵗʰ 1919 Richmond, Virginia

Father Molinari stood in a patch of moonlight, divided into slanted squares by a tall, multi-pane arch window. A feeble attempt at Virginia snow drifted through the night sky, though it had succeeded only in imparting the look of a light frost to the ground. He did not often enter the house proper, but the spectacle of winter had summoned him from the inner sanctum.

The patter of Sabine running barefoot over the marble behind him brought a smile to his lips. She careened past, in pursuit of a galumphing Gaston, who seemed to be gaining weight. Her puffy white dress gave her the look of a glowing spirit. The laughing child turned right and vanished beyond a grand staircase to the upper floor. Carved gryphons supported the ends of the banister railings, clawed feet clutching five-inch orbs.

I never imagined vampires could exist… perhaps there are such things as gryphons as well?

A wooden bump preceded a rattle of pottery. Sabine yelped, but nothing smashed.

"Be careful. You probably should not run in the house." He didn't quite shout, but his voice echoed.

"Yes, Father."

He considered chiding her for her lack of shoes or leggings, but it wasn't as if she had to worry about catching cold. The thought weighed down his heart, and he returned his attention to the slow-drifting snow, tinted azure in the moonlight. His eyes tracked the fall upward, until he stared into the clouds.

God, I place my trust and faith in you always. I pray that you guide me as your will commands.

"*Bonjour*, Thibodeaux." Sabine's merry chirp preceded a meow.

"Hello Miss." The man's baritone echoed into the second floor.

Father Molinari peered through his reflection at the weather, gauging the man's approach by the increasing volume of muted footsteps. "Good evening, Thibodeaux."

"Father."

He turned from the window, a pleasant greeting stalled in his throat at the serious look on Thibodeaux's face. "What troubles you, friend?"

"I have heard t'ings, Father, while I was in town today. A priest not of the area 'as been askin' questions. He 'as a man with him to do the speakin,' for his English is not the best of t'ings."

"*Il sacerdote ha parlato in questa lingua?*" asked Father Molinari.

"I'm sorry, Father."

He smiled. "Did his speech sound like that?"

"A bit"—Thibodeaux nodded—"yes."

Father Molinari closed his eyes. *Thank you, Father, for your sign.*

"Dere be rumor 'bout a family wit' two small girls who told of a strange happenin' in the night. Dey found a woman's body weeks ago in an alley... 'void o' blood.'"

"That poor woman." He sighed. At Thibodeaux's widening eyes, he raised a hand. "A vampire came from Europe, hunting for us. We stumbled upon him... I was not fast enough to save her, God forgive me."

"What became of dis creature?"

"Destroyed." Father Molinari blessed himself.

"I do not t'ink you are prepared to do de same to a livin' priest."

"No, Thibodeaux, I am not." Father Molinari closed his eyes, pondering the letter he had sent to Rome, which never received an answer. If Cardinal Benedetto's successor had any intention of helping, he would have responded. *No, they have not sent an emissary… this man is here to purge.* "As I would have done in his place."

"Pardon?" Thibodeaux raised an eyebrow.

Sabine ran over, trailed by Gaston. She stopped a few paces short and bit her lower lip, worry clear in her face.

"I will sign the documents, Thibodeaux. This house, this land, belongs now to you. We will be gone by the twelfth. You have my thanks for everything you have done for us."

Thibodeaux bowed and walked away.

Father Molinari stood in silence, listening to the fading steps. At the *click* of a distant door, he held a hand to Sabine, who grabbed it in both of hers.

"Father, I am happy here." Her expression fell to a pout. "*Je ne veux pas partir. Pourquoi devons-nous partir? Je veux rester.*" She clung to him and wept.

He let her cry until she quieted some minutes later. Gaston rubbed himself against her leg, purring. The cat paused to give Molinari a half-wary glance and ground his head into her calf.

"I am sorry. I know you like it here, but we must leave. It will be all right. Sabine. Listen to Gaston. He knows."

She rambled through a litany of reasons to stay. Her language shifted with the intensity of her mood, French in the most emotional moments, English in fleeting seconds when she collected herself. After a few minutes, he carried her through the house to the sitting room and the sofa. She threw herself down on her front, feet in his lap, and sulked.

"Why can't we stay?" Sabine folded her arms and hid her face.

"Do you remember the bad priests?"

"Yes."

Gaston bounded up and walked on her back.

"*Miaou,*" said Sabine.

"There is another priest in Richmond who is looking for us. I am afraid he is a member of the Order."

"So?" She rolled onto her side and gathered Gaston in her arms.

"He is dangerous, and will think of us the way those priests thought of you."

Sabine pouted.

"I am sorry. The man who came for you from France knew where to find us. The Vatican also looks for us here. But, even if it did not, we cannot stay in the same place for long."

Sabine sat up. "Because I am not growing up?"

He closed his eyes and let off a defeated sigh. "Yes. It will be strange to people."

She ran her hands over and over Gaston's fur, eliciting a contented purr. After some minutes, she looked up at Father Molinari, opened her mouth, but seemed to decide against saying anything. A short while later, she pulled her feet up on the cushions and fell sideways against him.

"People don't like what they don't understand. Men like Henri and Thibodeaux are few and far between."

"I like Henri." Sabine smiled. "Ooh, can we visit him?"

His jaw tightened. "Europe is still too dangerous for us."

"Oh." She frowned. "Do you think Josephine has had her baby yet?"

"I imagine so." He put an arm around her. *And if she has, they are likely parents as well... if the war didn't take them.*

"Where will we go?" Sabine drew a deep purr from the cat by scratching under his chin.

Father Molinari thought, picturing maps and considering a mixture of security and curiosity. "Away from the coast, perhaps a little north."

"Okay. Are we to walk, or take a coach?"

He smiled. "I think we shall try this thing they call a train."

She perked up. "Many coaches in a line. How do they get the horses to follow the rails?"

He chuckled. "There are no horses. It is like the streetcars in the city."

"Can we bring Gaston?" She grasped his arm, seeming about to erupt in a frenzy of pleading.

"Of course." Father Molinari drew her into a hug. "He is part of our family."

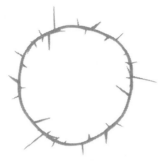

CHAPTER TWENTY-SEVEN

THE DEVIL'S PATIENCE

January 22nd 1929 Chicago, Illinois

The little yellow house on Kostner Avenue disappeared from a list of foreclosures after Father Molinari put in a 'good word' with a bank man during a surprise visit at home. The elderly Mrs. Sheehan had agreed to let them stay, though she found it odd they wanted to room in the basement. Sabine had the old woman wrapped around her finger without even trying, though this had the side effect of many cookies finding their way into the hands of neighbors from a mysterious benefactor.

Two years after settling in, the old one cottoned on to them. At least, she figured out something wasn't quite right. Of course, being in close proximity to the child, she'd noticed the girl hadn't changed in the slightest. She'd taken the news well, horror fading to pity and then to curiosity. By that point, she'd known them long enough not to panic. Since he had saved her house from 'the evil bank,' and because Sabine asked nicely for her to trust them, she had not made a fuss of it.

Father Molinari leaned back in the tired spring-loaded chair and rubbed his eyes. Creaks and groans emanated from the filthy bare wood overhead. A dense, musty smell permeated the air, tinged with traces of varnish, coal heat, and old paper.

The city library had a handful of occult books and others written by those who claimed to know of vampires and similar 'creatures of legend,' though none of the pages he'd looked at over the past months had offered the slightest hope. Theories abounded on how to 'cure' vampirism; alas, at best, they sent a 'freed' soul to Heaven, and at worst, what they described seemed like agonizing torture. He would *not* be injecting Sabine's veins full of powdered silver suspended in glycerin. Father Molinari did experiment a little on himself with silver, finding no more appreciable effect than stabbing himself with steel.

Perhaps because God had not abandoned him?

Sabine shrieked from the far side of the basement, out of sight behind a threadbare sofa a ghastly shade of orangey-brown. Her scream melted into heart-wrenching sobs. He leapt up and ran over, finding her kneeling by Gaston. The old black cat lay on his side, mouth open, wheezing in a desperate battle for air. He shuddered while making a noise half-meow and half-moan, tinged with pleading. The sound *felt* painful.

Sabine patted him. "Gaston!" She twisted around and looked up. "Father! Gaston is sick. Please do something!"

Father Molinari approached and took a knee behind her. He put his hand on the cat's side. Gaston emitted a low, keening wail, and huffed. It seemed as though he'd been holding on for some time, almost as if he'd waited for her to be with him for his last moments. The agony in the cry caused Sabine to shiver.

"What is wrong? Gaston!" She burst into tears, stroking his fur. "Gaston!"

Gaston twitched, rubbed his head against her hand once more, and let out his final breath. The motion of his little heart ceased under Father Molinari's hand, which he moved to her shoulder.

"Gaston?" She nudged him. His body flopped, limp. "Gaston! No!"

Sabine collapsed over him, wrapping her arms around the black furball, and sobbed. Father Molinari rubbed and patted her back. Minutes later, she sat up, cradling the dead cat and muttering, "*Leve-toi! S'il vous plaît! Leve-toi!*" over and over.

Father Molinari sat on the rug, pulled her into his lap, Gaston and all, and rocked her. Blood tears stained her cheeks and patted all along the front of her plain white dress.

"Why?" She looked up at him. "Why did God take Gaston away?"

"He had a long and happy life, Sabine. You took wonderful care of him, but it was his time."

She sniffled a few times, and burst into tears again.

"The best thing we can do for him now is to remember him. We'll give him a proper burial in the yard, and you can visit him there."

"Can cats become vampires?" She lay Gaston across her lap, and pet his head in gentle strokes. Before he could answer, she shook her head. "*Non.* I should not think such things."

He smiled. "It is in God's plan for every living creature to return to Him someday. Death is not the end of things, but the moment we reunite with Him."

Sabine sniffled and rocked Gaston like a baby. "Is that why I do not grow up? Because God does not want me?"

He watched her pet Gaston for a while, searching for how to answer that. His time ran out when she looked up at him with fresh blood leaking from her eyes.

"Did my father make me a vampire so he would not feel sad like I feel for Gaston?" She scratched under his chin the way he adored, the way that had always caused such deep purring, but Gaston remained silent. She skritched him more urgently, sniffling and falling into sobs again at his lack of purr. She calmed in a few minutes and resumed stroking him in long, slow passes. "That would hurt more than a cat, would it not? For him to hold me when I am dead?"

"No pain on this earth can compare to the loss of one's child." *It is a sin to lie.* "Sabine... your father was not the same man who loved your mother. The creature he was when he did that to you... I do not think love had anything to do with his decision."

She circled her thumb about, petting Gaston's ear. "What do you mean?"

"He was angry with your mother. The creature he had become wanted to keep you as you were: a possession, a child who could not think, feel, or have a life and mind of her own." He pulled her hair away from her face. "The bad part of free will is that sometimes people do things against God. I believe He has a place for you... but it is not your time yet."

"Is it bad that I do not feel sad for my father?" She stopped petting Gaston and bowed her head. "When you made him into ashes, I was happy."

"Your father died before that night, Sabine. That fiend was not him."

"Am I no longer me? Am I a creature who looks like Sabine Caillouet?"

"You are sad for Gaston? You love your mother still? You do not listen to the bad feelings."

"*Oui, oui, oui.*" She shivered. "Sometimes, it is not so easy."

He squeezed her shoulder. "What tempts you?"

"When I am angry." She clutched Gaston to her face and sniffled into his fur. "*Maman* does not talk to me anymore. It wants me to think she is upset with me."

"The Deceiver wants to trick you. Do you remember when we saw your mother?"

Sabine wiped her cheeks. "*Oui.* She smiled at you and went away."

"That's right. I believe she was happy. Keep her in your thoughts for perhaps she has not followed us here because she is with God now. I have read much since I have found you. Your mother's spirit could not rest because she worried for you. Perhaps she has put her faith in God through me and has gone to a better place. If nothing more, it proves her soul remains."

"*Je suppose.*" She rocked the cat back and forth. "We should bury Gaston so he can rest. Will you say a nice prayer for him?"

He stood. "I will." *I will pray for all three of us.*

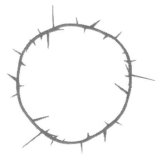

CHAPTER TWENTY-EIGHT

MYTHS

March 4ᵗʰ 1929 Chicago, Illinois

Clouds of fog rolled across the end of the alley. A light rain that had been falling all day continued into the night, leaving the air thick with humidity and a last-hurrah wintry chill. Father Molinari flipped up the collar of his coat to act cold and not appear out of place. Like a lesser version of Europe during the Great War, this city in America had seemingly lost its mind. People warred over alcohol of all things. Men shot dead in cold blood for no other reason than greed.

"Protestants," he muttered. "Do they not have anything better to focus their energy on?"

He crossed an alley, wary of traffic. 'Cars' still did not sit well with him. Too fast, too dangerous, and lately, they often had machineguns poking from their windows. At Sabine's admission the darkness had grown in its effort to claim her soul, he resumed asking her to feed with the intermediary of a cup or glass between her mouth and the donor. Together, they prayed when they woke and when they settled down to sleep.

She still twitched at shadows, expecting to see Gaston come trotting over. Each time the trick of light disappointed her, she cried as if watching him die all over again. As much as his inability to break her curse, watching her tiny body wrack with sobs over her beloved cat wrenched his heart. He could no more bear to watch her suffer than he could bring Gaston back from the grave, or pray the touch of life once more into her heart. In those moments, he could only hold her and comfort her until her weeping ceased to quiet sorrow.

He tried to focus on keeping the day to day as normal as he could, all things considered.

The shadows of the next alley wrapped around him. *How is it possible to feel so alone among such a massive gathering of humanity?* He gazed up at the high-rises. *People have walled themselves off from each other.* He thought of home, of Italy, of total strangers stumbling into an hours' long conversation while passing on a dirt road. Here, everyone hurried, caught in their own little universe of need and importance. No one walked with leisure in their step.

Of course, machineguns had that effect on people.

A man's panic-stricken shout rang out from a nearby street. By now, he knew the sound all too well: crime. Father Molinari followed the scuffing of shoes on pavement and ran from the alley to a street abutting a small park. A stocky man in a dingy coat and floppy cap stalked after a black-clad figure. Moonlight flashed from the blade of an outstretched knife.

The victim whirled about, raising an arm to shield his face. Molinari—and the mugger—gasped at the sight of a priest's collar about the neck of an aging figure who still had a touch of ginger in his greying hair.

"Shit. A damn priest. Figures. Sorry, Father." The armed man punched the clergyman in the head, knocking him down. "Nothin' a little confession won't fix, right?"

Molinari ran up behind him. "Hey."

The mugger spun and stabbed him in the chest without hesitation. "You should'a left well enough alone, pal." He smiled and yanked the blade clear. "Now you're dead."

"You missed that boat by quite a few years." Father Molinari touched his fingers to the wound, and rubbed the blood against his thumb. "I believe God is trying to send you a message, Frank. In a former life, I was a priest."

"H-how the hell do you know my name?" The trembling man lost his grip on the knife, which vanished amid the wet grass with a *thump.*

"This is Chicago. I took a lucky guess." Father Molinari forced his will over the man. "Forget."

Frank's eyes glazed over. He stared into space while fangs pierced his neck. Father Molinari nearly gagged on the flavor of cigars and cheap scotch tinted with desperation. No sense of inebriation came on. It had likely been several hours since the man drank, but a long drinking habit had made it part of his essence. Once more, Molinari flew along a crimson river, headlong into the rush of a roaring waterfall. For an instant, a twinge of indignation that this man would assault a priest made him consider sailing right past the foaming tempest and drinking a fatal amount. The city would be down one criminal, and it would lengthen the time necessary for him to feed again. Once he resolved to resist the lure, the shadow in the back of his mind squirmed in frustration. His sense of 'justice' had not been of God. Molinari pulled his fangs loose. Frank collapsed in a heap.

"Judge not, lest you be not judged. For with judgment I pronounce I will be judged, and with the measure I use, it will be measured to me."

A wheezy cough rose from the ground. "Why do you see the speck in your brother's eye, but do not see the log in your own?" The priest's smile evaporated when he looked up.

Father Molinari retracted his fangs and offered a hand.

"Did you kill him?" The older priest glanced at Frank.

"No, Father. He will recover, and I will not harm you."

"You are a priest?"

Father Molinari pulled the older man to his feet. "I was. Perhaps I still am. That is a question I leave to God."

"Regardless of His opinion, He sent you here at the right time tonight." The man bowed. "James Flaherty."

"Antonio Molinari."

The grasp of assistance became a momentary handshake.

"Well now, Antonio… Not that I wish to impose further upon your kindness, but would you indulge an old man?"

Gunshots sounded off in the distance.

"Let us move," said Molinari.

Father Flaherty fell in step at his side. "I may be old, but I can still walk, and that sounds like something I should be walking away from."

"Old? What are you, fifty?"

"Two." Father Flaherty chuckled. "Should I even ask?"

They hurried to the end of the park, found no traffic, and crossed the street.

"I was born in 1853, and yes… we exist. I spent half of my ordained years investigating claims of possession, supernatural creatures, psychics, visions, werewolves, and vampires."

"Werewolves?" Father Flaherty blinked.

Molinari chuckled. "I have yet to meet one of those… perhaps they are merely stories."

"So are vampires… I thought the Church disregarded such tales as myth."

A car passed unseen a street over, hissing over wet road, its engine emitting a belabored purr.

"The Vatican sent us out to look into such things. There was… perhaps still is a group dedicated to this, one cardinal removed from the Pope."

"I have had my suspicions. In my younger days, I saw some things, but no one believed me. Whoever or whatever was responsible, I had thought it left Chicago years ago… You weren't here in 1907, were you?"

"No."

"Well, I'd offer to buy you a drink so we can talk."

Molinari chuckled.

"So how much of it is true? Holy water? Crucifixes? Stakes?"

"For the most part, yes. For years, I thought all vampires were the same. There appears to be another layer: choice. I am, perhaps, weak by the standards of most. I do not fly, nor are my muscles capable of any more strength than they were in life."

Father Flaherty kept pace as they traversed another block. A police car sailed past, heading back the way they came, siren wailing like a wounded duck.

"How did it happen? Did one such creature find irony in turning you?"

Molinari smiled. "It was an act of love."

"What?" Flaherty gasped.

Again, Molinari shared his tale. The telling, particularly of Father Callini's death, felt like a confession this time... and welcome.

Father Flaherty nodded. They paused at cross street, waiting on traffic.

"For the life of me, I cannot understand how Cardinal Benedetto got a hold of Henri's letter. So many layers of bureaucracy."

"I see the church has not changed much..." Father Flaherty offered a somber laugh.

"I've spent the past several decades seeking a way to break the curse before it sets in."

Father Flaherty summoned the kind of sympathetic look one gives to the next of kin when news is bad. "And you are sure it hasn't?"

"I have to believe it hasn't. She wears a crucifix. Holy water does not burn her. She... has no sense of time. Events that happened in 1885 she describes as if they occurred days ago. She still thinks Josephine is expecting babies."

"I don't know if I should regard that as a kindness or cruel." Father Flaherty sighed. "How long do you expect the mind of a child to hold out against Satan's temptation?"

"As long as it takes or..." He bowed his head. "I have to believe God sent me to her for a reason. It would be nice to have some help finding it. I am sure the Church has the answers I seek, yet I cannot set foot on holy ground."

"Perhaps I can help?" Flaherty raised two fluffy eyebrows. "I assume since you're telling me all this, you either plan to kill me or you are as you say."

"I do not intend to harm you." He scratched at his chin and glanced up. "I must be getting back. I still must find blood for her."

"Do you think it possible for me to see her?"

Father Molinari looked at the priest. A desire for knowing opened a flood of thoughts in his mind. The man's intentions were genuine: pity, curiosity, a touch of pride at being validated. A few faces appeared, higher-ranking priests and one bishop, writing off his suspicions of something 'unexplained' as the fraying of a weak mind.

"I will bring you to her, but may I ask if you would allow her to take of your blood."

Father Flaherty hesitated.

"You will not be bitten." He oriented himself in the direction of the house, and walked to the right.

"My curiosity overwhelms my common sense." Father Flaherty waved his arm about in a casual attempt at blessing himself.

Father Molinari jogged up the steps of Mrs. Sheehan's porch. Flaherty glanced down the street at the spire of a small church visible beyond distant houses. Molinari opened the door and held it open for his guest.

"A curious place to live... so close to a church."

Molinari lowered his voice at a peak in the old woman snoring upstairs. "Perhaps I miss being able to visit His house."

He led the man down a narrow staircase. Sabine ran to the bottom of the stairs, grinning. Her daisy-yellow dress, even in the dim light of a single incandescent bulb, blinded him. A touch of grey in her skin, visible cheekbones, and hunger in her eyes made his unliving heart thud in his chest.

"Father!" she bounced, grinning. At the sight of Flaherty following him, she tilted her head. "Who is this?"

"A local priest. He is going to help us research the curse. Tonight, he has agreed to help you more directly."

She flashed a toothy smile at their guest and ran across the basement to a shelf, from which she retrieved a shoebox and a metal cup. Sabine rushed to a square table and set the items down, sat, and swung her feet back and forth.

Father Flaherty lowered himself to sit opposite her. He reached across and took her hand, rotating her arm palm up. "She looks..."

"I'm hungry," said Sabine.

Molinari sat with Sabine on his right, Flaherty on his left, and opened the box. He withdrew a length of rubber hose and a needle. Sabine stared through her hair at Father Flaherty, sporting a creepy smile.

"Is there an advantage to this?" Flaherty examined the medical kit.

"It keeps the process a step removed from her... makes me feel better. For all I know, it doesn't matter." Molinari frowned at the needle. "She thinks this takes too long."

"It does." Sabine glanced up and right.

"Do you clean it?" asked Father Flaherty. "Reusing a needle can spread disease and infection."

"Sabine, please fetch a candle."

She pushed herself back from the table. "He is afraid of needles, and would rather I bite him."

Father Molinari dropped the tubing into the box. "It seems I am outnumbered. Sabine, I only want you to have as normal a life as possible."

"I know." She hopped off the chair and hugged him before returning to the shelf to retrieve a candle. "But our life is not normal."

"Don't lose hope." He drew her into another embrace by a hand around her head. *She feels so brittle. She must feed.*

She squirmed through his grip to smile at him. "I have not lost hope. I do not want to make this man sick." Sabine twirled hair around her finger. "And I am hungry. The needle is slow."

"Very well." Father Flaherty unbuttoned his coat. "How does this work?"

"From the wrist," said Molinari. "We can feel energy within the blood of a person."

With some caution, Father Flaherty extended his arm. Sabine looked at Molinari for a nod of approval before standing at the man's side. She grasped his arm and raised his wrist to her lips. Father Flaherty offered a somber sigh when her fangs appeared and a slight wince as she bit down.

"The pain is fleeting. I feel lightheaded already." He stared as if mesmerized at the girl feeding from his arm. "An analgesic effect?"

"No medicine here, Father. I'm afraid this is as close to 'magic' as exists."

"Are you sure?"

"Vampires who have given themselves to darkness are burned by holy water. Can medicine explain how ordinary water altered only by the Will of God behaves like acid?"

"No... I suppose not."

Color spread through Sabine's face. Within a few minutes, she regained a living appearance, and withdrew her teeth. She licked blood from his arm while the wound closed.

"This is quite fascinating," said Flaherty. "What do you occupy yourself with, child?"

"I have books, and dolls. Father teaches me languages, math, and music." She said several random things in Italian, German, and Latin.

Flaherty smiled. "You live the life of a monk, my friend. Perhaps you should look into a television."

Molinari shook his head. "A toy for those with too much money and not enough sense. In a few years' time, no one will remember what the word even means."

"I will get you something to eat," said Sabine. "Since I had so much."

After a lingering grin, she darted off and scampered up the stairs.

"There is no doubt in my mind you are plagued with guilt." Father Flaherty put his hand on Molinari's. "Hers is such a tragic situation."

"I believe I can save her yet... somehow. We both have faith, but she has innocence. Soon after I became a vampire, Sabine told me her mother had prayed and prayed for God to help, to break the curse upon her daughter." Molinari stared down at his crucifix pendant. "I have to believe He had a hand in Henri's letter reaching the Order. He guided me to her. Dare I believe I am the answer to her mother's prayer? I do not know what I am expected to do."

"It is a paradox, my friend." Father Flaherty chuckled. "To become closer to God sometimes requires one to become closer to darkness. By meeting you tonight, my faith has been bolstered a hundredfold. I will do as much as I can to help."

Sabine crept down the stairs with a plate of toast and sliced apple, as well as a glass of orange juice. She glided to the table and set it before the priest. "Do you think Mrs. Sheehan will mind?"

"No, of course not." Molinari smiled.

"Can I go visit Gaston?"

Father Molinari glanced at a wood-faced wall clock hanging from the rafters under the stairs. "The sun will be up in about two hours."

"I will not be long." She darted off.

"Her cat," said Molinari. "His death is still fresh in her mind."

"I'm sorry." Father Flaherty ate and drank. "Thank you for the snack."

Molinari smiled. "I trust you will not speak of us. There are too many who would see her only as a monster."

Father Flaherty offered a handshake. "You have my word, and my help."

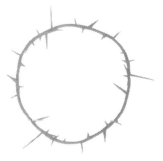

CHAPTER TWENTY-NINE

AT THEIR HEELS

July 16th 1929 Chicago, Illinois

Two full nights spent in prayer, reflection, and contrition produced no immediate visible effects. Much to Father Molinari's surprise, he did not feel as though he'd wasted time. Intermittent letters slipped under the door from Father Flaherty kept him up to date on the man's efforts. A credible bit of information concerned a case dating back to the Civil War, where legend stipulated some manner of creature—now thought to be a vampire—had run amok at the Battle of Antietam, gorging itself on the bodies of the fallen.

One man, a Lyle Thomas of Gatlinburg, Tennessee, claimed his brother Billy had been brought back as an undead by the same fiend. By virtue of comparing the dates of several records, a tale of tragic happenstance played out. To Molinari's opinion, a vampire had been involved, and had likely turned Billy Thomas. At the same time, Union Army soldiers in pursuit of the 'aberration' managed to confront and destroy it. Details were sparse, though one diary excerpt mentioned the body 'immolated itself until only ash remained, much to the chagrin of the field surgeon.'

At almost the same time, Lyle Thomas attempted to prove his brother's condition by shooting him through the heart, a wound a vampire would survive. Billy didn't. Lyle wound up hanged for murder. Had he fired minutes earlier, the world would have known proof of vampires.

Father Molinari rubbed his eyes. "So, slaying the source *might* work? Is there a time limit? Billy had not been undead for that long... days perhaps at most. Or..." He pounded his fist on the desk. "Auguste was not the source. *Sono stato un idiota!*"

Sabine padded down the stairs, hair soaked to her back and wearing a towel wrapped around her from armpit to knees. "Why are you calling yourself stupid, Father?"

"Why are you wet? Have you bathed yourself?" He smiled.

"No. Mrs. Sheehan gave me a bath. She has a lovely purple shampoo that smells like flowers." Sabine walked over to the trunk where they kept her clothes. "She asked me to send you upstairs. There are two men she would like you to meet."

"That's curious." Father Molinari stood, leaving Sabine to dress, and made his way up.

A pleasant floral aroma hung in the first floor hallway, riding a current of humid air from a bathroom painted in pea soup green. He found Mrs. Sheehan in the living room, entertaining a pair of besuited men who sat rigid on the cream-colored sofa. The man on the left seemed to be trying to count the small white dots on her dark navy blue dress. Between them on the floor stood a monstrosity. It resembled a block of silver metal with a can atop, connected to a broom handle from which a cloth sack dangled. One of the men idly spun around an electrical cord.

"Oh, this is my friend Carla's son, Mario." Mrs. Sheehan stood and wobbled over to him. "These nice men were showing me their fancy electric cleaner for the third time this month... Do you believe it's *only* forty dollars?"

"Only? That is a small fortune." He glanced from her mischievous eyes to the two hopeful salesmen.

"It's a Hoover," said the man on the right. "The rotating brush beats the dirt right out of the carpeting."

"Speaking of beating," muttered Mrs. Sheehan. "Are you hungry, my dear?" She winked at Molinari. "Help me in the kitchen a moment." She looked over her shoulder. "I'll be right back, gentlemen."

Father Molinari followed her through a short, arched hall. "Are you suggesting what I think you are suggesting? Isn't it a little late for salesmen?"

"Of course, dear. I'll get you a cup for the little one." She reached up on tiptoe to grab a tall highball glass from a cabinet. "And I would be grateful if you could make them forget I exist. They are pleasant enough, but all they want is my money, and they have been at my door every day this week. I honestly only let them in in hopes they would give up, but I can't seem to convince them I have no interest in buying anything."

"I'd hate to stain your lovely sofa." He chuckled.

"Well, you can test their electric thingamabobbin." She waved at the wall, smirking.

"I don't think it can extract blood from fabric." He pinged his thumbnail on the glass. If nothing else, feeding from these two would save some time. "All right."

He walked back to the living room. The salesmen perked up as he entered, misinterpreting his smile as a done deal.

"Gentlemen... a moment of your time."

Father Molinari descended into the basement, a glass of still-warm blood in his left hand.

"Good night, boys," said Mrs. Sheehan upstairs. The front door closed with a firm *thud*. "Don't come back."

Sabine had curled up on the dingy sofa, bare feet tucked under a throw pillow at her side. She'd changed into a fancy white dress with a tied ribbon at the small of her back. Father Molinari grinned at how it made her look like a larger version of the porcelain doll she held in her lap.

He walked the glass over to her. She set Véronique down with care to take it in both hands.

"Be careful not to get any on that dress."

Sabine nodded, already drinking. She draped herself over the armrest, so any dribbles would hit the floor.

A doorbell chime pealed overhead.

"I'll bite them myself," yelled Mrs. Sheehan. Thuds crossed overhead.

Father Molinari chuckled, and fell into the chair by the desk, reaching for the next stack of papers. Despite the distance, Flaherty's voice reached him. Distracted, he looked up. The door at the top of the stairs opened with a squeak.

"Father M?" asked Mrs. Sheehan. "There's another priest here to see you."

"It's all right." He stood, waiting to greet Father Flaherty with an outstretched hand.

The man descended the stairs in a heavy, rushed gait. He walked straight into an abbreviated handshake. Molinari gestured to an empty chair and started to sit, but Flaherty shook his head.

"I've snuck away to warn you. It's my fault, but not my intention." His face reddened, his rapid heartbeat echoing in Molinari's head. "They must have noticed my research... somehow. I overheard Bishop McEwen on the phone this morning. The Vatican is sending a 'special consultant' to the area. He's to arrive in a few days."

Sabine pulled the glass from her lips, and licked a blood moustache away. "We are leaving again, aren't we?" She pouted. "Can we bring Gaston with us, or would it be a sin to dig him up?"

Father Molinari looked at Flaherty, nodded, and walked up behind the sofa. Sabine bent her head back to peer straight up at him.

"Yes. I cannot allow the Order to find us." He heaved a heavy sigh, and found solace in the normality of it. "Gaston should remain at rest. He will watch over Mrs. Sheehan."

"I want to say goodbye to him."

"Of course."

Sabine slurped down the rest of the blood and licked at the glass until her tongue could reach no more. She all but leapt into her shoes and ran upstairs. Father Molinari gathered his books into a large duffel bag and pushed the library copies to one side.

"These are from the library; would you be so kind as to return them for me?"

Flaherty nodded. "I've brought you something that you may find helpful."

"What's that?"

"An automobile. I believe they call it a 'Model-A.'"

Father Molinari waved him off. "I cannot take such an expensive thing from you. Besides, I haven't the faintest idea how to operate it."

"Come, I will show you." Flaherty started for the stairs. "Do not worry about the cost. Someone left it near my church. It sat there for days, untouched. The man who owned it is likely with God now."

"Thou shalt not steal," said Molinari.

"I found... bullets under the seat. I am sure God brought it there for a reason, and right now, you don't have any room to question His will."

With that, Father Flaherty jogged upstairs. After a pleading look at the ceiling, Molinari followed. He paused at the door and stared at a sky-blue Model A coupe with whitewall tires and black fenders parked by the curb. Sabine's soft sniffles echoed from the backyard down the narrow gap between Mrs. Sheehan's house and the next. Father Molinari shook his head and walked outside.

The following night, Fathers Molinari and Flaherty wedged the trunk containing Sabine's belongings in the back end of the car. Flaherty closed the hatch cover and twisted the handle to secure it. Sabine, in a plain blue dress, frilly pink socks, and black shoes, waited on the steps next to Mrs. Sheehan. The child still wore a trace of pout at Molinari's insistence she leave Véronique in packaging lest the delicate doll break. She'd settled for clinging to a ragdoll. Since Papi had disintegrated from age, Véronique had become her most dear.

Mrs. Sheehan dabbed at her eyes with a tissue kept in service long beyond its acceptable lifespan. "Oh, heavens... what shall I do with the next batch of incorrigible salesman?"

"Goodbye, Mrs. Sheehan," said Sabine, getting a sad laugh from their old landlady. "Thank you for letting us stay with you."

Father Molinari walked to the porch. "I hope you will be all right without us here."

"Oh, I'll figure things out. I managed for sixteen years after Edgar passed away... I can manage two or three more till it's my turn."

"Don't talk like that." Father Flaherty winked. "I'll drop by every few days to keep you company."

"Bless you." Mrs. Sheehan stooped to kiss Sabine. "You take care of yourself, precious. I'll pray for you."

Sabine curtsied. "Thank you."

Father Molinari went to the car and opened the passenger side door. Sabine climbed in and sat, glancing around. He rounded the nose end and got behind the wheel. Father Flaherty leaned through the window and gave him a quick refresher to the two-hour driving lesson from the previous night. Molinari started the engine, eliciting a sharp intake of breath from Sabine as vibration rattled through the machine.

"Is it supposed to do that?" Her fingers dug in to the seat.

"Yes." Molinari studied the controls, lack of confidence clear in his voice.

Flaherty extricated himself from the car and made the sign of the cross at them. "May God bless you and keep you, and guide you on your journey."

"Keep yourself safe, James."

"Take care of that little girl." Flaherty bowed his head in a sober farewell, equal to equal.

Sabine waved at Mrs. Sheehan as they pulled away, twisting in the seat to keep waving out the back window until the house was too far away to see. She slumped back in place, and stared at her lap. "Will we always be leaving our friends?"

He gritted his teeth, not wholly comfortable without his driving instructor. He was not so worried about a crash per se, though the idea of being trapped amid a raging gasoline fire kept his grip tight on the wheel. "If we are careful, perhaps we can spend more time in the same place."

"Then you will not find what you are looking for." Sabine adjusted the doll's dress. "I think Henri would like Mrs. Sheehan, but she is perhaps a bit old for him."

"I believe they would get along." Father Molinari smiled.

He expected their constant settling and moving would have an ill effect on the child at some point. Perhaps she would forget Mrs. Sheehan in time, filing her away in the non-space in which everyone she met seemed to live forever and no sense of linear time existed. Had Gaston's death broken that illusion? The glare of oncoming headlights blinded his sensitive eyes; the other driver leaned on the horn.

"Headlights, jackass!" screamed a man as the other car passed.

Father Molinari hunted for the button.

"Look out!" screamed Sabine.

His head popped up. A pedestrian halfway across the street zoomed toward the hood. He swerved left, tires squealing, and corrected. The motion flung Sabine into him. Father Molinari prayed inside his head, refusing to blink for another two minutes.

"Sabine, please find the headlight switch."

She crawled over his lap and tugged on something. Blinding light spots painted the road ahead.

"Thank you."

He slowed a bit to avoid attracting notice, and turned northward. The engine sputtered and purred with a rhythmic, repetitious sound that, were he mortal, would surely have lulled him to sleep. The child occupied herself with the ragdoll, tugging at his heart by reassuring the little cloth person Mrs. Sheehan would be okay without them. Traffic at that hour was sparse. Any pedestrian who spotted them ducked for cover, suspicious of a lone car. Molinari kept his eyes open, praying that the vehicle's former owner did not have enemies who'd recognize it.

"Sabine?"

"*Oui?*"

"Would you like to get another cat?"

She combed the doll's yarn hair with her fingers for a few quiet minutes. "Will it die?"

"Eventually, yes."

Sabine set the doll in her lap and crossed her arms over it. After making a series of pensive faces, she looked over at him. "If we make a vampire cat, will it suck the blood from mice?"

He opened his mouth, but she broke into giggles. Father Molinari smiled.

Her expression became serious. "I will not make a cat into a vampire. I would want him to go to Heaven."

"I'm not angry with you because of what you did for me."

"I know." She managed a somber smile. "But you are no cat. And you were hurt because of me."

He reached over and held her hand. "I would not change anything."

"*Non?* Nothing?" She blinked.

"Well... if I could change anything, I'd stop Auguste from hurting you and your mother."

Sabine smiled. "I am glad you are with me, too."

"I will spend the rest of my days finding a way for you to enter Heaven." *If it is the last thing I do on this Earth.*

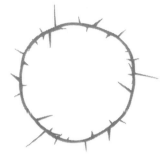

CHAPTER THIRTY

LA RIVIÈRE CHAUDIÈRE

May 2ⁿᵈ 1967 Saint-Georges, Quebec

Cool wind carried the fragrance of water and grass over a strip of park along the south bank of the Chaudière River. The moon hung full and bright in an otherwise inky sky, hiding on occasion behind drifting gossamer cobweb clouds. A shimmering gleam danced along the undulating blackness, mesmerizing Father Molinari away from the din of people.

Some stood apart in couples and kissed, others lingered in small groups discussing everything from poetry to fashion to music, and the Vietnam War. A pair of scruffy, bearded men in flannel shirts walked past him heading in the opposite direction. Judging by their American accents, he assumed they'd crossed north to avoid the draft. He agreed with them. Father Molinari thought World War II would satisfy Satan's need for blood. Stories of such horror had emerged from Europe, he'd wondered if the End Times approached in the 1940s. Alas, the Devil never ceased to find new ways to influence the world.

He had felt safe in Maine; however, after Pearl Harbor, he took Sabine into Canada despite there being no sign of Vatican hunters in the area. *A man should not walk upon the Earth for this many years. A 'war to end all wars' should occur only once in a lifetime.*

"Hey there, tall, dark, and delicious," said a woman in French-accented English. "You look lonely. You are Italian or American?"

He glanced away from the water at a blonde in a black bikini top, a tiny skirt, and shin-high brown suede boots with Native American style fringe. The smell of marijuana saturated her little purse.

No sooner had he made eye contact with her, he saw into her life. *Angelique, eighteen years old, lives with her mother, prostitutes for 'throwaway' money.*

"I was born in Italy, but I've spent more time here than there."

"Oh?" She approached. "You are the most handsome man I have ever seen. Say something to me in Italian."

He glanced around, gauging the scarcity of other people. *"Dovresti aver maggior rispetto per te stessa."*

She purred and threaded her arms around him, interlacing her fingers behind his neck. "That sounds sexy as hell. What did you say?"

"I said you are young and beautiful, and have an entire life ahead of you."

Angelique laughed. *"Vous parlez comme ma mère."*

He remained motionless, letting her kiss at his neck. "Your mother is a wise woman."

"Oh!" she gasped, one hand over her mouth. "You speak French? I'm embarrassed."

"I have had a lot of time to study. Once, I considered myself a scholar of language."

She stopped nuzzling him to look up at his eyes. "Would you like to find a nice little place we can be alone?"

"I think we already are."

"Oh, you are adventurous," she said in English. "I've never done it outside before. That might cost a bit more."

"I'm sure it will." He leaned in and kissed the side of her neck.

She squealed and snuggled against him. Urgency stirred within his chest. His fangs grew long. Angelique's fingers dug into his back as he found her jugular and his teeth entered her flesh. Her initial squeak of shock melted into contented 'oohs' and lustful moans. Hot blood surged into his mouth with the taste of peach and vanilla. Her heartbeat thundered in his head. Warmth gathered in his loins as she gyrated, rubbing herself against him.

The feeling welled up. It wanted to bask in her blood and carnality. Her essence swept through his veins. He encircled her in his arms, squeezing tight as he hardened against her leg. Angelique moaned and grabbed him through his pants, letting off a shuddering moan.

For fleeting instants, the riverside park flashed into scenes of an orange bedroom. The girl, a year or two younger, bounced up and down on top of a boy the same age. Her first time. The scene changed to the same boy laughing at her. She'd mistaken a one-off for true love. Crushed, she'd gone wild and promiscuous, certain every man in the world would treat her the same.

His hand cupped her breast before he returned from the inherited memory. Darkness beckoned him. He shuddered with desire, but pushed her away. Angelique swayed on her feet. The sight of blood on her bare skin, running down her front between her breasts, drew a snarl from deep inside him.

He looked away, and filled his mind with thoughts of his vows, his love for God, and his duty to Sabine. Father Molinari's heart rate slowed. He held her upright by a grip on her arms while composing himself.

"Whoa." Angelique reached up and put a hand on her face. "That was intense... Did we... are we done?" She looked down. "Oh, God, I'm bleeding. That's blood, right? How did I get dressed so fast?"

Father Molinari locked stares with her. "Angelique. Forget me. Forget Paul. You are not a prostitute." A sense as though a delicate bubble burst within her mind preceded a release of energy, which seemed to slide out through his eyes.

She gazed into space. "I'm not a prostitute."

"You should respect yourself."

"I should respect myself."

He ceased concentrating, took out a handkerchief, and wiped the blood from her. Father Molinari guided her to a nearby bench and walked away before the fog lifted from her mind. She would not remember him, and with any luck, would go home.

Electric lighting kept people out later, a change he still had not adjusted to. It made hunting easier: more people out and about in the dark. It also made it more difficult: more witnesses.

Worry nibbled at his heart. He had gone farther into Angelique's mind than he had with anyone before, making her forget something that had happened two years and some months prior. He swirled Élodie's comment around his brain like a snort of brandy in a glass. Did intent affect the darkness? Had he stumbled, or had his urge to help been noble enough? Was it her life to throw away, or had he done the right thing?

More pressing matters came to the forefront of his mind. Sabine needed to eat. Would he fetch her from the little abandoned house they'd made their own and escort her, or dare he bring a meal to her and again wash the memory from the mind of an innocent victim? Making a person forget a feeding had been *de rigueur* for as long as he'd been a vampire. Compared to the other two options—killing them or starting a mass panic—it seemed harmless.

They did not hurt anyone; the people had no need to remember.

He picked up his step, intent on fetching Sabine and letting her have some air. With this many people out, it wouldn't be difficult to find someone. Of course, these days, people questioned an eight year old out past midnight. Did he want to risk another near-fiasco like the one that forced them out of Montreal?

Father Molinari walked in silence. He'd ask her to wait in the car, out of sight.

After a twenty-minute journey, the cube-like outline of a freestanding white house emerged from the darkness of the wide-open field that surrounded it. A '62 Chrysler Valiant in hospital green lurked in the shadow beyond, headlights poking out from the wall as if the car itself was afraid of the dark. He didn't even remember the name he used to buy it. Perhaps the salesman hadn't asked too many questions when presented with $2,200 in cash.

The Chaudière River passed behind the house, near enough to see from the second story. Despite the rundown appearance of the place, Sabine had fallen in love with it. She had especially liked not having to destroy another vampire before moving in. The dandelions littering the field behind it reminded her of home, and her much-adored garden.

The squish of a shoe on mud behind him made him stop. His usual reaction to someone sneaking up on him, a fast whirl, startled a yelp from a small dark-haired boy in a yellow shirt and tan pants.

"*Je suis désolé!*" The boy jumped back with his hands raised. "I'm sorry."

"What are you doing here?"

He lowered his hands. "Forgive me, sir. Do you know the girl who lives in that house? I have seen her in the window, staring at the water. Why does she always stay inside? She looks sad."

Father Molinari relaxed and glanced at the house. *How long has it been since Sabine had contact with another child? Perhaps I am wrong to shut her away from the world.* He exhaled. *No. They will ask too many questions. Children can be cruel. I cannot risk her being tormented to darkness.*

"She is not well." Father Molinari took a step, but stopped. The boy was alone. He spun, surveying the area. No one would see them. For an instant, bringing the child to her as a meal struck him as less than reprehensible. Sabine would be horrified. He clenched his hands into fists. "Go home, boy. She is very sick and cannot be around people... especially other children."

God, please steel my mind against Satan. He grows stronger.

He stomped in the direction of the house.

"What's her name?" asked the boy.

Father Molinari whipped his head around. "Go home."

The boy's mind gave way like pushing his hand through a bowl of warmed butter.

"I... uh, gotta go home." He waved. "Bye."

Head down, the maybe ten-year-old trudged off. He looked back at their home twice as he crossed the grassy field on his way to clustered houses a quarter mile or so away where the line of 'civilization' started.

Sabine's soft voice filtered through the front wall as he strode up on the porch. He paused, listening to her singing along with The Monkees' *I'm a Believer*. Though the words were cheerful, her voice rendered them sad and lonely.

He brushed the front door open, knocking several flakes of peeling white paint to the ground. The music, and the child's singing, grew louder as he made his way inside to the living room. Must and mold, the scent of a house near the water left for years without solid windows, permeated everything. Transparent plastic sheets stapled to the windowsill crinkled in the wind, swelling and sucking out as if the building had some twisted version of lungs. A new knife slash through one fluttered with an upsurge in the wind.

"*Allo*, Father." Sabine knelt on the floor, still in her nightdress with Véronique perched on her lap. The gloom around her evaporated at the sight of him, and she grinned.

On either side of her lay two unconscious teenagers, a boy and a girl. Both had brown hair, torn jeans, and tie-dye shirts. The young man had a small knife attached to his belt in a leather case, and a silver transistor radio hung from the girl's wrist by a strap, from which The Monkees continued playing, despite the lack of Sabine's guest vocals. A cluster of innocuous-looking white pills scattered on the rug, evidently fallen from the boy's jean pocket.

Sabine pointed at him. "He tasted funny, so I did not drink. I fed from the lady."

Father Molinari took a knee, feeling at their necks. Once satisfied both were alive, he clucked his tongue. He looked from the damaged plastic to the girl's unbuttoned jeans to the pills. It didn't take long to figure out why they'd break in to a house that looked abandoned.

"They weren't mean." Sabine stood and moved to his side. "She wanted to bring me to the police, but he wanted to take her pants off first. They started yelling, so I made them sleep."

Not as defenseless as she looks. Father Molinari grasped her shoulder with a one-handed hug. "You did well. Go and wait downstairs while I make them forget us."

"Okay." She pulled away and walked to the kitchen.

Why does it bother me so that she fed on her own? He stooped over the boy and grasped him by the chin. *I am not Auguste. I do not fear her independence... she has not matured. I fear where her mind may go if something frightens her.* He glared into the boy's eyes, forcing the teen to forget seeing a little girl in this house. *I should not leave her alone. The next person to break in may not be a horny teenager...* He buttoned the girl's jeans and forced her eyes open. The house shuddered in the wind; tattered plastic sheeting flapped like a rattlesnake.

Unconscious minds proved easier to manipulate. He worked her thoughts with the finesse of an artist sculpting clay. The argument over taking the 'poor little homeless girl' to the police became a disagreement over Quaaludes. She refused to take them. He implanted the feeling the house was 'too creepy,' and she never wanted to come back here again. Upon noticing neither teen had brought shoes, he added a memory of rats crawling over her feet for good measure. She would think she'd fainted, and the boy passed out from too many pills.

Father Molinari stood, switched off the radio, and retreated to the protection of the locked basement door. Three extra deadbolts could keep away casual explorers and promiscuous teens, but would it be enough to fend off a more formidable threat? As he plodded down the stairs, he thought of the small boy from the street. How much longer could Sabine withstand the isolation? It pained him to think of how much like a child she remained, despite existing for eighty-some years.

The feeling nudged at his anger. How could God make her suffer so? What part of His plan included torturing children? At the bottom of the stairs, he grabbed two fistfuls of hair and stifled an anguished cry to a hiss. How many children had suffered through two world wars, Korea, and Vietnam? How could he possibly think Sabine was worse off than the families crushed under this 'new world' of machines and technology? A new world that ground up everything in its path, reducing trees and fields to hot ashes, and cities to rubble. A world where a lunatic exterminates millions of innocent people, and God lets it happen.

One blood tear crept down his cheek. Sabine's plight tortured him because she was his to protect and safeguard. She mattered more than a legion of faceless tragedies talked about in the news, people he had never known or seen. A memory of Josephine in the field behind Henri's house flashed by, her head half-turned back over her shoulder, smiling at him. He had only one regret over joining the priesthood, and the demon within her had known it. How much had it known? Molinari gnawed on his knuckles, a pained grimace across his lips. Josephine told him he would die, and die he had. Had the Hellspawn within her known he would find Sabine? Could this have all been planned due to his work with the Order? To neutralize him?

Father, forgive me the sin of vanity. I who am unworthy to serve you.

Sabine crept over, a fearful expression peering out from under loose hair. Her toes sank into the thick rug he'd added to make the space livable. She opened her mouth, but seemed fearful to make the slightest sound.

Molinari released his worry. This child could in no way be part of Satan's machinations. He offered a reassuring smile.

"Father? What is wrong?" She hesitated. "Are you angry with me?"

He held his arms out. "No, Sabine... I am not."

She rushed into his embrace. Her fruit-scented shampoo reminded him of Mrs. Sheehan. He offered a brief prayer in her memory, knowing it a veritable certainty she'd passed on by now, though the child still spoke of her as if alive. He shuddered, clinging to her small form as if to hug life back into her. For an instant, he worried about crushing the air from her lungs. *She no longer needs to breathe...* He wept.

His reaction to the discovery of vampires had once made him sure of God's presence. If a supernatural being, long dismissed as simple fantasy, existed... so too should the divine. *One cannot know light without darkness.* Father Molinari slumped to his knees, fists in his lap. Sabine remained at his side, deciding to fuss at his hair. *Have I given my life to a lie?* He gazed up at the ceiling, at dangling strands of insulation and wires ravaged by weather and wildlife.

"Why are you crying?" Sabine wiped at his face. "Did something bad happen outside?"

The memory of war protestors from several weeks back haunted him. Men and women, teenagers, even small children, waved placards decrying involvement in Vietnam and claiming 'God is a Lie.' The same rage that had washed over him then returned, only this time, he couldn't tell if it pointed inward or at Heaven.

Eighty-two years as a vampire. Eighty-two years trying to save this child from Satan. Eighty-two years of nothing changing. What if the sign was right? What if God *was* a lie?

"I don't know what to do…" He clasped her hand. "I…"

She leaned close to whisper in his ear. "Don't listen to the bad feeling. It wants you to be sad."

"You hear it too…"

"Yes." She stared down. "But I know it lies. Every night, I pray for God to help you… like *Maman* prayed for him to help me."

He isn't listening. Father Molinari closed his eyes. When she brushed her hands through his hair again, he shivered.

"Do you remember when you told the bad priest he did not have faith?"

Father Molinari smiled. "You remember that?"

Sabine gave him an incredulous look. "Of course! It was not so long ago. I am not an old lady. Mrs. Sheehan forgets her bread in the oven." She giggled, bit her lip, and put on a serious face. "He is with you." She poked a finger into the crucifix amulet around his neck.

Her touch set off a ripple of hope through his body, a tingle strong enough to feel.

I must trust in God. He pictured Auguste shrinking away from the crucifix. There was only one explanation for how a lump of metal, or water treated with only humble words and strong faith, could have any effect on a vampire.

"We should go outside tomorrow." Molinari smiled.

"*Oui!*" Sabine bounced on her toes.

"What would you like to do?"

Without hesitation, she shook her head. "I do not wish to see a film."

He pulled her close and kissed her atop the head. She'd been terrified of 'going to the theater' ever since that night. She'd even become upset at the sight of that old purple dress. Despite that the garment remained in Richmond when they left, Sabine still feared it lurked at the bottom of her trunk. Taking a child her apparent age into the city too late at night these days would attract unwanted attention. Whatever they did, they'd only have a few hours.

"We'll figure something out." Hope lifted his spirits, and he smiled.

Sabine darted around the basement to the shelf and grabbed the fat storybook. She didn't seem to notice how yellow it had become. He followed her to her bed, and sat on the edge after she climbed in.

"What story would you like to hear?" He grinned as he asked, despite knowing the answer.

"*La Souris et la Bougie.*" She offered him the book.

Father Molinari traced his fingers over the binding, examining every crack and flake. He slid a hand over the well-worn pages, to the top where the gilt edge had faded to bare paper. With great care, he opened the old book. Sabine's face lit up at the sight of the illustrated mouse in farmer's clothing.

He put his arm around her as she snuggled to his side.

"Philippe le petit was a mouse. He lived in the walls of a farmhouse, which he shared with a man. Philippe was happy to have a neighbor, but Jean-Claude was not happy to have a mouse in his walls."

Sabine giggled.

"For men, you see, do not understand mice." Father Molinari winked. "Philippe did not care. The clumsy farmer was easy enough to avoid. What he wanted, more than anything, was to reach the candle set upon the table so far above his head. For it would bring light to his little home. Each day when Jean-Claude set out to tend his fields, Philippe would emerge from his hole and gaze up at it, hoping one day, the candle would be his."

"*Souris bête,*" said Sabine.

"Why do you think the mouse is silly?" asked Father Molinari.

"Because he cannot climb the table. He wants and wants and wants, but he cannot have the little light." Her serious expression broke into a grin. "But he tries."

Is that mischief in those green eyes? Or does this child truly not remember how the story ends?

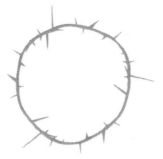

CHAPTER THIRTY-ONE

THE DARE

May 6th 1967 Saint-Georges, Quebec

Laughter emerged from the darkness; a small girl's giggling pulled Father Molinari forward, hand over hand along a wall he could not see. Singing followed, a child reciting a lullaby. Fear squeezed his heart, drawing him ever onward despite a building sense that he did not want to see what lay ahead.

A sliver of light along the ground appeared at the end of an impossibly long corridor. Black walls oozed with tar and the odor of sulphur exuded from all around him, clinging amid a thick blanket of heated air. A woman screamed. Molinari pulled his hands from the sticky wall and sprinted. The thin band of light grew and stretched forth into the hall; the world around him took on color and shape. White plaster walls, a threadbare green rug, a blurry painting of a meadow landscape.

Henri's home, upstairs.

He burst through the door of Josephine's bedroom. The young woman, still seventeen, lay at his feet inches from the threshold, gasping for air. Her blood seeped from the side of her neck and pooled on the floorboards. Beyond her, tiny bare footprints in blood led to an overturned crib. Sabine, grey and withered with death, cradled a fidgety infant who looked huge in her delicate arms. Dark blood smeared her mouth and chin, and ran down over her baby doll nightdress.

"Sabine, no!" he shouted, but his voice came from far behind him.

"I saved you one," cooed Sabine. She held up the second baby as if offering it to him. "They are delicious."

She stepped away from the bed, where the boy's twin lay drained and still. A little arm pointed at him, glassy eyes accusing.

Father Molinari shot upright, the thunder of his heartbeat in his brain deafening. Sabine turned to look at him, already awake in her bed, catty-corner against the wall. She smiled. In the delirium of waking before he should, the expression on her face seemed malicious.

Thump.

He looked up at the ceiling when something struck the floor.

"Hunters," he wheezed.

Sabine hopped out of bed, hiked up her nightdress, and ran to the steps.

"Sabine, no..." He collapsed. His stiff muscles refused to obey until the sun went all the way down. His brain spiraled between the panicked notion that she raced off to murder an infant or she rushed into the arms of a hunter.

The feeling tempted him. He could overpower the sleep if he wanted to in such a dire moment. How could he not listen? Sabine needed protection.

He pushed up from the mattress, focusing every morsel of thought on God.

"Children, father," said Sabine.

"What?" His arm failed him, and he fell on his side. She crouched at the top of the stairs and pressed her ear against the door. He could not keep his eyes open. "Children?"

"I can hear them. They are calling each other cowards because they do not want to come through the window." She put a hand over her mouth to suppress a giggle. "They are afraid of our house."

The burden of sleep crashed into him, pinning him down like a blanket of lead. "Go... back to bed..."

His arm gave out and he fell through the bed, through the floor, and into a bottomless void. His body spun head over feet, twirling, with no sense of direction. Despite the speed of his plummet, he landed without pain. A child's bare feet stepped in front of his face, surrounded by deep green carpet. He grunted and raised his head, his gaze ascending over grey skin to the mid-shin hem of a little girl's pink nightdress. Many people tromped on the ceiling upstairs, as though the teens had gone and returned with all of their friends. He squinted up at the tiny figure before him, a faint red light aglow in her eyes.

Sabine smiled down at him, clutching Véronique. The porcelain doll turned its head and grinned with vampire fangs. He cried out in shock and shoved himself up, rolling into a seated position on the floor with his back against his bed. A pair of girls emerged from the shadows at the far end of the room to stand behind Sabine, the daughters of the Richmond family, still eight and ten years of age. They flashed menacing smiles and opened their mouths, baring fangs.

"I am lonely, Father." Sabine set the doll down on its feet and walked backwards until she stood between the girls. She put her arms around them. "Now I have forever friends. I hope you don't mind."

"We'll be good," said the younger.

"You'll protect us, right?" asked the older.

Véronique pointed a stubby little finger at him. Her laughter sounded like a happy baby on fast forward.

He woke for the second time that night with his heart racing. Sabine's giggling echoed through the ceiling from upstairs; he flew from the bed and rushed across the basement. A different child's voice spoke in French.

"You aren't supposed to take that much. It is against the rules."

Molinari scrambled up the steps with the nightmare still fresh in his mind.

"I will put it back," said Sabine.

What have you done? Molinari shoved the door open and sprinted down the hall to the living room.

"You cannot just put it back," said the other child.

Father Molinari tripped on a peeling rug, falling forward into a grip on the doorjamb. Sabine jumped with a startled yelp, dropping a handful of cards on a Monopoly board. The boy from the park sat opposite her, cross-legged. He jumped back with a look of abject terror. Molinari calmed at the sense the boy was alive. He straightened and let his arms fall slack. Without a word, he returned to the basement. The children remained quiet for a while; only the fluttering of plastic broke the stillness. Molinari stood at the center of the basement, staring at his wardrobe.

"I should go," said the boy.

"*Non*. Stay. Father is not angry. He is worried."

Something tapped on the ceiling. Father Molinari snapped out of his fog and stepped into a pair of jeans.

"Sorry about the window."

"It is only plastic," said Sabine. "And it was already cut."

Molinari pulled on a long-sleeved white shirt and went back upstairs, disregarding shoes or socks. The boy juggled dice, but went motionless when he walked in.

Sabine collected the dropped cards and put them at the bottom of a small deck. "Father, this is Sébastien. He lives across the field. He brought over a game. Can he please stay awhile?"

The boy summoned a sheepish smile. "I am sorry for sneaking in. The house looked abandoned. My friends thought I was making up stories about a little ghost girl."

"Hah!" Sabine clamped her hands over her mouth and laughed. "I scared them good."

"I was worried." Sébastien set the dice down, stood, and walked up to Father Molinari. He hadn't even taken his green windbreaker off yet. "She's lonely. I know you told me to stay away, but she looked lonely." He glanced back at her. "Can I get sick from her? I'll go home if I have to."

Sabine stooped over the board to pick up the dice. Her silver crucifix dangled forward from her neck. "You cannot catch what I have."

The boy relaxed a little. "Are you sure?"

"Yes." Sabine sat back on her heels and smiled. "God does not like children to have this sickness, so He will not let you have it."

"She is correct." Father Molinari rubbed a finger back and forth over his lips as he forced the nightmare out of his mind. He could not get past how happy she seemed. "I suppose you can stay for a little while."

Sabine cheered. The boy smiled, thanked him, and rushed back to kneel by the board. Sabine handed him the dice, and he rolled. Father Molinari went downstairs again, and selected one of the newer books he'd discovered on occultism. The claim of 'true and genuine' knowledge on the back all but guaranteed it pure fabrication, but the best lies grew from a grain of fact.

He carried it upstairs and sat reading while the children played and talked. Sabine's remark that they'd 'recently arrived from France' raised his eyebrow. Her expression and tone felt sincere.

"What is it like?" asked Sébastien.

She shrugged. "I do not remember much." She hopped a piece around the board and rambled on about her mother and the servant girl Élodie, as if only weeks had passed. He lost focus on the words printed in front of him, wondering if the wispy blonde had survived two world wars and whatever repercussions arose from her helping them flee.

The memory of her tortured eyes haunted him. Élodie had given in. Despite the innocence her appearance conveyed, she embodied what he feared Sabine might one day become. Demons oft emulated the voices of children to lure the soft of heart to their deaths. He looked up as Sabine giggled. *And I walked right into it.*

Molinari pinched the bridge of his nose. *No. She is no demon.*

"Do you have any sisters or brothers?" asked Sabine. "Mrs. Sheehan is my almost-grandmother. She is nice, but lives far away."

"No. I'm an only child." He counted out play money and put a wooden house on the board. The building shifted around them with a gust. He looked at her bare feet and pulled his jacket tighter. "Aren't you cold? The house has no windows."

"*Non.*" Sabine rolled the dice and counted her piece seven spaces.

The game seemed to be going nowhere. Sébastien clearly attempted to let her win, but Sabine had no idea how to play, and had all the capitalist acumen of an eight-year-old. Father Molinari amused himself with an internal jab at the French, and turned a page without a word.

"Is it because of being sick?" Sébastien reached over. "May I?"

Sabine nodded. He put a hand on her forehead.

"You don't feel sick. Maybe a little cool." He looked at Molinari. "Sir, what time is it?"

"Hmm." He glanced at the collapsing walls. "That is a good question."

"I will look." Sabine hopped up and ran to the kitchen, returning in a moment. "It is three numbers from twelve and the little hand points at almost ten."

"Fifteen minutes to ten," said Molinari.

"Oh, no." Sébastien hung his head. "I am late. I must go home."

"It is okay." Sabine helped him put the game away. Once he tucked the box under his arm, she hugged him. "Thank you for visiting me. It is nice to have a friend."

Father Molinari's fingers dug into the paperback. His mood further darkened at the current chapter's great and lurid details of the practices of one Aleister Crowley. He flipped through, not too concerned if they tore.

The front door closed with a soft *tap*. Sabine padded over and climbed up next to him in what had once been a recliner. His first attempt to pull the lever on the side had broken it off in his hand. The discarded stick remained beside him where he'd dropped it months ago.

Sabine lay her head against his chest, and sniffled.

He set the useless book on the small table to the right of the chair, and held her.

A distant boat on the river sounded its horn, briefly overpowering the rush of wind through the empty second floor. He looked at the cracking plaster overhead, wondering how much longer the house would remain standing.

Sabine gazed into nothing. "Sébastien will be like the cat, yes?"

"I do not think he will scratch the chairs."

She smirked with a trace of a fleeing smile. "I mean he will grow up, become old, and then God will take him to Heaven... but I will be the same."

"Yes, Sabine. He will do all of those things in time."

Such sorrow overcame her that her expression bored a vacuous hole through his heart. He pulled her tight. *God, please grant me the wisdom to see that which has escaped me. Please give me the strength to help this child walk from the shadow into your preserving light.*

"Will He forgive me?" Sabine looked up at him. "For keeping you out of Heaven?"

Father Molinari grasped her hand, turned it palm up, and set her crucifix pendant atop it. The metal radiated more heat than he remembered, but not to the point of being painful.

"Does it feel hot?"

She put her other hand over it. "Warm like a hug."

"Then he has forgiven you." He smiled.

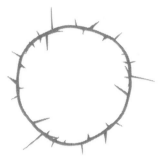

CHAPTER THIRTY-TWO

NON

November 28th 1967 Saint-Georges, Quebec

O f everywhere in the small house, the plastic over the kitchen windows remained the most intact, perhaps because they were the smallest. Books littered the white Formica table, spotted with blue abstract blobs and red zigzag lines. A man's voice echoed somewhere outside amid static crackles and pops. Rapid French criticized Lyndon B. Johnson for dragging his country into Vietnam, and questioned the credibility of the government's claims of progress in the war effort.

Molinari stood and crossed to the rusting sink. His vampire's senses soon locked on the source, a pack of teenagers near the river's edge with a portable radio. As a woman launched into a tirade suggesting Canada openly encourage young American men who objected to the war to cross over, one of them switched the station, and *Sunshine of Your Love* blared.

"Another war." Having no interest in staring at dancing teens, he returned to the table and rearranged the books. He considered reading, but couldn't bring himself to open any of them. "For what do they fight this time? No one seems to even know."

Perhaps God had grown weary of humanity trying to kill itself off. He looked down with the resigned detachment of a father faced with watching his children make mistake after mistake, hoping they would learn before they died. Was it too much to wish for Him to step in before humanity hurtled over its waterfall?

He closed his eyes and imagined the sensation of feeding. Always, the roaring loomed ahead, the feeling of approaching doom. What would it be like to cross that point? He tried to reason out if Sabine had experienced it when she passed on the gift. She had not drained him of blood; his death rode in on a steel point. A day in each direction from that moment remained a blur. Whenever he thought of it, all that came to mind was pain, darkness, and an ephemeral childish voice singing *Frère Jacques*. The strongest memories he could summon of the little church were the heartrending stare Sabine had first given him when the cell door opened, the scent of sausage lofted on a belch, and the horrified look on Father Callini's dead face.

Sabine's clothing changed through the years, but the innocent smile on her face remained the same. Ever happy. Ever a child. If God could give up on humanity, what chance did she have? None of the books from the Montreal library had helped. If he had not *been* one, he would have thought vampires to never have existed. Years and years of research, yet he was no closer today to breaking the curse than he had been while hiding in Henri's basement.

It would be a mercy. He tried to picture himself sneaking up on her with a stake. Without a doubt, he knew one look from her would stall him in his tracks. The imagined betrayal on her face brought him to tears. "Have I been staring at the answer for almost a century? Is your will simple mercy rather than the torture of experimentation?"

Nausea churned in his gut as he pictured the sight and feel of her little body disintegrating to ash in his arms. Her look of shock at what the only person in the world she trusted had done to her brought forth an anguished scream.

He could do only one thing after such a horror: embrace the sun.

"*Père?*" yelled Sabine. The front door squeaked open. "Father?"

Father Molinari thought of his two remaining stakes, down in the basement in a packed duffel, where they'd spent the past forty years.

She'd never expect it. Never see it coming. Never believe he could—

"Father!" Sabine appeared in the doorway between kitchen and dining room, clutching a calico cat. She grinned.

Guilt crushed him into the table. He hid his face in the crook of his arm to conceal his tears.

"Is something wrong, Father?" Sabine grunted as she adjusted the cat's weight.

A shadow coiled around his soul, fanning his resentment toward God. Was that the test? To kill the person who had become as dear as his own child? *Do you test me as you tested Abraham?* He wiped his face on his sleeve and looked up. *The angel stayed his hand.*

Sébastien peeked in from the doorway.

"You have found a cat." Molinari forced a smile through his sorrow. "What will you name him?"

The boy approached after a hesitant pause and no sign of disapproval from him.

"I think the cat is a she." Sabine's shoes scuffed on the floor as she shuffled over. "May I name her Betty?"

"Betty is a fine name for a cat." He positioned his arm to hide the bloody sleeve.

Sabine bounced, cheered, and spun about. Her dress and the cat in her arms flared outward. "We will need to purchase some food for Betty."

The feeling taunted him. It knew, as did he, that he could never bring himself to harm her. He could no sooner stake her now than he could stand by and watch Callini do it years ago. Father Molinari struggled for words, and nodded at her request. She went with Sébastien to the living room where they plopped down on the floor in front of the sofa. Sébastien spoke of watching television, and tried to interest Sabine in something called *Star Trek*. She asked him about it, though whether motivated by genuine curiosity or her desire to have someone her own 'age' to spend time with, he could not tell.

Hmph. Television. It's everywhere now. What else have I been wrong about?

Father Molinari hurried to the basement to change his shirt, deciding on a black button-down that reminded him of a priest's uniform. The gold crucifix sat on the table by his bed, where it had been for some months. Below it lay the bag containing the tools of the Order. Holy water, the sacred book, stakes, and his transcribed notes of the more useful parts of Gustav's journals.

"Of course," he muttered. "One like Gustav had little interest in breaking the curse. He reveled in it. I've been going about this the wrong way... I must find one who wishes to break it."

He slouched. The odds of that seemed ludicrous. If he *did* find a vampire who yearned to escape the grip of darkness, it would prove the task impossible, for if it were possible, they would no longer *be* a vampire. Perhaps, like Sabine's mother, they all met the same sort of end.

Would God consider it suicide to run headlong into the sunlight? He picked up the hot crucifix and draped it around his neck. It hurt a little, but not so much as to be intolerable. He knelt and prayed God to forgive him for his thoughts of murdering the child he had been sent to care for. He refused to see it as a mercy.

"You are my light and my salvation. Of what shall I fear? The Lord is my strength in darkness. I trust in Him."

He recited the Lord's Prayer, and stood. After a lingering glance at the bag, he went upstairs.

The children seemed morose, sitting together with their backs to the couch, holding hands. Betty wandered around the decaying structure, pawing at crumbling plaster and thin slat boards in the wall.

"I'm sorry," said Sabine. "Do not get in trouble because of me."

Father Molinari took a seat on the couch, closer to Sabine. "What is it?"

"My parents don't like me staying up late so much. When I told them there is a girl here, they didn't believe me. They think I'm lying and want me to see a doctor."

Sabine smoothed her dress over her legs, something to do with her hands while pouting. "You should let them believe I am a dream. If they know of us, they will make problems."

Sébastien frowned, and squeezed her hand. "I like having you for a friend. It sucks you're a vampire."

Father Molinari coughed.

Sabine giggled so hard she fell over sideways against his leg.

"What's so funny?" Sébastien's eyebrows scrunched together.

"Sucks," whispered Sabine, and clamped her mouth around his arm without teeth. "Mmm."

The boy chuckled. "Oops." He cringed from the glare Molinari focused on him. "Uh, sorry. She... I guess you're gonna make me forget now. Okay."

Sabine looked up. "He is my friend. We traded secrets."

Sébastien blushed, hard.

"I suppose I can guess what his secret is." Molinari couldn't decide if he was amused or angry.

"I'm not telling." Sabine folded her arms. "It is a secret."

"You should go home to your parents, boy. If they already think you are in need of a doctor for seeing ghosts, I would not recommend you mention vampires."

The boy grabbed the sofa arm and pulled himself standing. "I dunno when I can come back... Mom's gonna read me the riot act when I get home. I'm prolly gonna get grounded."

Sabine walked him to the door. They talked in quiet whispers for a little while longer, facing each other and holding hands. He kissed her on the cheek and ran off. She wiped at her face and glared after him.

"Eww!" She marched back to the couch with such an indignant expression he burst out laughing. "*Ce n'est pas drôle!*" Sabine stomped. "Not funny. Stop laughing at me."

Betty meowed.

The somber thought that her reaction to a boy's kiss would forever be 'eww' killed his mirth. He looked away as she wiped her hand over her cheek thrice more and huffed.

Betty yowled at the window by the front door. Her tail fluffed and the hair on her back stood on end. She hissed.

Molinari pulled Sabine back, putting himself, and the couch, between her and the door. "I asked you not to go outside alone. Someone might want to hurt you."

She peered around him. "I will make them go away."

Betty hissed again and zoomed into the back of the house.

Sharp footsteps, hinting at dress shoes, clomped over the porch. Father Molinari stood.

The front door opened in a slow, creaking motion. A fair-skinned man in a suit made of shimmery grey fabric appraised the pair from the porch with a raised brow of clinical detachment. Wind teased at the loose folds of a light tan raincoat. Silvery hair clung tight to the curve of his skull, cut short and slicked back. Pronounced crow's feet lent an air of age to an otherwise smooth face. His hard, grey eyes regarded Molinari with the sort of malice an eagle reserves for a mouse that bit it.

He waited a few seconds, and stepped inside.

"So, you are the one," said the visitor in French while glancing around. "My, my... I thought that whole vow of poverty thing was intended for show. I always wondered what God needed with so much money... gold chalices, expensive robes, artwork..." The man clucked his tongue. "You could have stolen this house and overpaid for it."

Heat rippled over Father Molinari's back, centered at the base of his skull. The feeling floated around, as if a serpent on his shoulder stared him in the eye. Every sense he had about this man warned him. Any chance he had to survive this night hinged on a plunge over the precipice. *Would I give up my soul for this child?*

"Yves..." said Molinari.

"I am impressed, *priest*." Yves folded his hands behind his back. "Don't bother rambling on about how you will not let me have Sabine. I have not come here to take her back to France. Your fortune at my distaste for the hassle of boats has ended with the convenience of air travel."

The child clung to Molinari's back. "I don't like him."

Something crashed in the kitchen. Betty screeched.

"They've had aircraft for some years now." Molinari squinted.

"Indeed. I hoped a few more years might allow you to develop a sense of security in order to make this more enjoyable for me." Yves paced in a leftward circle. "Once, I had simply wished to kill you for what you did to Auguste." He stared fondly at nothing. "He was, you know, my favorite. I had thought we would spend many years with each other before I bored of him." He pursed his lips. "Perhaps I may not have. But, that is something I will never find out."

"Auguste killed his own wife and daughter." Father Molinari clutched the crucifix, adoring the heat in his hand.

Yves seemed to suffer only a facial tic from the presence of the holy item, though he did not look directly at it. "Véronique was easy to seduce. She gave herself to me willingly. Auguste never could understand I regarded her as little more than a pastime. After he had given her the blood, the fool took it as an act of betrayal." He made a clicking noise with his tongue. "Auguste was never very good at sharing. What else are women for?"

"Sodomites?" Father Molinari squinted.

"Oh, how gauche." Yves rolled his eyes. "That implies an attraction of mere flesh, *priest*. What Auguste and I had was"—he waved a slow hand through the air in front of him, spreading his fingers—"transcendental. Our souls were entwined."

"You forget your kind do not *have* souls."

Yves paused his pacing about, eyes closed and head bowed. "I came here because I wanted to destroy you. I had to settle the anger that has so long dwelled within my breast. The Americans have no loyalty to the old ways. *La Accord de l'Ombre*, sadly, holds little influence among vampires who care only for personal wealth and power. It took me a long time to find you, Antonio."

Sabine pulled on Molinari's arm, trying to drag him away. Her feet slid over the carpet.

"You didn't learn when you sent your man to Richmond. God is my sword and my shield."

Yves let off a patronizing laugh that rankled the shadow lurking in Molinari's mind. It seized on the anger and pulled, teasing him with visions of claws and strength sufficient to rip a man in half. It horrified him with an image of what this creature might do to Sabine if he let himself stay weak. His hand trembled around the crucifix. What if God wasn't enough? He had taken so long to answer their prayers.

"I have changed my plans, *priest*." Yves pleasant demeanor iced over. "I will not simply destroy you. I will spend the next four hours causing your little pet to make such beautiful screams that you will beg me to kill her. I will force you to experience every second of it. Perhaps I will let you keep her skull as a token of my displeasure."

Yves blurred. Tremendous force struck Molinari in the side of the head with a sickening *crunch*. One instant he stood in the living room, the next, he found himself embedded up to the waist in the wall of the dining room. Splintering cracks raced through his head as his skull knit back to normal shape.

"If you behave yourself," said Yves, "and watch as I tell you to, *and* show sufficient remorse for what you did to poor, sweet Auguste, perhaps I will end your miserable existence. Cross me, and you shall spend the rest of eternity hearing this unfortunate mistake shriek in your dreams."

Sabine screamed. Father Molinari struggled at the wall pinning his arms to his sides and wriggled until he fell to the floor. Yves held Sabine off the ground, a hand under each arm, spinning her around as though waltzing. Her scratching and kicking didn't faze him in the slightest.

Father Molinari staggered to his feet and charged. Yves moved with such speed he seemed to disappear and reappear a few yards away. Molinari ran headlong into the opposite wall, crushing the plasterboard and sending a legion of spiders swarming out of the hole and upward to the ceiling. The mass of insects moved together, a diaphanous living shadow. He spat a few out and growled.

"Help!" screamed Sabine. "Father!"

"Yes, child. Scream for him."

A pronounced *snap* came from her chest as a rib broke under Yves's grip. She wailed and sobbed.

Molinari raised the crucifix. "In the name of G—"

Yves smeared into a streak of tan and silvery grey, leaving Sabine hanging in the air where he had been. Claws raked down Molinari's chest, scraping over breastbone and rib. The crucifix chain snapped, though Yves's fingers flared with smoke and flame as he made contact. Sabine hit the ground and curled into a ball, cradling her arms to her side and wailing.

"Beautiful music." Yves rammed his fingers into Molinari's gut, lifting him off the ground by a clawed hand grasping at his innards.

Two of Molinari's punches may as well have hit a statue for all the effect they had. Bladed fingers tightened around the bottom of his ribcage. Yves twisted, and hurled Father Molinari across the house. He punctured the wall to the left of the archway between the dining and living rooms, skipped off the table, and crashed face-first into an old glass-doored china cabinet. Fire swam through his cheeks on the points of shattered fragments.

Sabine let off a short, high-pitched shriek.

"Scream, child," said Yves.

She complied. After the initial shrill, she begged and pleaded.

"What shall I break first? Tell me, girl. Arm or leg?"

Soft grunts came from her as she tried to wriggle free. "Please don't hurt me."

"Ah, no dignity. Begging is so beneath the station you were born to. That shall make for two breaks. Arms, legs, or one of each? Come now, Sabine, make a choice... They'll knit. You have such delicate little wrists. Shall I snap them?"

Father Molinari snarled. He sprang to his feet, and brushed glass shards from his face with a hasty swipe. Sabine trying to speak through her tears drove him to a run. He stomped past the table, into the living room.

Yves had the child off the floor by a fistful of her dress, holding her left wrist up to inspect it. He closed his fingers over the back of her hand, forcing it to bend down, seeming intent on making her palm touch her wrist. She tugged at her arm, but could not pull it free. The harder he pressed, the louder she screamed; shrieks of fear became cries of pain.

Molinari let off an enraged howl. He dove into Yves from the side, wrapping his arms around the man and knocking him flat. Startled,

Sabine yelped and landed on all fours somewhere behind. He grabbed at Yves's suit, seizing the older vampire by the collar and throttling him, pounding his skull into the floor.

Yves punched him in the chest, knocking him up through the ceiling. Molinari, stunned from the massive impact to the stomach, gawped down through the breach in the floor as Yves zipped out of sight. His back touched the ceiling of the second-story bedroom for an instant. Gravity brought him back through the hole, burying hundreds of splinters in his arms and legs as he scraped the edges.

Sabine shrieked again, wailing, "Please, don't!" over and over.

Father Molinari smashed into the floor. Everywhere, the tickle of knitting bones erupted, pins and needles from the ninth plane of Hell. The gold crucifix glinted in a patch of moonlight leaking in through the front window. Sabine's desperate cries pulled him toward her instead.

He pushed himself upright.

Yves held Sabine out to arms' length with a grasp at her hips. She pulled at his hands, whining and squirming. Her bare feet pummeled his chest, though he showed little reaction.

"Do you hear your bones cracking, little one?" He sniffed at her. "You look so lifelike. You've got plenty of blood inside you... enough to play with you all evening."

Sabine reached up with both hands, grasped the neck of her dress, and tore it open.

The silver crucifix upon her exposed chest seemed to glow in the moonlight, tinting her pale skin blue.

"*Putain!*" Yves wailed and clamped his hands over his eyes. "*Pute!*"

Sabine fell on her back and scooted against the wall, clutching the little crucifix as if hiding behind it. Her left leg dragged limp and twisted at a wrong angle.

Father Molinari tripped himself going through a rapid about-face. He grabbed the couch back to keep from falling and sprinted for the larger gold crucifix by the door. Yves looked up with glowing yellow eyes and hissed at the girl.

"Vous appartenez à l'enfer! Le diable vous emporte!" shouted Sabine. Her leg rotated back into place with a *crunch*, and she tucked herself into a tighter ball, hiding behind the raised little crucifix.

Small wisps of smoke fumed from Yves's face. He let off a dark chuckle. "The Devil cannot take himself."

Molinari snatched his amulet from the hardwood and ran at Yves from behind. Consumed by anger, the older vampire lunged at Sabine, grabbing her by the throat and hauling her up with her back pressed to the wall. Yves's cheeks ignited; wild with rage, he seemed to disregard the pain. Molinari charged. All that mattered was protecting Sabine. He raised the amulet over his head like a dagger.

The elder vampire's motion slowed from blur to normal.

Father Molinari screamed with fury, and stabbed the long end of the crucifix into Yves's back between the shoulder blades. Undead skin burst into flames. Yves's hand opened. Sabine slid to the floor. Molinari grabbed the crucifix in a two handed grip and forced it an inch deeper, twisting.

Yves stumbled forward, shoved face first into the wall by Molinari crushing down on his back. Sabine scooted sideways out from under him, keeping one hand on her pendant as if it were a wall between her and death. Yves raked his claws down the plaster, tearing wallpaper into crinkling runners. He dropped to one knee, arms flailing in a useless attempt to reach behind him at the searing implement embedded in his back. Hissing and bubbling roiled from where the gold touched him. Molinari gagged on the reek of burning flesh, and kept grinding the Crucified Lord into him. Yves shrieked as though an ember of magma had lodged in his spine. He wrenched away, pulling the crucifix from Molinari's hands. Flame spread up and over his shoulders. Sabine leapt to her feet and ran into the kitchen, silver necklace bouncing against her chest.

The elder vampire spun around and pounced, but Molinari got his hands up fast enough to catch the man by the wrists. Still, Yves's far greater strength knocked him over backwards. Yellow eyes devoid of any trace of humanity flared. Smoke poured out of his mouth and nostrils; the glow of fire shone deep in his throat. Yves forced his teeth closer to Father Molinari's neck.

Focused on the fear he'd seen in the child's eyes, Molinari surged. He raised a knee to Yves's chest, holding back the fanged mouth. Their strength seemed to equalize; heat welled up in Molinari's muscles.

"I have not"—Father Molinari grunted—"spent the past eighty-two years watching over Sabine only to let an unholy"—his face burned red with blood as he wrestled Yves to the side—"unclean abomination destroy her soul."

Yves hissed and spat, beyond ration or reason, pure monster.

The tide of strength turned. Father Molinari traded his grasp of the man's arms for a grip on his shoulders as he rolled up on top. He pulled Yves a few inches off the floor, then thrust with his legs and slammed him flat to the ground. A half-inch of gold, the bottom tip of the crucifix, poked out of the older vampire's chest.

Little feet pattered over the kitchen floor. Sabine ran in carrying a stake in one hand and a bottle of holy water in the other. She stopped six steps away with wild, terrified eyes at the sight of Yves pinned to the floor, burning and writhing.

She tossed the stake to the carpet nearby. The small crucifix hanging around her neck still seemed to radiate light, causing Yves to shy from her approach. Molinari looked at her, only a slight trace of bruise remained where her rib had been broken. The glint on her crucifix hurt his eyes. Yves clutched his arm as he grabbed the stake. Anger at what this wretch wanted to do to Sabine welled up inside him. He disregarded the frantic claws, seized the wood in a grip near to splintering it, and plunged it down into Yves's heart. The stake twisted as it passed between ribs, and the satisfying shock of it striking the floor rattled his fingers.

Yves raked his hands through the air twice more before his arms fell limp. Sabine crept nearer, trembling as if he might spring to life at any second. When she got close enough, she poured the bottle of holy water over his face, aiming for the elder's gaping mouth. Wherever the stream touched, flesh and bone disintegrated.

She jumped back with a sharp squeal as the body erupted in a yellow-orange conflagration. Father Molinari rolled away, swatting embers from his pants. The girl stared at the smoldering skeleton, eyes wide, head held high. Wind passed through the house, lifting strands of her hair to the side and fluttering the torn front of her dress.

"I do not think the Devil wanted him," whispered Sabine.

"Are you hurt?" Father Molinari shuffled on his knees to her side, and wrapped her in his arms.

"I am more frightened than hurt." Her shivering lessened. "Why did he not turn to ash right away when you put the stake through him?"

He held her in a tight, protective embrace, staring with worry at the blisters on his hand from where his crucifix had left a red welt. Father Molinari closed his eyes. *By the grace of God, guard this child.*

"Father?"

"I… am not sure." He loosened his grip on her, and shifted to look at the remains. "Or why his bones have remained. Perhaps because he was very old."

He blinked, and whirled to face her, grasping her by the shoulders. "Sabine… I thought we could break the curse by killing the one who turned you. We destroyed the wrong vampire. Yves passed the curse to Auguste. How do you feel?" He twisted her left and right, studying her for a few seconds before pressing his ear to her bare chest. "I hear your heart beating! Do you feel different?"

Sabine looked at him when he pulled back. She smiled at him, baring fangs. "*Non.*"

Father Molinari slumped, and wept into his hands.

"Thank you for saving me." Sabine kissed him on the cheek. "Do not be sad. We are together still."

Betty trotted in, wound herself between Sabine's legs, and meowed.

Father Molinari looked up. The cat's tail fluffed, but after a wary glance, she settled.

"You're a pretty cat." Sabine knelt and scratched Betty along the length of her back. "I think she likes me."

"You have a way with animals... I've never seen anything quite like it." He cringed from the full-body itching of hundreds of small cuts sealing. Wooden shards, slivers of glass, and small splinters worked their way out and tumbled down his sleeves. Greyness swept through his skin as hunger grew. "Are you certain you want to keep her? You will be sad when she dies."

Sabine nodded. "*Oui*, but I will cherish the time I have with her. Maybe Gaston will have a friend in Heaven when Betty is too old."

He stroked her hair, gathering it away from her face and tidying it. "I must feed, and dispose of these bones. I don't want to leave you here alone."

"I do not wish to be alone." Sabine glanced at the remains of Yves. "We are moving again, aren't we?"

"Yes." He got to his feet and frowned at her ruined dress. "Go and change so we may go out."

Sabine knelt in place, patting Betty for a little while more before standing. She looked him up and down. "Go and change, so we may go out."

He regarded his shredded clothing, chuckled, and swept her into his arms. For the first time since he'd laid eyes on the little vampire, he had not a trace of regret at this course his life had taken.

Father Molinari wore an ear-to-ear grin as he carried her downstairs. "I think it is time to purchase some new clothes... for both of us."

He set her down on her feet in the middle of the basement and ruffled her hair.

"Tomorrow." Sabine trotted over to her trunk. "It is too late now."

"Yes." Father Molinari went to his own pile of folded clothes. Sabine, little more than a blur in the periphery of his vision, sang a happy childish song to herself while switching dresses. "Tomorrow, we will get some clothes to wear in our new home."

"Father?" Sabine turned once her head emerged from the top of her dress. "I think, perhaps, our next house should not be so close to falling apart."

"Yes." He fixed the last button of his shirt.

Sabine put on her shoes.

"Come, let us go find some nourishment."

She grinned, rushed to his side, and took his hand. "Will I have time to say farewell to Sébastien?"

Molinari tilted his head and licked one fang. "Perhaps I can convince his parents to give you a few minutes."

She peered up at him. "And I do not think Sébastien deserves to be grounded."

He patted her on the head. "Of course not."

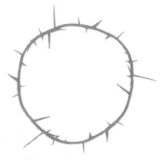

CHAPTER THIRTY-THREE

INNOCENT

April 12th 2014 New York City, New York

Haunting, repetitive music from Sabine's video game console mixed with the ceaseless thunder of people shifting about on the ceiling. The occasional *crack* of someone taking a shot at eight ball broke through the din, sharp enough to seem like it happened ten feet away rather than upstairs. Light flashed on the wall beyond a pile of stacked up folding tables. Patches of pink, green, and white created a larger-than-life silhouette of Sabine's head on the grey cinderblocks.

A siren passed outside, followed by a cacophony of blaring horns.

Father Molinari hovered over a MacBook, hands in fists save for dagger-like index fingers jabbing at keys. At least with all the noise going in the bar, the ever present buzz from a bright green shamrock sign bearing the logo 'Callahan's' escaped his notice. He finished typing out a search string: 'Vatican conspiracy + vampire,' and clicked the button. The page came up with almost half a million hits. Text, videos, and websites claimed to have information 'the Vatican is hiding' or 'things they don't want you to know.'

He clicked on a random link, which brought up the smiling visage of Pope Francis. He tapped a finger on his chin. *Something about him feels welcoming... Perhaps I should risk contact.* His brain chewed on the idea. The previous pope unsettled him. When last he'd thought of reaching out to the Order, under John Paul II, he decided against it. Had he been mortal, he would never have doubted serving God with him. Despite his 'condition,' Father Molinari thought of the much-beloved pontiff with nothing but respect. Respect tinted with fear. As conservative as that pope had been, the thought of open dialogue with a *vampire* struck him as laughable... even if said vampire had once been privy to some of the Vatican's real secrets.

A creak on the far right side of the basement preceded the *thuds* of a stocky red-haired man descending a creaky set of stairs made of unpainted lumber. Every day, the man wore the same sneakers, jeans, and green tee shirt with a Harp beer logo. He wandered around two pushcarts loaded with steel folding chairs, ducked a low-hanging beam, and stepped through a gap in the black curtains hung around the corner that now served as home.

"Evenin', Father."

"Neil." Molinari nodded in greeting.

"This came for you today." Neil held up a flat package with an Amazon logo and dropped it on the folding table.

Molinari twitched as someone upstairs broke a fresh rack on the pool table. At the confusion on Neil's face, he smiled. "The billiards game is painfully loud."

"Can't hear it." Neil pulled a folding chair over and sat. "Break time. Mind if I keep you company for a bit? I need a few minutes of silence."

"Please do."

"So, how goes it tonight, padre?"

"There are mysteries of the universe I am about ready to give up on." Father Molinari chuckled. "A hundred and twenty years, she learns four languages, learns to play one of those... guitar things, but gets bored with it, learns to play these... video games, and gets mesmerized by them. And yet, despite all the time I've spent sitting at this infernal box"—he held up two index fingers—"I cannot type but one letter at a time."

Neil raised a bottle of Harp in toast. "Old dog, new tricks and stuff. You know they say kids learn faster. Something about the way their brains are wired. Maybe she's stuck in programming mode."

Sabine emerged from behind the wall of tables in a blue sweatshirt, pink tights, frilly black skirt, and black converse sneakers. Shimmery violet stars dangled from her earlobes. She stopped at the edge of the table and leaned forward to peer at the package.

"*Bonjour*, Neil." She smiled.

"Hey kiddo. What'cha playing?"

Sabine's eyes gleamed. "*Child of Light*. I'm saving the kingdom."

"Sounds important." Neil sipped his beer.

"She's been 'saving the kingdom' every night for months." Father Molinari chuckled. "How can that little box devour so much time?"

"It's a PlayStation, Father." She grinned.

"You know, I used to ask myself what in the world an immortal would do with themselves... would they not get bored of existing after a time. That machine"—Father Molinari gestured at the glowing wall—"can compress months to hours."

"Is tonight a feeding night?" Sabine tilted her head.

"No, hon. Tomorrow."

"Okay." She smiled at Neil. "I'm sorry about making such a mess yesterday."

Molinari cocked an eyebrow.

"Heh. I had a couple of baking soda volcanoes when I was your age." Neil winked. "She's quite the little chemist."

Sabine bit her lip and shrank, as if about to be scolded. "Father does not think a girl should do science, but he did not tell me I couldn't read Nessa's old schoolbooks."

"Well." Father Molinari tapped at the table. "I also did not think television would last. Perhaps there are some old ways of thinking that I am better off discarding. She does seem fascinated by your daughter's texts."

Her expression lit up. Sabine spent the next ten or fifteen minutes rambling about things she'd learned regarding third grade science.

Eventually, she looked back and forth between the men. "I'm sorry. I have interrupted."

"S'okay," said Neil.

Sabine gave their landlord a quick hug before running back around the tables out of sight.

Within seconds, the music started again.

Neil shook his head. "Hard to imagine her being as old as you are."

Father Molinari lowered his voice. "Sabine has little concept of time. Things that happened in 1885, she talks about as though only days have passed. I'm still not entirely sure how long she had been cursed before I found her. Their house looked untended; for all I know, she may be older than me."

"That sounds like umm, dementia or something." Neil pulled his fingers through a ginger goatee. "My grandmother would forget what she did five minutes before."

"I remember things here and there. Unimportant things are gone... For example, I couldn't tell you what I ate before I met those two priests, but I remember meeting them. It is different for her. Events are strung along in no particular order, as if she can't register time passing between them. Josephine, Élodie, Mrs. Sheehan, Henri... in her mind, they're all still there. A century, a week... little different."

Neil mimicked an Irish brogue. "Is that why she still has such a strong accent? She sounds like she emigrated from France only hours ago."

"I cannot say why she retains some things and not others. It's more I think the timeframe that eludes her, but facts and events stay."

"Innocent." Neil took a long pull from his beer. "She's... innocent."

Father Molinari swiped a finger over the touchpad to keep the screen active. "It is a miracle she still is. I am starting to lose hope that I can save her."

Neil glanced in Sabine's direction. "Maybe you already did? Those two crazy French priests seemed like pretty bad dudes. You got her away from them."

"Most vampires give in to the darkness within a few days or weeks of being turned." Father Molinari picked at the keys on the MacBook.

"Sabine has not. I do not know how much longer I will be able to protect her soul from Satan."

"She's a li'l sweetheart; I don't think you gotta worry much." Neil went to drink from an empty bottle, and grumbled.

"It's not her I'm worried about. If something happens to her... if she gets attacked, scared, or even incredibly angry, there's always the chance."

"Angry?" Neil raised an eyebrow. "Better keep a close eye on the games you give 'er. Nessa smashes her PS4 controller at least once a month. Never did understand how some people get so damn pissed off about video games."

"Hmm." Father Molinari rubbed his eyes. "Some nights I think it would be kinder to let the Vatican find us."

"Aww, don't go talkin' like that. Father, you're a priest... you're not supposed to advocate suicide." Neil leaned forward, pointing the bottle at him. "An' don't give me no shit 'bout not fighting ain't the same. 'Sides, I think it's kinder for her to stay innocent. Ain't gotta worry 'bout shitty boyfriends, shitty abusive husbands, school, work, taxes... Hell, some days I'd give anything to be able to go back to when the worst decision I had to deal with was if I wanted to play with G.I. Joe or Transformers. I miss the eighties."

"You were to become an army electrician?" Molinari blinked.

"Forget it." Neil suppressed a belch. "Alls I'm sayin' is that maybe she's not got it as bad as you keep makin' it out to be."

"She will never know love, or a family."

"Same could be said for you, Father." Neil winked. "Vow of chastity and all that. But seriously, she loves you... That's family."

Molinari stared at the fake wood pattern on the folding table. "I mean the love of a husband, having her own children, experiencing life as God intended... and going to Heaven."

"Aye, well. You've got your work cut out for ya there. Me grandmum never heard o' no one comin' back." Again, Neil tried to drink from an empty bottle. "Dammit. Sorry, Father. I dunno why you'd want to. Half the people in this city would give their left nut for immortality."

"Perhaps you are right, though it is a sad statement of where humanity has gone. All the world is full of fear."

Neil tilted the bottle side to side; he held his breath for a second and let it out in a heavy exhale. "Welp. Gotta get upstairs before Tina and Darrel give away the whole damn bar. Oh, before I forget, I *did* hear some people talking about the one you pulled offa me last year and ashed."

"Upstairs? Here?" Father Molinari tensed.

"Yeah. Couple of young punks. I mean… I suppose they could've been discussin' some *other* guy with fangs and a sky-blue ten-inch Mohawk, but the eighties have been over for a long time."

"What did they say?"

Neil started to lift the bottle to his lips, but stopped with a grumble. "Not a lot. I caught a few snips of conversation while I had an armload of wings. Apparently, someone name o' Parrish is on the warpath over it. The way they talked about him, I got the feelin' he's like their boss or something. Fortunately, they didn't know me, so they probably won't track it back to you either."

"Argh!" said Sabine. "Stupid random encounters."

"Small miracles." Father Molinari returned his attention to the MacBook. "I am still amazed by this Internet. The libraries of the entire world at my fingertips, yet still there is nothing."

"Maybe you can hang out in some chat rooms, make friends with a conspiracy wonk or two? Info like you're searching for isn't the kind of thing people tend to post."

Father Molinari looked up. "Are these 'chat rooms' far from here?"

"Oh, man." Neil cringed.

"Got you." Father Molinari smiled. "But I am still not sure how to locate them."

Neil saluted with the beer bottle and jogged to the stairs. "I'll pop down tomorrow night and show you around."

"That would be much appreciated."

He settled in over the MacBook and resumed the laborious process of scouring the 'net for legitimate information on vampires. One link brought him to a website sporting red text on a black background.

Stylized thorn vines ran down both sides, with buds that swelled open to roses bearing menu text as he moused over them.

The site, 'The Blood Veil,' had the trappings of an online vampire-themed roleplaying board, where mortals pretended to be the accursed. He shook his head at the naiveté. *If any one of them knew what it was really like...* In the message forum, interspersed with an uncountable number of rules arguments between users and admins, a number of message threads appeared to contain truth disguised as references to the game. He skimmed over them, getting the distinct feeling the old guard in Europe still existed.

Some of the posts remarked about 'undisciplined Americans.' Though wrapped in the context of the fictional setting in which their game took place, the poster complained at how American vampires were anarchistic. He clicked on a reply titled 'they refuse the accord.'

The avatar of the poster resembled a girl he'd seen on posters advertising *Les Misérables*, only a teen. Her haunting, tragic eyes seemed familiar. On a whim, he clicked on a 'private message' link, but the site gave him an error about the feature only being available to registered users. He reached up to close the MacBook in a huff of annoyance, but changed his mind.

After searching around the page for a few minutes, he spotted a tiny 'register now' link at the top and muddled through the steps to set up a profile, using the name Caiaphas. He bypassed the 'upload character sheet' button, sandwiched between flashing red letters warning users that all characters had to be approved by admins before access to 'story forums' would be granted.

Fifteen minutes later, with a barebones profile, he again clicked on the private message link for 'TragicWaif81.' After thinking for a moment, he typed:

"The Americans do not honor the accord, even after you sent them a statue."

He minimized the browser and crawled through an article written by an 'archaeologist/historian' who maintained that Egyptian Pharaohs were, in fact, all vampires. Rubbish notwithstanding, he found it hilarious enough to keep reading for twenty minutes... at least until he got to the part where the man claimed Jesus had been a vampire, hence the 'resurrection.' He drummed his finger on the mouse, closing the browser window with disgust. Molinari stared at the desktop for some minutes, unable to decide what to do. Sabine cheered in whispers as her character in the game won another fight.

Ping.

The forum icon flashed, indicating activity. He clicked on it, causing the window to maximize. A box in the middle of the page indicated a new private message. He clicked 'read now.'

"I can't find a character sheet in your profile. How much you know about the accord would depend on your character's background. –TW."

He moved the mouse pointer over 'reply,' but a box popped up before he could click.

User TragicWaif81 would like to chat. Accept?

Father Molinari clicked yes.

‹ TW: Hi. Welcome to The Blood Veil.›

‹C: Hello. I noticed your post. Like any group of men who think they own the world, they have laws and decrees. Like mortals, they frown upon murder.›

‹TW: An interesting opinion.›

‹C: I may be mistaken, but I think it is yours.›

‹TW: The high priest who organized the plot to kill Jesus.›

‹C: I am impressed.›

‹TW: Don't be. I have the Internet.›

‹C: You've been nineteen for a long time.›

‹TW: A girl never tells her age.›

He smiled. ‹C: Sabine misses you.›

‹TW: ...›

‹C: Élodie?›

‹TW: Antonio?›

"Sabine, come here," said Molinari in a raised voice.

‹C: I am pleased you survived the wars.›

‹TW: The 1940s sucked... hard. Had a few close calls.›

"What is it, Father?" Sabine trotted around the table stack.

He waved her over and pointed at the screen. "I have found Élodie online, pretending to be a human pretending to be a vampire."

"*Mon Dieu! Élodie!*" Sabine jumped up and down. "How is she?"

‹C: Sabine is happy.›

‹TW: Do you have a cell phone?›

‹C: No. How is the climate?›

‹TW: Raining.›

‹C: Not what I mean.›

"Where is she now? What's she doing? Tell her the boat almost sank." Sabine grinned.

‹TW: I know. Things are messy, but at least I no longer have to keep my head down.›

‹C: Still trying to help Sabine. No luck. She wants to know where you're living now."

‹TW: It was you, wasn't it? In the late 60s. I'm in Paris.›

‹C: He attacked Sabine.›

‹TW: You did it then... if you beat him, you had to have...›

‹C: Jury is still out. Can you help?›

‹TW: I wish I could. No one has ever broken it. No one knows. Few even wish to speak of such a thing. All are quite happy being immortal.›

‹C: Please ask?›

‹TW: I will try.›

‹C: Thank you.›

A long number came through beginning with +33.

‹C: What is that?›

‹TW: Secure phone...›

Élodie walked him through downloading and installing a VOIP client. Fortunately, his MacBook had a built in microphone. Soon, Sabine and Élodie chatted in French almost too fast for his rusty command of the language to keep up. The former servant girl now existed among the wealthy elite of Paris, mingling with the fashion crowd and reinventing herself every twenty years with a new public name. She seemed to pick up on Sabine's weak grip of the passage of decades, and kept the conversation undetailed. At a few minutes past midnight, Élodie gasped at the time. Her clock read six in the morning. While she was at home, and safe from the sun, she would succumb to the sleep soon and wished to retire to her bed. They said their goodbyes. Sabine asked Élodie about Henri and Josephine. Father Molinari tensed, though Élodie said she hadn't seen them in a while but assumed they were okay. The answer appeared to satisfy the child, but she kept trying to ask questions to keep the conversation going. Her former servant politely excused herself and hung up.

Sabine cried, clinging to Molinari for about twenty minutes of sniffles. Heavy *thuds* and scraping chairs overhead announced a mild fistfight, which ended almost as soon as it started. He picked at the computer one handed, skimming a few other websites, but found only more of the same. Eventually, Sabine slid from his lap and returned to her game. Hours passed, website after website of uselessness. About ten of six in the morning, Sabine re-emerged from her little cubby behind the stack of tables wearing her ice blue *Frozen* pajamas. She padded over and tugged on his arm. The mere sight of the two cartoon faces on her chest put *that* song in his head. Fortunately, it had been at least a month since Sabine insisted on singing it all night long.

"Will you please read me a story?" She grinned.

Father Molinari closed the MacBook. "Of course."

He plucked a Kindle from the shelf to his left, and followed her to her bed, where he tapped the bookmark to jump to the beginning of *The Mouse and the Candle*. If not for them being in the basement of a bar, she'd have passed for a normal child in a normal bed.

"Father, do you think Sébastien is still in trouble?" She crawled under her blankets.

The 'boy' is probably creeping up on sixty by now. "I'm sure he's no longer grounded."

"Good." Sabine smiled. "I like him." After a moment, she took on a serious look. "I still don't want him to kiss me."

He chuckled.

Sabine swished her feet back and forth and frowned. "He's not a little boy anymore is he, Father?"

Molinari sat on the folding chair between the bed and the flat-panel monitor connected to her PS4. "No. He's grown up."

He braced himself for tears, a tantrum, or gloom.

"I want to grow up." She furrowed her eyebrows. "What are taxes and jobs?"

"Oh, so you *were* listening to Neil."

"He is as loud as ten moose." Sabine rolled her eyes.

After a brief explanation of taxes and jobs—which seemed not to deter her from her want—he held the Kindle up and read. Sabine smiled through the story, still reacting with shocked expressions and gasps whenever Philippe le petit almost got stepped on by a cow, crushed by a shovel, thrown in a bucket down the well, and when, at long last, he pulled himself up a towel the farmer had carelessly left draped over the kitchen table.

"There it was," said Father Molinari. "The candle which Philippe le petit had been gazing at for as long as he could recall. His furry little paws trembled as he touched it. Joy beyond his wildest dreams made his heart swell. And so, he dragged the great treasure to the edge of the table and threw it to the chair cushion. He jumped down and pushed it to the floor. From such a short distance, the wax did not break. Philippe le petit grabbed the wick with both hands, and scurried back into his dark home, a hole in the wall."

Sabine clapped.

"Philippe marched back and forth before the candle, wielding a match like the sword in the hand of a triumphant general. 'At last, I have brought light into my dark home,' he cried, and swung the match with a flourish over the floor. He raised the flame to the wick; his eyes grew wide with awe as the candle chased the shadows away."

"Father, isn't it dangerous to—"

Molinari held up his hand. "You asked me to read... It is rude to interrupt."

"Sorry," she whispered, half hiding her face with the blanket.

"Philippe le petit blew out the match. He leaned back and smiled at his victory over Jean-Claude. For so long, the man had withheld the light, but now, it was his. The man would not give him light; he had to take it. Soon, Philippe's joy became worry. For you see, the candle flame reached too close to the wood above. The mouse watched it blacken and smolder. Afraid, he tried to blow out the candle, but his little lungs were no match for the light he had so coveted. Fire spread over the ceiling of his little home."

"*Oh, non!*" She shivered.

"Thimbles of water did not help. Screaming did not help. It soon became clear to Philippe le petit that the candle did not like being taken. The great light would consume him."

"Run, Philippe, run!" yelled Sabine.

Father Molinari smiled and shushed her. "Philippe covered his mouth with his sleeve and darted into the man's part of the house. Above him, the entire wall blackened as the fire ate it from within. He ran as fast as he could to the door and dove for the gap at the bottom, but a great snore drew him back inside. Jean-Claude slept, unaware of the fire spreading through his home."

Sabine gasped and held a breath she didn't have need of.

"Smoke filled the little farmhouse, but Philippe le petit was unafraid. He raced up the bed sheets, stood on Jean-Claude's chest, and pulled on his beard. 'Jean-Claude,' squeaked the mouse. 'You must wake.' But, Jean-Claude kept snoring."

Sabine opened her mouth to blurt, but closed it. She drew the blanket up to her nose.

"'Jean-Claude!' shouted the mouse, yet still the man snored. Fire broke out along the ceiling. Philippe ran back and forth over the man's face, shouting his name over and over, yet still, the man slept. His great snores threatened to pull the mouse into his mouth. The cows and horses and chickens outside all shouted, yet still, Jean-Claude slept."

"Bite him!" yelled Sabine, her fangs growing. "*Oups!* Sorry."

"That's exactly what Philippe did." Father Molinari smiled, then cleared his throat. "The smoke came down from the ceiling, and it got very warm inside. Philippe looked at the door. He could save himself, but he did not want to be responsible for Jean-Claude's death. He leapt to the pillow and sank his sharp, mousy teeth into Jean-Claude's ear." He pinched her right earlobe and wiggled it.

"Ouch!" Sabine covered her ears.

"Jean-Claude awoke with a roar. He grabbed Philippe le petit who dangled by his teeth like a furry bit of jewelry, and bellowed, 'At last, I've caught you!' Jean-Claude started to crush Philippe in his hand, but the mouse pointed to the burning wall. '*Mon Dieu!*' shouted Jean-Claude. He ran outside only seconds before the house collapsed. 'Mouse,' said Jean-Claude, 'I owe you my life. I shall build a new house, and you are welcome in it.'"

Sabine smiled.

"Jean-Claude built a fine new home a short distance from where his old one had been. For many days, the mouse and the man lived as friends. Guilt weighed heavy on Philippe le petit. One day, the guilt became too great, and he decided to confess. 'I know how the fire started,' said Jean-Claude. 'But, you could have run out and left me to sleep. I still have my life, and a house is just a pile of wood.'" Father Molinari lowered the e-reader. "The end."

He stared at the Kindle, at the text describing Philippe le petit trapped in his home, burning to death, while the clueless Jean-Claude escaped after the ruckus of farm animals woke him. He looked up over the top of the device at Sabine. Her dark green eyes sparkled with adoration.

"Time to sleep now, *mon chéri.*"

He stood and started toward his bed.

"Father?"

"Yes?" he glanced back.

"I like the way you tell it better than what is on the page."

Father Molinari gawked at her as Sabine closed her eyes and went to sleep.

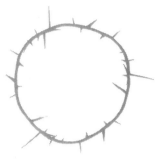

CHAPTER THIRTY-FOUR

ANOTHER STEP DOWN

June 20ᵗʰ 2014 New York City, New York

The harsh glare of artificial lights saturated the city, blotting out the stars and reducing the moon to a vague hint of a presence where clouds glowed from behind skyscrapers. A living river of people flowed along the sidewalk, serenaded by frequent blaring horns. It seemed no stretch longer than ten minutes could pass without the distant wail of a siren. Sabine had once been afraid to come to America because men 'shot each other from the backs of horses.' He sighed at the almost truth of it, though rather than horses, they shot each other in the dark of the city.

Perhaps God truly had given up on humankind.

Father Molinari followed the crowd, hands in his pants pockets. The suit jacket and dark slacks he'd gotten from a thrift store, the basic white shirt was a 'gift' from Sabine. She'd picked it out online, though he'd been the one to order it. His penny loafers were also new, another thing that magically appeared at Callahan's a few days after clicking a mouse. Part of him, the part that still clung to old, fading memories, missed talking to people and going to stores. The rest of him found relief in the ease with which this new way of shopping protected them.

His mind wandered to a little store in Paris, to an imposing, but beautiful woman who sold books. The fragrance of the place returned to him. He closed his eyes, lost in the deceptive sense of being elsewhere. Old paper, wood, the scent of paraffin, and the hint of food in the air from outside. He remembered her smile, her thick dark hair, blueberry and vanilla... the taste of her blood.

He kept his head down, smiling at the thought of Sabine's ever-increasing collection of clothes, shoes, dolls, and electronics. Her favorite, Véronique, she took greater care to protect. Seldom did she cling to it as she did at first. Did she realize the porcelain doll had become old and her dress fragile?

A red signal stalled the crowd at a corner. He huddled among them, stealing glances at faces lit by mobile phones. No one, not even a few preteens, took any notice of what stood among them. These days, he could bring Sabine out far later than he was comfortable doing. No one cared; if they did, they kept to themselves, not wanting to get involved. Two years ago, when they had first accepted Neil's offer to stay downstairs, she had locked herself out via the one-way door by the dumpsters.

New to the city, she'd managed to get herself lost merely trying to walk around the block. Not one person took notice of an eight-year-old out alone at close to two in the morning, until she walked in the front door of Callahan's.

Again, he thought of the doll and wondered if her gelatinous perception of time had solidified, or if while the events remained blurry to her, she had somehow gained understanding of age. She'd been inconsolable after Betty died, as though she had not witnessed Gaston's death. Despite the calico's passing being peaceful compared to Gaston—they had found her dead on the floor one evening without gasping or moaning—Sabine bawled and refused to eat for a few days.

And the mouse...

Father Molinari felt a bit like Philippe la petit himself. The light changed, and he moved with the crowd across the street. How long had Sabine known he'd changed the story? He remembered the first time he'd read it to her, trapped in a box with parts of the Statue of Liberty. She'd hated the ending... for all the little mouse's determination to make his dreams come true, a reward of a fiery death had made her cry. 'Ce n'est pas juste!' shouted a little girl's voice in his mind. His own lame reply, 'Not everything in life is fair,' taunted him from the corner of his memory.

The next night, as the boat rocked and swayed, she had asked him to read to her again, seemingly over her upset. When she picked that story again, he'd almost refused... but he had been unable to (and still couldn't) say no to those pleading green eyes. He'd done the next best thing—made up a new ending on the fly. *Does she know the words aren't quite the exact same thing each time? Does she wait for me to tell her the true story again? Is that why she keeps asking for that one?*

He grasped his cheek to hide an expected blood tear.

Perhaps she merely prefers the story of hope to a fable of what happens to fools who chase ill-conceived fancies? He slipped out of the busy street to a less-populated avenue. Cars and side streets passed as he pondered the connections his mind explored, uncomfortable with the idea of Sabine maturing mentally while her body remained that of a child. At the thought of preferring she remain innocent, he scowled.

I have no more right than Auguste to impose such a thing on her.

"God, grant me the clarity to see your plan." He traced his fingers over his chest, where his crucifix had hung for so long. People in this city reacted in strange ways to it. He couldn't imagine what 'flavor' had to do with wearing an eight-inch gold cross. "And the strength to carry it out."

The street, devoid of people, gleamed wet from rain that had ceased before sundown. Humid air saturated with the smell of trash and a lingering hint of food washed over him. He inhaled, savoring the fragrance of what had to be handmade marinara sauce. No mortal nose could have picked it out, and for a few seconds, he simultaneously enjoyed his abilities and lamented the dinner he could not have.

Thoughts of meals brought him back to the task at hand. He still did not much care to leave Sabine alone, though lately pulling her away from the 'video game' was quite the task. The girl had taken to feeding in Callahan's, in a back hallway by rooms reserved for special events and catering. Her use of mental influence had developed into a strong form of emotional manipulation. One look at her could have mortals paralyzed with 'aww.' Once rumors started of a child ghost haunting the inner rooms of the place, people wanted to go back there and look for themselves.

Sometimes, they saw her.

He ground his teeth at the thought. Did her streak of independence bother him? Was it even that, or was she only looking for an expedient feeding so she did not lose time from her game? Perhaps not as she always insisted he read to her at night. She often changed beds in the middle of the day, wanting to feel safe with his arm over her.

No, she was still a child.

A lazy child that will start rumors, which will force us to move. He picked up his pace, turned left into an alley, and set out to find a meal. As soon as he returned, he would ask her to stop feeding in the building, for no other reason than the practice attracted unnecessary attention. For now, people thought she was a ghost. He worried about the publicity. Once, a crew had come in with little handheld devices and asked questions of thin air. *I'm not sure what bothers me more. That they came looking for Sabine, or that they found something to talk to.*

He thought of Neil's suggestion of stealing blood from the hospital. The mere idea of it made him gag. They had tried that once in the early 1980s, and discovered it worse than hours' old cow blood. At least the cow's blood was not loaded with preservative chemicals. He'd rather gnaw on linoleum tile. Bags upon bags of it sat in hospitals and blood banks, but he'd sooner tear the heads from rats.

His stomach tightened similar to a mortal's sense of hunger. Blood was a vector, the liquid itself not the end, but a means to it. Similar to the way the acid within a battery held electricity, the blood carried a person's spiritual energy. The anima, the soul. Too long removed from the body, the life force faded, and the blood became stale and all but useless. It would keep a vampire from a final death, but weak, wretched, corpselike, and prone to blackouts as he had experienced when he killed Father Callini.

Father Molinari chose his food with care. Many out in the city at night had drugs or disease riddling their bodies. While the drugs did little to him but make the blood taste foul, the corruption of the soul so common in those individuals would alter his mood. Feeding from a man or woman who had lost the zeal to live left him in a similar state for hours.

Disease, on the other hand, would not affect him, but would linger for months inside his body. If Richmond had taught him anything, feeding from the soldiers had charged the blood inside him with what people now referred to as the flu. These days, they considered it a nuisance. The sickness he had brought from Camp Lee to Richmond proper in 1918 had been far more than a nuisance... despite not understanding what he had done at the time, the thought of it still came with heavy guilt. It may not have *all* been his doing; the flu would likely have spread like a brushfire without any help from vampire fangs. Still, he might have made things worse. How many of those from whom he'd fed perished because his meal had weakened them?

He avoided convenience stores with cameras. Each time he peered into a bright white space full of shelves, he laughed to himself about the mirror thing. Certainly they worked on him, and so too did cameras. Leaving a recording of his image was something he had grown rather paranoid about. A few alleys over, and still no closer to an explanation for how the whole 'vampires don't have reflections' thing started, he spotted a pair of police officers.

Two men leaned against the front fender of their car, enjoying coffee and complaining about the Mets. Father Molinari approached along the sidewalk, careful to stay out of view of the little camera on the dashboard.

"Perhaps they've got too much faith in deGrom," said Molinari. "I still don't think even someone of his abilities can save the Mets."

"Say what?" The closer cop pushed away from the car. His stance seemed aggressive, but he smiled. "They're already takin' bets he'll make rookie of the year."

"Whoa, slow that shit down, Chuck." The shorter policeman ambled over. "He's only been playing a month."

Father Molinari smiled. "A moment of your time, gentlemen."

The cops froze in place, staring dumbfounded at him.

He lifted coffees from their hands, which remained poised as if holding something, and set them on the trunk of the car. Molinari fed from one officer, then the next. Their blood tasted similar to steak; he had not consumed beef in so long, he'd forgotten where he'd last had it. Unexpectedly, it also carried fear. Curiosity piqued, he looked into their thoughts. Despite their outward bravado, both men grappled with doubt, a worry that any day might be the one they didn't get to go home.

When he finished, he reposed their hands around the coffee cups, and walked away. Twenty seconds later, their discussion of the Mets' newest pitcher resumed as though he'd never been there. Between the two, he'd fed enough to keep him for at least a week. He lowered his head, muttering a quiet prayer asking God to keep watch over them.

Molinari circled back in the direction of Callahan's, pulled by his increasing discomfort at leaving Sabine alone. Intermittent chats with Élodie had picked open a scab. The young woman walked the line between innocence and darkness. Though she had opined the Conclave had long since forgotten about him and Auguste, he found himself unwilling to believe it. Perhaps they had. Yves may have been the driving force behind the decree of destruction. Could they be even more incensed with him for destroying Yves? Certainly, even creatures such as vampires would recognize the act of self-defense.

If she had wanted to lure them back to Europe as some manner of offering to gain political power, would she not have suggested all was well and they should return? Maybe... or perhaps she feared that too indelicate and worried too much enthusiasm would arouse suspicion. Of course, she had helped them leave Europe in the first place, to escape the same group. It pained him to think the darkness could change someone to that degree.

Maybe I am the one that has changed? Perhaps Élodie is still the tragic waif. Hmm. Tragic Waif 81. 1881? The year she was turned. It matters not. I much rather an ocean stay between us and the Order.

The scent of blood distracted him from his thoughts. Curious, he walked into the wind, tracking the source a few blocks over. A body in a dark blue business suit lay half concealed in a pile of trash bags wedged between two overflowing dumpsters. The man appeared to be in his middle thirties with hints of Middle Eastern features. His purple silk tie dangled, torn, as was his shirt. The front and left side of his neck bore a gaping wound deep enough to expose a bit of spine. In spite of the massive hole, the amount of blood in the area looked minimal.

Father Molinari's ears twitched at a jingle of keys to the right. Footsteps, a casual stroll, became clear as he focused his attention in that direction. He moved up to a trot, following the rattling of tiny metal slivers.

"Come on, where is it?" A figure moved out of a side street, doubling back on his route. Brown ropey dreadlocks, gathered in a tangled mass at the back of his head, swayed with his stride. His black leather jacket creaked as he raised his hand, squeezing buttons on a small box attached to a bundle of keys. "It's gotta be close. Dammit."

"Lose something?" asked Father Molinari.

The kid, he couldn't have been older than twenty, jerked a handgun from the back of his jeans and aimed at him. He held it sideways and high up, with the barrel angled down.

"Yo, fuck off, dude."

Molinari locked eyes with him. The young man's thoughts floated back, a step removed from his ability to see as if protected by a thin bubble. At once, he knew him to be a vampire... and a weak one at that. New, but charged with the energy of a recent feeding.

"Quite careless of you, Kyle." Father Molinari flashed a patronizing smile and walked closer. The scent of eastern incense clung to the young man. "Anyone could find him."

"Fuckin' nuts, man." Kyle adjusted his hold on the gun, aiming it properly. "Glock .45 says proceed with the offing of fuck."

"You're not going to shoot me, Kyle. Put the gun down."

The punk clenched and released his grip on the weapon.

Father Molinari shook his head. "There is no need to kill when you feed."

Kyle blinked. "Yo, I ain't never seen you before. What kinda crazy you talkin'?"

"Skip the ruse." Molinari showed his fangs. "If you litter the streets with bodies, you'll soon find that playing coy won't help."

"Shit, man." Kyle let his arm drop, rattling several bracelets of wooden beads. A moment later, he stuck the weapon back in his belt. "Don't do that crap. I almost shot your ass."

"And?" Father Molinari raised an eyebrow. "All that would've done is made noise."

"Fuck noise." Kyle laughed. "People 'round here don't notice shit. So, what are you, like the litter pig? Gonna give me a 'talkin' to' for leavin' an empty lying around?"

"Well, that's one thing." He glanced down the alley toward the body. "For another, there's no need to kill them."

"Yah mon." Kyle raised his hands in a gesture of 'so what.' "But it's funner that way."

Molinari frowned. "There's nothing fun about taking a life."

"Come on... You're fuckin' wit' me. This is... Kathy put you up to this, didn't she? Yank the new blood's chain or some shit?" Kyle laughed.

"I am not here to do anything to your 'chain.' It is a simple matter to sense the ebb and flow of life while feeding, and know when you approach that point where you must stop."

Kyle scoffed. "I used ta do all sorts o' shit, but the purest smack ain't nothin' compared to how it feels to glide through dat membrane. S'like their life breaks free of their body with the force of an atomic bomb. When I'm slurpin' up all that energy, I can eat the sun. I am the world."

"God would be saddened by your callous disregard for human life."

"Hah!" Kyle swiped a hand under his nose. "God? Right? Now I *know* you're fuckin' with me."

"Do you have a little feeling or voice in the back of your head tempting you? That is Satan trying to pull you away from God." Father Molinari reached into his back pocket and pulled out a metal cigarette pack case.

"Are you for real, man?" Kyle held his arms out to the sides and puffed his chest. "We're vampires. God is just bullshit, dude. Some asshole Roman made the whole thing up. It's all"—he tapped two finger to his temple—"mind control."

"I fear it may be too late for you, Kyle. If you will not restrain yourself from killing everyone you feed from out of fear for your soul or respect for God, do so to keep our existence a secret. There are people out there who hunt us."

"Kathy sent you." Kyle stomped about. "I already told her I got this vampire thing down. We are the masters of the world. Humans are like fruit on the motherfuckin' vine. They so clueless, man. Just there for the taking." He laughed. "You should'a seen the look on that dude's face when he saw my fangs."

Father Molinari opened the case, threaded his finger around a string of beads, and held up a rosary with a small, pewter crucifix at the bottom a few inches below his hand. The trinket spun clockwise, paused, and rotated the other way. He held it up.

"I charge thee before God, and the Lord Jesus Christ, who shall judge both the living and the dead."

Heat radiated from the spot below his hand, both warming and threatening.

Kyle recoiled, raising his arms. The skin on his hands and face smoked; he screamed. The punk leapt back, fangs bared, eyes glowing, and hissed.

"To what sad state has the world arrived that one who is not yet a month removed from the presence of God has given himself so completely to the darkness."

Kyle growled, and charged.

Father Molinari raised the rosary. "Satan has no power over those who repudiate sin."

"Gah!" Kyle covered his face. He swerved to the side and crashed into the unyielding wall of a skyscraper. After a few seconds of moaning, he scrambled through a stack of wooden pallets and stood. "It burns! What the fuck you doin'?"

"Showing you the fate that awaits you if you continue down the path of darkness." Father Molinari dropped the rosary into the case. "Dwell among mortals as invisibly as you can. If you cannot resist killing because it is the right thing to do, resist it out of fear for your own existence."

"Is that a threat?" Kyle seized a pallet and hurled it like a massive shuriken.

Molinari leapt to the side. The wooden square shattered against the building behind him.

"You're fast for an old man." Kyle leaned forward with a diabolic grin. He licked at his fangs, lips flickering between menacing leer and smile. "That burning shit *hurt*. Time for a little payback."

Kyle ran at him again, jumping into a claw-tipped tackle. Father Molinari slipped to the right, evading him like a matador. The young man skidded to a halt before kissing another building. The instant he spun around, Molinari pounced, grabbing him by the arms and pinning him against the wall. The younger man squirmed and howled, trying to break loose.

"I am trying to help you, Kyle." Molinari glared. "It was once my sworn duty to destroy those who could not be saved. I have not forgotten my vows. You will cease your wanton killing."

The punk thrust his face forward, trying to bite him. Molinari leaned back; Kyle's teeth snapped closed with a hard *click*.

"After I kick your ass, I'm gonna go work out my frustration. Find some nice little high-end place in Brooklyn Heights and have an entire family for dinner." Kyle grinned, and rammed his forehead into Molinari's nose.

Father Molinari staggered back a step, but recovered his bearings in time to catch Kyle as he leapt. He swung the young man around and flung him face-first against the skyscraper, creating a *slap* that echoed three times through the concrete canyon. The punk bounced away and landed flat on the pavement, wheezing. Blood welled through the fingers of a hand he clamped over his mouth.

A large scrap of pallet wood with a sharp point caught Molinari's eye.

"Fuck, man. You broke my goddamn fang."

"Thou shalt not"—Father Molinari picked up the wood, tossed it up, caught it with the point facing down, and jumped on top of Kyle. He rammed the impromptu stake through the front of the leather jacket—"take the name of thy Lord God in vain."

Kyle's body immolated to a dusty cloud of light grey ash in a hair less than four seconds. Molinari took a knee and recited the Last Rites over the swirls of dust carried off in the breeze. He spent a moment staring at the handgun. It, and the soles of Kyle's sneakers, were all that had survived the burn. Back and forth, he replayed the fight in his mind. How simple it had been to maintain the upper hand. The feeling plagued him still, noticeably more subdued. *It tempts me not to take a first step upon the path to damnation, but another.*

Father Molinari sat in quiet reflection for a while, wondering if the ease with which he bested the new vampire had been how Yves had felt throwing him around. What path did God guide him on that he sliced away a part of his soul? Had he not, the fiend would have killed them both, and only after torturing Sabine for hours. The memory of her pitiful begging brought shaking to his fists.

Forgive me Lord for I could not save this young man. Lost was his soul; gone was his regard for life. His carelessness would have brought the Order to New York. As you commanded me in Quebec, again I had to protect the child, and whatever other innocents his path may have crossed.

He stood, brushed ash from his pant legs, and picked up the Glock.

"I should not leave this here..."

A narrow aluminum thermos in his right hand complicated the task of opening the door leading to Callahan's basement. The heavy plastic bag in his left bumped against his leg as he made his way downstairs. The music from the PlayStation ceased a few seconds before Sabine peered around the stack of folding tables. Her wary glance became a broad grin, and she ran over. His heart swelled at the sight of her safe. In the midst of one of her 'lazy days,' she hadn't bothered to change from the shin-length blue tee shirt she'd slept in. A whimsical yellow bunny on her chest had its head tilted to the side.

"There were people looking for the ghost." Sabine giggled into her hands. "I wanted to scare them, but I did as you asked."

He smiled and handed her the thermos. "Drink quick. It is almost fifteen minutes old."

Sabine flipped up the straw-like top and sipped. "Mmm. It's sweet. A woman? Is she pretty?" She took another sip and smiled. "I think so. She tastes nice and caring."

"Considering where I met her, that is understandable." Father Molinari stuck his hand in the outside pocket of his suit jacket. "I brought you something else."

Her eyes widened with gratitude as her cheeks sank in from sucking on the straw. Air hissed through the tiny hole in the thermos lid.

Father Molinari withdrew his hand, and presented her a little beige kitten. The animal leaned forward in his palm, as if trying to get closer to her already.

"Mmm!" She coughed and a trickle of blood ran out of her nose. "He is adorable! Thank you!"

"You do not seem yourself without a cat around." He winked.

She hugged him. He patted her shoulder and prayed in his head, asking God to keep her from sensing the change in him. After setting the kitten on the floor, he put a large bag of dry cat food down and went to his workstation.

Sabine flopped in place, legs wide, petting and playing with the new arrival while she upended the thermos with her other hand. Watching her warmed his soul, and eased the worry nibbling at his heart. He did not seek darkness, nor did he crave power. The gradual erosion of his qualms worried him most. It began the night Yves attacked. He no longer cared what he had to do in order to protect his child.

She set the empty thermos down and gathered the kitten to her chest. For a while, she lay flat on her back, letting the cat prance around on top of her. Sabine's giggling mixed with the delicate *mews* he made every so often. Father Molinari thanked God for this time with her. This existence of theirs was not so bad after all.

"Father." Sabine, still lying on the floor, held the kitten up over her face. She made a series of coos, eliciting another *mew*. "I will name him *Crème*."

Warmth spread through his heart; he took his seat behind his computer and smiled. "That is a perfect name."

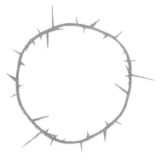

CHAPTER THIRTY-FIVE

EMISSARY

August 9th 2014 New York City, New York

The MacBook flickered and went dark. Molinari pulled his finger back from the power button and rubbed his face. Another chat with Élodie further confused the issue of the Conclave. He decided to stop dancing around it and asked her if Yves's death had caused problems. It had, but none directed his way. A group of Yves's lessers, almost fifty years later, still quibbled over who would take his place in the social hierarchy.

They knew Yves had gone to Canada to destroy him, and evidently, many had *felt* the elder's death. He'd read and re-read Élodie's explanation of its chilling effect. Some could not believe he defeated Yves, while others did and now feared him. His doubts regarding her intentions settled when she suggested no further harm would come to him if he remained in America. There, he was not a threat to their order.

Of course, this suited him just fine.

Sabine ran about, chasing *Crème*, ribbons in her hair and wearing a gossamer, pleated babydoll top with black capris covered in quarter-sized Hello Kitty heads. The patter of her barefoot pursuit circumnavigated the basement.

He'd had enough of computers for one night. Neil suggested he try a game to break the boredom, though the first suggestion, some game involving World War II and tanks, soured the topic completely. Molinari thought it wrong to make entertainment of such a tragic time in history, and launched further into a grumble at how so many video games glorified war and killing. Even the little girl character in Sabine's favorite game ran about with a sword fighting monsters.

Neil laughed it off, saying 'they're just games,' but Molinari had not relented.

Sabine ran up to him, holding *Crème* tight to her chest and looking worried. "Someone's coming, and it doesn't sound like Neil."

He focused his attention upward. Sure enough, the click of a woman's high-heeled shoes crossed the room overhead in the direction of the cellar entrance. Sabine crawled under the table and scooted against the wall, hiding behind his chair. The door opened with the *squeak* of a dying hinge, and a red shoe with a four-inch heel landed on the first step.

Father Molinari raised an eyebrow when shapely legs moved into view, as though someone had poured milk into the form of a woman. The hem of a red skirt-suit, quite far up her thigh for his comfort, followed. She navigated the steps as if born in such impractical footwear, pausing at the landing to appraise her surroundings.

Red hair with a hint of curl draped over her shoulders, cut even with her elbows. A frilly white shirt collar poked out of her jacket, accented with a tiny, pink flower that might have been carved from kunzite. She looked in her later twenties, and carried herself as though quite used to getting whatever she wanted. Sapphire eyes locked on him, and she smiled.

Crème hissed and spat.

"Well, well..." The woman approached to within three strides and put her hands on her hips. "I thought those Vatican fools had a hunter sniffing around, but... never could I have imagined they'd have the balls to use an 'inside man.'"

Sabine lost her fight to hold *Crème*; the animal became a yowling, beige streak, which disappeared into the back of the cellar.

"Inside man?" Molinari slipped a hand into his pocket, grasping the cigarette case. The big crucifix sat above and behind him on a shelf, covered with loose papers and notes from decades of fruitless research. "I'm not sure what you're talking about."

"Before I twist you in half, I'd love to hear how they convinced you to allow yourself to be turned." The woman's pink-painted lips glistened with high gloss; fangs peeked through her smile.

A presence weighed upon the forefront of his consciousness. The woman's eye twitched, yet the pressure seemed no greater than a person leaning against a wall.

"Interesting," she said. "You are either a unique situation or much older than I thought."

Father Molinari held up one hand. "Whoever you are, I think you have been misinformed. The Vatican did not encourage me to become a vampire. Quite the opposite. I am convinced they would prefer to 'save' my soul with a bit of wood rather than have me do their bidding."

"I don't like her," whispered Sabine.

"What's that?" The woman stooped enough to peer under the table. "Oh, how precious. I thought priests preferred boys."

Father Molinari sprang from the chair and grabbed at her. The woman was fast, but not so much faster. He snagged a fistful of her jacket and glared into her eyes.

Sabine let out a short scream.

An inkling of fear appeared in her expression. "A bad joke."

"Do not insinuate me capable of such diabolism."

"You *are* older than I thought." The woman grasped his wrist and worked his fingers free of her jacket. "Must you? This is Versace."

Father Molinari cocked an eyebrow. "You named your jacket?"

The woman rolled her eyes. "Do you live in a bubble?"

"No, a basement." He took a step back.

"Forgive my intrusion then." She offered a hand bearing a ruby rose ring. "My name is Katherine Parrish, and I run things here."

"'Run things?'" He shook her hand. "You'll forgive me. The only rings I kiss are on the hands of cardinals or popes."

She narrowed her eyes. "Didn't you just say—"

"The Church may have no further use for me, but my fealty lies only with God."

"I see." Katherine opened her jaw a touch, but kept her lips closed. After a moment, she chuckled. "Among our kind, I am the one who decides how things happen in this city."

"You were... elected?" Molinari smiled. "I did not think American vampires had any sense of organization."

"I saw what I wanted, and took it." She cast a glance about the room, emitted a faint scoff, and paced. "Given your age, I will grant you some slack. America is not Europe."

"I know that, and I'm eight," muttered Sabine.

"Adorable." Katherine spun, sending a smile and finger wave at the child. "I suppose to them, we're still the Wild West. They would find it unthinkable to seize a position of power by overt force. They much prefer their backstabbing and political manipulation. At least we have the balls to let our enemies see us."

"I hadn't thought any semblance of... 'law' existed among our kind here. How many of us are there in the city?"

"Not many... two dozen perhaps, and it's not the same everywhere. Florida is an absolute nightmare." Katherine approached the table. "Come here, child. Let me have a look at you."

Sabine backed out the other side, stood, and flattened herself against the wall. Her toes whitened from their grip on the floor.

"Oh, sweetie, I'm not going to hurt you."

"Please leave us alone," said Sabine.

Crème hissed from deep inside the basement. Molinari twitched as someone broke a rack at pool upstairs.

"I did not think it even possible to make a vampire of someone so young." Katherine took a step closer to her.

"Please give her space." Father Molinari put himself between them. "I'm quite protective."

Katherine frowned. "What tortured soul did this to such a small child?"

Sabine, her unblinking stare locked on the woman in red, ducked to cross under the table, and clung to Father Molinari's arm.

"It's a long story, and I'm not sure I'm inclined to share it with someone who came here intending to kill me."

"Respect is reciprocal," said Katherine. "I can make existence here easy for you, or difficult. Your man Neil upstairs had some rather interesting memories. You destroyed Samuel while wielding a cross. Of course, I assumed you were an adversary. I am impressed at your sleight of hand. Neil never saw the UV lamp."

"What is a UV lamp?" Father Molinari tilted his head.

"What did you do to Neil?" Sabine yelled.

"Nothing, girl. He's fine." Katherine looked from her to Molinari. "She is absolutely adorable. When did you make her?"

Sabine looked down.

Father Molinari pulled her close with a hand at the back of her head. "I didn't turn her."

"But I can feel the bond..." Katherine glanced back and forth between them for a few seconds; her eyes widened. "You... Oh, I simply *must* hear this."

"Are you going to fight?" Sabine's fingers clenched into his clothes.

"That depends on the story you have to tell, but I am almost ready to believe you." Katherine appropriated the folding chair Neil always used, and crossed her legs.

"Very well." Father Molinari sat in his usual spot and pulled Sabine into his lap, both arms wrapped about her. "I once *did* work for the Vatican... but that was many years ago."

Katherine seemed moved. Blood tears gathered at the corners of her eyes at several points during Molinari's explanation, though they did not fall. Sabine stared at her the whole time. Her heart raced under his hand.

"So you've spent all your time hiding, trying to break her curse?" Katherine smoothed her skirt. "I hate to be the bearer of bad news, but this is a one way trip."

Father Molinari forced through the shadows of doubt. "I have to believe that He will welcome us into the light. Through Him all things are possible."

"Well, who am I to come between a religious man and his delusions." Katherine stood. "You have convinced me you are not the hunter I thought you were. Your church has someone in the area." She started away, but turned back. "Oh, if you ever get tired of dealing with a child, I'd love to take her for a while. A little girl needs a woman in her life."

Sabine leaned back, whispering, "*Je n'ai pas confiance en elle.*"

Crème's hiss came from farther away in the dark.

Katherine scowled with a hint of playfulness at the girl. "Did not your father tell you it's rude to speak a language around people who don't understand?"

"But I did not want you to understand me." Sabine glared.

"Aww." Katherine smiled. "She is too cute."

"There was a new vampire killing people left and right... If you are wondering why there is a hunter in the area, that would be the cause. He should not be a problem anymore. If, as you say, you have sway over the rest of our kind in this city... I think you should have them keep to themselves for a while, and the Church will lose interest."

Katherine's eyes flared open, a hint of azure light flickered within. "*You* destroyed Kyle?"

"I gave him every chance. He was taken by shadow and bloodlust. I warned him he should not kill every time he feeds. The boy was an addict, first to mortal drugs, and then to the final spark of another's lifeblood. When he would not see reason, I had no choice. He would have left a trail of bodies the Order would follow straight to your doorstep."

"You're right." Katherine narrowed her eyes. "The hunter will not be a problem. As for what you did to Kyle..." Her heels *clicked* as she crossed the basement. The way she walked, placing her feet in front of each other, made her butt sway. She paused at the bottom of the stairs to wave at Sabine. "I'll come back to visit you soon, sweetheart."

Crème hissed.

Katherine ascended the stairs. A moment later, the pointed *tap tap tap* of her stride crossed overhead.

Sabine looked up. "Are we moving again?"

"I fear we must, lest things escalate. It would not be fair to Neil or his family for us to endanger them. Though, I wonder if I should try and send a warning."

Crème scurried out of hiding and climbed Molinari's leg.

Sabine picked him up. "Warn who?"

"The priest Katherine is going to kill. I'm not sure the Order knows what they're getting involved with here. Almost thirty vampires... when I was alive, the idea of dealing with *one* kept me up all night. It seems a sin not to at least try to convince him to flee."

"Won't the bad priests try to kill you again?" Sabine looked down, petting *Crème* and whispering reassuring things to him in French.

He tapped a finger against his lips for a few minutes, thinking. "Perhaps you are right. It may be best for him not to become aware of us. He would likely force a conflict I have no interest in. God forgive me, but I think it better for us to slip away. We shall begin packing tomorrow, and I will figure out where we are going. Until we leave, it would be best if we do not venture outside for any reason."

"You will feed in our home?" She tilted her head, making a face of mock accusation.

Father Molinari thought. Between the primary restrooms upstairs, Callahan's had a single-person room rigged for wheelchair-bound patrons. It would be a simple matter to confound someone, take blood in private, and send them on their way.

"For a little while. It is still risky, but I fear such measures are necessary for the time being."

Sabine nodded. "I am frightened of that woman, Father. I do not like her. And I will miss Neil, but I do not want him to get hurt. Can we live in a place that is not so loud? *Crème's* ears tick whenever the table game cracks."

"Nor do I." He squeezed her tight, and buried his face in her voluminous hair. "As to the ambiance, I am sure we can figure out something. If only *Crème's* sake."

She giggled when he kissed her atop the head.

He rocked her, taken by a surge of love and protectiveness. It soothed him to think that despite Sabine's age, the child had no concept she could become more powerful than Katherine at the mere wanting... for the low, low price of her immortal soul.

By God, I will not allow it.

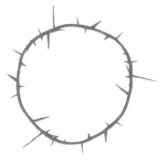

CHAPTER THIRTY-SIX

A FATHER'S LOVE

August 11ᵗʰ 2014 New York City, New York

I **dreamed of the sun yesterday," said Sabine. "I was at home** with *Maman*, and we ran in the garden. She told me not to be afraid." Father Molinari shut off the Kindle and kissed her on the forehead. "Sleep well, my child. May your head be filled with happy dreams again."

"Good night, Father." She smiled, and closed her eyes.

He watched her for a few minutes, praying in silence for God to protect her. Soon, the tug of dawn pulled at his consciousness. Molinari forced himself to stand and staggered to his bed about ten paces from hers, along the same wall, but separated by a modest freestanding cubby. Rather than books, games and DVDs packed the shelves. He'd never get used to that.

He stared past his feet at it as the pillow engulfed his head. *Shelves are for books.*

The blank void of vampiric repose devoured his mind.

Sabine's high-pitched scream hit his brain like a knitting needle through the ears.

"It's awake," whisper-shouted a man. "We should have come at noon. This is reckless."

A different man coughed into his hand. "You're the one who objected to breaking in while the place was closed. We could've dealt with the man then, and waited."

"This is not the time! We are to bring the child to her alive. Even now, it may be light enough to harm her." Another voice grunted in time with Sabine's whimpering. "I got it. The little one's not very strong."

Father Molinari tried to force his eyes open, but his lids clamped down like leaden blankets.

"Are you sure it's one of them?" asked a different man.

The unmistakable sound of a hand muffling a child's scream shot a surge of energy through Molinari's limbs. His eyes snapped open and he sat upright.

"God save us, the other one's moving," yelled a man in black, abandoning all pretense of stealth.

Of three men in the garb of priests, one grabbed Sabine about the chest with a hand on her face while the second fought to contain her kicking legs. Her *Frozen* pajama shirt pulled up in the struggle, exposing her belly. The last man raised a four-inch silver crucifix at Molinari.

"Back, fiend. God commands it!"

The presence of divinity washed over him like a wave of boiling fresh-brewed tea. It hurt, but he did not smolder... much.

"Sabine!" shouted Molinari. "You do not understand. She is innocent. I will not let you!"

He lunged at the cross-bearer. The too-early hour left his limbs wooden and burdened. The priest caught him by the shirt and wrestled him to a standstill. He grabbed at the intruder's neck, fighting to get past him while the other two hauled Sabine into the air.

Crème leapt on one, but the teeth and claws of an adolescent cat had little effect. The man yelled and kicked, launching the animal away. Sabine screamed into the hand on her mouth. Blood seeped through the priest's fingers.

"The fiend bit me!" yelled the priest.

"Leave *Crème* alone!" shouted Sabine. "He is just a cat! You are—"

The hand clamped over her mouth again.

Snarling, Father Molinari tried to force himself to wake. The vampire in Vienna never made it out of his bed. Desperate panic seized him at the thought the burden of the hour would render him unable to protect her. He wrenched to the side, and hurled the man grappling with him to the floor. Unsteady legs gave out, and he collapsed next to him.

"Go, go, go!" yelled the one holding Sabine's legs.

Father Molinari dragged himself after them as they rushed to the stairs. Two thoughts clashed in his head. One, they lacked the ability to plunge a stake into the heart of a little girl, and believed the sun would be a more peaceful way to destroy her. Two, the rarity of a child vampire piqued their interest and they wished to poke and prod and test and torture.

Wait; what? She wants the kid alive... Parrish! He roared and pulled his feet under him.

Before he could get upright, the third priest jumped on his back and knocked him flat. A searing crucifix pressed into the side of his head. Sabine's shrieking drew distant as heavy footfalls clambered up the stairs.

Molinari snarled, feeling rage swell into his eyes, imparting them with a deep red glow. He drove his elbow backward, smashing it into the priest's head and knocking him away. He scrabbled at the floor, dragging himself upright, and sprinted for the stairs. The door at the top was not locked, though it refused to open. Still, Sabine's muffled screams reached his ears. Molinari bashed through the door, splintering the chair that had been wedged under the knob and sending bits of wood skittering across the bar.

The scent of gunpowder lingered in the air, lofted on wispy clouds of smoke. Neil slumped over the bar, alive but bleeding from the temple, a revolver a few inches from his hand. A trail of spilled drinks, upended chairs, and askew tables led to the wide-open front door. Molinari sprinted past the billiard area and bee-lined through the room, knocking furniture out of his way rather than going around it.

Car doors slammed outside, where the last vestiges of orange-purple sunlight drained out of the sky.

He had not seen the sun, or any hint thereof, for over a century, but the majesty of fading orange in the west did not dawn on him. Without hesitation, he careened out the door onto the sidewalk, and slipped through a hard left turn toward Callahan's parking lot. A white Mercedes cargo van backed into the front bumper of Neil's green Honda in their haste to flee. Molinari ran after it, squinting at the brightness overhead. Somewhere between the heavy clouds and tall buildings, the daystar weakened enough to cause only pinpricks of discomfort on his face.

The third priest came thundering up behind him. Molinari spun about, desiring speed. The man's rushing charge dragged down to a stall. Arms and legs moved as if in slow motion, face warped in a cry of determination. Molinari caught the raised arm attempting to bring a stake down at his heart, and redirected it into the priest's own chest. The stunned man, Italian by looks and not yet thirty, gurgled up blood and collapsed.

Molinari snapped his gaze back to the street, spotting the van in the distance. A matching white Mercedes sedan remained in the lot. He ripped the priest's pockets off, praying he was the one with the keys for the car. When a fob bearing the Mercedes logo clattered to the paving, he grabbed it and rushed to get in. After losing a few seconds hunting for a keyhole, he spotted a button labeled 'start,' and pushed it. The car started, engine barely audible. He smoked the tires backing out of the spot, cut the wheel, and drove over the dead priest's legs on his way out onto the street.

Horns blared; three cars plowed into parked vehicles and trashcans across from Callahan's as he lurched into traffic. Pedal down, he ran a red light and skidded through a right turn a block later.

"God, please... Guide me."

Ahead, the van weaved lanes, emerging from in front of a metro bus. Molinari rammed a taxi out of its lane and accelerated. A cart full of street meat, papers, and condiments went flying as the cabbie lost control and jumped the sidewalk. Molinari sped up, managing to force himself not to bump a motorcyclist. The van swerved to the right, cutting off a number of small cars while careening through a hard turn that tilted it on two wheels for a few seconds.

Molinari's car skimmed off an old Buick that tried to pull out, and fishtailed around the same corner.

"Please, God. Keep her calm. Give her the strength not to repeat my mistake. Don't let her give herself to the shadow. Let her know I am coming."

He laid on the horn to warn pedestrians as van and car shot through another red light. Something clipped his rear bumper, knocking his car around in a 360 degree spin, but his tires gripped at a miraculously well-timed instant, and propelled him straight again. Two blocks later, other drivers steered for cover, opening a clear stretch of road between them, and he gunned it. His face bounced off the steering wheel when he drove into the van's rear bumper. The boxy thing changed lanes fast enough to totter up on two wheels again. The driver overcorrected, and it came down hard, swerving to one side and going up on the other pair seconds later.

A police car whipped around the corner up ahead, lights ablaze. The van didn't attempt to slow down, t-boning the cruiser and sending it spinning into a shrouded bus stop bench, which folded like a house of cards. Molinari anticipated a turn coming when the crazed priest in front of him made a rapid two-lane change to the left. He swerved after it, accelerating.

He drove into the rear corner of the van as they pulled into the turn, slamming it hard enough to send the back wheels skidding faster than the front. His car stopped dead in the road on impact while the van spun through the curve and slid sideways into a streetlamp post with a deafening *whump* of bending metal.

Molinari reached for the door handle, but the van pulled away. He cranked the wheel and got his car moving again. For minutes, they weaved through thick traffic. Their reckless demolition derby created a snarl of cars and cursing behind them, which bogged down a handful of police cruisers trying to chase them. The van pulled a hard left onto 5th avenue, nearly bowling down a group of pedestrians.

He pursued, taking the turn wide to avoid the scattering people, downshifted, and stomped on the gas pedal. The battered Mercedes purred and pinned him to the seat. Central Park shot by on the right. The van dodged buses, cars, and pedestrians at over sixty miles an hour. Seconds later, the blurry grey of city replaced the park green. Molinari's desperation grew. Someone's blue paper cup struck the windshield, belching a spray of pale coffee across his vision. Molinari fumbled for the wipers. Any second now, Sabine could fear enough for her life to give in to Satan.

I will not allow it.

The engine roared as he focused on the van. Seventy. Eighty. Ninety. The boxy white doors came up faster than he expected. *Wham.* This time, the airbag went off in his face, though it may as well have been a pillow slapping him. His car wobbled along at a mere twenty miles per hour after the collision. The van squealed in a serpentine, leaving black squiggles on the road as it went up on the curb, where its nose crumpled around a metal streetlamp. With an eruption of sparks, the pole collapsed downward, crimping the van's roof.

Grinding came from the front end of his car when he tried to accelerate. He flung the door open and bailed out, rushing on foot down the street. Some people screamed, some ran, and others held up mobile phones. The sight of the building beyond the crash site terrified him as much as it filled him with longing.

Saint Patrick's Cathedral.

Molinari sprinted up behind the van, and tore the twin doors from their hinges as though they were aluminum foil. He flung the twisted scraps of metal to the road. His heart slammed in his chest at the sight before him.

Sabine, bound hand and foot, huddled in the front corner, her back pressed to a partition separating the cargo area from the seats. One priest hovered over her with a stake raised. Blood oozed down his face from a smashed nose and a cut over his eye. He swayed on his knees as if in a trance. The child squirmed and struggled at the rope, not taking her eyes off her assailant. His arm shuddered; the guilt she undoubtedly forced into his mind stayed his hand.

A yell to the left snapped Molinari's gaze to the priest who had been driving. The man, bleeding from the mouth, pulled a short cutlass out from behind the seat and held it aloft.

"In the name of God, I send you—"

Molinari pounced before the priest took two steps. Rage consumed him. The pathetic look on Sabine's face made his blood boil. He palmed the man's skull in one hand and caught his sword arm in the other. Fingertips cracked into bone. With a snarl, he lifted the priest off the ground by his skull and gave it a wrenching twist, shattering the man's neck. He flung the body to the side, and it seemed to hang in the air as he blurred around the van.

Sirens in the distance dragged out to bizarre demonic moans.

The last priest grasped Sabine by the knot between her ankles and pulled her forward so she lay flat on her back. She twisted and thrashed in slow motion, whimpering as the Vatican Hunter held the stake over her chest. Red light began to form in her eyes, but faded once she noticed Molinari leaping in the back doors.

He lunged at the priest, grabbing him by the shoulders and hauling him away. The priest swung his arm at nothing, kicking and howling. The scent of urine flooded Molinari's nostrils as he hurled the man past him onto the road. He hit the pavement hard, a pronounced *crack* emanating from his body, his right arm twisted into an agonizing shape. Molinari gave the priest only a second to scramble to all fours and raise a pleading hand before he leapt down on him. Warm blood sprayed over his hands as he gripped the would-be child-killer by the throat and crushed. His fingers curled around the slippery hardness of spinal bones, piercing the rubbery strands of vein and tendon. Molinari lowered himself to whisper at the gurgling man.

"You will not harm my child."

In the second their eyes met, Father Molinari's mind filled with Katherine Parrish demanding they bring Sabine to her intact. The priest had flown face-first into the wall during the crash. At the sight of Saint Patrick's, the entrancement broke along with his jaw. His conditioning took over. Sabine was once again a creature of darkness the church mandated he destroy. His daughter... this man wanted to destroy *his* child. Molinari squeezed his fingers deeper into his victim's neck.

Blood burbled from the priest's mouth, and he lay still.

Father Molinari rose to his feet, keeping his back to the van, and glanced down at the sharp yellow claws extending from his fingers. Rage dissipated under a tidal wave of horror. Leaden weight enveloped his throbbing heart.

I am lost.

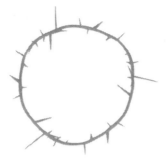

CHAPTER THIRTY-SEVEN

THE KINGDOM OF HEAVEN

August 11ᵗʰ 2014 New York City, New York

Saint Patrick's Cathedral radiated heat like a great mass of magma, waves of dread and discomfort billowing from its walls. Most of the curious onlookers, even those taking pictures, had run away at the sight of blood. Father Molinari stared down at the twitching, dead priest. He had protected Sabine. These men would have killed her. They deserved to die. He had to destroy them. Victorious. Justified. Thrilling.

He... enjoyed it.

Molinari stooped and wiped his hands clean on the dead priest's jacket. He considered Élodie's opinion, and perhaps God could have forgiven him for using the power to save Sabine. He had, to a point, done so with Yves. But here... He gazed down at the twisted remains of the priest. Anger had killed him. Molinari had been furious that the man *dare* threaten his child. She was safe, well, momentarily safe, and yet he had presumed to punish. *Vengeance is mine, sayeth the Lord.*

"Father," yelled Sabine, grunting as she struggled to move. "Help. I cannot get loose."

After a glance down to ensure his claws had receded, he turned. Sabine scooted to the end of the van. Two wide-eyed, innocent faces on the chest of her *Frozen* pajamas had nothing on the pleading look of fear on the child wearing them. He picked her up and clung like a little boy clutching a teddy bear.

"I will never let anyone harm you, Sabine."

He carried her to the side where the driver lay face down, grasped the cutlass, and cut her bindings. She reached up and wrapped her arms around his neck, shivering. He glanced at the church before staring down the street. Already, sirens closed in, echoing through the vast canyons of high-rises all around them. They had perhaps a minute or less before the area swam with police. He did not want to kill innocent men and women doing their job, but he would not let anyone take Sabine from him.

Visions came of the carnage he would wreak upon them if they dared get in his way.

The rosary in the metal cigarette case burned like an ember in his pocket. He held Sabine with one arm pressed to her back, and clenched his free hand into a fist. *I have fallen. As hard as I have tried, I am weak. If one ordained can fall...* Blood tears ran down his cheeks. Utter defeat wracked him. He would let no one corrupt this child—not even himself. Shuddering, he took a knee and set her on her feet.

"The street is cold and dirty, and I have no shoes." Sabine pushed at him. "Please, pick me up. I wanna go home."

He thought about walking hand-in-hand into the church.

If she does so of her own choosing, it is suicide.

Sabine pulled back and looked him in the eye. "Father, why are you crying? I'm okay." She smiled. "I-I knew you would save me."

He pulled the neck of her pajama top down, smiling at the small silver crucifix sitting against her skin—and not burning her. Exposing it hit him like a heat lamp to the face. Molinari looked into her deep green eyes. A spark of fear seemed to lurk within her gaze. *Can she sense that I have fallen?*

Sabine glanced to the side, and back at him. "Father, the police are coming. Don't you want to run? Why are you looking at me like that?"

"A test. I understand now."

He stood, lifting her in his arms. She clamped on; her adoring smile faded to a look of worry.

"Father... we must run."

A swarm of police cars squealed around both sides of the cathedral, cutting off the streets. An uncountable number of flashing lights glared in the darkness.

"I am sorry, Sabine. Perhaps I have failed already. Perhaps it has been God's will all along that I bring you to Paradise, and I have been too stubborn to see it."

"You're scaring me. Please, can we go home?" Sabine squirmed, trying to get down.

Molinari tightened his grip around her and closed his eyes. "I love you like my own daughter."

"I love you too, Father." She whined. "I want to go home."

"Put the girl down and back away from the van," yelled a man.

Jesus must welcome her.

At his desire, energy permeated his body, the power he had so long denied. He leapt forward into a sprint, giving himself to the urge, so that his speed would be imperceptible: to the police, so they did not shoot Sabine; to the child, so she did not suffer the anticipation of what was coming. The world appeared to hang in frozen time around him. Police officers mouths stuck open, twisted in authoritative grimaces, guns pointed still at the spot where he stood seconds ago. Sorrow flowed from the corners of his eyes. Nothing mattered anymore but protecting this child's soul. She was his Gaston, his Betty... the little cat he could not save. It was too much of a coincidence where this chase had ended. For decades, he had begged the Lord for a sign. This *had* to be it.

Father Molinari raced at the doors of Saint Patrick's. Each footfall *thudded* into the ground like blocks of stone falling from on high.

Flames blazed up his front as he ascended the stairs.

"Suffer little children and forbid them *not* to come unto me," he shouted. "For such is the Kingdom of Heaven!"

He rushed through the open front doors as a blazing comet of yellow fire. Beautiful agony washed up and over him. Sabine shrieked and screamed, squirming and writhing in his arms, but he would not let go. Tiny hands squeezed at his shoulders, as she tried to pull herself out of his grasp.

"*Non! Non! Père, que faites-vous!?*"

Her agonized cries wounded him like no pain he had ever felt. He was doing this to her. *No! I am bringing her to God.* Flames cored into his body. Bubbling fire spread through muscle and sinew. Threads of pure elation seared through him. Flesh fell away, bones melted.

Ahead, the altar glowed with golden radiance.

A euphoric grin spread over his face, even as the sense of his skin peeling away numbed it.

How long have I yearned to again enter the House of God?

His legs disintegrated from under him. Sabine ceased shrieking; her form went limp in his arms, which, like the rest of his body, no longer existed as a solid thing. He drifted in vertigo. Floating, feeling nothing. Sound and pain faded away.

Bless me Father, for I have sinned. Into your hands, I commend my spirit.

He collapsed into darkness.

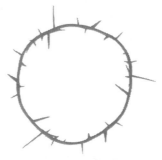

CHAPTER THIRTY-EIGHT

ASHES

August 23ʳᵈ 2014 New York City, New York

Warm sunlight shone through the garden, shimmering among white, yellow, and red blossoms. Sabine ran barefoot between rows of bushes, white dress glowing in the early afternoon. The fragrance of grass and roses made her grin, and she laughed.

"*Sabine? Où es-tu?*" said *Maman*.

She ran toward the voice. "I am here, *Maman*, but where are you?"

At the end of the row, she stopped, peering left and right down a crossing path. Seeing nothing, she twisted and looked at the house. Billows of black smoke came from the windows and the color looked *wrong*. A deep, foreboding rushing noise emanated from the windows, as though the building devoured the air. The decaying manse stood apart from the verdant surroundings, appearing in tones of sepia. Daddy was in there. She didn't want to be anywhere near it.

"*Maman?*" yelled Sabine. "Where are you? I'm scared!"

"I am here, my daughter. You are almost there."

Sabine, crying, hurried on through the roses. "Mommy!"

The noise from the black-smoke windows grew louder; a dread

presence seemed to close in on her from behind. She ran as hard as she could to get away.

"Here," said *Maman*.

The child followed the voice to the left past another row. As soon as she passed the end of the shrubs, the horrible noise pursuing her stopped. Sabine glanced back at a tunnel of rose bushes and grass. In a few breaths, she calmed and advanced around the next turn of hedge-maze at a cautious creep. Two right turns and a left later, she emerged at the clearing in the center of the garden. Birds chirped and tweeted above, unseen in the endless crisscrossing branches.

Her mother sat with her back turned on a curved bench that wrapped around the basin of the fountain. Their home in Briançon. Three granite angels raised their wings and harps to Heaven. Her mother's gauzy white dress and hair fluttered in a gentle wind as she traced her fingers in the water.

Sabine tiptoed closer, reaching a hand out. "Mommy, I have missed you."

Her mother glanced up. Baby's breath and wildflowers decorated her hair on either side. She extended her arm, but did not grasp Sabine's hand. "He has heard my prayers, my sweet."

"Mommy? The house is scary. Is Papa going to come and hurt us?"

Véronique Caillouet stood and stooped forward, eye level with her. "This is no longer your home, my dear Sabine. I will wait for you here."

"Where is the nice priest? Where is Father Molinari?" Sabine clutched her hands to her chest, and cried.

"Do not cry, my sweet. He forgives."

Her mother kissed her on the forehead. Lips charged with tingly energy made her dizzy, and her body fell backwards, outstretched hand unable to grasp her mother.

"*Maman!*" Her yell echoed again and again, fading into silence as she fell flat in the grass.

Sabine coughed on the taste of ashes. Distant voices murmured, though she could not make out what they said. Crackling static snapped and popped from portable radios, and everything sounded warbled as if submerged in water. Her feet were cold, toes numb. She opened her eyes, staring up at a slab of wood less than her arm's length over her head. Chill seeped through her pajamas from the stone beneath her. Distant voices hovered too far away to make out words, interrupted by the occasional spit of radio static or crunch of boots on brittle debris.

She clasped a hand over her mouth, and coughed. Hunger swirled in her stomach. She slipped a hand under her pajama shirt and rubbed her belly. Where was the man who had been taking care of her?

Dim light let her see a hint of wood overhead, and her fingers found glass-smooth marble beneath her. A few seconds passed before the fog of sleep left her, and she realized she lay underneath a long bench in a shadowy corner closest to the wall. A yawn forced its way out of her, and she wiped at her eyes. After rolling onto her side, she crawled all the way to the other end of a church pew. She stuck her head out into the wide central aisle and knelt staring up at a ceiling so high over her head, her mouth hung open in awe. Confusion danced through her mind. For an instant, she cringed, thinking she should be terrified of being inside a church, but the idea struck her as silly. Why would anyone fear a church?

"*Meow.*"

"*Crème!*" she whispered, as the beige cat trotted up to her. She gathered him and buried her face in the vibrating side of a hard-purring feline.

"Where am I, *Crème*?"

"*Mrow.*"

She stood, teeth chattering from the frigid floor under her feet, and stepped onto the aisle near an ashen mark in the general shape of a man spread out over a dark burgundy runner. Fluttering yellow plastic tape surrounded the area. The carpet ran all the way from the foyer to the altar far to the left. She crouched by the ashes, overwhelmed by sorrow.

Sniffling became crying; transparent tears patted on the stone. "I was wrong. When *Maman* prayed for me, God *did* listen." She bowed forward, whispering at the ashes. "He sent you. Thank you, Father. I know you are in Heaven now."

Sabine scrunched up her face. She didn't remember how long she'd been with the nice priest, or much of anything beyond living in New York. She smiled, wiped away the last of her tears, and stood. With *Crème* in her arms, she padded to the door. Faces of the buildings across the street popped with red and white light in staccato flashes. The first signs of morning sun peeked over the skyline in the east, infusing indigo with cyan and orange. She wandered the length of the cathedral, heading for the wide doors from which the tweets of early morning birds echoed.

The stone steps outside set her teeth chattering despite a hint of warmth in the breeze. She crept to the edge and looked around at a mass of blue and white police cars. Adults swarmed everywhere, examining a crashed white van. Something lay on the street covered by a black plastic tarp. Sabine shied away from it and kissed *Crème* upon the head as she made her way down the steps to the sidewalk.

"Hey, kid?" A man in blue looked from her to a cluster of other cops. "Hey Louie, where the hell did that little girl come from? Don't you jackasses know how to secure a scene?"

She ignored the yelling man, clutching her cat and smiling at the brightening sky. *Crème's* purr vibrated through her chest. Her attention lingered on the brightening spot in the clouds. For some reason, it felt as though she had not seen the sun in a long time. A fleeting glimpse of a sprawling meadow dotted with flowers came and went, capped with a strip of bright mountains. How could such a place feel like a memory if she had never been there?

"Didn't our pyro have a kid with him?" asked another man.

A woman made an odd frustrated grunt. "Yeah, but we've been all over this place for hours. Where the hell was she?"

"Kid?" A dark-skinned police officer with a shaved head took a knee at her side. "Hey kid? You speak English?"

"*Oui.*"

The man's eyebrows drew together. "Huh?"

"Sorry." She looked to her left at him. "Yes."

"Are you all right, kiddo? What's got you crying?" He blinked at her. "What are you doing out here in your PJs at quarter after six in the morning?"

Sabine smiled. "I am watching the sun come up."

The cop scratched *Crème* on the head. "Do you know your phone number or address? Where are your parents?"

"My parents died." Her smile faltered.

"Hey, some of the wits said that lunatic carried a little kid into the church. She fits the description." A woman officer jogged over. "Hi, sweetie. What's your name?"

"I am Sabine Caillouet, and I am eight years old." She leaned back to heft the animal in her arms. "This is my cat, *Crème*."

"Didn't that kook light himself on fire?" The male cop scratched his head. "How did they miss finding her?"

"Probably terrified and found a good hiding spot." The second officer extended her hand. "Hello, Sabine. I'm Officer Benitez. You don't need to be afraid."

"Damn good hiding spot," said the male officer. "Someone's gonna hear it if they missed her."

Sabine looked up as the sun broke free of the skyscraper's grip, and bathed her in warm light. "I am not afraid."

"Did someone hurt you, sweetie?" asked the male cop.

"*Non.*"

"For Christ's sake, Reed, get her out of here, this is a crime scene," yelled a disagreeable sounding man with a white shirt and silvery hair.

"Come on, honey." Officer Benitez took her hand. "Would you like to get something to eat?"

Sabine licked at her teeth. "*Oui.* May I have toast and jam?"

"I think we can arrange that." Officer Benitez winked. "Would you like to ride in a police car?"

"*Je ne sais pas.*" Sabine shrugged. At the confusion on the woman's face, she smiled. "I don't know, but I do not think you are really asking as I am not having a choice. It is okay. I am little, and should not be alone. I will go with you."

The cop picked her up and carried her toward a patrol car. Sabine rested her chin on *Crème's* head, and stared at the receding church. At the *clunk* of an opening car door, she twisted around to squint at the sun, and smiled at the heavens. He *had* to be there now.

Sabine bowed her head. *Thank you, Father.*

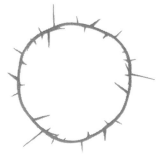

ABOUT THE AUTHOR

Born in a little town known as South Amboy NJ in 1973, **Matthew Cox** has been creating science fiction and fantasy worlds for most of his reasoning life. Somewhere between fifteen to eighteen of them spent developing the world in which Division Zero, Virtual Immortality, and The Awakened Series take place. He has several other projects in the works as well as a collaborative science fiction endeavor with author Tony Healey.

Matthew is an avid gamer, a recovered WoW addict, Gamemaster for two custom systems (Chronicles of Eldrinaath [Fantasy] and Divergent Fates [Sci Fi], and a fan of anime, British humour (<- deliberate), and intellectual science fiction that questions the nature of reality, life, and what happens after it.

He is also fond of cats.

THANK YOU
FOR READING

www.matthewcoxbooks.com

Please visit http://curiosityquills.com/reader-survey to share
your reading experience with the author of this book!

Nine Candles of Deepest Black, by Matthew S. Cox

She saw it coming. She knew it would happen—but no one believed her. Almost a year after tragedy shattered her family, sixteen-year-old Paige Thomas can't escape her guilt. Her father hopes a move to a quiet little town will help them heal, but Paige doesn't believe in happiness anymore. Paige's new friends decide to dabble with magic, unaware her gift will make it real. Alas, they soon learn the darkness they set loose will give them what they asked for—whether they want it or not.

Yea Though I Walk, by J.P. Sloan

Linthicum Odell, a Union Army deserter, seeks atonement by hunting monsters in the untamed West. His road to redemption leads to Gold Vein, a mining town with two afflictions: a corrupt justice named Lars Richterman, and a horde of cannibal wendigo in the surrounding hills. Odell joins forces with Denton Folger, a newspaper man intent on exposing Richterman's schemes. Odell soon realizes that Folger's darkly mysterious wife, Katherina, may hold the secrets to saving this valley from a war between devils...and the true reason Odell was called to this valley.

The Vampires' Last Lover, by Aiden James with Patrick Burdine

Txema Ybarra should be enjoying college life and her entrance into adulthood. And for a moment she does...until the vampires show up. Txema is one of only a handful of females who bear an unusual 'twin teardrop' birthmark on her neck. Caught in the middle of this war after all the other bearers of the birthmark are murdered, Txema must race to save her blood, as well as her very life, to ensure the survival of Les Amantes de Vampire. Otherwise, Txema will be the last one...the vampires' last lover.

The Other Lamb, by Katie Young

Incarcerated on Earth as punishment for breeding with humans, the Watchers found a way to escape. Zach is living proof of that... even though someone has cut out his heart.

Zach is a Naphil, the forbidden offspring of a mortal woman and a Watcher. When those who seek to destroy him snatch Kim, Zach is forced to embark on a journey of discovery spanning continents and ages. With the help of a mysterious stranger named Sam, Zach must unearth the truth about his parentage, find Kim, and discover who has stolen his heart... before he triggers the apocalypse.

CPSIA information can be obtained
at www.ICGtesting.com
Printed in the USA
LVOW10s1236210217
524936LV00002B/450/P